HELL ON HEELS

BOOK THREE OF THE HOT DAMNED SERIES

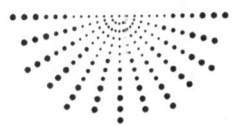

ROBYN PETERMAN

DEDICATION

This book is dedicated to my kids. Thank you for understanding that mom holes up in her office for days at a time and you're cool with eating a lot of peanut butter when I'm on a deadline. I promise that you'll be able to read my books eventually... Just know that I love and adore you and none of this would be worth it without you two in my life.

ACKNOWLEDGMENTS

Writing may be a solitary sport, but putting a book out is not. I am grateful and blessed to have many amazing people in my life. *The Hot Damned Series* is the series of my heart and writing it is a joy.

Donna McDonald, you are the bomb... literally. Your patience and support mean the world to me.

Audrey Peterman *aka Mom* you are the best freakin' proofreader in the world. For Real. Thank you and I love you.

My beta readers Candace, Donna, Kris, Christi, Kellie and Jennifer are awesome. I adore all of you and thank you for the time you gave me.

Rebecca Poole, my cover is everything I ever wanted and more. We are a warped team and I am so grateful for your creativity and your friendship. To many, many more!

My readers are amazing! You delight me and I write for you!

My critique partners, JM Madden, Donna McDonald and Kris Calvert—you ladies are brilliant, and when I grow up I want to write like you.

And my girl-crush, Darynda Jones... your cover quote humbled me and made me cry. You are an amazing writer and a beautiful friend.

Last but not least I want to thank my family. Hot Hubby, you are my real life hero and you are hotter than Satan's underpants. My kids, I love you. You are my finest accomplishment. None of this would be any fun without you guys.

BOOK DESCRIPTION

Where does a Demon go when she gets deported from Hell?

Kentucky. Eden, Kentucky to be more specific—where nothing is exactly as it seems.

My name is Dixie. I'm a Demon—a lousy Demon. I'm a twenty-one year old virgin and I have a battery operated boyfriend. My magic is iffy at best and downright dangerous at worst. Leaving Hell to represent my race is not high on my list of things to do.

Hell was exact. Hell was simple. All I want to do is get to home base with the hotter than Hades Demon of my dreams and work on my dark side so Satan, my dad, will get off my ass.

Instead I end up in Kentucky looking for the Balance of Chaos, avoiding pole dancing classes with Mother Nature and finding out my invisible friend is a silver skinned destructive weather pattern.

And if that isn't craptastic enough, the damn Sword of Death is missing again and who ever has it wants the King of the Underworld dead. Seriously.

With new powers emerging daily, keeping my Demon side, horniness and general disgust under wraps doesn't make it any easier to fit in with the humans. Thankfully my priorities are in line: get laid...save world...try not to blow up kitchen appliances...and get laid again. I was ready to rumble.

All I want to do is go back to Hell, but with the balance of good and evil in my hands, I'm stuck in the garden of Eden. Oh well, what the Hell.

Someone has to save the world before there's no world left to save. Might as well be me.

CHAPTER ONE

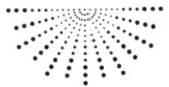

"WHAT EXACTLY ARE YOU DOING?" I ASKED MY FATHER. HE HAD A deck of playing cards laid out on his massive mahogany desk and he was putting tiny dots on the backs of the aces, queens, kings and jacks.

"It's Thursday," he replied.

"Yes... and?" I flopped down on the plush leather couch and waited.

"That bastard Hemingway won last week. That was unacceptable," he huffed. He put down the red pen and picked up a blue one.

"So you're going to cheat?"

He gave me a smile that had melted the hearts of thousands of women. Literally. "But of course."

Being the daughter of Satan had its challenges. This was only one of many. I knew that explaining to him that cheating at poker was wrong would be like running up the down escalator for eternity, so I kept my mouth shut.

Furthermore I was fairly sure that Hemingway cheated too. Poker Night in Hell usually consisted of Ernest Hemingway, Mr. Rogers, my dad and occasionally Mother Teresa. Since all of the players, my father excluded, resided in Heaven they basically took a bi-weekly field trip to Hell for game night. For real.

He finished his deceitful art project and gave me his full attention. "So, my beautiful girl, are you ready?"

I picked at my nail polish and considered my answer. Pleading had not worked, nor had crying or throwing a tantrum. Actually, the tantrum was a total bust. We ended up laughing because it was so far out of my character and I sucked at it. I suppose I could try the truth.

"Dad, being deported from Hell is not my idea of a good time. I'm not ready. I have no real power yet and I know I'll disappoint you."

"Dixie, the only thing that disappoints me is that you will be graduating from Demon College as the valedictorian and your obsessive need to do good." He sighed dramatically and ran his hands through his jet black hair.

He was gorgeous. He was evil. And I loved him.

"Your sisters… "

"My sisters are thousands of years old. College didn't even exist when they were of age."

"Point," he agreed. "I just don't understand why you couldn't learn what you wanted and then flunk the tests on purpose. We have a reputation to maintain."

"I know." I let my head fall back and stared at the mirrored ceiling. What the…? When did he have the ceiling in his office mirrored? The reality was too much to take in. I shut my eyes and tried without success to block out what I'd just seen. I was from the most over-sexed family in history and I was a twenty-one year old virgin.

"I've done my best to help you past that little hump. No pun intended," Satan said innocently.

"Get out of my head, Dad," I snapped.

He wasn't lying, and he *intended* every pun he made. He'd thrown the cream of the crop at me. Of course they were smarmy and way too old. The last Demon he'd set me up with had ridden on the Mayflower, had no clue who Maroon Five was and smelled funky.

"Dixie, darling, all of your sisters popped their… "

"Hell to the NO," I yelled as I slapped my hands over my ears. It was beyond unnecessary to hear about the sexual exploits of my sisters, the Seven Deadly Sins. It was bad enough that one of them was named Lust.

"Dixie, I'm just trying to help," he pouted.

"Look, Dad… there is a guy. And, um… well."

There actually was a guy—an amazing perfect guy, but I had no intention of telling my dad about him. He would ruin it. My dad thought it was hilarious to threaten the lives of all my sisters' paramours. And what did it matter anyway? I was leaving. All Demon Princesses had to do their time on Earth and my number had come up. The only thing that made it bearable was that I'd get to see my cousin Astrid. She was very pregnant and furious that no one could tell her what the gestation time was for a half-Vampyre half-Demon baby. She'd apparently caused so much property damage that her mate Ethan had everything breakable in the compound nailed down.

"Do I know him?" my father inquired casually.

My stomach clenched. Nothing my dad did was casual. "Nope." I smiled and stood up. "And you're not going to. I don't like him anymore."

"This happened in the thirty seconds since you announced his existence?"

"Yes. Yes it did."

"Dixie, Dixie, Dixie, you are so like your mother."

Considering no one had the testicles to tell me who my mother was, his comparison drove me to grind my teeth. "And that's a bad thing?" I challenged, hoping for once he'd slip up and give me a clue.

He paused and watched me for a moment. "Not good. Not bad. Interesting."

I went back to work on my nail polish and bit back a nasty retort as the tears threatened.

"Will you attend the poker game tonight?" he asked as if nothing important had passed between us.

"Sure," I muttered.

"Bring your guy. I'd love to meet him." With that my frighteningly beautiful father disappeared in a blast of black glitter and smoke. He was insane if he thought I'd bring my *friend* —completely insane.

CHAPTER TWO

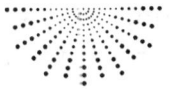

"How was the poker game last night?" my best friend Stella asked as we tried to find something edible in the college commissary.

"Dad won."

"Your dad always wins."

"He cheated," I muttered as I grabbed a sandwich and a bag of chips.

"So? He's Satan."

"Does anyone have morals here?"

"Dixie, we're Demons. We live in Hell. What do you expect?" Stella asked logically. The crabby Demon with the unibrow behind the food counter slid a nasty-looking bowl of what could pass for beef stew onto my BFF's tray. Stella, never wanting to cause a scene, accepted the offending bowl and moved on.

She was correct, and I didn't quite fit in. I never had and Hell knows I tried. I slid my tray quickly past the lunch lady and avoided the rank-looking stew.

"The commissary sucks," Stella lamented as she tried not to gag at the aroma rising from her tray. "I should have gone to college on Earth."

"Agreed." I nodded as I made my way through the crowd to a table.

The Demon College looked more like a high school than a college—lockers and all. The commissary looked like a freakin' high school lunchroom because up until a couple of years ago it had been. Most Demons, if they chose to pursue a higher degree, went to Harvard, MIT, Princeton, Yale, or Northwestern on Earth. From what I understood Angels tended to prefer the party schools. Since my father decreed I wasn't ready to go to Earth four years ago, he created the Demon College—where my old high school formerly stood. While the education was top notch, the accommodations left a lot to be desired.

"Holy Hell, your boyfriend is staring at you," Stella whispered gleefully.

"He's not my boyfriend," I hissed.

"Does he know that?" Stella's smile broadened as she enjoyed my discomfort.

Glancing around the commissary, I spotted the person I dreamt about on a nightly basis and I debated my next move. Did I stay or did I go? Being near my secret fantasy made me stupid. I'd far rather be mysterious than idiotic. He made me feel hot, cold and tingly at the same time and I'd barely uttered a word to him all year. Go. I would go—just put my tray down and be out of the commissary in a minute flat—or I could dematerialize… but then I could end up anywhere. I didn't quite have the hang of dematerializing to places I was actually trying to go. Last week I tried to travel to the mall and ended up in my father's chambers while he was getting busy with his pregnant consort Amanda. Bleach couldn't remove that one from my brain.

"I'm out of here," I muttered as I started walking. Speeding up my pace, I hightailed it to the tray drop praying to every deity I could think of that I didn't run into the man of my dreams. In all of my inexperience I was liable to either drool or bodily throw myself at him.

"He's still watching you," Stella whispered as she followed close on my heels.

I rolled my eyes. "He's not watching me."

"Wrong," she trilled happily.

"Stella, hush. Someone will hear you." She was my best friend, and if I didn't love her so much I would take great pleasure in killing her.

"Oh please." She waggled her eyebrows and made smooching noises. Pretending I didn't know her was impossible and I seriously considered dematerializing, but a healthy fear of seeing my father's naked ass stopped me.

"He is totally gone on you," she informed anyone within hearing distance—which was everyone—as she chased me. "And you are so gone... watch out," Stella yelped.

I stopped short to avoid running into Vincent van Gogh, my art teacher. Dressed in a purple velvet cape and a frighteningly poufy hat, he was weaving his way toward the open bar. It was Hell, after all, where mixing alcohol and academia was the norm. Van Gogh had a very close relationship with his absinthe. When the great master died he had the choice between Heaven and Hell. He chose Hell, much to my Uncle God's disgust. Van Gogh, while brilliant and extremely funny when he wasn't morbidly depressed, was clearly intoxicated. Did no one notice or care about these things besides me? Much was overlooked in Hell, but drunk was drunk.

In an attempt to avoid body-slamming the great artist I veered left and unfortunately Stella had the same idea. She slammed into my back, covering what used to be my brand new hot pink Juicy sweat suit in rank beef stew.

"Shit," she moaned as she tried to remove the potatoes, carrots and meat from my hair and the inside of my hood.

I froze and closed my eyes. As a child I used to think if I couldn't see anybody then they couldn't see me. It didn't work when I was five and I was fairly sure it wouldn't start working at twenty-one, but one could always hope. I also used to think that there were actual people in the TV.

"Hey Dixie." An insanely sexy voice broke into my invisibility fantasy.

I pried open one eye, and much to my great horror and delight stood the object of my desire in the flesh. The most beautiful man I'd ever seen—Hayden Black.

"You okay?" he asked.

My stomach flipped, my tongue became sandpaper and I felt lightheaded. I shakily tucked my hair behind my ear in a move that I knew looked good on me and came back with a fistful of beef stew. "I'm great," I lied. The heat crept up my neck and settled squarely on my cheeks. Holy Hell, could it get any worse?

"I'm going to skip the rest of the day and go cliff diving south of town. You want to come?" He smiled a lazy smile that made my breath hitch and all my unused lady parts tingle.

"I can't," I stammered. "I have a calculus exam… and I smell like beef stew, and I don't have a swimsuit and I… "

"Another time then." Hayden grinned and my heart skipped a beat. He reached out and ran his fingertips along my jaw line and his thumb across my lips. The shock of his touch jolted through my body and my knees buckled a little. "Another time."

He stood for a moment and stared, then turned and left the commissary. I watched his perfect butt in his loose-fitted faded jeans walk away from me. I didn't like him walking away from me —it felt wrong. What the Hell was that about? Why was I so drawn to him? I was leaving and those were the most words I'd said to him in a year. My hand automatically went to my still tingling lips, which I silently vowed to never wash again.

"Dude." Stella bounced like a ball. "He just asked you out!"

"No he didn't. He asked me to skip class. You know I don't skip."

"You need to pull the steel rod out of your ass and loosen up," she chastised as she futilely attempted to remove the beef stew from my hair.

"I've been telling her that for years," my sister Sloth chimed in as she appeared in a burst of silver glitter dust.

I rolled my eyes and smiled at my beautiful lazy sister. She was by far the nicest of the Seven Deadly Sins and I adored her. "What are you doing here? Is everything okay?" She never came to the Demon College. Academia gave her hives. Literally. Panic knotted in my stomach.

"Everything is fine," she assured me. "Dad's got his panties in a wad and he wants to see you. I've been sent to bring you to the Dark Palace."

"But I have a calculus exam and I… " I began to explain my schedule but petered off, realizing it was useless.

"And?" She raised her eyebrows as she began to scratch the welts that had popped up on her arms.

"Fine," I acquiesced quickly. As laidback as my sister was she got really grumpy and occasionally deadly when she was itchy. Furthermore, my dad waited for no one, certainly not his youngest daughter.

"You can't see Dad or Grandma like that." Sloth referred to my stew-splattered attire.

I paled considerably and clutched my sister for purchase. "Oh my Hell, Gigi is there?"

"Yep, and Dad is in a tizzy." She grinned evilly. "Let's get the unidentifiable lunch product off of you."

"That's my fault," Stella offered apologetically.

"No worries," my sister told Stella as she affectionately squeezed her cheek. Sloth raised her arms and flung them towards me. In a flash my hair was clean and my hot pink sweat suit was gone, replaced by the requisite black my father expected us to wear.

I hugged Stella goodbye and wrapped my arms around my sister. Sloth moved her hands in a circular motion. The glitter engulfed us as my beautiful sister and I vanished in a cloud of magic.

~

My day was going from mortifyingly bad to really scary bad.

The Dark Palace, my father's main residence, was normally a gross display of wealth and questionable taste. At the moment it had been transformed into a wild garden that resembled a blooming jungle on crack as opposed to the lush manicured gardens that populated Hell.

I grasped my sister's hand in terror and peered through the vines and flowers. "Is she here?"

"I don't sense her yet, but she's definitely on her way. Her garden usually precedes her by about five minutes," Sloth mumbled as she disengaged her hand from mine. "Dixie, I love you, but I wasn't summoned by our certifiable granny. Do you mind if I go?"

"Um…"

"Great! Call me later," my traitorous sister said as she disappeared in a blast of glitter. So much for counting on a Sin. The smell of jasmine and lilies permeated the air. There was no trace whatsoever of the grand ballroom which was where I knew I stood. Mother Nature, aka my Grandma Gigi, had a very bad habit of destroying my dad's homes. My guess was that he had missed his weekly visit to Nirvana to kiss her butt and she was pissed, but that didn't explain why I had to be here.

"Dad," I called out in the largest whisper I dared.

"Over here," Satan said quietly.

I made my way toward my father's voice and found him hiding behind a large ivy covered rock. My stomach dropped to my toes. The most terrifying and powerful Demon alive was hiding from his mother. This was beyond bad.

"Um, Dad?"

"Dixie," he hissed and pulled me behind the rock with him. "Thank sweet Hades you're here."

"Why exactly am I here?" I asked as I peeked around the rock.

"Your grandmother is the definition of unstable insanity, and if I knew why she summoned us we wouldn't be hiding behind a rock," he answered logically.

"Dad, you're my rock and this is making me very nervous."

He considered me for a long moment and stood up. He was magnificent. He stood six feet six inches tall and had long raven black hair like mine. Our eyes were gold, although they turned ruby red when we got excited or angry. My skin was more peaches and cream in comparison to my dad's beautiful pale mocha color.

"You're correct Dixie, I am your rock. She's so damned horrific I forget myself. Everything will be fine—I hope," he muttered.

His total lack of conviction was unsettling. I rose to my feet and waited. What the hell did she want with me? She'd shown me no attention at all in my twenty-one years in Hell.

"Don't look her in the eye and stand at least ten to twenty feet away from her," my dad instructed. "She's crazy and prone to blistering and deadly fits of rage."

"I heard that, you little shit," a glorious melodic voice shouted. "Just because you're the King of the Underworld doesn't mean I can't take you over my knee and tan your ass."

I gasped and held on to my father.

"Son of a bitchass motherhumping asshats—arghhhh!" she screeched as she fell ungracefully from the sky. It wasn't until that moment I realized the roof of the palace was gone. The musical voice did not match the language flying from her mouth or the otherworldly glamour she possessed.

The disheveled beauty got to her feet and glanced around impatiently. She wore a gown of sheer golden gossamer that floated around her magically. Her hair was a mass of fiery red curls and her skin was a pale porcelain, but it was her eyes... Her eyes were the clearest blue I'd ever seen and they sparkled. She was quite simply the most gorgeous crazy woman in the universe.

Her power filled the room. It was earthy with a dangerous sensual undertone to it. I would give anything to be back in the commissary covered in stinky beef stew. Anything.

"Satan, you little bastard," she snapped as the gentle breeze in the room shifted into a slightly menacing wind. "I know you're here. I want to see my granddaughter. Now."

"Mother," Satan bellowed joyously as he stepped out from behind the rock. "To what do I owe this pleasure?" He placed me firmly behind him and waited for her next move.

"Cut the shit. You were supposed to visit me and I made a cake," she yelled. "You didn't show up and I ate it. I ate the entire cake. Do you have any idea how many hours I had to pole dance to work off an entire cake?"

"Seven?" he guessed.

She froze, stared at him for a tense moment, and then threw her head back and laughed with delight. "You're right! I always knew you were smarter than your brother. He guessed three."

My father stood even taller, clearly pleased with himself that he'd bested his brother, God. Forget about my Grandma Gigi—my entire family was nuts.

"Mother, while it's alarmingly wonderful and highly destructive to see you," he said, gesturing to the wrecked ballroom, "why are you here and what do you want with Dixie?"

"I want to see her," she pouted and stamped her small foot.

"You've not wanted to see her for twenty-one years. I don't see... "

"You know exactly why I've ignored her, Satan," she said in a deadly quiet voice.

My father had no reply. He bowed his head and shook it. What was going on here? Something was wonky and I'd bet my embarrassing virginity that no one was going to enlighten me.

"I know she's behind you. Dixie, come out and greet me," Gigi demanded.

My father turned to me and his golden eyes burned into mine. "It's all right. She won't harm you. Go to her."

Sucking in a huge breath, I stepped out from behind my dad and warily approached my grandmother. My fear disappeared and was replaced by curiosity... the kind that was deadly to cats.

"Oh my," she giggled, completely disarming me. "You are exquisite. You look like your father, but you have so very much of her in you."

She caressed my face gently. I automatically leaned into her warm and delicate hand. My maternal upbringing had been virtually nonexistent—attention from a mother figure was addicting, no matter how insane she might be.

"Do you mean my mother?" I asked tentatively, hoping she didn't remove her hand. "Do you know her?"

"Well of course I do. She's a crazy irresponsible assbuckle. The next time I see her I will... "

"Mother," Satan roared.

"Well, she is," she shot back. "Anyhoo, I got a phone with cells. Would you like to see it?"

"Um... " I was hoping she would continue her tirade on my mother. It was the most information I'd ever heard.

"You mean a cell phone," my father corrected her.

"That's what I said." Her gaze narrowed dangerously and the wind in the room kicked up a few notches. Her fingers began to shoot little orange sparks, and I worried for the health and welfare of my dad and his home.

"I'd love to see it," I insisted quickly before she caused a Hellquake or leveled the Dark Palace completely.

"I want you to take a selfie of me," she demanded as she handed me a jewel-encrusted cell phone.

"Um, a selfie means you take it of yourself," I explained as she shoved her new toy into my hand.

"Exactly. Take a selfie of me."

Deciding further explanation of a selfie could end in violence I took several as she posed obscenely with a flowering vine.

"While it's wonderfully disturbing to watch you hump the vegetation, would you like to explain your presence?" my father asked as he partially hid himself behind a boulder.

"Yes, of course," Gigi said as she disengaged herself from the plant and planted a huge wet kiss on my cheek. Glancing at her phone, she grinned. "These would go positively viral on YouTube."

"Mother," Satan warned as he stepped up next to me.

As calming as my father's presence was, I realized to my utter shock I was not at all afraid of Mother Nature. It was clear that she loved me, which only confused me more.

"Why haven't you ever wanted me?" I asked her and she froze.

My father tensed beside me and his magic began to swirl with his mother's.

"Dear sweet child," she cooed. "It was for your safety, but now since you're leaving I needed to see you and tell you… "

"Enough," Satan shouted. "You know the rules. Would you put her in more danger than she's already in?"

This was unwelcome news to me. I was in danger?

"You're such a douchewanker—I wouldn't say anything to harm her. I love her," Gigi shot back angrily.

"Then I think it best you leave," he said in a voice that made the hair on my neck stand up. However, his mother just giggled.

"Have her powers come in?"

"No, but they will," he snapped and advanced on his mother. "You will stay out of this. Do you understand me?"

"It's not nice to backtalk Mother Nature," she hissed.

"I thought it was fool," my father replied dryly.

"Whatever. I'm late for a marathon pole dancing exhibition, otherwise I'd smite your ass for being rude."

"You've done quite enough. Dixie, say goodbye to your grandmother. Now."

I scurried forward and embraced my slightly unhinged grandma. She hugged me tight and whispered in my ear, "Your father is an assmonkey. Don't worry about a thing. I will see you on Earth. I promise."

With that she disappeared, taking her jungle with her—almost. The roof of the palace was missing and I was quite sure that was not an accident.

"Son of a bitch," Satan yelled and stomped around, throwing a fit. "It had better not rain before I can get a new roof or I will send ten thousand giant goats to Nirvana to eat your gardens, you heinous woman."

"Um, Dad?"

"Yes, Dixie?" he answered as he reined in his tantrum with difficulty.

"What kind of danger am I in?"

"At this exact moment, none. But tomorrow is a new day."

"Is that supposed to help? Because it doesn't," I replied as I frantically began to pick at my woefully under-manicured fingernails.

"Dixie, look at me."

I did. He was magnetic and scary and beautiful and mine. I knew I would do anything for my father.

"I am sending you away from danger. You have a mission, but you are capable and ready. It's not for public knowledge because it fucks with my reputation, but I love you. I will kill for you and I would die for you. Now, your sisters? Not so sure, but I would not send you directly into the firing squad. You have to trust me."

Sucking in a huge breath, I nodded. "I trust you, Dad, and I love you too."

"Come here," he said.

I slid into his strong embrace and wished I could stay forever, but that was not how life went. If he said my powers would come, they would come. If he said I was ready… Hell, I just hoped he was right.

CHAPTER THREE

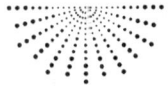

I GO TO GROUP THERAPY.

When you live in Hell and you're not considered to be evil enough, you have to do therapy.

I have to do therapy with a group of others who have an evil deficiency.

That group destroyed my cute bungalow yesterday.

They were insane misfits and I'd grown to love them in the same way one loves a puppy who chews up your couch and eats your walls. Prone to destruction, we'd been banned from meeting anywhere but privately. I'd spent every afternoon at three-thirty for the last year watching them destroy meeting rooms, offices, classrooms, convenience stores... you name it, they could trash it. The convenience store wasn't actually a session. We'd gone for Slurpees after a grueling hour of therapy and they thought the Demon at the cash register looked at them funny. It was bad. Our newest therapist—*we'd had many*—had threatened repeatedly to quit unless we started doing at home meetings. Hence my ruined house. And hence their solution.

I should re-name my group The Wrecking Balls. Janet the formerly Bearded Lady, Carl the Strong Man, and Myrtle the...

I'm not really sure how to explain her. I like her a lot, but she was difficult to describe. Basically she was a tiny Goth girl with more hair in her face than Cousin It. They were all quite funny but bordered on homicidal.

Today they arrived in a big van loaded with tools, wood, a window and paint to repair my bungalow in Hell. Yesterday's therapy session had turned violent when a debate over *The X Factor* versus *The Voice* ensued. Our therapist had been hospitalized for blunt head trauma from a toaster. Myrtle was one tuff cookie and psychotic to boot. She clearly thought the therapist was out of line when she commented on Simon's man boobs, hence the beating, followed by the destruction of my home. As much as I found my group amusing, their ability to trash every place we met was starting to ride my last nerve. Not to mention my horror that they were coming to Earth with me and posing as my family.

A furniture truck arrived soon after they descended on my home, loaded with brand new furniture to replace what they had demolished. The new stuff wasn't nearly as nice as my old furniture that they'd destroyed. When I tried to kindly explain this to the Strong Man *aka Carl* he just shrugged and began doing the Moonwalk. Normally he flipped people off, but he liked me. He was fond of flipping people off. It seemed to give him joy. He moonwalked for about thirty-two counts and then slid very slowly into the splits, arms raised above his bald head.

I stared at him in silence. I was definitely going to have a word with my dad about this group posing as my family on Earth. These people were C-R-A-Z-Y. It didn't help that Carl was wearing something akin to a mauve wrestling uniform with black socks and brown earth shoes. I had no idea how to respond to his performance. Was I supposed to clap or was I supposed to challenge him by busting out my own moves? In the end I nodded at him, he nodded back and I walked away. Quickly.

The furniture delivery guy, Wolf Boy, the hairiest Demon I'd ever seen, lined up all the new furniture on my lawn. I'd have to say Demons were a very attractive race. My therapy group and their friends were an anomaly. Wolf Boy then explained as he shed all over said furniture that he'd be back in a couple of hours to put it in my house.

After winking at me lasciviously, he meandered over to Myrtle and copped a feel of her butt. This earned him a bone crunching solid right hook to the face. She knocked his nose clear up into his forehead. *God, that had to hurt.* Amazingly undeterred by this painful rejection, I watched in shock as he then palmed her boob. Ya'd think he would have learned his lesson…

Myrtle easily picked him up even though Wolf Boy was twice her size and threw him to the ground. She then viciously crunched his testicles with the large hard heel of her combat boot. My dad would love that move. It made me bend over in sympathy for Wolf Boy even though our plumbing was entirely different.

Wolf Boy lay crumbled on the ground moaning for a long time. With his nose where his forehead should be and his testicles lodged somewhere near his chest I didn't blame him. All the others worked around him as if he wasn't there.

I sat down on the front steps of my bungalow and watched in horror as my therapy group turned my beautiful little house into a bad home-improvement project. I felt a cool wind on my face and I closed my eyes and smiled. The air shimmered around me and out of nowhere Blanche magically appeared on my front lawn. She stepped over Wolf Boy and made herself comfortable on my new and highly unattractive couch. She happily held one-sided conversations with a bunch of Demons that didn't even know she was there… because she was invisible. Blanche was mine and I was the only one who could see her. Although I'd told my dad and sisters about her, none of them believed me. Stella was the only one who was convinced of her existence. Stella loved hearing about Blanche's adventures and Blanche loved Stella. It pissed her off to no end that Stella couldn't see her. She would curse a blue streak trying to figure out a way to become corporeal for Stella. If I could behave a little more like Blanche, my dad would be so happy. However, every time I tried to copy her I either ended up with hives or laughing uncontrollably.

"Excuse me, Dixie," said Janet with the voice of a shy ten year old girl. Poor Janet was wearing a fake beard and mustache. Up until a few months ago her beard and stache had been real, but our former therapist had them permanently removed as punishment. Janet had been devastated. She'd been sporting her beard for hundreds of years and clearly felt naked without it. Her mate, Carl, loved her both hairy and hairless and had bought her an impressive array of beards. Focusing on her eyes instead of her lopsided facial hair was difficult, but she was sweet. "Would Your Highness like the walls the same color as before or do you want something new and fresh and not so dated?"

I was fairly sure I was just insulted by a child locked in a hairy adult's body, but I decided it was in my best interest to let that baby go. My hairy female friend was going to help me redecorate.

"I don't know. What do you think?" I felt my eyes go red with excitement.

"I think we should look at this!" She whipped out a color chart and squealed.

Blanche cleared her throat to get my attention and mimed shaving her face. Damn her, I was almost able to pretend that Janet was normal. Then Blanche had to go and ruin it by reminding me that Janet had more fake hair on her face than I had on my entire body. Well, screw her. Janet was my friend—she couldn't help that she was a hairy destructive mess.

While Janet and I bonded over paint colors, Carl and Myrtle got into three rather violent fights.

"Carl." I stopped him as he went to replace my window. "Why do you two hang out if you're just going to keep trying to kill each other?"

Carl paused, contemplated, flipped me off and then started break dancing. I was beginning to think he was brain damaged.

"Oh, for goodness sakes," Janet piped up. Her mannerisms were so dainty for such a hairy gal. "Carl is a little… well, he's just Carl. He's a wonderful Demon, just not a good conversationalist." She paused and waited for Carl to finish with his splits. That was how he ended all of his routines. As he wandered out of earshot Janet continued.

"Actually," she went on, "he's very smart and kind. He smells good and he's champion in the bedroom."

"Oh, Good Lucifer Almighty, no!" Blanche screamed as she slapped her hands over her ears. "That's disgusting." I was so glad that Janet couldn't see or hear my non-corporeal imaginary friend, but I had to concur. Blanche vanished in a huff of disgust.

"Oookay, Janet," I said, deciding to use this as a teachable moment for my hairy buddy. "That is way too much information. That's not really an image you want to create for others."

"You're right," she answered solemnly in her childlike voice. "No one should know that Carl is Superman in the sack. If anybody tried to steal my Carl away I'd tear their limbs off, decapitate them, shove a spike through their heart and burn them for the Hell of it."

She stopped for a moment, clearly considering what she just said. She was normally so sweet. I was positive she was going to yell "joking", but no.

"Actually I'd rip their limbs off first then burn them because they would be conscious for that and it would hurt." She seemed pleased with the new order of torture. "Then after they're dead I would decapitate them and run a spike through their heart to make absolutely sure they could never ever get a piece of Carl's manmeat. That goes for you too, so don't go getting any ideas." She was dead serious.

I was seriously unsure of why she was in my therapy group. That sounded pretty evil to me. I needed to reconsider the sweet thing. She was making it increasingly difficult to be friends. I could have possibly gotten past the fact that she glued on facial hair but this was a deal breaker. Janet the Fake Bearded Lady had succeeded where many had failed. She had rendered me speechless. Not to mention implanted visions in my head that would take years of therapy to erase. I really tried to speak, but my voice was gone.

Janet giggled and braided the left side of her mustache. "I think mustard yellow paint would be lovely in your den."

I nodded, still in shock.

"How about a mossy green in the bathroom, a candlelight yellow in the kitchen, and a warm peach in your bedroom?"

I nodded again. She could have said she was going to paint my entire house crap-brown or lime green and I would have nodded.

"Great!" She hopped up and hugged me, tickling my neck with her beard. It was not soft and silky. "It was soooo much fun talking to you. I'm going to go mix some paint, and if Carl's in the van… " She giggled. "Well, you know."

Oh Holy Lucifer, unfortunately I did know. I watched in abject terror as Carl did lewd hip-hop moves all the way over to the van —followed by Janet, seductively twisting her gnarly beard with her stubby fingers.

"Carl's really got moves," a wistful voice behind me said.

I whipped around to find Myrtle watching Carl longingly as he and Janet raced to the van for their love fest.

"Myrtle, if I were you I'd stay away from Carl," I said as I tried to save her from a sure death.

"Oh I know—Janet's already beaten up twenty-two low level Demons and a zombie over Carl."

"I heard she would mutilate and kill anyone who even looked at Carl," I casually informed Myrtle, fearing for her life. It was difficult to kill a Demon, but Janet's recipe would definitely work.

Myrtle laughed. "She wouldn't really kill anyone—she's too

sweet for that. Plus, I don't want Carl that way. I want to dance like he does."

Weird didn't even begin to describe that statement so I backtracked to something even weirder. "Did you just say zombie?"

"Yeah," Myrtle said, "and you think we're disgusting and gross."

"I don't think you're disgusting or gross."

Myrtle peeked out from behind her hair and stared at me. She took a long pause and simply said, "Maybe you don't, but everyone else does. We're the freak Demons—we're not beautiful like the rest of you." With that she picked up a hammer, stepped *on* instead of over Wolf Boy, and went back into my house.

Carl, Janet and Myrtle weren't freaks, they were just alarming looking semi-violent Demons who had the same problems that I did. Well, some of the same problems. My father would kill me if he found out how much compassion I felt for others, including my violent and bizarre little therapy group. Truth be told, I liked my therapy group and I did fit in with them. Why was life so damn complicated? Myrtle was a person, no matter how stinkin' weird she was or looked. She had feelings—they all did. I turned just in time to see the van roll over onto its side due to the disgusting and illicit activities within. Well, some of them did.

CHAPTER FOUR

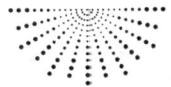

My commissary disappearing act with my sister Sloth the other day had caused quite the stir. I was going for a low profile today. Being Satan's daughter made it kind of difficult to blend in, but I tried. It was a little strange when underclassmen bowed to you, insisted on giving you their lunch money and offered to carry you. Not my books. Me. I shoved stuff into my messy locker and swore for the millionth time I'd clean it out.

"He's going to the library." Stella ran up and knocked me into my locker, causing an avalanche of the entire contents to come falling out.

I glared at her. "Stella, look at what you've done."

"I did you a favor," she retorted, grinning from ear to ear. "Now you don't have to clean it. Did you hear what I said?" she panted, out of breath from her sprint down the hallway and her flying leap into me and my locker.

"No. I was busy getting nailed in the head by my *History of Mortals* textbook," I sarcastically explained as I began to pick up the mess on the floor.

"I said he's going to the library," she repeated impatiently.

"Who's going to the library?"

"Your boyfriend," she yelled eagerly.

"Be quiet." I rolled my eyes. "He's not my boyfriend. I've barely ever talked to him."

"That's about to change." She yanked me up by the arm and shoved me into the middle of the hallway. "Okay, Dixie," she screeched at alarming decibels. "You go to the library like you said you were going to. You know, go to the library and... um... study. Okay? In the library, like you said."

Everyone in the hallway stopped what they were doing to watch our exchange. I had never wanted to die so much in my entire life. And every bone in my body sensed that Hayden Black was standing right behind me.

"So you're going to the library, Dixie?" Hayden chuckled, circling me until his entire beautiful self was standing in front of me.

"Um... well," I started, flustered and mortified.

"Yes," Stella shouted. "Dixie is definitely going to the library. She just said 'Stella I'm going to study in the library'. That's exactly what she just said. Just now."

We had entered the realm of shitty sitcom. "Stella," I hissed through clenched teeth.

"Yes?"

"You can stop shouting now."

"Oh, right." She laughed, clearly unashamed of her appalling behavior. "My bad."

"Well, it just so happens I'm going to the library too." He winked conspiratorially at Stella. "Can I walk with you?"

He turned his green gaze on me and waited for my answer. The speech part of my brain ceased to function. All I could do was stare at him like an idiot.

"Yes," Stella chimed in and gave me a push. "She'd love to walk with you and maybe even sit at the same table, regain her power of speech and exchange a few words."

Stella was evil. I gave her a look that would have scared most

Demons to death. I was Satan's daughter after all. She just stuck her tongue out at me and giggled. She was going to pay later.

"Shall we?" Hayden asked.

"Um… sure," I stammered and started walking toward the library.

"Dixie." Hayden's silky voice stopped me.

"Yes?"

"Do you want to bring some work with you?" His eyes twinkled.

I looked down at my empty hands and for the second time in a matter of minutes I wished I was dead. "Yes," I replied in a very businesslike manner. I made my way back to my locker, squatted down and picked up the first two things my fingers touched. "Okay." I smiled, having no idea what was in my hands. "I'm ready."

"Great." He grinned. "I was born ready."

SITTING ACROSS FROM EACH OTHER IN THE DEMON MAGIC SECTION of the library, I stared at my fingernails while Hayden stared at me.

"Dixie," he said softly. "Look at me."

"I can't." I continued my love affair with my fingernails. "I get stupid when I look at you."

"I find that extremely flattering and very sexy," he said.

My eyes shot to his and my stomach dropped to my toes. "No, you don't."

"I do." He captured my chin in his hands and forced my gaze to stay on his. "It's not every day that the most gorgeous girl I've ever seen in my life gets all flustered around someone like me."

"Are you kidding me?" I gasped. "Someone like you? You're the most… " I slapped my hand over my mouth before I permanently destroyed any vestige of cool I might own by telling him I loved him and that I had memorized every single thing he'd worn to class—*down to sock color*—for the last three semesters.

"I'm the most what?" he asked quietly.

Change the subject, change the subject. "So why don't you have a girlfriend?" *Help me Cousin Jesus, did I just say that?*

His grin was lopsided and the hottest thing I'd ever seen. "Haven't found the right girl yet."

"Oh." I was usually more eloquent.

"I'm working on changing my status." He let go of my chin and took my hands in his. I felt a tingle run through my fingers and all the way up my arms. Not only was I physically attracted to this guy, apparently I was chemically attracted too. "Do you have a boyfriend?"

"No." I was caught in his web and couldn't get away if my life depended on it. "I'm working on changing my status too," I whispered. Was I flirting? Oh my Hell, I was. My sisters would be so proud.

His eyes flashed red with desire and his smile broadened in approval. "Am I in the competition?"

"Do you want to be?" I lowered my eyes and watched his thumb caress my knuckles. His hands were beautiful and strong, slightly calloused and very gentle.

"More than you'll ever know," he replied with such seriousness my eyes shot back up to his and my insides did a triple lutz.

Whoa Betty, I needed to slow down or I was going to tackle him to the ground and see if his lips were as soft and tasted as good as they looked. My entire body thumped like a heartbeat and the need to lean into him was overwhelming. I disengaged my hands from his and tried to regain some composure. His smirk made me think he could read every thought in my head.

"I'd like to take you to dinner," he said, watching me closely.

Stella was going to freak. "But you don't even know me." I really wished the idiotic dumbass in my brain would stop talking.

"We could remedy that," Hayden leaned in.

28

Hades, he smelled yummy. "How?"

"Well…" He took my hands again. "We could ask each other questions."

Damn, I was hoping he would say we could play tonsil hockey.

"What's your favorite color?" he asked, drawing me back in.

"Green," I quickly replied. The heat crawled up my neck as I realized I'd chosen the color of his eyes.

"Why's that?" He tilted his head, very aware of my reasoning. I couldn't speak. "Mine is gold," he offered. His emerald green eyes bored into my gold.

"Is it hot in here?" I gasped as I pulled my hands back and put them in my lap.

"Nope." He grinned, quite pleased with himself. "Tell me what you like."

"Well…" I needed some noncombustible territory here. I wasn't about to tell him I liked the way he filled out his jeans or that his mouth was beautiful and the way his muscular arms looked in his long sleeve t-shirt was making me weak. Nope, not going there. I decided to tell him about the real me. Which would probably end with him walking away in boredom, but… "I like animals, especially strays. I love to run. I adore my family and I read constantly." I knew my tone was defensive, but I couldn't help it. I waited for him to glaze over and fall asleep.

"I love to read," he offered quietly.

"You do?" I was surprised.

"Does that shock you?"

"Well…" I bit my lip in embarrassment. Hot guys could read too.

"Is it because I skip school, wear ripped jeans and go cliff diving that you think I'm illiterate?"

"That's not what I meant," I sputtered. My cheeks burned. How many times could a person want to die in one afternoon?

"Dixie, I'm teasing you," he said gently.

"Oh… okay." He had to think I was such a dumbass.

29

"I think you're amazing and beautiful and sweet." He walked around the table and sat right next to me. "I love to read. I collect first edition books. I have some that are thousands of years old."

That piqued my interest. "Like what?" I adored old books. My father's den was loaded with them. I'd spent a great amount of my childhood curled up in his den reading till my head spun.

"I have an original bound copy of *The Beginning of Time.*"

"Holy Hell, I didn't know that even existed."

"It does. I'd love to show it to you if you'd like."

"I'd like." I smiled. "What's your biggest fear?" I asked. Now that the door was open, I wanted to know a few things about him. He might be hot, but maybe I wouldn't like him. Maybe he was a jerk...

"My biggest fear," Hayden repeated as he ran his hands through his thick blond hair. "My biggest fear is being alone through all eternity."

Damn, that was deep. I was going to say spiders.

"What's something you dream about doing?" He changed the subject to something far lighter.

I took a long pause while I considered my answer. The first thing that came to my mind was silly, but if he could be that honest, so could I. "Flying," I answered shyly. I knew Demons couldn't fly, but that's what I dreamed of. "I've always wanted to be able to fly. Sometimes when I run and I feel the wind race around me and through me and in me I pretend I'm flying."

He was quiet for a moment, just watching. "Perfect," he murmured softly. "Please, Dixie, let me take you to dinner tonight. I promise I'm a good guy and I like you a lot."

"Hayden, do you know who my father is?" I assumed he did, but maybe not.

"Yes Dixie, I absolutely know who your father is."

"And that doesn't... um, bother you?"

"No, should it?"

Was he crazy? Everyone was terrified of my dad. Wait... Didn't

Satan tell me to start being promiscuous? Something I had no intention of doing, but a date… I could go on a date. I wanted to go on a date. I'd never ever been on a date. No one had been brave enough to ask me. I wanted to go on a date with Hayden, and against all odds he wanted to go on a date with me.

"I'd love to go to dinner with you," I blurted a little louder than I intended. I wanted to nail down my acceptance before he changed his mind.

"I'll pick you up at seven." He looked so happy I started to giggle.

"What should I wear?" I asked as my mind raced through my closet.

He got up, gathered his books and whispered in my ear. "Flying clothes. Wear your flying clothes, Dixie."

CHAPTER FIVE

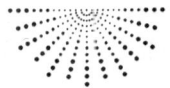

"I'M AFRAID TO ASK, BUT WHAT IN THE HELL HAPPENED TO YOUR house?" Stella wrinkled her nose and put her hands on her slim hips.

We both looked around my bungalow in dismay. Only days ago it resembled a chic yet cozy high-end home of someone with excellent taste. Now it looked like a house decorated by someone on crack who'd gone to a yard sale.

I shook my head and grimaced. "I didn't realize how bad it was."

It was so bad it was almost funny. Almost. It would have been hilarious if I didn't have to live in it.

"It's pretty damn awful."

"It's a long story, but suffice it to say group therapy got a little violent," I said.

"How does that explain the butt-ugly furniture?" She sat on my scary new lavender and green tartan plaid couch and bounced up and down. "Hmm, it's appalling, but at least it's comfortable." She moved to the floral chair.

"Myrtle beat the crap out of the therapist over Simon Cowell's man boobs and then all Hell broke loose. They destroyed my house and everything in it, so they brought me new supplies. I hesitate to call it furniture." I piled six outfits on my brand spankin' new blonde pressboard dining room table. Stella was here to choose an ensemble for my date.

"Ooo," Stella squealed as she clapped her hands gleefully. "She nailed the shrink?"

"Yep." I grinned as I examined several pairs of jeans, wondering which ones Hayden would like the best.

"I always liked Myrtle. Do you want your old furniture back?" she asked as she ran her hands over the super-sized black lacquered Asian-style coffee table. Not only was it shiny, but painted right in the center was a large bloody fire-breathing dragon destroying a village of unsuspecting mortals. The stuff of which nightmares are made.

"I can't get my old stuff back." I sighed. "They demolished it. Besides, I don't have the time or the energy to redecorate my entire house. I leave for Earth soon. I'll get around to it eventually."

"But," Stella interjected. "If you could have it back in its original form... would you?"

What was she talking about? "Of course I would, but that's impossible."

Stella's excitement was palpable. "Watch this," she sang with delight.

She threw her arms into the air and lightening struck inside my small bungalow. I shrieked in terror while Stella cackled like a crazy woman. Every time she flailed her arms a new bolt of lightning struck and thunder roared through the house. The walls trembled and the floor buckled. Sparks flew and bounced off the walls like a meteor shower. I continued to scream until I realized with each crash of lightning the ugly furniture was being replaced with my beautiful old furniture. How in Satan's name was she doing that?

The violent storm lasted about twenty minutes. When it

ended, my home was perfect again. Stella flopped down on my chocolate velvet cushy couch and promptly passed out.

"Dude," I gasped and poked her. "Are you asleep or dead?"

"Neither." She refused to open her eyes. "Just exhausted. Did it work?"

"Yes, it worked," I said as I moved around the room and touched all my stuff. No more scary plaids and florals. No more highly lacquered tables with scenes depicting death and destruction. It was elegant and comfortable.

A thick Persian rug covered the hardwood floors. Chocolate velvet mixed quietly with pale rose silks and creamy coffee linens. Dark hardwoods complemented rich brown leather. It was peaceful. It was mine again.

"How did you do it?" I eased her over and sat down next to her. She was wiped out. I gently pushed her hair back from her face and gave her an arm tickle.

"Ooo." She happily sighed. "That feels good."

We'd been giving each other arm and back tickles since first grade. Oftentimes we made it a contest. If you moved, flinched or giggled, you lost. The loser had to tickle the other person. Right now, it was purely for comfort.

"How," I repeated, "did you do that?" I stared at my wiped out insane best friend.

She pried her eyes open and gave me an exhausted grin. "You like?"

"I like." I grinned back. "Now explain."

Stella slowly sat up and pulled her knees to her chest. "I got really mad at my dresser drawers the other day. You know, the one that's three hundred years old. Literally." Stella's mom was an antiques freak. "Anyway, the stupid thing sticks and my underwear drawer wouldn't open." I nodded and waited. "I simply wished I had a new one and BAM—lightning struck and I got my wish."

"What did your parents do?"

"They weren't home." She grinned evilly. "So I took the opportunity to redecorate the entire house."

I pressed my lips together to keep from laughing. Didn't work. Stella's home was a grand mansion filled with antiques dating back thousands of years. I feared touching anything when I was over. It was very formal and quite honestly, cold. "What happened when they got back?"

"Dad was proud that my powers had arrived and Mom was pissed. Royally and spectacularly pissed. Apparently I got rid of some priceless antiques. Her head practically flew off."

"Holy Hell." I laughed and fell back on the couch.

Amusement flickered in her eyes as she continued, "After a showdown and a lot of threats, I re-conjured her icky old antiques, but not the dresser drawers."

I popped back up and grabbed her hands. "What else can you do?"

A sinking feeling of jealousy reared its ugly little head inside me. I tamped it down quickly. I didn't begrudge her magic, I just wanted some of my own. Stella was my best friend and I loved her. I was proud of her powers even if I was still power-free.

"That's it so far," she replied as she squeezed my hands reassuringly. "Dixie, don't worry, your magic will come. Mine's just a freakin' parlor trick. Someday soon you will be a real power, just like the rest of your family."

I hugged her tight. There were many reasons she was my best friend and always would be. She was beautiful inside and out.

"That's a little more than just a parlor trick, my friend. You scared the living Hell out of me." She looked entirely too pleased with herself so I punched her in the arm. "Have you done anything else?"

Stella's laugh was infectious. I began laughing with her before I even knew what she was going to say.

"I changed the color of my mom's car while she was getting her nails done," she squealed. "It took her an hour in the parking lot to figure it out. She called the Demon Police and everything!"

She laughed with sheer joy and triumph. I joined her, but sobered as I realized I would have to leave her soon.

"Dixie, you are so lucky you get to live on your own."

"Yeah, it's great." I smiled and lied.

Satan believed all his daughters should be independent. At sixteen I received many gifts, the bungalow being one of them. As lovely as it was to have my own space, I was lonely. The Dark Palace had been a wonderful place to grow up, but it was always so busy and filled with hundreds of Demons I didn't know. As I got older I began to notice some of the murky and horrible things that often took place in the palace. We were in Hell after all. I was fairly sure my dad thought I'd be safer and happier in my little home. The truth was I longed for a family. A traditional family, even one as uptight as Stella's.

"Sooo," Stella said as she knocked me out of my pity party. "What hot sexy outfit are you going to wear tonight?"

"I was thinking about jeans," I replied, moving toward the pile of clothes I laid out.

"Jeans?" She groaned in dismay as her eyes went wide with concern. "I was thinking more along the line of Prada or Gucci."

"Nope." I smiled. A warm glow settled in my chest as I thought about Hayden. "It sounds pretty casual. I don't want to overdress."

There was no way I was going to tell Stella he wanted me to wear flying clothes. Hell, I didn't even know what that meant. I'd never told anyone about my desire to fly except Hayden and Blanche.

"You don't think he's going to take you cliff diving, do you?" Stella began to sort through the pile, discarding what she didn't like.

"Lucifer, I hope not." I prayed that wasn't his idea of flying. Nevertheless, I was definitely wearing jeans.

Stella pulled a rockin' pair of dark brown Doc Maarten

combat boots, a pair of True Religion jeans, a sleeveless, sheer pale mocha flowing top with a lacy chocolate camisole for underneath. Kind of delicate, feminine biker chick.

"You will be totally hot in this," she decided. "He'll be on his knees. Your boobs and ass will be amazing."

"Maybe I should wear something else."

"Nope." Stella laid down the law. "It's this or you go naked."

"Fine." It was absolutely no use to go against Stella once she had her mind made up. With her new powers she could probably dress me however she desired. Furthermore, she had a great fashion sense and I liked what she picked out.

"Go take a shower," she commanded. "Use that lemony grapefruity shampoo." She plopped back down on my couch and grabbed the remote. "I'm going to watch me some *South Park*. I love those guys."

I rolled my eyes and left her to her program.

AN HOUR LATER I WAS READY. CLEAN, DRESSED AND NERVOUS AS Hell. I never wore much makeup, but Stella insisted on mascara, a little blush and some pale pink sparkly lip gloss. I glanced in the mirror and liked what I saw. Stella was a genius and she wasn't afraid to remind me repeatedly. She repaired my chipped black nail polish with some quick dry stuff she had in her purse. We agreed to let my hair fall loose and wild. I did feel pretty and was grateful she was here.

I let myself go to that bad place for a moment realizing Stella was doing all the things a mother should be doing. Motherless children often ached for a maternal figure, I had read. I needed to get over it and buck up and be grateful for what I did have… and I was grateful. Not everyone had a father who loved them, a ton of sisters that they adored for the most part and the greatest best friend in the universe.

"Damn girl, you are so pretty it makes my teeth hurt." Stella admired her handiwork.

"Shut up," I groaned. The reality of what I was about to do hit me. "I think I'm going to hurl."

I sat down on one of the dining room chairs and put my head between my knees. Stella rubbed my back and made tsking noises.

"I believe I told you to shut up." I mumbled from between my legs. "I can't do this. I need to call him and tell him not to come." I shot up and searched for my cell phone.

I spotted it on the coffee table. As I went to grab it, lightning struck and it turned into a banana.

"Stella!" I screamed. "Turn it back. Are you trying to ruin my life?"

"Nope," she informed me unsympathetically. "I'm trying to help you get a life."

"You suck." I sat down on the coffee table with the banana and pouted.

"You suck," she retorted as she unsuccessfully tried to suppress her laughter.

"It's not funny," I yelled, attempting to bite back the smile that was threatening to split my face.

"You need to stop dating BOB."

"Bob?" Who was she talking about? I wasn't dating anyone named Bob...

"Your battery operated boyfriend," she replied with an evil grin.

I blushed from head to toe. "I like BOB," I muttered.

"Dixie, do you like Hayden?" Stella's voice grew very serious.

I ran my hands through my wild mass of hair and sighed. "Yes, I like him. I'm afraid I like him too much. Every time he touches me I feel a jolt of electricity shoot through me and I'm terrified I'm going to say something mortifying."

"There's a good chance you'll say something dumb," Stella agreed.

39

"Thanks for the vote of confidence." I laid back on the coffee table and peeled the banana. "Is this edible?"

"Totally," she assured me. "Look, if you're worried about being stupid, just let him do most of the talking. Ask him questions about himself. Guys love to talk about themselves. By the way, Little Missy, this is not just about if he likes you. You are also free to figure out if you really like him," she said with authority.

"Where'd you learn all that?"

"*Cosmo.*"

"Does that apply to Demons? That's a mortal magazine," I said with a mouth full of banana.

"A guy is a guy is a guy. Mortal, Demon, Angel, whatever."

Stella stood up to leave. She walked over to my landline and ripped it out of the wall. I groaned.

"I'm simply saving you from yourself," she smugly informed me. "Your cell phone and land line will be fixed by the time you get home so you can call me and thank me for making you go." She curtsied and walked to the front door.

"Hey Stella," I called.

"Yep?"

"Thank you."

She smiled and left.

CHAPTER SIX

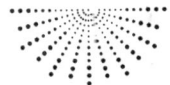

I KNEW HE WAS HERE. NO SOUND, NO PURR OF AN ENGINE, NO BEEP of a horn… I felt it. It was as if I was connected to him on some bizarre level. It completely freaked me out. My heart beat faster and I was short of breath. I wondered for a brief moment if I was having a panic attack, but the feeling of perfect calm amidst the storm in my mind made me realize I wasn't panicked at all. I couldn't name what I was feeling. I'd never felt it before.

Holy Hell, if I was this much of a mess before I saw him I was worried I'd self-combust in his actual presence.

The soft knock at the door jerked me back to reality. Adrenalin shot through my veins. I jumped up and ran to the front door, took two deep breaths and opened it.

Hayden stood in the doorway, hands in his jean pockets wearing a faded green t-shirt that made his eyes appear more emerald than the jewel. His beauty stole my breath and I was grateful I had the door to hold me up.

"Hi Dixie." He smiled and I melted. "You look beautiful."

My voice decided to take a vacation. I stood there and mutely stared at him.

He chuckled and extended his hand. "Are you ready?"

"Yes," I whispered. Hades, I sounded like a baby. I cleared my throat. "Yes, I'm ready. Do you think I'll need a jacket?" I asked, trying to behave like a rational, mature twenty-one year old woman.

"I've got one in the truck if you get cold." He nodded to his big black pickup truck.

Dang, I love pickup trucks. Was there anything I was going to discover about this guy I didn't like? I somehow doubted it. He took my hand and a tingle shot up my arm.

"Did you feel that?" I gasped.

"Yep." He held my hand tighter so I couldn't pull away.

"What was that?"

"Not sure, but I like it a lot." He grinned and pulled me along. I giggled and followed him to the truck.

The interior was black, buttery custom leather and the truck smelled like him. I took a deep breath to commit his scent to memory. If I kept acting like an ass, I feared this would be my one and only date with him. I needed to remember every detail.

He got in the truck. I kept my eyes glued straight ahead, afraid if I glanced at him I would say something stupid like "I love you." I waited for the engine to rev up, but nothing happened. I felt his gaze on me. It made me both happy and uncomfortable.

I peeked over at him. "Is everything okay?"

"Yep," he replied.

"Is the truck... um, broken?" I asked.

"Nope."

"Oh, okay."

He continued to stare.

Did he change his mind about the date? I felt sick. Should I get out and go back inside? Should I say thank you and shake his hand before I get out? Stella would know what to do. Maybe I should ask him questions about himself. I was a little unsure about putting my dating skills into the hands of *Cosmo* magazine, but I certainly wasn't doing well with my own skill set. I didn't have any freakin' skills. Questions. I'd ask him questions.

I plastered a smile on my face and turned my body toward his to start my interrogation. I opened my mouth to speak, but the intensity of his stare rendered me speechless.

"I love looking at you." His voice was smokey and my heart lurched.

"You do?" The dreaded heat began to crawl up my neck.

"I do," he said. "You make me feel happy and strange and nervous and excited."

My wildly beating heart was the only thing I could hear. This could go one of two ways—I could laugh and act like he made a great joke or I could be honest.

"You make me feel all those things too," I said softly. My eyes dropped to his mouth.

"You scare the Hell out of me, Dixie, in the best way possible."

His breath smelled delicious and it took everything I had not to slam him against the door to taste him. "You scare me too, so we're even."

He exhaled an overly dramatic sigh. "Well, now that we got that out of the way, we can relax and have a great time. Okay?" His eyes were full of amusement as they searched mine.

"Okay," I agreed. "Where are we going?"

"It's a surprise."

THE DRIVE TOOK ABOUT FORTY-FIVE MINUTES DOWN WINDING roads I'd never traveled before. My voice came back with a vengeance. Thankfully it was mutual. I kept forgetting how handsome he was because he was so smart and funny. We talked about movies, books, music, school, drunk teachers and how the Underworld was the greatest place in the universe.

I told him how Ernest Hemingway scared the Hell out of me

when I was five by describing bullfighting in graphic bloody detail. Of course Hemingway resided in Heaven but was quite fond of the atmosphere in Hell. Satan and Hemingway were known to go at each other with gusto and pitcher after pitcher of mojitos with the occasional Cuban cigar thrown in. Hayden sheepishly informed me that *Gone With the Wind* was one of his all time favorites, so I let him off the hook by professing my love for Barry Manilow.

We argued theology and laughed about the mortals' obsession with Vampyres. I giggled so hard I snorted when he imitated movie scenes depicting Demons. *Rosemary's Baby* and *The Exorcist* were the best. My snort made him laugh so hard he had to pull over. I felt my face grow hot, but my embarrassment disappeared as he swore to me it was cute and begged me to do it again. I refused, called him an asswipe and punched him in the arm, which only made him laugh harder.

Cosmo magazine was full of it. I didn't need to grill him about himself. I just need to be me. I only stopped breathing a couple of times when I caught him staring with something in his eyes that looked like wonder.

"We're here," he said, his excitement was contagious.

"Where's here?" I peered out the window.

We were parked at the edge of a monster field of wildflowers. There was no moon, but the stars were out and bathed the scene before me with a soft glittery glow. It was exquisite.

"Is there a restaurant here?"

"I brought the restaurant with us." He gave me an irresistible grin.

"Okay." I was confused.

"Come on." He got out of the truck and went around to the back.

He handed me a soft blanket and pulled out a large cooler. "Follow me," he instructed.

I did. If he had told me to stand on my head and yodel, I would have done that too.

He spread the blanket on the ground and opened the cooler. It was filled with all sorts of yummy food. He laid out plates and napkins, patted the ground next to him and waited for me to join.

Was I nuts? I was alone with a guy I barely knew in the middle of nowhere. It was an awfully pretty flower field in the middle of nowhere, but nowhere nonetheless. The flowers were not the prettiest thing here... he was, but that was beside the point. I was having insane urges to touch him and my stomach was flipping around like it was hosting an international gymnastics competition. This was a recipe for disaster.

My body tensed and I considered running away, but I had no idea where we were. My grip was tenuous at best on all of the emotions ping ponging around inside me. Just as I was about to give into my fear and run, he started to sing one of my favorite Barry Manilow songs... badly.

"Oh Dixie, well you came and you gave without taking, but I sent you away

Oh Dixie, well you kissed me and stopped me from shaking

And I need you today, oh Dixie..."

"Stop," I laughed, and dove toward him to cover his mouth with my hand. "You're destroying Barry!"

I tripped over the blanket and onto Hayden. I knocked him to his back and ended up right on top of him, nose to nose. Time stopped along with my breathing capabilities. My world was right and I felt happy. I was safe all tangled up in his big strong body. I knew my eyes were beginning to glitter with tears. It was so perfect that it scared the Hell out of me. Way more than Ernest Hemingway did when I was five.

"You don't like my singing?" he whispered, our lips almost touching.

"Um, no. It was awful."

His green eyes sparkled in the starlight and he took a shaky breath. Was he as affected as I was? Did he feel the same things?

"You've mortally wounded me," he teased. "My secret ambition is to be a rock star."

"You're going to need to rethink that one."

My voice sounded wobbly to my own ears and my eyes were glued to his mouth. I carefully eased away and attempted to squash down my raging hormones. Wasn't working.

Disappointment flashed in his eyes. I couldn't tell if it was because I moved or because I had insulted his singing. He didn't try to stop my retreat, which was a relief. Kind of.

"Are you hungry?" he asked, sitting up, seemingly unaware of my inner turmoil. He moved to the cooler.

"Sure," I replied as I removed imaginary lint from my jeans. I watched him through lowered lashes and picked at my manicure. I thought about sitting on my hands to keep from reaching for him, but I worried that might look weird.

"What do you want?" He held up two sandwiches. "I've got turkey and gouda or ham and brie. I also have cheese and crackers, bruschetta, wine, strawberries and dark chocolate."

I wasn't sure I could keep food down with the circus performing in my stomach, but I was hungry. I certainly didn't want him to think I was one of those girls who didn't eat. I loved to eat. "Ham, please."

"Coming right up," he smiled. He made two heaping plates. I grabbed a glass of wine and my plate and dug in.

"Mmm," I said after taking a bite of my sandwich. "This is amazing. Where'd you get it?"

"I made it," he told me as he bit into his own.

"Really?"

"Dixie," he laughed. "You're going to give me a complex. First you think I'm illiterate and now you're shocked I can make a sandwich."

"I'm sorry, it's just that you're so... " I stopped, unable to tell him how beautiful and amazing and smart and funny I thought he was.

"Just because I'm Satan's gift to women." He grinned evilly and flexed his considerable muscles. "Doesn't mean I'm as dumb as a box of hair," he teased as he continued to flex and make ridiculous sound effects.

"I don't think you're dumb at all," I protested, rolling my eyes at his macho display. "You just keep surprising me."

"In a good way?" He tilted his head and ran his finger down my arm.

My arm tingled with his energy. "In a very good way."

We ate in silence. A gentle breeze caressed my bare arms and flowers danced in the field like colorful little fairies. I was happy. I kept stealing glances at the beautiful boy who made amazing sandwiches. Every time I peeked, he was staring at me.

"Do you want anything else?" Hayden asked.

Boy, there's a loaded question. "Um... no, I'm good."

Dots of brilliant purple light quietly filled the grass and trees and sky. Fireflies glowed purple in Hell. Some were a lighter violet and others boasted a deep indigo. The trees looked like they'd been strung with sparkling amethyst. They were my favorites. I put my hand out to catch one, but Hayden was quicker.

"Here you go." He delicately placed the fragile bug in my hand. "A sapphire for the Princess."

"Thank you, my loyal subject." I uttered grandly, behaving like some of my older sisters who thought they were the bomb. "Hayden." I bit my lower lip to hide my smile. "You have mustard on your mouth."

"No, I don't," he shot back in mock offense.

"Yes, you do."

"Where?" he demanded.

"On your lip," I said, pointing to my own.

"On your lip?"

"No, dorko." I laughed. "On yours."

"Come and show me," he challenged. One side of his mouth lifted into the sexiest smirk ever. "I dare you."

"You should know better than to dare one of Satan's daughters, pretty boy," I informed him as I crawled across the blanket toward him. He tensed as I neared and his eyes went from emerald to red. He had never been more beautiful, mustard and all. "Should I use my finger or my tongue?" I asked silkily.

Holy Hell, when did my inner ho-bag decide to show up? My dad would be so proud.

"Your finger would be fine," his voice was husky. "But your tongue would be much better."

"Tongue it will be." I leaned into him, knowing my golden eyes had turned as blood red as his. The power I felt was overwhelming. I was scaring myself silly, but I had no desire to stop. I wanted to press my lips and my body to his from the very first moment I saw him. If he never called again because my inner slut had taken over my body, then his loss. Besides, I was only going to kiss him.

I very carefully ran my tongue along his bottom lip. He inhaled sharply at the contact. His body was as tight as a coil about to spring.

I pulled back and smiled. "Good mustard."

"I think you might have missed a little," he replied in a tone that sent shivers through me.

"You think?" I didn't move an inch.

"I think." He stayed as still as I did.

Ball was in my court. I slowly closed the slight distance between us and pressed my lips to his. It was magic. A hot spiral of something unfamiliar made my bones feel watery. I grasped his broad shoulders for balance.

He didn't stick his tongue down my throat or try to grab me anywhere inappropriate. His kisses were featherlight and his tongue gently traced the fullness of my bottom lip. My heart hammered furiously and I knew I was a goner. He cupped my face in his strong hands and pressed soft kisses on my lips, my nose, my cheeks and my eyes. I was dizzy and falling madly in love.

"Dixie," he moaned. "We have to stop."

"Why?" I touched my forehead to his.

"Because I want you to fall for my intellect and charm before I let you ravish my body."

I giggled and brushed my fingertips along his cheekbones and jaw. "What if I only want you for your hot bod?"

He chuckled, "I won't be used that way. Well... maybe once or twice." He grinned. "I'm looking for something lasting. I plan to make you fall head over heels, no turning back in love with me."

I knew he was joking, but I was already there.

He kissed me once more and my toes curled. He stood and pulled me to my feet.

"I want to make one of your dreams come true."

"You kind of already have," I said, unable to tear my eyes away. I leaned into him and laid my head on his chest. I tentatively wrapped my arms around him. He was so broad my hands didn't touch.

"Oh Dixie, you're killin' me." His voice was unsteady.

"Really?" I was amazed I had the power to make such a strong man so vulnerable.

"Really." He reluctantly pulled away and held me at arms' length.

"I'll race you to the pond," he challenged.

"What pond?" All I could see was flowers.

"It's two miles that way." He pointed across the beautiful field.

"What's at the pond?"

"One of your dreams," he smiled.

"You're on."

CHAPTER SEVEN

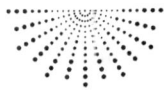

WE RAN THROUGH THE FIELD WITH WILD ABANDON. THE WIND
whipped through my hair and I felt free. All Demons were blessed
with speed, but my speed was unusual. To the human eye, I
completely disappeared. To the Demon eye, I looked like a blur.

I was amazed and delighted Hayden could keep up with me.
Then I got pissed when I discovered he was beating me. Then he
vanished.

He was sitting nonchalantly on the ground near the pond, legs
crossed, hands behind his head with a big smile on his face. With
both hands on my hips I slowly circled him. My eyes narrowed as
he basked in his victory.

"How did you do that?" I continued to circle him.

"I'm fast." He grinned.

"No," I corrected him. "I'm fast."

"But I'm faster." He hopped up, grabbed me and swung me in a
circle.

"Put me down, you cheater," I shrieked, trying to stifle my
laughter.

He put me down and I took in my surroundings. It was unlike
anything I'd ever seen. The pond shimmered as if covered in a

thin layer of diamonds. Huge weeping willow trees with giant crimson flowers adorning them blew in the breeze. Wildflowers dotted the bank, but it was the smell. I couldn't find words to describe it. The closest words were wind, summer rain and promise, but even that didn't do it justice.

"What is this place?" I whispered reverently.

"It's my home," he smiled and took my hand.

"You live here?"

"Well, not exactly here." He laughed. "I have a house about ten miles away, but this is part of my property."

"Do you live with your parents?" I realized I knew nothing about his family.

"No, my dad gave up on me a long time ago and my mom is gone."

His matter of fact tone didn't hide his sadness.

"I'm so sorry," I sputtered. "I didn't know."

He squeezed my hand and pulled me into a hug. "It's okay, Dixie. It's been a long time. I'm good."

"Do you have any brothers or sisters?"

"I have a brother, but we're not close. I haven't seen him in years." He paused. "This is getting too serious. I'm starting to sound pathetic to my own ears." He grinned. His mood abruptly changed from pensive to silly. He picked me up and carried me to the edge of the pond.

"If you throw me in," I threatened. "I will make your life a living Hell for all eternity."

His eyes twinkled with mischief. "That hadn't occurred to me, but now that you mention it..."

I wrapped my arms around him in a vise-like hold. If I was going in, he was coming along for the ride.

"Dixie?"

"Yes?" My face was buried in his neck. His scent was making my tummy tingle.

"First of all, I would never throw you in the pond, and second, you're cutting off my circulation."

"Whoops." I grinned and eased up on my hold. "Where's my dream,—or was that just a story you made up so you could kick my ass in the race?"

He laughed joyously and gently pushed my hair out of my face. "No Dixie, your dream is right here. I simply have to show you."

"So show me." I was getting a little nervous. I had no clue what he was going to do.

"Can you keep a secret?" he whispered against my hair.

Little fissions of magic whooshed through my body and I felt lightheaded. I wasn't sure if I caused it or if he did.

"I can keep a secret," I assured him.

"You can't tell anyone or question me about it."

What in Hades was he about to show me? "I won't," I said, wondering if this was such a good idea. He was making me nervous.

"Promise?"

"Promise," I whispered. If he killed me, at least I'd already kissed him.

Hayden put me down and took a few steps back. "Close your eyes, Dixie," he instructed.

I did.

As soon as my lids shut, an absurd amount of magic filled the air. I'd grown up around magic and power and I knew the real deal when it happened. This was the real deal. I felt raw, alive and alarmed. What in Satan's name was he doing to create such a strong enchantment?

"Open your eyes." His voice was deeper and sexier. Like that was even possible.

I slowly opened my eyes and I gasped. This couldn't be real. I closed my eyes and reopened them to make sure they weren't playing tricks on me. They weren't. My knees buckled and I sank to the ground. He was glorious—I'd never seen anything so magnificent in my life.

"Are you trying to impress me?" I asked, awestruck.

"Maybe," he replied. "Is it working?"

"And then some."

His eyes were closed and his arms were outstretched, reaching to the sky. His shirt was gone and his body seemed to glow, but that wasn't what astonished me.

He had wings.

Huge, breathtaking golden blond wings that matched his hair. They shimmered like spun gold in the starlight and blew gently in the breeze.

I stood up on wobbly legs and approached him. His eyes stayed closed, but a smile touched his lips. I circled him again, but this time in shock and reverence.

I felt small and inconsequential compared to the beautiful creature that stood before me. Magic hung thick in the air. I walked slowly around him to really see his wings.

"You can touch me, Dixie," he coaxed. His voice was richer and more seductive. My already weak knees weakened some more. He sounded older and wiser, but I knew he was still Hayden.

I reached out and stroked his wings. He sighed in contentment. They were soft. Softer than cashmere, softer than puppy fur, softer than anything I'd ever touched. I ran my hands through them as tears poured down my cheeks.

"Why are you crying?" Hayden turned his body, his face full of concern.

"You're so beautiful," I murmured, stepping back from him. The very air around him was electric. How could someone like him possibly want someone like me?

"Don't back away from me, Dixie," his voice was soft. "Not now. Not like this." He held his arms out to me.

I didn't hesitate or even think. I ran right into his arms, the only place I ever wanted to be again. The tension left his body as he wrapped his arms and wings around me.

"Would you like to fly with me?" he asked, still holding me tight.

"More than I've ever wanted anything in my life," I whispered.

NOT IN MY WILDEST DREAMS COULD I HAVE IMAGINED WHAT IT really felt like to fly.

I laid on his back, my arms around his neck and my legs around his waist. I nestled between his downy wings. My heart beat so loudly I was sure he could hear it.

"Are you okay?" he asked. I heard the smile in his voice.

"I don't know," I admitted.

"We're not even in the air yet." He laughed.

"I know." I was grateful he couldn't see the blush that had covered my whole face. "It's just that... um, I'm not sure what I'll dream about anymore."

"You'll dream about me, Dixie," he said so quietly I wasn't positive I heard him correctly.

His wings expanded with a whoosh. They had to be six feet of gleaming gold on either side. His skin felt hot to my touch and the feeling of anticipation skittered down my spine like little mice. He took several running steps toward the pond and we were airborne.

I shrieked with delight as we glided low over the water and I felt his body shake with laughter.

"Go higher," I urged, locking my knees around him tighter. His feathers tickled my nose so I raised my head. The view was tremendous.

We soared up like a roller coaster and my tummy dropped. I squealed in sheer terror and joy. The wind roared through my hair and his wings. The ground below looked like a fairy tale, moving and sparkling in the starlight.

The beat of his wings was reminiscent of a calming

metronome. I let one of my hands loose and ran it through his hair.

"None of that, Little Missy. I'll lose my concentration."

"Sorry." I giggled and wrapped myself back around his neck.

The peace and happiness I felt was new to me. I was meant to fly. In my heart I'd always known. I just never knew it would take a beautiful boy with golden wings and green eyes to get me there.

We soared so high the stars were our traffic. Wanting desperately to touch one, I reached out. Although I knew they were millions of miles away, I swear I felt their heat. He rolled and dipped, flying at extreme heights and almost touching the ground. I held on for dear life. Even though I knew a fall wouldn't kill me unless I got decapitated on the way down, I didn't want to let go of him. I loved the way his body felt under mine. It was sinful.

We flew for hours. I was positive I'd have no voice tomorrow for all the screaming and laughing I did. The terrain below began to look familiar. We were at my house. He landed smoothly in my front yard. I hopped off, ran around to his front and threw myself into his arms.

"That was the most amazing thing I've ever done," I babbled. "It was beautiful and you're beautiful and I…" I stopped abruptly. Hell's Bells, I was about to tell him I loved him.

"You what?" Hayden bent down so we were nose to nose.

I couldn't think straight with him so close. "I… um, I don't know." I pulled back a little bit so my brain would work. I touched his lips and gently ran my fingertips back and forth. "This was the best night of my life."

He closed his eyes and leaned into my touch. "Mine too."

"Really?"

"Yes Dixie, really, really." He chuckled. "Would you like something to remember it by?"

"Yes." I knew even without a memento I'd remember this night forever.

He removed a small feather from his wing and handed it to me. It glistened in my hand like a jewel.

"Thank you." I would treasure it forever. "I'll see you at class tomorrow?"

"No," he said regretfully, tucking my windblown hair behind my ears. "I have to take care of something tomorrow, but I'll see you on Friday."

My disappointment was embarrassing, but it seemed to make him happy.

"It's only one day." He pulled me into a tight hug. "I promise I'll be thinking about you the entire time we're apart."

"Okay," I said as I tried to hide my disappointment.

He lifted my chin and brushed his mouth against mine. My lips tingled with need. "Go inside now."

"Your truck," I remembered. "It's at the field. How will you get home?"

Hayden laughed and spread his wings. "I have several modes of transportation."

Hades, after an entire night of amazing, I had to end it with something stupid. "Right," I murmured.

"Dixie." He stopped me as I was about to go into my little house. "Tonight was perfect. You are perfect and I've never been so happy in my life."

My breath caught in my throat. He gave me one last intense kiss, turned and flew into the night.

He was right. It was perfect.

I felt his absence keenly and my cozy bungalow made me more lonely than ever. I grabbed my now working cell phone and quickly texted Stella a big thank you and a semi play by play of the highlights minus the flying part. I wandered to my room and crawled into my bed fully dressed. I clutched my feather to my chest and fell asleep.

That night I dreamt about flying, but for the first time in my life... I wasn't flying alone.

CHAPTER EIGHT

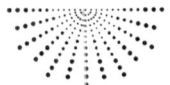

CLASS WAS BORING WITHOUT HAYDEN THERE. I FOUND MYSELF
unable to concentrate on anything academic. My father would be
delighted. Stella had a field day giving me crap, but nothing could
rip my mind from reliving the most beautiful night of my life.
Well, nothing except another round of group therapy.

Due to the fact that we were scheduled to leave Hell soon, we'd
graduated from therapy to combat training. As usual anything we
did turned into a royal cluster... and of course we were back at
my bungalow.

Not having heard Carl speak much in the months I'd known
him, I remembered why when he tried to persuade the group to
take up hip-hop instead of combat.

"You thould all realithe that fighting ith dangerouth and hip-
hop ith good cardio," he explained as he busted a few moves,
trying to impress.

"I really don't think hip-hop will protect us from Angels and
all sorts of other things that will want to kill us on Earth," Myrtle
volunteered as she tried to imitate Carl's moves.

"Angels really want to kill us?" I asked in a strangled voice.

"Sweet Lucifer's bouncing balls, of course they do! Angels, other Demons and Hell knows what else," Janet chimed in happily.

Why she was happy was a mystery, but I was not. "Guys, what would you say if we decided not to go to Earth and we just stayed in Hell and opened a dance school?"

Carl looked intrigued, but Janet and Myrtle shook their heads impatiently.

"No. Satan has said Earth and to Earth we shall go," Janet declared.

"Your dad may be a whack job, and *please* don't tell him I said that, but he's been around for millions and knows the score. If he's sending us there it's for a reason. And I prefer to keep my head," Myrtle said.

"What if we open a danth thcool on Earth?" Carl suggested as he did a tremendously horrid split leap that made my groin hurt.

"I don't want to go," I said quietly. "I have no power yet."

I wondered if this new wrinkle would cause a violent episode. I knew if they demolished my house again Stella would come to my rescue. My odd little group didn't even seem to notice the bungalow had reverted back to its former glory or even care that I was powerless aside from a few normal Demon tricks. Whatever. I hadn't been able to figure out a kind way to dump them and I wasn't sure I really wanted to. So here we all sat back in my bungalow debating kick lines as opposed to kickboxing.

"Your power will come," Carl said gently. My nutty group surrounded me protectively. "Bethides." He grinned evilly. "We've been holding out on you."

"Wait. What?"

"Carl," Janet admonished as she put her stubby little hands on her cute curvy little hips.

"Jutht remember, what the eye theeth is not alwayth true."

"Enough," Myrtle mumbled grumpily. "I like my life even if you don't. Can it."

"Besides, if you think Hell is safe… " Janet muttered worriedly.

"Why does everyone know more than I do?" I demanded, tired of all the cryptic bullshit I had dealt with my entire life.

Carl smiled. He actually had beautiful teeth and cute dimples, but the lisp. Hoo baby, now I knew why he preferred to communicate through interpretive dance. On Earth he could have had speech therapy, but in Hell you were stuck with what you got.

"Pathienth is a virtue and withdom cometh with time and maturity," he said as he patted my head like a dog.

At loath to admit it, he might be right. I hadn't behaved like the grown woman I'd become. I was stuck in adolescence. Could I change? Did I have a choice?

"We're Demons. We are born of Hell and sin. We are destined to make sure the balance of good and evil remains. Without one the other distorts and becomes the end of the world. Simple and impossible," Myrtle stated.

When in the Hell did she get so smart? Had they really been holding out on me?

We'd all been born in Hell. However there were different levels in Hell, same as Heaven, from what I'd heard. The lowest level, or the Basement, was truly horrifying. That was the Hell from nightmares. The Hellfire and brimstone, screaming in agony, burning for eternity Hell. That was where the very evil went when they died. They were punished in fire until the end of time. Nobody could give me a definition on what the end of time actually meant. You would assume that my dad or his brother God would have an idea on that one, but if they did they were incredibly tight lipped. I'd never been to the Basement and I never planned on going. A couple of my sisters, the ones from the seventh and eighth centuries, seemed to enjoy visiting the Basement, but it just wasn't for me.

The next level up was the Sub-Basement, another place I'd never been. The Sub-Basement was for lesser evil souls when they died. There was fire there too, just not as hot. The lucky people who resided there were not quite bad enough for the Basement, but not quite good enough for Purgatory. I knew many doubted Purgatory, but it existed. I'd been there and trust me, you don't want to go. It's boring and beige, it smells stale and they play bad cheesy elevator music twenty-four seven..

There was also an area in the Sub-Basement that my dad preferred to ignore. It was an area where souls did penance so they could leave Hell and ascend to Purgatory... then possibly Heaven. It was a major long shot, but there were some who I did think ended up in Hell by mistake. Not that I would share that with my dad—my outstanding grades were about all he could take. The flip side of that was that some in Purgatory end up becoming violent and had to descend into Hell. Personally I think the constantly piped in elevator music caused some souls to snap. It would make me want to tear my own head off.

And then there was the main floor—where we all had been born. It was as big as the United States, but most of the action took place in the northeast corner in an area about the size of Washington D.C. This was where the Demons lived. We were born in Hell and we were the loyal army of Satan, my dad. Many Demons took the portals back and forth to Earth for pleasure and work. I'd never been allowed to go. Besides, I'd rather stay in Hell with my family no matter how dysfunctional we might be.

It was a huge misconception that my father created all the chaos and evil on Earth. Mortals were given free will by my Uncle God, and they created evil all by their lonesome. My dad got to punish the you know what out of those idiots who choose to be heinously bad. And quite honestly some of them deserved my dad's wrath. He loved his job.

Another misconception is that Hell is below and Heaven is above. What does that even mean? Nothing is up or down, that's just human mythology. Most likely the mistake was made because Hell was occasionally called the Underworld. Hell and Heaven are simply on different planes, accessible through portals. Earth was modeled after a combination of the seasons, climates and terrains of Heaven and Hell. We all shared the same moon and sun and stars.

I'd been raised to be grateful to evil-doers, because without them Demons would not exist. Demons derived their power and magic from the chaos and evil of others. So while we don't necessarily cause it, we thrive on it or feed on it so to speak. Lest anyone forget, my dad's brother God dealt out the free will thing, not my dad. And now to combat his error in judgment, God and his army of Angels keep trying to end evil so my dad and his people, *including me*, will cease to exist. No offense, but God really screwed himself by letting men and women choose their own paths. If he wanted everyone to be good, he should have come up with a better plan. My dad finds this particular subject hilarious.

I was the black sheep of my family. There was my dad, me and the Seven Deadly Sins. My dad had been around since time began, and as history implied he was quite the ladies man. It was an irony that he had no sons, but as I learned in sex ed, the sperm determines the sex of the child so my dad was to blame for the overload of estrogen in Hell. However, his pregnant consort Amanda was possibly pregnant with a boy. That small fact could upset the hierarchy in Hell and had sent the Sins into a tailspin, especially my sister Wrath.

After a particularly violent and ugly episode where she'd tried to off Amanda and failed thanks to my cousin Astrid, she'd been punished—harshly. She and two of my other screw-up sisters, Lust and Greed, had been sent to Nirvana to be taught a lesson by Mother Nature. My stomach roiled at the thought. I knew Gigi liked me, but punishment by her hand even scared my dad.

My black sheep status stemmed from my inability to derive pleasure from evil. I assumed that was why I had no power or magic. This infuriated my dad to no end. He told me I had the potential to be the strongest of all his children. That was definitely a responsibility I didn't want. My punishment, as I saw it, was to attend group therapy to learn to become a harbinger of evil.

Well, I suppose everyone had to start somewhere. "I'm ready to kick some ass," I blurted to the shocked trio.

Myrtle grinned with excitement. "Now you're talking."

I prayed silently to my cousin Jesus that I wouldn't regret my new and improved attitude and that I'd be able to walk later.

CHAPTER NINE

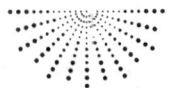

I WAS SORE AND BRUISED, BUT AMAZINGLY I'D HELD MY OWN—OR they'd just taken it easy on me. Carl punched like a bomb and Myrtle was no slouch. The big surprise was Janet. She was the reason I would have difficulty sitting for a few days. As a Demon I healed fast, but a beating is a beating. The pride they took in the black eyes and bruised ribs I dished out was encouraging, but I felt terrible for injuring them. And now on top of everything I'd been summoned to the Dark Palace for a party. My father's shindigs were infamous and I hoped to Hell I wasn't going to be featured this evening. Being summoned to the Dark Palace was not always a good sign. More often than not it was a very bad sign.

The Dark Palace was Satan's main residence and the home I grew up in. It was a sight to behold, and to me it was the loveliest place in Hades. It was nestled on about a thousand acres of the most beautiful and fertile property in Hell. Trust me, Hell was fertile and I'm not talking about the fact that I have seven sisters and a sibling on the way… Our climate was warm, breezy and balmy year round. Hell had more varieties of exotic plants, trees and flowers than Heaven did. My dad shoved that in his brother's face every chance he had.

The palace property was loaded with streams, ponds, rolling hills and meadows filled with blindingly colorful wildflowers. My bungalow was tucked into the far northwest corner of my father's land. My corner boasted huge weeping cherry trees, orchids and scads of bougainvillea.

The palace itself sat on forty very manicured acres. It looked like a giant Gothic cathedral. It was the grandest castle in the world including Heaven, Hell and everything in between.

I arrived early, handed my Porsche over to the valet Demon and made my way to the palace entrance. I was a little nervous. I was guessing my deportment date would be handed down this evening, but I couldn't imagine my Father would make it such a public event.

I'd dressed with care. My father expected no less from his daughters. My smokin' hot Stella McCartney dress and my Prada stilettos were the typical uniform that was expected. I carefully made my way to the huge carved teak doors guarded by the vicious Hell Hounds.

Vicious, my rear end. Another very well kept secret in Hell... the Hell Hounds were just big ugly puppies with razor sharp fangs and claws. I loved them and they loved me. The two that normally guarded the Palace entrance were my favorites, General George Patton and Bambi. They'd slept in my room when I was a child and I'd secretly pretended Bambi was my mother—a five hundred pound snaggle-toothed mother.

I was tempted to run up and bury my face in Bambi's fur, but I knew better. Appearances counted, and no one in Hell was to be privy to how sweet the Hounds really were. Not that they weren't deadly... they were, but only to the enemies of my father.

I was disappointed that General George wasn't standing duty, but I was delighted to see Bambi. She purred as I passed. I blew her a quick kiss. I missed them terribly. Their fur was so soft and silky and they smelled like brownies.

"Hi Bambi," I whispered when I was sure no one was watching. "I wish General George was here too."

"He's a little busy, but he sends his love."

I froze and gaped at her.

"Did you hear me?" she asked excitedly.

Her lips never moved, but her eyebrows waggled like crazy.

"Is that you, Bambi?" I asked, sure I was going nuts.

"Yes! Your powers are near if you can hear me. I've waited so long for this, my sweet child."

"Um... are you talking through your eyebrows?" I didn't want to insult her, but I had to know.

"Oh yes, dear. We eat with our mouths and talk through our brows. Never have bad breath that way." She leaned in and quietly informed me, "And we've been known to poop rainbows."

I bit down on my lips hard and tried to stifle my laugh. She made bizarre sense and that concerned me, but I was so happy to talk to her I ignored the oddities and the ass shooting rainbows part.

"Have you always been able to talk?"

"Yes, of course, but you couldn't hear us until you were ready," she replied.

"Can everyone hear you?"

"No, no, only the special ones. Your cousin Astrid could hear us," she said as she giggled joyously.

That didn't surprise me at all. Astrid was a True Immortal and as special as they come. I couldn't wait to visit her on Earth no matter how crabby her pregnancy had made her.

"I feel like crying," I told her as I leaned in for comfort. "I used to pretend you were my mom."

"I know, baby. I love you like my own and I always will. Go in to the party before someone sees us. Maybe I could come over for a sleepover before you leave."

"I would love that. Do you promise?" I asked.

"Do I promise what?" a thin and nasal voice demanded. "Dixie, what are you doing loitering on the front steps with the animals? It's not fitting and your father will not be pleased."

My father's pregnant consort Amanda looked me over with disdain.

"I was just… " I mumbled as I tried to think up a legit lie.

"Were you talking to your imaginary *friend*?" Her condescending laugh grated on my ears and brought tingling to my fingertips. My sisters could give me all the crap they wanted about Blanche—they loved me. This bitch could not.

I turned and leveled her with a stare I'd learned from my father. To my great delight she backed off in fear. "What I do and to whom I speak is no concern of yours, Amelia," I said in a voice I didn't know I possessed.

"My name is Amanda," she hissed, drawing up to her full height, which was a good six inches less than mine. At five foot nine I dwarfed her.

"Whoops." I smiled and shrugged. "My bad. And *Amanda*, I wouldn't call the Hell Hounds animals. They get insulted easily and they're always hungry."

Her overly made up eyes widened in terror and she made a hasty retreat back into the palace. Why the Hell my father decided to knock this one up was beyond me. Sure, she was beautiful, but he'd had some fantastic consorts over the years. For the life of me, I didn't get this one.

"You might want to try being nice to your father's lover," Cole, my father's second in command, admonished me as he stepped out of the shadows. Geez, this freakin' guy was everywhere.

"Yep, you're right. However, that goes both ways, Cole, and my father's consort is rude."

"She's an elder and should be respected. She carries the heir to Hell in her body," he said reverently.

That was up for debate according to my sisters, who were

positive the child wasn't my dad's, but I had no desire to debate that rumor with the humor-free Cole.

"You're right, Cole."

His eyes shot to mine in surprise. "So you will apologize?"

"I certainly will," I gushed sweetly. "As soon as she apologizes to me."

With that I brushed past him and made my entrance into the palace. I could swear I heard Bambi giggle as I left a shocked Cole in my wake.

"DIXIE," STELLA SQUEALED AS SHE RAN UP TO ME. "DAMN, YOU LOOK hot!"

I was so glad to see a familiar face I was shaking. I hadn't realized how nervous and uncomfortable dealing with Cole and Amanda made me, plus I was thrown by the electricity in my fingertips and Bambi's talking eyebrows. I squeezed her hard. "What are you doing here?"

"I'm not sure." She giggled and adjusted her black Armani shift. She was the cutest Demon in Hell, with her wild ginger curls and freckles on her little turned-up nose. "Mom and Dad informed me about an hour ago that we were coming to the Dark Palace. What gives?" she asked as she tucked a stray hair behind my ear.

"I have no clue." I was bewildered and getting worried. Still no sign of my dad. That was not so unusual, as he did love to make an entrance. "I thought I was coming here for my deportment date."

"Your dad wouldn't announce that in front of this many people."

"My thoughts exactly," I agreed, but I was still uncertain.

"Is Blanche here?" Stella asked as she ran her hands through the air and tried to grab my invisible friend.

"I don't... " I began.

"Yes, I'm here, I'm here, I'm here." Blanche appeared. "You

think I'd miss an overblown array of disgusting wealth and power like this?"

"She's here," I told Stella.

"Hi Blanche," Stella whispered as she desperately tried to see her.

"Tell her hi back," Blanche said.

"Blanche says hi." I grabbed Stella's hand as she started to trip over her very high heeled Manolo Blahniks.

"Holy Hell," she gasped, clutching my arm like a vise. "Does Blanche look a whole lot like you, but with ice blue eyes and better boobs?"

What was she talking about? Blanche's boobs weren't better than mine. They might be a tad bit bigger, but… "Oh my Satan, can you see her?" I was shocked.

"I think so." Stella was thrilled and so was Blanche. "She's gorgeous."

"Of course I am." Blanche laughed and tossed her locks. "And so are you."

Stella let go of my arm and moved toward Blanche. "No!" she cried. "Where did she go?"

"She's still right there," I said as I pointed to Blanche, who hadn't moved.

"I can't see her anymore."

"Have her hold your hand, Dixie," Blanche instructed. I grabbed Stella's hand and wondered if any of the Demons around us were paying attention to our bizarre conversation.

"She's back," Stella whispered reverently. "I have to touch you to see her. It's like she's another part of you."

Blanche approached us, smiling. She did look a lot like me except for her eyes. They were a crisp, clear icy blue and mine were as gold as they came.

"I can't stay," Blanche told us. "But it's so nice to finally meet you, Stella. You are so special to my Dixie, and for that I love you." She disappeared as quickly as she had appeared.

"Can you call her back?" Stella asked.

"Sometimes, but Blanche has her own agenda. I'm glad you can finally see her."

"Yeah." Stella sighed wistfully. "I wish we had figured out the touch thing a long time ago. There's something really different about Blanche."

"What do you mean?" I agreed, but I was curious for her answer.

"I can't put my finger on it," she mused. "I'll figure it out." She smiled and hugged me. "People are headed to the Grand Ballroom. Shall we?"

I cracked all the joints on both my left and right hands, leaned back and popped my aching sternum and finished off with my sore hips. "Yes, we shall."

CHAPTER TEN

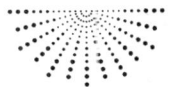

THE GRAND BALLROOM WAS A GROSS SHOW OF OBSCENE WEALTH and my father loved it. The marble floors were encrusted with precious gemstones: rubies, sapphires, emeralds, and diamonds and ten of the most gorgeous crystal chandeliers ever created spilled down from the ceilings.

Everyone of note in Hell was here and I had a bad feeling that I was going to be in the center ring of the circus. I gave Stella a quick hug and promised to catch up with her at the end of the evening. I moved to the back of the ballroom to an area that was reserved for Lucifer's family. I spotted my sisters Sloth, Pride, Envy and Gluttony all smiley and waving. It was difficult to miss us. We were quite tall and reeked of magic—well, at least they did. Oftentimes my sisters resided on Earth, reporting to my dad and making sure the Demons on Earth didn't upset the Balance of Chaos. Today they were here except for Wrath, Greed and Lust who were spending some frightening quality time with my grandma.

I spotted Carl and Janet. What the… ? She had forgone her beard and was wearing a pretty dress. Carl proudly had his arm around her and they looked so happy it made me grin. Blanche was gonna have to eat it about Janet's hair issues. Myrtle followed them like a third wheel and wore black jeans and a concert T. That was about as formal as she got.

They were too far away to get their attention and I quickly lost sight of them as more Demons filed into the Grand Ballroom. My favorite sister, Sloth, grabbed me in excitement.

"I think you're going to get your deportment date tonight," she said with her lazy sexy smile.

"I'm not ready, and thanks for leaving me with Gigi the other day."

"Oh honey child, I was fourteen when I got assigned—you're ready. Besides, I heard it went well with Gigi, short of her leaving Dad with no roof." Sloth laughed and kissed my forehead.

"You were deported eight hundred years ago," I said, reeling from the thought of my life changing so drastically. I glanced up and noticed the ballroom had a new mirrored ceiling. Oh my Hell, I held back a gag. My father's taste was truly appalling.

"You're twenty-one." Sloth stated the obvious. "And for whatever reason, Daddy thinks you're going to come into an assload of power very soon."

"Wouldn't it be better if I was at home when the assload arrived?"

"Nope," Gluttony, my second favorite sister, said as she smiled and ran her beautifully manicured hand down my cheek. "There are things happening that need to be dealt with and Daddy thinks you're the gal to do it."

"I haven't had any training and I pretty much suck at being a Demon."

"Oh baby," Sloth cooed as she pulled me close. "You're a beautiful Demon. None of us were trained before we were deported. Lucifer believes in on the job training. You can't conquer the world without failing miserably first, sweetie."

My stomach roiled at the thought of my impending assignment. "What if all I do is fail?" I whispered.

"You won't, my darling," Gluttony said as Pride and Envy nodded in agreement.

"Do you realize your sexy pet name is Donkey Booty?" Envy asked me as she played with her phone.

My sisters were obsessed with the name games on Facebook. The dirtier the better.

"I'm Smelly Booty," Gluttony moaned. "I don't like that one."

"Because it's accurate?" Envy asked with an evil smirk.

"I will kick your ass after the party," Gluttony shot back sulkily.

I did not want to be there for that. My sisters could take down cities when they fought.

"Mine's Honey Booty," Pride said gleefully. "I'll take that and keep it."

"I win. I'm Fire Booty. Trumps all you beeotches." Sloth laughed and then went silent.

Daddy had arrived.

The room quieted as Satan entered. His power was stunning and his beauty was absurd. Demons were a glamorous race, but my father put all to shame. His black Hugo Boss suit fit to perfection and he wore his black silk shirt open at the neck. He had an aura that was unexplainable. It instilled rabid loyalty, adoration and fear. He was beloved by his people and despised by his enemies, and he was good with that... very good.

"Good evening, my Demons," Satan laughed, showing even white teeth and dimples that brought women to their knees. My sister Sloth made a gagging sound as all the women in the room swooned over our father. I grinned and grabbed her hand.

"Do you know anything about me being... " I began.

"Shhh," Sloth admonished. We had to have exemplary behavior, and speaking while our father held court would not fly.

"Sloth" I whispered, panicked. "I've lived in Hell my whole life. I'm not ready to leave."

"Yes, you are," she whispered back. "Now, hush!"

I did, but it wasn't easy.

"Welcome, my people," my father's voice boomed through the Grand Ballroom. His second in command, Cole, stood on his right and his consort Amanda stood on his left. It was surprising he let her stand so close in public, but she was crafty at weaseling her way into the forefront of everything.

"Tonight is a night for celebration." He grinned. "My consort becomes more swollen with my son every day and my youngest daughter will soon go to Earth and do me proud."

Amanda smiled at the crowd and rubbed her belly. She was disgusting and in her glory. The crowd eyed her with distrust. The applause continued, but there was much speculative whispering. Amanda ignored it and mooned at my father. He gave her a short nod and turned away, much to her embarrassment. The crowd's chatter increased with the slight.

"Was it this bad with my mother?" I asked.

"We never met her," Envy replied. "You didn't come to us until you were three."

Right. Another mystery in my life that no one wanted to explain. I had no recollection of my first three years of life, hence no real clue where I truly came from.

Gluttony tensed beside me and her magic swirled. My sister had a gift for telepathy. She was the only female Demon I knew who could send her thoughts, and she could target who she wanted to communicate with. Right now it was me, Sloth, Envy, and Pride. *"Did Amanda not get the memo that once you bear Satan's child, he kicks your ass to the curb?"*

I put the mystery of my first three years on the back burner and I laughed. Clearly big fake-lipped and silicone-boobed Amanda didn't think that would apply to her since she was supposedly carrying a boy. Maybe she was right.

"If she blows out a boy, Daddy might keep her," Pride surmised.

"Possibly," Sloth agreed. "But I just don't see it."

Sloth had visions. Unshareable visions. Violent and terrifying

76

visions. She refused to speak of them because not all of her visions came to fruition. Free will had a habit of changing destiny constantly. So instead of scaring the crap out of everyone she kept them to herself. The only person privy to her visions was Satan. Sloth and our father were very close—he trusted her with enormous decisions.

As the crowds murmuring died down my father continued, "But the main reason I have called you here tonight is to celebrate my beautiful daughter, Dixie."

The crowd whistled and clapped. Amanda seethed and I blushed. I might not be very evil, but I was certainly very well liked. My dad held his hand out to me and I went to him. I was truly mesmerized and I adored my Prince of Darkness, my father. I would do anything for him, anything he asked of me.

"Your deportment draws near," he told me. "You shall transport to Earth and serve me well."

"I know and I will serve you proudly," I whispered, trying not to cry, but fear and abandonment were forefront in my mind.

He pulled me close and hugged me. "This is for the best."

I nodded, unable to reply.

I didn't want to leave my home, my family, my friends or Hayden. I could feel my eyes go crimson red beneath my closed lids. I slowly opened them and met my father's gaze that blazed red with emotion.

I heard Amanda hiss her displeasure at my father's attention to me. He turned on a dime and cut her to shreds with a look that sent her to her knees in fear. The crowd edged forward with excitement. She had better have a boy and it better be his or Amanda was dead. Satan raised his eyes to the room, clearly dismissing her. "The ones that have agreed to go to Earth with my child and protect her—come forward."

There was snickering as Carl, Janet and Myrtle stepped forward. My insides boiled with rage at the way they were treated, but they seemed to be oblivious. Many of the caretakers of Lucifer's daughters ended up dead. For real dead. Every time my siblings went to Earth, Uncle God sent a gaggle of Angels down to destroy us. I'd almost lost several of my sisters to God's wrath.

To be fair, Demons killed Angels on sight also. Of course since we were all immortal and difficult to kill it took some doing. So even though a Demon may gain Satan's highest praise by protecting the fruit of his loins, said Demon may not live long enough to enjoy it.

"Yes," he said, his melodic voice booming through the room as my caretakers approached. "You are brave and well-suited for this journey. Myrtle, Keeper of Secrets, Carl the Destroyer and Janet the Atrocity Maker, you will go with my child and protect her. Kneel to me," he commanded, and they did. He laid his hands on each of them and gave them another gift of Black Magic power. The Demonic audience hissed with jealously. I was hoping he'd give me a little extra magic hoohoo but he didn't. Apparently I had an assload of powers on the way.

"You will leave three weeks from today," Satan proclaimed. "Go and prepare."

With that the crowd began to disperse. I quickly thanked and hugged Carl, Janet and Myrtle. I still couldn't get over how pretty Janet looked without her fake beard. It really made me want to take a stab at Myrtle. I made my way back to my dad as I waved bye to Stella, miming a phone--international signal for *I'll call you*.

"Dad?"

"Yes, Dixie?"

"I don't want to leave," I whispered.

"I know, baby," he whispered back. "It won't be for long and I will never be far from you. It's time for you to come into who you are. When you were born I made a deal and part of that deal requires us to be parted for a while. Trust me, if I could keep you with me for eternity I would."

"I'm going to go out on a limb here and guess if I wanted you to expand on what you just said, you won't." I watched him closely.

"You guessed right. I've said more than I should have already. Just remember that I love you and I always will, no matter what path you ultimately choose to take."

"You're kinda freakin' me out, Dad," I told him. I wanted him to keep talking as much as I wanted him to stop.

He grabbed me and hugged me hard. It felt so good. As he let me go, Amanda slithered over and took me into an embrace purely for my father's benefit. Cole and several other high-ranking Demons drew his attention away.

"You're a spoiled rotten little brat and you will fail. You will disappoint your father greatly, but I will be there for him when he realizes how much time he's wasted on you," she hissed viciously in my ear.

For the first time in my twenty-one years I knew true dislike, actual hatred. I wasn't sure why, but this woman brought out the worst in me. The need to destroy her was intense, but that would be a cluster of epic proportions. A bizarre rush of power came alive inside me and manifested in my fingertips. I remembered how my cousin Astrid had popped Amanda's collagen lips with magic…

Did I dare? Would it even work? It would be quite reckless and out of character, but I had a hate-on for the smug Demon hissing evil in my ear. I grinned. I would not copy my cousin Astrid. I would do one better. Glancing over and making sure my dad was engaged, I raised my fingers and pointed at her overly-blown silicone chest and I flicked.

I held my breath. I watched a glittery mist fly from my fingers and head toward my target at alarming speed… and they popped. I think. I might have made them disappear. Shit.

Amanda's scream of fury was nothing short of earsplitting.

"What's wrong?" Satan demanded of his consort impatiently. I wasn't sure he liked her any more than we did.

"Cramp," she said as she crossed her arms quickly over her chest. "Excuse me."

She left, but not before she gave me a glare so vicious it actually unsettled me. She was horrid and I couldn't believe my dad couldn't see it. My father nodded to Cole, who followed quickly on her heels.

"All right, off with you. I have to dole out punishments and you've never enjoyed that much," Satan said as he gave me a quick hug and a gentle push toward the door.

I leaned in, gave him a kiss and glanced over at my sisters. They loved the punishments and I knew they would stay and watch every last bit. They were clearly delighted with the Amanda boob pop. I couldn't wait to tell Astrid… she would be so proud.

CHAPTER ELEVEN

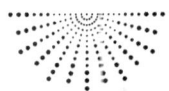

I walked quickly down the hallway away from the Demons still milling around and hoping for an audience with my Father. I decided to stay the night in my old room at the Dark Palace. I felt impatient for something familiar as my life was hurtling towards the unknown. I slipped off my heels and started to run. Running gave me joy. My sisters called me the Tasmanian Devil when I ran as I tended to be oblivious to things I knocked over or destroyed while I moved at crazy warp speeds. Rounding the corner at a fast sprint, the violent force of two large hands yanked me into an alcove.

I screamed and reared my fist back to punch my abductor's nose up into his forehead as I'd seen Myrtle do to Wolf Boy. I froze mid-punch when a strong hand grasped my arm in an iron grip.

"Dixie, it's okay. It's me." Hayden grinned as he gently halted the arm that was about to rearrange his face. In the dim light of the alcove, he looked more beautiful than I remembered. How was that possible? His black Armani suit and black silk shirt fit him beautifully. He put every male model I'd ever ogled to shame.

Furthermore, how did he catch me when I was moving at a speed that almost rendered me invisible?

"Satan forbid." I was breathing hard from shock and fear. "I almost punched your gorgeous face."

"So you think I'm gorgeous?" He chuckled and moved a step closer.

"Well... um, you know," I stammered as I tried to regain control and moved a step back from him. He seemed different, more mature. I couldn't put my finger on it. "You're definitely not butt ugly." Oh my freakin' Hell, my choice of vocabulary stunned even me.

"Thank you. I think." Hayden laughed. "Dixie, do you know why I'm here?"

His skin was perfect and a sexy light stubble covered his cheeks. His lips were full, but it was his eyes--those green eyes caught me and held me immobile. My body involuntarily began to lean into his. Wait. Did he ask me a question? What was wrong with me? My brain wasn't working right.

"Did you ask me something?" I choked out as I slid myself a little farther away until the wall halted my progress. It was strange to be with him in my father's home.

He threw his head back and laughed. Help me Satan, he was even more beautiful when he laughed. "I asked if you knew why I was here."

"Because you're in trouble?" I guessed and hoped I was wrong. My dad could be heartless when it came to punishing his people for digressions.

"Yes," he whispered. My eyes shot to his in fear. "But not the kind you're thinking of," he assured me. "I'm in a good kind of trouble."

He moved closer and ran his hand through his sandy blond hair.

I was jealous of his hand. Holy Hell, I wanted my hands in his hair and on his face and on his chest and arms. What was it about him? I was losing myself—couldn't think straight. Didn't want to. Hayden stopped inches from me and I felt my body tighten in anticipation. Of what? I had no idea. This felt different from our date. He seemed more serious, more of a man and less of a boy. I was out of my league.

I stared at him and considered trying all the things I'd been too much of a goody two-shoes to enjoy. My dad would be so proud.

Hayden moved closer. I closed my eyes. I knew they had turned blood red with desire for him. Fervently I hoped if I couldn't see him, the need to knock him to the ground and strip him would disappear. Maybe if I couldn't see his beautiful lips and eyes my body could relax.

Nope.

Damn, he smelled good—like soap and wind and summer rain. I opened my eyes to find the object of my desire so close to my lips I got dizzy. His eyes were intense, having changed from green to red. My breathing became erratic. His eyes flashed in delight and the corner of his mouth lifted into the sexiest smirk I'd ever seen. I was a goner.

I had to do or say something fast or I was going to embarrass myself by jumping him and professing my undying love. "Why are you here?" I put my hands on his chest to put at least an imaginary semblance of distance between us. Big mistake. He moaned and his body contracted under my fingertips. A jolt of electricity shot through me at the contact. Quickly I removed my hands.

Hayden took a huge breath. "I'm here because I needed to see you." He was so close I could taste his breath and it tasted good. I knew how perfect his lips felt on mine and it was Hell not to feel it again. "I was going to go slow with you and do every single thing right with you."

A shiver of delight ripped through my body and landed low in my stomach at his words. "Why?"

"I'm older than you think I am, Dixie," he said.

He was being a little too vague.

"How old?"

"Old enough." He grinned and my tummy flipped. "Old enough to know exactly what I want." He looked at me pointedly.

"You want me?" I asked shakily.

"I more than want you, Dixie. You're my soul mate," he whispered into my mouth.

Now I was definitely going to pass out. Demons rarely mated for life. Mostly because we have really loooong lives and are simply too untrustworthy and promiscuous. Many of my sisters have been mated more times than I could count. Of course it wasn't called marriage in Hell. Marriage was a sacrament sanctioned by Uncle God. In Hell we called it Bonding and Dissolving. Every so often Demons found their soul mate, but that was rare and most think it to be myth.

"I'm not ready... " I was getting panicked.

"I know," Hayden said, placing his hands on either side of my face which forced me to look at him. "I know," he repeated. His frustration and need pierced me and unsettled me. "I need you to know how I feel. I've been waiting for you for so long and now you're leaving. I didn't expect you to be deported so soon. I thought I had more time."

He stared at me with a desire and intensity that made me feel more alive than I'd ever felt. "What do you want from me?" I asked. My voice sounded small and so far away to my ears.

"Everything. I want everything from you... but I'll wait." His hand caressed my face and I leaned into his touch. "Dixie?"

"Yes?" I raised my eyes to his.

"I need you to promise me something."

In this moment I would have promised him anything he asked of me. I nodded.

"When you are ready, it will be me. No one else. It has to be me. Do you promise?"

I stared into the eyes of the beautiful Demon who wanted me

to be his, but before I would promise he needed to up the ante even higher. "Will you love me?" I asked.

His eyes turned a deeper red than I thought possible. "Oh yes, beautiful girl, more than anyone else ever has or ever will."

He pressed his hand to the small of my back and trapped me against his body. I couldn't get away if I wanted to. I didn't want to. Reaching up I wrapped my arms around his broad shoulders and threaded my hands into his hair. It was soft and silky. I cupped the back of his head and tentatively pulled his mouth toward mine. He teased my lips with the tip of his tongue. I could hear my heart thundering in my ears. He ran his tongue across my lower lip and my knees buckled. I grasped his shoulders as he pulled me tighter against him.

He gently parted my lips with his tongue, sending shock waves through me. He took his slow sweet time. These were different than the kisses from our date. A warm heat suffused my body. I had no idea kissing could be this amazing. He tasted so good. I melted against him... into him. As the kiss deepened, I clung to his shoulders and gave back as good as I got. My tongue tangled with his and I had an out of body experience. I was amazed at how my body and lips knew just what to do. I had to stop.

Before I could push him away he stepped back. As much as I knew we had to stop, I was devastated that he pulled away first. My heart was beating like a rapid fire machine gun in my chest.

His voice was thick. "If I don't stop now I won't be able to."

I couldn't find my voice to save my life. My body trembled and feelings I didn't understand consumed me. How in such a short time did I feel like this? All I wanted was to be in his arms again, but I stayed still. I was not ready for everything he wanted from me.

"So, do you promise?" Hayden's voice was hoarse with desire.

"I promise," I whispered.

His smile took away what little breath I had left. How could a boy this beautiful and amazing care for me?

With my promise secured, he leaned in and pressed his lips to mine. My eyes fluttered shut and all my good intentions along with my brain cells melted away. I wrapped my arms around him and tried to deepen the kiss, but again he pulled back.

I gasped at the loss and watched him struggle with himself to be a gentleman. It was in a Demon's nature to take what we wanted. I was blown away by Hayden's restraint. It did make me more curious about his age. A young Demon could never do what he did. Nevertheless, I was glad to see he was as affected as I was.

He took my face in his hands, running his thumbs along my cheekbones. "Not the time or the place, Dixie. You could take me down, beautiful girl." He smiled and shook his head.

I tried to look away but he made it impossible. "You should probably go," I told him quietly.

His eyes searched my face for a long moment. "You're right, but I'm going to see you every day until you leave. I want to teach you how to protect yourself on Earth."

"Have you been to Earth?" I asked.

"Many times." He gently placed one last kiss on my lips. "I'll be seeing you soon. Make sure you keep your flying clothes handy." He winked and my body clenched in desire. Maybe I was ready to be his. Maybe…

Hayden stepped back and vanished, leaving behind a cloud of beautiful black glitter mist. My hand went automatically to my lips as my body slid to the floor. What exactly had I just promised him? My virginity? My soul? My life? I wasn't sure, but whatever it was, it felt right.

CHAPTER TWELVE

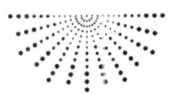

"Sloth, what do you think about love?"

My sister stopped raiding my refrigerator and gaped at me.

"What?" I said defensively. "It's just a hypothetical question."

"Oh." She heaved a sigh of relief. "In that case, it's messy—causes unwanted attachments and real emotion. I stay away from it at all costs. Do you have any chocolate in here?"

"It's eight in the morning."

"Yes. And?" she said.

"Try the freezer," I told her as I heaved my own sigh. Did Demons even know how to love? Was I slated to be like my sisters and doomed to only feel lust? I knew my dad loved me and in her own warped way Sloth did too, but that wasn't the love I was talking about. If at first you don't succeed... "What about soul mates?"

Sloth choked on the wad of chocolate in her mouth. "Soul mates?" she croaked. "Why in the Hell did I roll out of bed this morning? You're giving me indigestion. Do not under any circumstances find a soul mate. It completely ruins the fun of orgies."

"Hmmm, hadn't considered that issue," I snapped sarcastically.

As much as I loved her, her morals were skanky, but then again so were the rest of my sisters.

"What have you done, Dixie?" she asked as she drank straight from the pitcher of lemonade in my fridge. "Tell me you didn't bond with a college boy."

"I didn't bond with anyone," I informed her as I wondered if I had indeed bonded with Hayden by making my promise to him. Surprisingly the thought didn't frighten me. It filled me with something warm and unfamiliar.

Sloth's eyes narrowed and she pulled a tub of ice cream from the freezer. "Get a spoon and sit," she demanded. "You're gonna talk while I eat my breakfast."

"Your healthy eating habits overwhelm me." I handed her a spoon and parked my butt across the table from her. I needed to talk, and as much as her choice of breakfast food grossed me out I trusted her.

"Yep. Now spill it."

"Um… " Maybe talking was a bad idea. I grabbed another spoon and joined her.

She watched me consume half the carton and waited.

"How would you know if someone was your soul mate?" I asked as I pressed my fingers to the bridge of my nose and tried to ward off the brain freeze that the mint chocolate chip had caused. Hell, no matter how hard I might try, I could never be like my sisters. I was always going to be different—right down to my inability to enjoy a crappy breakfast.

"Satan's balls, I'd hoped my vision was wrong," she muttered.

"Do you have to refer to Dad's testicles this early? My brain is frozen and now my stomach is churning."

"It's just an expression. However, you have now put a visual in my head that made me lose my appetite." She laughed and dropped her spoon to the table with a clank.

"I didn't say it. You did." I grinned at my favorite big sister and tried in vain to wipe the vision of my Dad's privates from my head.

"Subject change. Now," she said. "Enough about Daddy's nutsack. Why do you think you're in love?"

"Wait. What vision?" I asked her. She rarely shared her visions with anyone but Satan.

"You first."

"I'm just trying to figure out if soul mates exist."

"That didn't even come close to answering my question." She crossed her arms over her chest and pursed her lips in annoyance.

"Fine," I huffed. "I've had feelings for someone for a year, but it feels like I've known him my whole life and then some. When he touches me I feel tingles up my arms, and when I'm not with him I feel empty."

"Shit," she muttered and retrieved her spoon. She stirred the now melting ice cream and her demeanor changed to serious. "Since you came to us a dark presence has followed you. I've never caught a glimpse of him, but whatever he is, he adores you and has acted like a protector."

"Like a guardian Angel?" I asked, confused.

"Possibly, but Demons don't have Angels. At least not the Heavenly kind. Is this boy blond, built like a brick shithouse, more powerful than all get out and as tall as Dad?"

"Yes," I whispered.

She ran her hands through her hair and stared at the ceiling for a moment. "Have you slept with him?"

"No."

"Good—don't. Because he is your soul mate, and if you bond it might all come crashing down around you."

"He'll hurt me?" Why did even asking that question feel ridiculous?

"I would really love to lie to you, but I won't. If you were any other sister of mine I would lie my ass off, but you're not... " She got up and paced. Her energy made me tense and I made a grab for the chocolate she'd left on the table.

"Please just tell me."

"He would never hurt you. Ever. But your bonding could rile up the order and all Hell would break loose. Winged jackasses will start showing up everywhere. Just because you're supposed to be with someone doesn't mean you should. Not that you won't possibly end up with the flying bastard, but you need to sow your wild oats, start eating shitty breakfasts and maybe commit a few crimes. Nothing major—I don't think you have that in you, but you can't grow up without being incarcerated a few times. At least try for public intoxication when you go to Earth."

"What does that even mean? And how do you know he can fly?" I threw my hands in the air and accidently pelted her with a Hershey's bar.

"Nice shot," she said and then stopped dead in her tracks. "I was right?"

"About what?" I yelled. "I have no clue what the Hell you were talking about."

"He flies?"

"Yes, he flies." My brain still reeled as I tried to decipher her bizarre and alarming advice. She grabbed my hands and pulled me to the couch.

"Fucking Hell, you're too young. Actually you're not, but you've been protected. Dad has watched you like a hawk since he brought you here. I always thought he was worried your mother would come for you, but it's so much more."

"You're making me nervous and I'm pretty sure you've cut off the circulation in my hands."

"Sorry," she mumbled as she lightened her grip. "It's not that what you feel isn't real. I'm very sure it is. Certain people were created for each other and are destined to be together, but it's always more complicated than that. You've been different from the rest of us since you were brought to Hell. I thought you'd grow into your Demon... and you have," she added quickly as I tried to pull my hands from hers. "But there's more to you. Dad knows what it is, but my guess is that you will have to figure it out for yourself."

"So I can trust what I feel?"

"Yes," she said slowly. "But find out who you are first."

"Do you know more than you're telling me?" I asked.

"I wish. My visions aren't like movies. Sometimes I see faces and locations, but most of the time I have feelings. Dad helps me piece them together."

"But not everything comes true like you see it," I said, knowing she kept much of what she saw to herself for that very reason.

"True, which is why I don't advertise."

"So Hayden might not be my soul mate then," I said as a wave of depression washed over me.

"His name is Hayden?" Sloth hissed. Her demeanor went from sisterly to Demony in a hot second.

"Um... yeah. Do you know him?"

"Not sure," she answered too quickly. "I'm sure there are lots of Demons named Hayden."

It was my turn to pace. She'd gone quiet and I knew she was done talking. The cryptic nature of my family made me want to tear their heads off, followed by my own.

"If you're not going to talk I want you to leave," I told her.

She nodded and stood. "Just... be careful. Do you adhere to the notion of pre-destiny?"

I thought for a moment. I'd never actually considered it, but the answer came to me with clarity. "No. I believe we make our own. I will make my own."

"Remember that and choose wisely."

With that she disappeared and left me with a Hell of a lot to think about.

∾

"How long have you known me?" I asked a confused Hayden.

In his worn jeans and faded t-shirt, he stood in the living room of my bungalow and filled the entire house with his power and size. Not to mention he looked as if he just walked off the cover of a magazine.

"Is this a trick question?" he asked as he leaned in for a kiss that I swiftly avoided.

"No. Well, maybe."

He sat down on the couch and rested his chin on steepled fingers as he watched me. "What exactly are you asking me?"

"Have you known me longer than a year?" His thoughtful expression made me uneasy.

"I have dreamt of you for eternity. I've seen your face and heard your laugh for more years than you could imagine and—yes, I've known you."

"Since I was a child?"

He nodded and waited.

I was torn between elation and fury. My emotions ran riotous in my head and I had no clue what I really felt.

"How old are you?"

"A bit older than you," he hedged and grinned sheepishly.

"Like fifty or a hundred years older?"

"Something like that," he said. "Does that scare you?"

"Isn't that a little pervy?"

He threw his head back and laughed. Hell, that was so unfair. He was so beautiful when he was joyous and I wanted to curl up next to him and trace his lips with my fingers.

"Um… " He struggled to regain his composure with little success. Patting the couch beside him, he gave me a sexy lopsided grin. "Sit, please."

I did, but I kept a respectable amount of distance between us so I didn't jump him.

"My dreams of you gave me the hope of a happily ever after—not that I necessarily deserve one, but it has kept me going for many years. When you live a long time the desire to end oneself occurs frequently." He paused and ran his hands through his hair. "The knowledge that one day I would find you is the only reason I'm still here."

This was far larger and more overwhelming than anything I could have imagined him saying. The thought of him destroying himself was unthinkable to me. I picked relentlessly at my fingernails as I wondered how much more I wanted to hear.

"Yes, I have watched you grow and I knew you were the one I had waited for, but I can guarantee you it was by no means *pervy*. Instinctually my need was to protect you. I would have never come into your life as a man until you were a fully grown woman. My love for you transcends physical desire. It's far more than a sexual need for you."

"So you're saying I'm not hot?" I teased and scooted closer. I was no longer angry or confused. I was awed and head over heels in love with someone who was in love with me. Fast? Yep, but not really if the pieces were put together.

"Hades," he hissed. "If you were any hotter Hell would cave in on itself. Keeping my hands still at the moment is more challenging than a lone Demon fighting an army of Angels."

His body was taut and his eyes flashed with desire. It took a massive amount of control on both our parts to not attack each other.

"What does bonding mean?" I asked. His quick intake of breath and his immediate move off the couch was exhilarating. The sheer fact that I affected him the same way he affected me was some powerful hoodoo.

"Bonding," he said as he backed farther away. "Means exactly as it sounds."

"I would be yours?"

"Yes. And I would be yours," he replied. "Forever."

The sexual tension in the room made my breath hitch and heat unfurl low in my belly.

"How do you bond?" I whispered as I watched him like prey.

"Sex," he replied just as quietly. "And blood exchange."

That was a little surprising—and gross. We were Demons, not Vampyres.

"At the same time?" That didn't make popping my cherry too appealing. I wrinkled my nose in disgust.

He heaved a sigh and chuckled. "No, but it has to happen within a week or so I'm told."

"So we do the nasty and then bite each other?" I wasn't quite as horny as I had been only moments ago.

"No. Hell no." He laughed and joined me again on the couch. I went willingly into his strong arms and laid my head on his chest. "I suppose if we were into kink we could do it that way, but a simple slice on our hands and a firm handshake will also work."

"Well, that's good to know. I'm not into massive amounts of pain," I muttered as I snuggled closer.

"There's a fine line between pleasure and pain, Dixie," he said in a voice that made my tummy flip with desire. "But biting and drawing blood doesn't really do it for me."

"Good to know," I quipped sarcastically.

"I want to bond with you more than mere words can describe, but I won't until you are ready to commit to what it truly means."

"So we're not doing the nasty today?" I ran my hands over his broad chest and reveled in the tingles that ran up my arms.

"First of all," he said as he gingerly removed my hands. "It will not be *nasty* when I make love to you. I will make love to you until you don't know your own name and then I will fuck you until you can't see straight. It will be perfect and you won't be able to walk for a week."

I was rendered speechless and the need to tear my clothes off was mindboggling. As I searched for my voice he moved off the couch and walked across the room.

"You're pretty cocky," I choked out. "Shit. No pun intended."

His laugh almost sent me over the edge into the land of not

walking for a week. "It's taking all I own at the moment to be this close to you and not make you mine," he said gruffly. "I know that you would come to me willingly right now, but you still have a journey to take and I won't deny you that. I can't."

"My body feels like a heartbeat and I literally ache right now. So unless you have a ginormous bucket of ice water or you can morph into a disgusting troll, you'd better leave," I said in frustration.

"I have a better idea," he said as he held out his hand to me. "Let's fly."

I blew out a huge breath and grinned. "Yes. Let's fly."

CHAPTER THIRTEEN

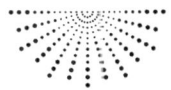

Time had moved far too swiftly and the thought of leaving Hayden made my heart hurt.

"Do you want to play baseball?" Hayden asked as we lounged on my couch in my bungalow. With only a day left before my deportment, we'd spent almost every waking moment together.

"Will baseball help me live?" I asked, confused. Possibly handling a bat?

"Not that kind. Another kind," he said in a voice that woke up all my yet to be used lady parts.

"Um... okay," I whispered.

"Now baseball is complicated, but with practice you could be a pro."

"Not really my goal," I murmured as I slid closer to him.

"It's a very handy sport," he said as he pinned me with a stare that made my insides squishy and the need to crawl all over him intense.

"Interesting."

"Right, well the first thing you need to learn is about the bases. Do you know what first base is?" His eyes hooded and I prayed he wouldn't stop this time. I knew he would, but maybe...

I gently fingered the feather at my throat and considered my next move. Hayden had taken the feather he'd given me and had it made into a necklace. It now hung on a delicate golden chain. I swore I felt his energy inside me when I wore it. I secretly vowed to wear it for the rest of my life.

"I think it's this," I purred as I crawled on top of him and pressed my lips to his.

My softer, smaller body melted into his harder one and I knew I was where I was supposed to be. The evidence of his need pressed against my stomach and I hissed with delight.

"Baseball," he groaned as I wiggled my body closer, "is very difficult. You have to practice running the bases before you hit a home run."

"Am I doing it wrong?" I asked as I ran my tongue along his full lower lip.

"No, you're doing it right." His breathing was uneven as his tongue tangled with mine.

"If I'm not mistaken," I said as I took his large hand and placed it on my breast. "This is second base."

He closed his eyes and gently massaged my breast until it grew taut and tender under the touch of his hand. A familiar, yet to be fulfilled need coursed through me and I instinctually ground my hips into his.

"Oh God," he hissed as his hips moved in reply in a rhythm that was far more serious than the one I'd teased him with. His mouth captured mine and his teeth nipped at my lips.

I was so freakin' done being a virgin.

I pulled my shirt over my head and frantically tore his from his body. Sometimes having Demon strength rocked. His eyes widened and his grin almost undid me.

"I want you," I said as I took his face in my hands. "I need you."

The light sprinkling of blond hair on his chest that veed into the no-man's land I was desperate to visit tickled my breasts and stomach as I rubbed against his strong body.

"You are killing me," he said as his hands grabbed my ass.

Heat traveled through me and landed squarely between my legs. I whimpered and tried to crawl inside him. His hands were everywhere and with each touch I climbed higher... closer.

Until he pushed me off of him and held me at arm's length.

"Are you ready to commit to me for the rest of your very long life?" he demanded gruffly. His eyes blazed and his breath came in short spurts.

"Oh my Hell," I shouted. "You're a Demon. You're not supposed to have morals. How did I find a Demon with a conscience?"

"Answer my question."

"Can we at least get to third base before I have to answer?"

"Oh Dixie." His eyes crinkled and I wanted to slap the smirk off of his face. He pressed his lips to mine and I felt the kiss all the way to my toes. "I'll be back in a few hours to say goodbye."

Baseball sucked.

Sexually frustrated and ready to scream, I opened my suitcase and began to pack everything I owned. I wasn't sure how different Earth would be from Hell. I was panicked. I picked my nail polish clean off and started on my cuticles. Blanche hadn't been around in days, which was highly unusual. Even if I wanted to, I couldn't talk to my family about her absence. They didn't believe she existed.

"Dixie," a voiced hissed ominously.

"Grandpa?"

"It's Pee Wee Herman."

Pee Wee Herman wasn't dead. "Show yourself," I yelled. I was in no mood for this and I wasn't a hundred percent sure it was my grandpa.

"I've come to get you," the voice growled.

"Really?" I snapped. "You're not doing a very good job then."

"Dixie." The voice sighed in exasperation. "Are you really going to have conversations with things that want to kill you?"

"Are you going to kill me?"

"Well, no."

"So your point is?" I asked the empty room.

"My point is that you should have tried to destroy me. What in the Hell are you going to do on Earth when your Uncle God sends the do-gooder winged jackasses down to kill you?"

"Grandpa, PeeWee Herman isn't really scary. I'd suggest you get up to date on pop culture if you want me to try and kill you."

"Point," my grandpa said as he materialized in a cloud of glitter.

My grandpa was the cutest man alive. He was part Sprite and part Demon. I pressed my fists into my sides so I wouldn't squeeze him. He spent a lot of time in traction because my sisters had squeezed and loved on him too hard.

"You want to hug me and stroke me," Grandpa informed me with great delight.

"Ewwww." I groaned. "Do not say stroke. That sounds so wrong."

"Oh, for the love of Mother Nature's rack, how did my son sire such a prude?" He shook his head and gave me a wink.

"I don't know, but he did and don't say rack." I grinned and blew him a kiss. "I also happen to know that although you may protest, you love me to pieces." Damn, I wanted to grab him and squeeze him. "Are your ribs healed?" I asked as I debated if I could at least pick him up and cuddle with him.

My grandpa was a tiny little thing, approximately the size of an Oompa Loompa. He was as irresistible as they come and almost as powerful as my father but not quite. His son was my dad, Satan. Dad and Uncle God were actually half brothers. They shared the same mother—Mother Nature.

"So, are you excited, my sweet?" he asked as he examined the contents of my suitcase.

"Um, no," I said quietly as I sat down on my bed and shoved my hands under my bottom so I didn't grab my grandpa and break him.

"You and your cousin Astrid are the only ones that can control yourselves around me," he muttered as he refolded some of my clothes that I had sloppily thrown in. "The Balance of Chaos is missing and the Rogue Demons are out of control."

"I'm sorry, what?" I asked, getting a sick feeling in the pit of my stomach. Grandpa loved dropping time bombs.

"The Rogue Demons on Earth are wreaking havoc and they must be stopped," he relayed as if he were reciting a laundry list of chores. "Of course the one who should be stopping them is useless."

"Rogue Demons?" I asked, knowing for sure I didn't really want the answer.

Grandpa clasped his little hands together and bowed his head. "They are Demons who don't follow our rules." He paused and squinted.

"Don't you dare sugarcoat."

"Fine," Grandpa huffed and rolled his eyes. "They are Demons that roam Earth killing and maiming mortals, Angels, Demons, Vampyres, Fairies. You name it. Basically they're destroying the Balance of Chaos. They have become uncontrollable and it's come to our attention they want to destroy your father and supposedly God."

"That's not possible," I replied sharply.

"It's possible," he said. "But highly improbable and quite difficult."

"Is Heaven behind this?" I felt restless, irritable and freaked out.

"Very good guess, my child, but no," Grandpa sighed. "The Demons have been ravaging Angels in the most heinous ways even in neutral territories. God is definitely not behind this. We need to find the Balance of Chaos."

"Did you say Fairies?"

"I did," he replied.

"How in the Hell did I not know that Fairies existed?" I moaned and dropped my head into my hands.

"Trust me, they do and they're not sweet and they do not grant wishes easily. I'm not even sure how they got involved in this mess," he mumbled.

"And I'm supposed to fix the shitstorm of a bunch of immortal asswipes, including Fairies that I didn't know existed?"

"You forgot a part."

"Oh right, and find the elusive, stupid, freakin' Balance of Chaos?"

My grandpa raised one eyebrow and stared at me in silence.

"I'm sorry," I whispered. I was trembling and furious with my father. "Why would Dad send me into something like that?"

"He doesn't have a choice. It's part of the deal he made. In fact, I think he's a couple of years behind on that deal," he answered.

I waited for more but none came. I'd about had it with my family's love of cryptic bullshit. "Would you like to tell me what that means?"

"I'd love to." He smiled and clapped his little hands.

I waited.

"But I can't," he said as he produced a wicked-looking dagger out of thin air and placed it in my suitcase.

"What's that for?" I asked as I tried not to laugh hysterically or scream in frustration and terror. Was I supposed to use that to slice up the Rogue Demons to save the freakin' Fairies? If they thought I was going to cap that problem they were seriously mistaken.

"If I did something repulsive for you, would you honor me by going along with it?" he inquired as he continued to conjure weapons out of the air and pack them carefully in my suitcase.

"Is this a trick question?" I wondered what in the Hell the most adorable man in the world could do that would strike me as repulsive.

"No, Dixie, it's not a trick."

Crap. "Um, okay..."

My delightfully scrunchy and addictive grandpa produced yet another knife from out of nowhere. This one was different. The handle was encrusted with diamonds. It shimmered and winked at me—a perfect combination of beauty and death. He raised the knife to his neck and sliced.

I screamed.

"Holy Hades, Grandpa," I screeched, trying to pry the knife from his fingers before he took his head off.

"Dixie, stop," he commanded. Occasionally his adorable factor made me forget he could level a continent with a flick of his fingers. I froze and watched the blood gush out from his neck. "I want you to drink from me."

"Like a Vampyre?" I was in shock.

"Yes, like a Vampyre." Grandpa grinned and used two fingers to pretend they were fangs.

"Oh my Hell." I gagged as I turned my head away from the sight of my beloved grandpa bleeding all over my favorite down comforter. For Satan's sake, did he slice into an artery or what? "Can I ask you a question?" I choked out.

"Make it quick. Feeling a little queasy here," he replied.

"Oookay, drinking your blood seems kinda cannibalistic and beyond disgusting since I'm not a Vampyre. You want me to do this why?" I tried desperately to keep a tight rein on my gag reflex.

"Your cousin Astrid did it," he informed me.

"My cousin is a Vampyre. She likes blood. Why do I have to do it?"

He swayed from blood loss. "Your father isn't allowed to because of the deal he struck, but no one said anything about me."

"I am so confused and grossed out I don't know where to begin."

"Drink my blood, Dixie. If you want to survive Earth, you must do this. Trust me, I find it as unappealing as you do, but there's no faster way."

"Faster way to what?" I felt the bile rising in my throat.

"To give you Black Magic."

I gasped and grabbed my bedpost to steady my quaking knees. Only the highest level Demons had Black Magic. The only ones I knew for sure that possessed the gift of Black Magic were my father, my grandfather and my cousin Astrid. I suspected some of my dad's top generals might have a small amount, but me? Why in the world did they want me to have Black Magic?

"Does Dad know?" I whispered.

"He suspects," Grandpa muttered. "He would do it himself if he could, but as I told you he can't. Now drink before I faint," he insisted.

"I have to?"

I really did not want to do this.

"Do you want to live out the next week?"

I thought about my family and my friends and Hayden's green eyes and soft lips and the ridiculous fact that I still hadn't experienced third base. "Yes, I do."

"Then drink," he hissed.

I slowly bent down and pressed my tightly closed lips to my grandpa's throat. I shut my eyes and hoped that if I couldn't see what I was doing I could pretend I wasn't doing it. I'd tasted blood before—my own. The many times I bit down on my lip trying not to laugh at something that wasn't supposed to be funny and drew blood. Blood tasted like metal, kind of like vitamins. I would pretend I was drinking liquified metal vitamins. It would make me stronger, smarter, possibly make my boobs better than Blanche's. Not to mention it would give me the ability to destroy cities with the blink of an eye. Crap. I jerked back and my eyes shot open. They locked on my grandpa's.

"There's more at stake than just your life," he told me with a gentle urgency. "The future of Hell will soon rest in your hands. You have to do this."

"I might throw up," I told him.

"For the Love of Hatred, please don't. I have a very active gag reflex, and if you go I'll go too."

I started laughing. I'd had many bizarre conversations during my short life in Hell, but this one took the cake. "Okay Grandpa, I'll do my best not to hurl." I took a tentative lick. It wasn't good, but it wasn't as bad as I thought it would be.

"Latch on and drink." Grandpa grasped the back of my head and forced my lips to the gaping wound on his neck.

I drank.

The second his blood entered my system something strange happened. Bolts of heat ricocheted through my body, down to my toes and out through my fingertips. It was violent. I tried to pull away, but Grandpa held me fast. As much as I wanted to stop drinking, something compelled me to continue. I was losing control, of myself, my mind, my body, my soul.

I convulsed and shook as if I were having a seizure. It quickly subsided into a gentle hot wave churning inside me. It didn't hurt. It was surreal, floaty and powerful.

I knew now that I possessed a power I had no business owning. I wasn't old enough or mature enough to wield Black Magic. Only the strongest beings in the Universe were blessed with Black Magic, and now I was in that club.

"Um, Grandpa, I'm guessing I shouldn't share the arrival of my new super powers with anyone?" I gave him a small smile as I floated down from my bizarre blood high.

"That would be correct, although some will know." He grinned as he ran his fingertips over the gash on his neck. It magically closed.

"Could I have done that?" I asked, referring to his healing.

"Yes, you can now," he replied as he retrieved a small silver book from thin air. "In this tome are some of the things you need to know. Don't read it all at once or you'll die."

Laughter burbled from my lips. I waited for him to join me. I waited some more. He didn't join. My laughter died in my throat.

"For real?"

"Yes." His cute little dimples appeared and I couldn't help myself. I squeezed him, but not too tight.

"What's in the book?" I ran my hands over the cover and I could swear it had a heartbeat. I jerked my hands back. "Grandpa, it's breathing," I shouted.

"Oh, how wonderful." His eyes were shining with glee. Of course he would think that was awesome. What in the Hell was wrong with my family?

"Wonderful," I agreed sarcastically as I moved away from the freaky silver book with a pulse. "What's inside that book?"

"Spells, how to cope with your gift, how to cure magical hangovers, how to destroy the world."

"Great. That's just frickin' great," I muttered as I attacked my now raw cuticles.

"Isn't it?" Grandpa giggled and hugged me tight. "I love you, little Demon Princess. I really do." He slowly let go and then disappeared in a breathtaking mist of black glitter. I looked down at my suitcase loaded with sharp, glistening weapons and I shook my head. I tucked the book into a corner, carefully zipped it shut and prayed I wouldn't have to break in any of my shiny new toys any time soon. I walked to my closet, yanked out another suitcase and continued to pack.

Ahhhhh, just another effed up day in Hell.

CHAPTER FOURTEEN

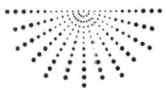

"I'M GOING TO GO TO EARTH TO KICK SOME ASS IN A TIMELY manner and then come home. However, I'd like to go on record and say that I'll probably do something horrifically embarrassing to Hell and get my Demon card revoked." I paced my bungalow as a wave of apprehension crashed through me.

"Duly noted. Mine's been revoked at least a dozen times."

I laughed and threw myself into Hayden's strong arms. He wrapped himself securely around me and buried his face in my hair.

"You smell so good." He ran his lips along my jaw and kissed the corner of my mouth.

I placed my hands on either side of his face and touched my forehead to his. Being so close to him sent shivers of delight through me. I eased away and searched his eyes. "Will you come see me?"

"I will." He captured my lips and made me forget my name. I wrapped my legs around his waist and tried to wrestle him down on my bed.

"Oh no you don't." Hayden laughed as he flipped me over and

locked my arms over my head while trapping my legs under his thigh. His desire made me bold.

"Well, I like this too." I fought to free my arms so I could wrap them around his neck.

He slowly lowered his face to mine. Butterflies were having a smackdown in my stomach. My lips parted willingly under his and I gave myself freely to the passion of his kiss. He raised up and gazed into my eyes, "I have waited so long for you, Dixie." His voice was low and intense.

"Was I worth the wait?" I whispered, completely lost in his eyes.

"Without a doubt," he said.

"Hello, Dixie darling."

"Holy shit," I screeched as I sat up and conked heads with Hayden so hard I saw stars. "Dad, you're supposed to knock!"

"Why should I knock on my own daughter's door?" he asked, truly stymied.

"Because I'm an adult and I was busy." I was mortified.

"And who is the young ma…" My father froze, his fists clenched at his sides and the room got chilly. Literally. It dropped about thirty degrees. "What are you doing here?" my father hissed at Hayden, giving him a brutal and unfriendly stare.

"Hello, Lucifer, it's nice to see you again too," Hayden replied as he made himself more comfortable on my bed.

Something was really wrong here. Why wasn't Hayden afraid of the Prince of Darkness?

"I believe," my dad spoke slowly through clenched teeth, "I asked you what you were doing here. I'd also like to know what in the Hell are you doing with my daughter."

"I'm here because I've finished my task and I'm with your daughter because I'm in love with her."

Hayden stood up and went toe to toe with my dad. Sweet Baby Beelzebub, Hayden really was as tall as he was.

"Impossible," Satan bellowed. The room shook as his power

bounced off of my walls like a ping pong ball on crack. I shrunk back into a corner, not liking where this was headed. I felt certain it would not end well.

"Not impossible," Hayden countered. Holy Hades, I could feel his power dancing all over my room along with my dad's. Who in the Hell was he—or better yet, what was he? Why in the world would he challenge my dad like this? He either had a huge amount of power and magic or a gargantuan death wish. "You knew she was mine yet you sent me away all these years."

"She's just a child," my father fired back at him.

"She's a woman."

"Exactly," my Dad shouted. "Young. Woman. And she's mine. My little baby girl."

"Helloooo," I said to the two "Tug on Dixie" participants. "She's sitting right here."

"Quiet," they yelled in unison. Well, alrighty then.

"She is not yours, she's mine," Hayden smugly informed Satan. Ooooh, my dad hated smug.

"I could destroy you so quickly and it would be so much fun." My father bestowed an icy smile on Hayden. He was stunningly beautiful and viciously evil at the same time.

Hayden laughed, his beauty as riveting as my father's. "Try it, old friend. See how far it will get you."

I was confused and pissed off. Clearly Dad knew Hayden. And Hayden must have some major magic mojo if my dad couldn't kill him. How in the hell old was he? Had I been lip-locked with somebody that was around before mortals roamed the Earth?

"Lucifer, if you don't approve of me… " Hayden stared pointedly at my father. "Are you prepared for the alternative?"

He got right up in Satan's face. He was either really brave or really stupid.

My dad turned his back on Hayden in a show of disrespect and walked away. He leaned against my wall and ran his hand through his thick hair. "No," he conceded. "The alternative is unacceptable."

"Good, then it's settled." Hayden reached for me but I backed away.

"I'm glad you guys worked that out," I told them, my voice heavy with sarcasm. "But you forgot one minor detail. You neglected asking me what I want."

My father laughed and Hayden looked pained.

"I thought you wanted me," he said quietly.

"I did," I said. "I mean, I do. I think. But you won't own me. Ever. And neither will you," I informed my smirking father. I turned my attention back to Hayden. "Who in the Hell are you, anyway?"

He was going to straighten a few things out before he stuck his tongue down my throat again.

"You haven't told her who you are?" My father was positively gleeful.

"Shut up, Satan," Hayden retorted.

"Tell her," my dad taunted. "Tell her who you are."

A warning voice whispered in my head. How bad could it be? As long as we weren't related. "Are you my cousin or something?" I felt like I was suffocating.

"No," Hayden quickly interjected, then paused for an eternity. My dad bounced up and down like a three year old at a birthday party. "I'm the Angel of Death."

The wings made sense now and I realized his lack of fear of my father stemmed from the simple fact that he was an unkillable True Immortal. Both men waited for my response. I waited for the other shoe to drop. It didn't. "Yeah, so?"

"That doesn't bother you?" Hayden asked uneasily.

"Why should it?" I shrugged. "I'm a Demon Princess, my father is Satan, most of my sisters are raging sluts, I have an invisible friend named Blanche and I've been in therapy for what feels like half of my life because I'm not evil enough. I'm not sure I'm such a great catch either."

Hayden threw his head back and laughed joyfully. My first highly inappropriate reaction was to tackle him to the ground and have my way with him. Of course my dad being in the room kind of killed that one.

"Fine," Satan rolled his eyes and threw his hands up in disgust. "Have you slept with him yet?"

"AHHHH," I shrieked. "You so cannot ask me that."

"Why not? I'm your father." He was truly confused.

"That's why," I yelled. "I am not talking to you about these things!"

"All your sisters do," he huffed.

"That's so gross." I shuddered.

My dad pulled me down on his lap and hugged me tight. "It's okay with me if my *adult* daughter is sexually active with the Angel of Death. I will always love you no matter how distasteful your choices are."

"Oh, for the love of abomination, I'm not *technically* sexually active. And you shouldn't be encouraging your daughter to have sex."

"But I'm Satan," he grandly explained.

I tried to wiggle off his lap, but he held me fast and laid a big sloppy wet one on my cheek. I giggled and hugged the most important man in my life. I eyed the second most important man in my life as he leaned on my bedpost and watched me with my dad.

"We'll be sure to let you know when her status changes." Hayden grinned and my father made gagging sounds. I punched him in the arm and laid my head on his shoulder.

"If you hurt her, I will destroy you. I don't care who you are," my father threatened. He then gently lifted me off his lap, kissed my forehead and disappeared in a lovely black glitter mist.

"Well, that certainly went better than I anticipated." Hayden blew out a breath and flopped back down on my bed as he pulled me along for the ride.

"Are you serious?"

"Yep." He smoothed my wild hair back from my face. "I was sure he'd try to kill me."

"But that wouldn't have worked. You're a True Immortal." I was no longer curious about his utter lack of fear of Satan.

"Correct, but it would have been quite messy."

"But he said he would destroy you."

"Oh Dixie, there are many things worse than death," he explained and then changed the subject by running his fingers along my lips. The left side of his mouth lifted into a sexy crooked grin. My breath caught in my throat and my pulse started to race.

"You have four hours left. What would you like to do?" he asked with a twinkle in his eyes.

"Do you really want to know?" I asked.

"I really, really do." His eyes turned red, as did mine.

"I wanna go to third base."

He considered my request and gave me a lopsided smile that made my insides dance. "Done."

"Really?"

"Really. Come here," he said in a voice that set my panties on fire.

"Nope. Come get me," I countered as I hopped off the bed and slowly pulled my shirt over my head. His breathing hitched and his eyes blazed as he hopped off the bed and made a grab for me. He was fast, but this time I was faster. Why the thought of being chased and ravished by the Angel of Death was turning me on to a degree I'd never felt was a mystery, but it clearly turned Hayden's crank as much as it turned mine.

His eyes narrowed as he began to stalk me like prey. I removed my clothing piece by piece and avoided his grasp. I knew he could catch me just as well as he did, but the thrill of the chase was as erotic as what I imagined would come next.

"You're playing a game you can't win." His voice was rough as he tore his shirt over his head. His broad shoulders and muscular chest made my insides clench in anticipation and a moist heat pooled between my legs. He was smoking crack if he thought we were only going to third base.

Something inside me came alive—something I'd never owned about myself. And I liked it. I liked her.

"I win either way," I purred as I unsnapped my bra and let it fall to the floor. The only thing that covered my body was a scrap of silk that barely passed for panties.

His eyes were glued to my breasts and the power I felt was intoxicating. My chest heaved and my nipples tightened to the point of pain. Hell, is this what I'd been missing by being a good girl? Good girls sucked. I slowly touched my aching breasts and he expelled a hiss through clenched teeth.

"Dixie," he warned as he held on to his restraint by a thread.

How in the Hell was I going to get my way if he was still standing across the room watching me? Time to play dirtier. I had no plans to lose tonight. I was a Demon and I wasn't above cheating or doing anything in my power to get what I wanted, and I wanted him. For a brief moment I wondered who I was, but the throbbing in my body squashed the thought quickly.

Turning around to show him my backside, I shimmied out of my panties. Hands at my ankles and ass in the air, I moaned as I slowly stood and ran my fingertips over all my intimate places. He was on me so fast I didn't see him move. His grip on my hips was painful and I gloried in his possession.

"You're playing with fire," he ground out through clenched teeth before he took my nipple into his mouth and suckled hard.

My body jerked and I gasped as heat shot through me and straight to my core. I arched into him and offered my body in a way that came so naturally I was shocked. My hands grasped his hair and I held on for dear life as he bit and sucked at my breasts till I was sure my vision was gone.

"Hayden," I gasped. "Oh my Hell. I need… "

"What do you need?" he demanded as his large hands cupped my ass and trapped my willing body against a huge, jeans-covered erection.

"You. I want you. All of you." I cried out as he pushed a strong thigh between my legs and pressed against the part of me that was on fire. I rocked against him as little shocks traveled through my body.

"Am I overdressed?" he asked as he bit and sucked at my lips.

"I don't know. Are you?" I shot back, unable to stop moving obscenely against his thigh.

"You tell me, Dixie. And tell me now, but know if I remove my clothes I will bury myself so deeply within your body you will feel me inside you for eternity."

My body stilled and I searched his eyes. It wasn't just the sex. It was him. I wanted him. I wanted to be with him and I wanted him to remember me if I died on Earth. Selfishly I wanted to experience making love with someone I loved in case I didn't come back.

"You're overdressed, Hayden—very overdressed."

His head fell back on his shoulders and the growl he made low in his chest sent me into a mini orgasm. I felt the loss of his thigh acutely, but I knew what was coming would be even better.

His clothes were gone in a flash and my excitement became tempered with fear. His erection was huge and all of a sudden I wasn't so bold anymore.

"I've never done this before," I blurted as he effortlessly picked me up and tossed me on my bed. "And I had no idea you were so, um… humongous and I don't think that's gonna fit, so maybe we should just go to third base."

He grinned evilly at me and my body spasmed in response. Why were the bad boys so freakin' hot?

"What did I tell you would happen if I took off my clothes?"

His eyes were hooded and his erection stood at attention on his stomach.

"That I would feel you inside me for eternity," I whispered.

"Touch me," he said. "Feel what you do to me. I plan to have you and I promise after what I do to you, you will beg for me to take you—but if you want to stop, I will. I will stop at any point, Dixie. This is more than sex."

"Are we bonding?" I asked as I crawled across the bed to him. I wanted to touch him. I needed to. His beauty was like nothing I'd ever seen.

"No. Not until you do what you need to do on Earth, but I will make love to you tonight. I will mark you and I will make you mine."

"Will it hurt?" I asked and realized I didn't really care if a little pain was involved. The ache between my legs was becoming painful and the need to have him inside me was overwhelming.

"Possibly," he said as he took my hands and wrapped them around his cock. It was smooth as silk on the outside yet as hard as steel. "I'll try to go slow, but you completely undo me. Lie back and hold the headboard," he said.

"But I want to touch you."

"You will." His smile was positively sinful. "But the first time it's all about you."

If I'd been standing I'd have dropped to the floor like a sack of potatoes. My body went liquid and my brain was functioning at half-speed.

I did as he instructed and he skimmed his hands over every part of my body, followed by his mouth. I writhed and moaned under his touch, which seemed to increase his need. His lips took mine in a crushing kiss and his hand slid between my legs. The heel of his palm pressed against my clit and I bucked and gasped. His sexy chuckle was almost my undoing, but he was just getting started.

"You are so beautiful," he said as his mouth made a trail from my lips to my neck.

As the pressure of his palm increased, his finger slipped inside me and the pleasure was intense. A second finger followed and I tightened in protest.

"Relax, Dixie. Let me in." His voice was hypnotic and I let my legs fall open. His head dropped to my breast and his lips trapped my nipple. His tongue ran lazy circles around the rock hard nub and my back arched trying to make him increase the pressure. He took the hint—happily. The harsh pull of his mouth on my breast sent me into meltdown and he pushed a third finger inside me. The burn from the stretch was obliterated by the fireworks his mouth was causing. Despite the pain I rocked almost violently against his hand. My brain said wait, but my body had other ideas. The sounds coming from him were the sexiest things I'd ever heard and my need for more skyrocketed.

It came on fast and it lasted a long time. I closed my eyes and screamed as my body detonated.

"Look at me," Hayden demanded. "I want to see you and I want you to see nothing but me."

My eyes blinked open and his smile was feral. Ohmyhellohmy-hellohmyhell, this was the scariest, most amazing thing I'd ever experienced.

"More," he said gruffly as he slid down my still shaking body.

"More what?" I choked out. "I thought it was your turn now."

"Not until you come three more times. Then it's my turn."

"I might die," I told him honestly. "I'm pretty sure I just suffered brain damage during that one."

He threw back his head and laughed. I wanted to slap him and kiss him, but he had very different ideas. His mouth replaced his hand and I was sure my entire body blushed.

"Um… I don't know if you should… you know," I mumbled.

"Should do what, Dixie?"

"Well, that."

"This?" he asked as his tongue and teeth did things to me I didn't know were possible. My exhausted body was no longer exhausted and to my shock and his delight I wrapped my legs around his head. "You like?" he chuckled as he continued to rock my world.

"I like," I gasped as he sucked and I exploded for the second time in the space of fifteen minutes. I was certainly going to die at this rate, but it was a Hell of a way to go.

"Hayden, no more. I can't." I begged.

"You can and you will," he said softly before he went back to work.

"You're mean," I snapped as the motion of my hips belied my words.

He grinned and shrugged. "I'm very mean—very, very mean."

He was right. He was mean and I came three more times before he worked his way back up my trembling body. I should be dead or at the very least unconscious. I knew my voice was gone from all the screaming I did. Why wasn't I tired and how did my body want more?

"I do believe it's my turn now," he said as he took himself in hand and pressed the broad head of his cock inside me. "Are you sure you want this?" he asked through clenched teeth. The veins in his neck were taut and I knew it took all he possessed to show restraint. But he did—and it made me love the beautiful man even more than I did a moment ago.

"It's what I want," I whispered, removing my hands from the headboard and wrapping them around his neck. I rocked my hips forward, taking more of him into me. I was full and stretched, but I wanted more. I wanted all of him.

"I'll try to go slow," he ground out as he pushed farther inside. The feel of him filling me so slowly was excruciating. I might be inexperienced, but I knew what I wanted and I wanted it now.

"Not slow... more. Please."

"Tell me. Say it. Beg for it," he said as he stilled inside me and waited.

"You like dirty talk?" I giggled and wiggled my hips.

"I like dirty talk. I'm the freakin' Angel of Death. I'm supposed to like dirty talk." He grinned and rotated his hips, making me see stars.

"Fuck me," I whispered so softly I almost didn't hear it.

"I'm sorry, what did you say?" His delight in my foul mouth was contagious… and I liked it. It was freeing and sexy.

"I said fuck me. Now."

"Well if that's what the lady wants… "

His lips captured mine as he sheathed himself fully inside me with a guttural moan. The pain was sharp and intense. I cried out and his body froze.

"Shit, did I hurt you?" He was torn. His Demon instinct to take exactly what he wanted was so close to the surface, but the man who loved me would wait. I was suddenly glad he was older. How much older was a discussion we would have when my brain functioned properly again. In about a year.

I relaxed my body and expelled my breath. The pain slowly morphed into something so magical tears threatened. "I'm okay," I said. "Better than okay. Please, please don't stop."

He gauged my expression for truth and clearly saw what he was looking for—and then all bets were off. With a power only a Demon possessed, he took me in ways that words were inadequate to describe. The slap of our bodies, the moans, the kisses, the nips and the sheer speed of the motion was otherworldly.

I begged and muttered incoherent words as riotous colors ripped across my vision. My body, mind and soul became one with his. It was more than sex—more than making love. It was like our essences mixed and neither one of us ended or began without the other.

"Look at me," he hissed. "Watch me. Watch what you do to me."

Never had I felt more vulnerable and alive as I did in this moment.

"I see you and I love you," I said breathlessly as the speed of his thrusts increased to inhuman levels. My body gripped his like a vise and the beginnings of the mac daddy of orgasms started low in my belly. Our coupling bordered on violence and I realized that was on my part more than his. I wanted him deeper and harder and just more. He obliged.

"Come with me," he said as he took my lips in a kiss I would never forget. "Now," he demanded.

I did.

He was right.

I would feel him inside of me for eternity and I didn't want it any other way.

CHAPTER FIFTEEN

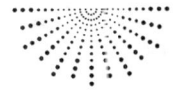

BASEBALL ROCKED AND EARTH SUCKED.

"Lizards smell with their tongues."

"What?" I was getting exasperated. That was at least the tenth piece of useless information Myrtle had passed on in the last hour. "Wait, is that even true?" I asked as I checked my cell phone to see if the battery was dead. Why hadn't Hayden or Stella called me yet?

"Yep," Myrtle said.

"How do you know?" I countered as I opened and began to unpack my suitcases in my new room, in my new house, in my new world, with my new family.

"Because I can shift," she muttered.

"Back up." I laughed. "You can shapeshift into a lizard?"

"Yep." She grinned and shrugged.

"And how does that work out for you?"

"Not so good." She pushed her newly bobbed hair behind her ears. Earlier I'd chased her for an hour and wrestled her to the floor so I could give her a makeover. Carl finally held her down while I had my way with her hair. I snipped and dyed for two hours. She bitched and moaned the entire time. No surprise to me, but clearly a humongous surprise to her, she was beautiful—too skinny, but beautiful.

"People don't really like lizards so much," she continued, still playing with her new hair. "They usually scream and occasionally try to kill me."

"Hell forbid." I giggled. "Can you shift into anything else?"

"Yep," she said as she smiled and exited my room before I could pry her secrets out of her.

"You suck," I yelled after her and heard her chuckle as she went down the stairs.

I sighed and tossed the t-shirt I was refolding back into the suitcase. I flopped back on my four-poster bed and stared at the ceiling. I wasn't so sure about this Earth thing yet. I glanced around the room and laughed. My dad had replicated my room from the palace down to the stuffed animals I'd had as a child. It was embarrassing but sweet. Thank Hell he didn't replicate the palace too. That might have been a little conspicuous. Instead we were living in a lovely old farmhouse. Actually it was more like a stately old Southern manor.

My father chose Kentucky for our destination—to be more specific, Eden, Kentucky. I told him I wanted to live someplace beautiful and be close enough to visit my cousin Astrid. I'd never seen fall or winter in my life. Hell was warm and balmy all year round. I couldn't even begin to imagine snow. I'd seen it on T.V. and in the movies, but I wanted to touch it and catch it on my tongue.

The other consideration had been language. Demons and Angels were hardwired from birth to understand and speak every language—even dead ones. I couldn't even imagine how limiting it must feel to only speak one or two. I loved speaking French and Russian, but English was my favorite language. So I requested an English speaking country. I wanted the United States. The

Americans seemed to get in the most trouble and have the most fun. Even though I was a kind of good girl, I was still a Demon and I much preferred spicy to bland.

My dad liked Kentucky a lot. He said it reminded him of Hell, plus there were portals all over the place. Kentucky, Tennessee and Ohio were apparently hotbeds of otherworldly activity. A triad, if you will, of immortal strength and power.

Kentucky in particular housed Mammoth Caves. Hundreds of miles of natural underground caves. The caves formed over ten million years ago during a time of great upheaval between Heaven and Hell. There had been a war for ownership rights. It was bloody and long. In the end it was a draw.

Because so many Angels and Demons died in the caves during Mammoth's formation, great magic was trapped within the limestone floors and walls. The Earth's natural magic combined with the trapped immortal power had opened many portals to both Heaven and Hell. It was like a Heaven and Hell-bound bus station. It was considered neutral territory for both Angels and Demons. Earth had certain areas of neutrality, places for my dad and Uncle God to negotiate treaties and threaten each other with obliteration without having to make good on the threats. Any given day you could find tons of immortals hanging out. Either absorbing the fallout of magic that constantly seeped from the caves or hopping a Portal back and forth to Heaven or Hell. Ironically the humans didn't even notice.

I rolled over and stared at all my shiny new weapons still nestled in my suitcase. They mocked me. Why Grandpa decided my parting gift should be an arsenal made my stomach roil. I had no freakin' idea how to wield a sword, much less how to strike a deathblow. Moreover, I had no desire to harm or kill anyone or anything.

I thought about Grandpa and Sloth and Stella and my dad... and Hayden. Hayden was my every waking and dreaming thought. And where in the Hell was Blanche? Had my invisible friend deserted me too? My old life was gone. My eyes welled up and fat salty tears slowly rolled down my cheeks.

"Are you okay, sweetie?" a child asked.

What the Hell? I didn't know we had brought a kid with us. "Oh, hi Janet." How come I kept forgetting she sounded like a third grader? I swiped at my tears and plastered a big fake smile on my face. No reason to bring everybody down just because I was miserable, horny and hated my life.

"Don't pretend," she said gently as she took my hand into her sweet little stubby one. "You should cry and get it out. Earth's really not as bad as you think."

"I want to go back to Hell," I whispered as I tried unsuccessfully to suppress my tears. I watched Janet search for reassuring words and was amazed at what a delicate beauty my bearded therapy partner turned out to be.

"Oh baby," Janet cooed. "It will be fine. You're here for a reason. I wish to Satan we knew what that reason was, but it will reveal itself in good time."

"What if I can't live up to whatever it is I'm supposed to do?" I made myself into a tight ball and hugged my knees for comfort. I waited for her to tell me the secrets to life, make me feel better and suggest we forget about Earth and go find a portal back to Hell.

No. Such. Luck.

"You have no choice. It's your destiny," Janet replied logically, in the same manner she would say the Earth was round or the sky was blue or Hell was way better than Heaven.

I decided to ignore her and continue to whine. "Why hasn't anyone called me?"

"They're not allowed to." She began to hang my clothes in my closet.

"What do you mean not allowed?" I demanded. I grabbed my phone and checked for voicemails. Nothing.

"Your father forbade any contact for a month so you could acclimate to Earth."

"He can't do that," I yelled at her as I punched numbers into my phone.

"I think he already did." She put her hands to her face worriedly and searched for her missing beard.

I dialed Hayden and held the phone to my ear. Lost connection. Shit. I dialed Stella. Lost connection. Double shit. One more time… Triple shit. I threw my phone on my bed. I wanted to smash it against the wall, but I wasn't stupid. I was just pissed.

He was ruining my life. I hated him. He threw me out of the only home I'd ever known. Got rid of me like I was trash. Just like my mother did. He tore me away from my family and my friends and the boy I was madly in love with. Although *boy* might be pushing it. Hayden was clearly older than dirt. As hard as I'd tried, he'd managed to avoid all my age queries.

My father ruined my life and more than likely his actions would get me killed. He condemned me to Earth where I was on constant watch for Angels who want to off me. Furthermore, as if avenging Angels weren't enough, there were a buttload of uber rotten Demons wreaking havoc and I was slated to ice them and find the freakin' Balance of Chaos. This sucked mostly because all my power hadn't arrived yet.

Fury rushed through me like high tide coming in. There was no stopping it. The more I thought the more inflamed I became. My chest burned and my eyes flashed red. Heat flowed through my body and I wanted to crawl out of my skin. Crying and screaming sounded like a grand idea. My hands started to tingle and brilliant sparks of red light flew from my fingertips.

"Holy Hell, what's happening to me? Son of a bitch shitshitshitshit," I cried out as I levitated. The wattage and frequency of my fingertip light show increased and my hair floated around my head as if I'd been electrocuted.

Janet turned from my closet and quickly plastered herself against my wall. "Good Satan Almighty! Look at you," she screeched. "Carl, get in here. Her magic has come and her language is outstanding! Not full Demon, but close."

She watched me like someone watches a bad car accident, which only pissed me off more.

"Are you going to help me down?" I hissed as a golden glitter sprayed all over my room.

"Hell no," she replied, slowly inching her way toward my door.

"If you take one more step," I threatened, "I'll fry your ass."

Janet laughed with delight, bounced up and down and attempted to pull on her nonexistent beard. Old habits die hard. "Ooooh, you're a nasty little piece of work. Your daddy's gonna be so proud!"

Carl burst into my room wearing tighty-whities. Only tighty-whities. I was fairly positive my appetite had been permanently destroyed.

"Whath going on?" he shouted as he assumed a kung fu pose in a deep squat. Not a good look while clothed. Definitely not a good look while practically nude.

"Look up." Janet pointed and giggled.

I tried with all my might to wrench my eyes from the heart-shaped mass of hair on Carl's chest. WTH?

"Carl," I said calmly, still spitting sparks from my fingertips. "Have I lost my mind or is the hair rug on your chest shaved into a heart?"

"It ith," he said with pride. "But look at thith!"

He turned around, and on his fur-covered back the word *Janet* had been shaved. The J started right above the elastic band of his underpants and the T ended at his neck.

"Oh dear Beelzebub," I gasped in horror, completely caught off guard by the shocking and disgusting declaration of love for Janet. "Did you shave or wax that?" Was that necessary information? No, but I needed to know.

Carl's eyes were earnest as he turned to me. He literally swelled with pride. "Neither. I did electrolthith. Ith permanent."

Janet blushed with delight and scratched Carl like a dog. I expected his leg to start dancing at any moment.

I didn't know what to say, which was rare. My ass was plastered to my ceiling, my fingers were still shooting red sparklies, gold mist had created an iridescent cloud in the room and I mutely watched Janet and Carl begin performing some foul, hairy mating ritual. Enough was enough.

"Hey," I shouted, throwing a metaphoric bucket of cold water on my overheated *family members.* "I appreciate your positive attitude toward body image and creative hair design, but I have a problem here."

"Right," Carl said as he grabbed my foot and tried to yank me down from the ceiling.

No go.

"Get me down or I'll rip out a map of Hell with all the excess hair left on your body," I ground out through clenched teeth. The fingertip fireworks increased. Purple and silver sparkles joined the red ones. They rained down on Carl, who was laughing at me and about to pull my left leg out of the socket. I was in pain, pissed off and at the same time seriously concerned I was going to set Carl on fire due to his excessive body hair issue. He didn't seem to notice or care. He just yanked harder.

"Let go of my leg," I yelled.

"I can't get you down." He was puzzled.

"No duh, dumbass." I couldn't find polite if it bit me in the butt. "You're going to pull my leg off."

"You can grow another one," Janet volunteered.

"That is so not the point," I shrieked. "I don't want to grow a new leg. I like this leg. I just want to get off the ceiling."

"I'm not thure how to handle thith," Carl muttered, rubbing his bald head a mile a minute.

"Clap," Myrtle said as she entered the room all business-like.

"What?" I rolled my eyes at her as more fire flew from my fingertips.

"Clap," she repeated and rolled her eyes right back at me.

"Fine," I snapped. I clapped and miraculously I steadily floated back down to my bed. The sparks subsided, but the room was covered in gold glitter dust. "How did you know what to do?" I asked as I grabbed onto the post of my bed just in case the light show and levitating decided to return.

"Because I'm Myrtle, Keeper of Secrets. I know lots of things." She smiled and plopped herself down next to me.

"Why did it happen?" I still maintained a death grip on my bed.

"Your magic came in, and it's just a guess, but did you get angry?" she asked.

"She told me she'd fry my ass and she's pissed at Satan," Janet trilled gleefully.

"And the told me the'd rip a map of Hell into my chetht hair," Carl added with pride.

"Ewwwwww. Well, there you go," Myrtle told me as she hopped off my bed and headed for my door.

"Wait just one minute, little secret keeper," I shouted. "How do I control this?"

"First of all, it's Keeper of Secrets, and if you wanna know what to do read the book." She raised her eyebrows at me.

"What book?" What the Hell was she talking about?

"The silver one your grandpa gave you," she replied, grinning evilly.

"The one with the heartbeat?" I moaned and hoped I was wrong.

"The one and only."

"It freaks me out that an inanimate object has a heart beat."

"How do you know it's inanimate?" she challenged. Myrtle pulled the silver tome with the bizarre heartbeat out of my suitcase and tossed it onto my bed. "Start reading." With that my bizzaro little family left me alone in my room with the leather bound freak show.

"Great," I muttered as I gingerly picked up the book and quite possibly my fate. "Just freakin' great."

CHAPTER SIXTEEN

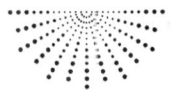

"You have got to be kidding me," I shouted as I shook my head in disgust and looked at the blank pages of my little silver book with the pulse. "What kind of joke is this?" I muttered as I tossed the empty book on my bed.

Either Grandpa was screwing with my head and playing a really mean prank or the book was alive and very unhappy with me. It was so angry it deleted itself. If I was a gambling gal, I'd lay my money on the book being pissed. It sensed my ambivalence.

I took a deep breath and glanced around to make sure no one was here. "Um, book... bookie, friend. Sorry for, you know, not believing." I rolled my eyes at how ridiculous I sounded and ran my hand gently over the cover, trying to reassure the little book of my change of heart. It purred.

"Holy shit." I quickly yanked my hand away and it growled. This was so not happening. I'd had a little too much crazy lately. I didn't have the patience or the time for some pissed off pile of paper. "You know what?" I glared at the book. "I don't need you. I'm going to find a portal and go to Hell. Some other idiot can come up here and kill the psycho Rogue Demons and find the dumbass Balance of Chaos." I had no use for a two-ounce instruction manual with a bad attitude.

"And you know what else?" I was on a roll. "You can take this Black Magic crap and shove it up your ass or... pages. I don't ever want to get stuck on a ceiling with sparkler fingers and hellacious hair again." I gave the book a hostile stare and turned my back on it.

What in the Hell was I doing? I was yelling at a book. I was stuck in a foreign world, yelling at a growling book. I was utterly alone in a strange, albeit pretty, new land and I'd become a gravity-deprived freaky electrical conduit. This sucked.

I stomped over to my window and laid my hot forehead against the cool pane. The picturesque landscape calmed my frayed nerves. Dad was right. Eden, Kentucky was gorgeous—rolling hills, graceful weeping willows, and white horse rail fencing as far as my eyes could see. Thoroughbred horses dotted the lush green fields and ponds glistened in the late day sun. It looked like paradise. Bizarrely enough, it felt vaguely familiar to me. I'd never been anywhere but Hell as far as I could remember but Eden, Kentucky made me feel safe and happy.

Maybe I'd stay a week or two, but first I needed to make nice with my book.

I slowly peeled myself away from the serene landscape and turned to embrace my destiny. It was gone.

"Damn it to Hell," I screeched as I sprinted to my bed and felt around for the book. "Oh no, no, no," I muttered, frantically looking under the pillows and behind the headboard. "I didn't know the stinkin' thing had legs."

I searched under my bed. Nothing. I ran over to my closet and tore through my clothes. Nothing. Could the stupid book fly?

"Where are you?" I yelled.

Nothing.

"Okay." I was going to have to eat it. "I'm really sorry. I treated you like an ordinary book and that wasn't very—well, you know, um—nice of me. So, ahhh…" Was this actually happening? "Clearly you're special. I've just never been acquainted with a living book, so I was a big gaping butt."

I heard something giggle. I quickly scanned the room. I couldn't gauge where the sound came from, but it seemed to enjoy my verbal self-abuse.

"That's right, I was a total loser jackass jerk-ass." The giggle got louder. I still couldn't locate its origin so I continued. "I am a colossal raging asshat assmonkey and I beg your forgiveness." Now I was giggling and the book started laughing.

Something changed—quickly and violently. An invisible pressure pushed me down on my bed. My room got hazy and blurry. The magic in the air was thick and it was getting harder and harder to breathe. I should have been terrified but I wasn't. I was excited. Clearly I'd lost it. My inner Demon was emerging more and more every day.

The book materialized and began to spin. The faster it spun, the bigger it got. A cascade of silver liquid flew from the pages and sprayed my room, making everything glow. I looked down at my t-shirt and jeans and gasped. They were covered in millions of teeny tiny lights—and I thought I was electric before…

The force from the magic in the room held me immobile. I could feel my heart beat in my throat and although I couldn't move, my body trembled. I was both hot and cold. It was difficult to focus, but I knew something important was about to happen. Whether I survived it or not, remained to be seen.

The book's binding shredded itself with a high-pitched squeal and pages flew everywhere. The liquid changed into a fine silver dust and began to swirl like the funnel of a tornado. A woman's arm popped out of the funnel. I screamed. Then another arm. Then a foot. Then it laughed. The laugh sounded familiar…

The pages danced violently around my room, obscuring my view of the morphing glitter-dust funnel. Being Lucifer's daughter, I'd seen a lot of hoo-doo, but this was nuts.

"Who are you?" I called out. There was no way in Hades the magic tornado could hear me. The wind from the flying pages alone was deafening. I'd just have to wait it out.

As quickly as it started, it ended. My room was eerily quiet, and as far as I could tell I was still alive. I sat up slowly, halfway expecting to see body parts and book pages strewn around the room. But no. I could never have imagined what I saw. It made no sense and at the same time it made all the sense in the world.

"Dixie," she said as she waited for my reaction. She looked exactly the same except her skin was silver.

"Blanche?" I whispered. "Who are you?"

"Not who," she whispered back. "The question should be what am I?"

"Okay, I'll bite." I wasn't sure I wanted the answer, but she looked pretty determined to tell me. "What the Hell are you?"

"I am what I have always been," she replied.

"And that would be?" Enough with the cryptic bullshit.

"What do you think I am?" she asked.

"I thought you were my imaginary friend, but now I'm not so sure."

"Oh, I'm still your friend." She walked toward me and I backed away. Hurt flashed in her eyes, but she quickly recovered. "Don't be afraid."

"Okay." I was still uneasy. It wasn't every day you found out your invisible friend was possibly a book, had silver skin and moonlighted as a tornado. "Are you a book or a person?"

"Neither."

She was beautiful in an alarmingly spooky way. We still looked alike, aside from her ice blue eyes and her silver skin, but she was slightly transparent. I couldn't see completely through her but I saw shadows. I wondered if her skin was going to stay silver.

"Yes, it will." She was very matter of fact.

"What will?"

"My skin will stay silver." She sighed wearily. "It's my natural color."

Holy crap, did I say that out loud? I'd swear I just thought it. I was truly going crazy now.

"You're not crazy."

"You're inside my head," I accused her as I slid off my bed to put some more distance between us. Did I even know her? I began to pace. I always thought more clearly when I moved.

"Of course I'm inside your head," Blanche laughed. "I've always been inside your head."

"Do you even exist?" I yelled. Confused didn't even begin to define how I felt. "Are you me?" I whispered.

"You're getting warmer." She was excited. "Guess again."

"I'm schizophrenic and you're a weird violent weather pattern?" I moaned as I ran my hands through my hair and continued to move restlessly around my room. I was feeling the need to burst out of my skin.

"Cold." She laid down on my bed and rolled her eyes at my stupidity.

"How about a little help here," I snapped.

"I'm not allowed to." She hesitated, torn by the desire to reveal what she was. She stayed quiet and pouted. She was unhappy with the rules of the game.

"Let me get this straight... You're inside my head. You're a what, not a who and I have to guess because it's against the rules for you to tell me."

"You got it."

"What will happen if you tell me?" I mean, how bad could it be? Surely no one would know.

"We'd both turn to dust," she replied.

That was bad.

"Look, if there was any way I could tell you I would. I don't like these rules either, but I have no desire to test them to see if they're accurate," she huffed.

"This sucks," I said as I sat down next to her. I was no longer afraid. "Can anybody else see you?"

"Nope."

"How come Stella could see you?"

"I'm not sure." Blanche was thoughtful. "Maybe because she loves you so much and knows you so well. Or maybe because she's young and not yet jaded."

We sat in silence. I stared at the ceiling and let my mind go blank. Blanche took my hand in hers. Light currents of power traveled from her hand to mine. It was strangely comforting. We lay quietly for a few more minutes. I began to try to piece the puzzle together.

The book was here to guide me—to teach me how to control my Black Magic, or so I thought. Blanche said I was getting warm when I asked her if she was me. She could read my thoughts as if they were hers. She was not a who, she was a what. That one threw me a little. She'd always been with me, but did I create her or did someone else put her in my life? She had always believed in me and given me the strength to make decisions, right or wrong. She never made my decisions for me, nor did she guide me. She was always there for the results. She wasn't my Guardian Angel. Demons didn't have Angels.

"Sweet Baby Satan, are you my conscience?" I gasped.

"You're so close." The tension in her body was palpable. I needed to guess correctly before she imploded.

I sat up and searched her face, and I knew. "You're my fate."

Her smile spread slowly and lit up her entire face. "Bingo."

CHAPTER SEVENTEEN

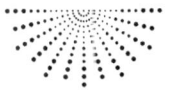

"Good morning, sunshine," Janet sang as she whipped up my window shades, temporarily blinding me.

"Get out," I grumbled.

"Why, aren't we a nasty Nellie this morning." She hummed as she poked at me.

"What time is it?' I groaned, throwing my pillow at her.

"Time to get up, sleepyhead!" She got a running start, tore across my room and took a flying leap onto my bed, successfully bouncing me out of my cozy nest and onto the cold hard floor.

"What in the Hell is wrong with you?" I hissed as I pulled my comforter off the bed and curled into a small ball.

She leaned her head over the side of my bed and got in my face. "You have fight training with Carl." She grinned and yanked my comforter off of me.

"Holy Hades, you suck," I moaned as I attempted to crawl under my bed just to get away from her and her upside down face. I was still exhausted from the night before with Blanche. We stayed up most of the night talking. As usual, when she decided we were finished she left. She disappeared and gave me no indication as to when I'd see her again. The rest of my sleepless night was consumed reliving the best night of my life with Hayden. Suffice it to say coherent thought escaped me at the moment.

Janet grabbed my foot and pulled before I could disappear to the relative safety of underneath my bed. Damn her.

"Carl's going to teach you some moves, then you'll practice with Myrtle and me." She straightened out my bed and muttered, "We're going to kick your ass."

Now she had my attention. "I'm sorry, what did you say?"

"Carl's going to teach you some moves."

"Uh huh." I narrowed my eyes at her. "And the other part?"

"Oh." Janet smiled sweetly. "I said we're going to kick your ass."

"You're sure about that?"

"Yep," she quipped and felt for her missing beard and stache. Her elation died. She deflated like a popped balloon.

"Janet." I could tell she was close to crying. "Is there a chance you could grow them back?"

"No." Averting her eyes and trying to hide her tears, she mumbled, "That horrid therapist had the hair removal Demons put a cease and desist spell on my follicles."

"That's, well that's... I don't even know what that is," I stuttered and tried to make sense of that one. I pondered why or who would create a spell like that. "I'm really sorry, Janet."

I gathered her little body in my arms, the same body that had just evilly bounced me off of my bed, and I hugged her while she cried. Tremors shook her and I held her tighter. I wanted to kick that therapist's ass. I wouldn't mind taking a pass at that bitch with a coffee table leg. The more I thought about that smarmy hag, the angrier I got. Yep. I was becoming more Demon with each passing second.

My hands began to tingle. Oh Hell, I knew what was coming. Small red sparks started to fly from my fingertips. I gently disengaged Janet. I had no desire to light the hair she had left on fire. I took a deep cleansing breath and clapped my hands.

It stopped.

Damn if Myrtle wasn't the smartest girl in the world. I grinned and wiggled my non-flaming fingers.

"Did you see me?" I blurted. I sounded like a five year old on her birthday, but I didn't care.

"You controlled it," Janet yelled, her hair issues forgotten. "I'm so proud of you."

"Me too." I grinned. "I'm ready to go downstairs and hand you your ass."

"You sure?" she challenged gleefully.

"So sure," I replied.

BEING SURE DOES NOT GUARANTEE SUCCESS, NOT BY A LONG SHOT. Just ask my bruised and aching body. Fight training was ugly and painful. My pride was the only thing that had kept me from giving up. I'd never admit it, but Janet was right. They were kicking my ass. The training room was state of the art. Leave it to the Devil... Who in the Hell would have guessed the basement of a graceful Southern manor housed a torture chamber? Oops, I meant a large gym, with every conceivable machine and weapon known to man. There was a large, mat-covered open area for martial arts training and Jazzersize. *Carl was addicted.* The walls were covered with weapons: swords, daggers, throwing stars, guns, grenades, bombs... You name it, we had it.

There was also an area for knife throwing. I was sure I'd spend many hours there, certainly after I'd nailed Carl in the neck with a nice-sized dagger. Thank Satan we're immortal. I was aiming at the wall. Carl just pulled it out of his jugular and kept on going, not even commenting on the unavoidable fact that he was bleeding profusely. I thought for sure I'd killed him. I even threw up a little bit in my mouth I was so upset, but Carl was fine. He wasn't even mad at me.

That's when Carl decided it was time to spar. He wasn't as sweet as I thought. Pay back for an almost decapitation was a bitch, and that son of a bitch punched as hard as a freight train. If I didn't have Black Magic I'd be so dead. After the third punch to my head, *which probably caused brain damage*, I understood why my dad sent Carl up to Earth with me. Carl the Destroyer was an apt name for him.

"Okay," Carl explained, sweating up a rather unattractive storm. "When thomebody runth at you to kill you, you have to fight back."

"I know, but Janet and Myrtle aren't really going to kill me," I patiently explained to Carl for the fifth time. "I don't want to hurt them." I referred to the still open knife wound on Carl's neck. I heard Myrtle snort.

"You might want to shut your cakehole," I politely told Myrtle. "Or I'll shut it for you."

"As if," she snapped.

Carl thought we should all take a break. I'd like to think it was because he was worried about what I would do to Myrtle, but even I couldn't live in that dream world. Carl helped me stretch out, which was something I'd never ask him to do again. I was certain my arms had been dislocated and my legs would need amputation. I moaned and tried to kick Carl in the head.

"You are such a wussy," Myrtle laughed.

That was about all I could take. I took my leg back from Carl, shoved him out of my way and gave Myrtle the evil eye. I'd been knocked around and beaten up for over two hours. I could take getting whaled on, but getting laughed at? Not so much.

"Get your skinny asscrack over here," I yelled. I mentally ran through all the moves Carl had taught me. I was a quick study and I was strong, but more than that… I was pissed. I was sick of getting busted on. I was ready to do some busting of my own.

A rush of energy and heat blasted through me as I sized up Myrtle. She looked smug and unconcerned. Not smart.

"Bring it," I shouted.

She did. She gleefully put me into a chokehold.

"You suck, you freakin' assclown," I grunted.

"Holy Hell! Assclown? You can't do better than assclown?" she barked. "You are the wussiest Demon ever born. There's no way you're Lucifer's daughter!" She forcefully threw me to the mat. As she was about to body slam me, I quickly rolled to my left, hopped up and gave her a roundhouse kick to the head. She staggered back and grinned like an idiot.

Hmm, this was actually getting fun.

"Oh," I informed all of them. "I am definitely Lucifer's daughter." Without even thinking I raised my hands and froze them. Wow, that was cool. I wondered what else I could do. Blanche hadn't taught me anything about Black Magic yet, so I figured trial and error would be my teacher today. I grinned evilly at my cute little frozen pseudo-family. The shock on their faces was priceless. I smirked and considered my options.

I slowly rotated my right wrist and my little frozen family began to spin—and spin and spin. The faster I moved my hand the faster they spun through the air. They were on an invisible vomit-inducing carnival ride from the Basement of Hell. Their shrieks were music to my ears and aching muscles. Not Lucifer's daughter, my ass.

As Carl's pallor turned green I backed up. Using my left hand I made little flicking motions, moving the trio closer together. Not touching, but close enough that they all could enjoy what was about to come out of Carl.

"Dixie," Myrtle screamed. "You win. We lose."

"Hades help us." Janet moaned as she started to turn the same shade as Carl.

I did feel kind of bad, but not *that* bad. I grabbed my phone with my left hand as my right continued to rotate and I set the timer for five minutes. That should probably do it.

"STOOOOOPPPPP," Myrtle shrieked as she clearly saw the

impending bile storm headed her way. Carl and Janet whimpered in agony.

Now I felt *that* bad. So much for being a heartless Demon…

I lowered my hands and they all dropped to the ground with resounding thuds. I was too nice for this crap. I went to my dizzy group and tried to help them to their feet. Too little, too late. Payback was a bitch… and so was getting thrown up on.

CHAPTER EIGHTEEN

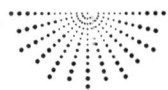

"I just blasted you with a volt of electricity and magic that should have killed you," I coldly informed one of my favorite people in the world. "You cannot sneak up on me anymore. Grandma Gigi will fry my ass if I off you."

"Yes, yes, she would." Grandpa's eyes sparkled with joy. Curls of smoke streamed from his singed clothing. "But you can't!"

"Can't what?"

"Can't kill me," he continued gleefully as he patted out a small fire on his crotch. "On any other Demon or Angel that would have worked, but not on me. In fact," he pondered seriously, "I believe there are only several beings in the entire universe that your power will not work on."

"And they would be?" I asked as I grabbed a bottle of water from the fridge and poured it over his head.

"Thank you," he giggled.

"No prob. Answer my question."

"Your magic kills anything except a True Immortal."

I ransacked my brain for the list of True Immortals. Grandpa waited patiently. All I had wanted was a damn midnight snack.

How did scrounging for Janet's Rice Krispie treats turn into a history lesson with a smoldering grandparent?

"A True Immortal can't die—I already knew that. I just forgot." I watched him stare lovingly at my snack and I sighed. "Do you want one?"

"Of course. I've been eating Mother Nature's cooking for weeks. I need something edible."

I cut him a huge wedge of Rice Krispie treat, slid into a chair at the kitchen table and attacked my own.

"Are you going to go back to my lesson?"

"I believe it was your turn. However, part of what you said was wrong." He grinned and began separating the treat—Krispie by Krispie. "True Immortals can die—they just can't be killed."

I tamped back my desire to slap him and then hug him. "Like that makes any sense."

"It makes perfect sense, my love. A True Immortal can only die if they choose to."

"Oh my Hell, are you going to eat that or just play with it?"

"Both. A True Immortal can die of a broken heart."

"For real?"

"For real. You know if you press on the individual Krispies it's a little like popping bubble wrap."

I dislodged a few Krispies to see if he was right. He was.

"Wait," I said as I cut two more pieces to eat since we were obviously going to play with our first round. "You just get a broken heart and poof, you're dead?"

"Mother Nature's bosom, that's satisfying," he shouted as he pounded his little fist into a large wad of Krispies. "Of course not —it's a three part finale. One, your heart must be truly broken. Two, you must choose to die and three, the Sword of Death must be plunged into your heart."

"They didn't exactly teach that in school."

"That's not information we want getting out," he replied. "In the wrong hands that could be a clusterfuck. And apparently the Sword has gone missing."

"Again? Mr. Rogers lost the damn Sword again?" I shouted as I grabbed the pan and punched the rest of the Krispies.

Why the Hell my father let Mr. Rogers guard the Sword was beyond me. Mr. Rogers was the former host of a mortal freakin' children's show.

"It was never lost the first time," Grandpa reminded me. "That was a test for your cousin Astrid. Fred Rogers is a formidable warrior and is one of the few men I know who can pull off a cardigan sweater."

I bit back my retort about asking if it disappeared while he was changing his tennis shoes and I began to eat the crushed mess on the table.

"Oookay, that seems like a bit of a problem."

"Oh yes," he agreed and pilfered some of my snack.

I picked at the marshmallow goo on my hands and debated asking any more questions. Curiosity won out. "Do you know who stole it?"

"Possibly." He leaned forward and licked the table. What in the Hell was he doing? His manners were disgusting. I wondered if he got away with this at my grandma's.

"You're not going to tell me."

"Correct," he smiled ruefully. "You are correct. Do you have any milk?" I nodded and got him the jug. I didn't bother with a glass—he wouldn't use it anyway. "Let's get back to your lesson."

"Can I guess who stole it?"

"Of course, but if you listen closely the answers are always there."

I watched him gulp from the container and grinned. How did he make disgusting etiquette look cute? I waited for more. More would certainly come, it just might not make any sense.

"So, where was I?" he inquired as he wiped his mouth with the edge of the tablecloth.

"Let me see… Mr. Rogers is a sucky guard, True Immortals can bite it if a date goes bad and the freakin' Sword of Death got ripped off."

His mouth quirked with humor, "Yes, yes, of course. How many True Immortals are there?"

"It's undefined."

"So very smart." He chuckled and brushed all the crumbs to the floor. "There are eight established Immortals at the moment, but there are more in our midst."

"Grandpa, I'm sure you're not telling me this for my health."

"Actually, I am."

We sat in silence while I waited for him to continue. It was clear I was going to be waiting a long time and I didn't want him licking any more surfaces.

"Fine. Satan, you, God, Angel of Death, Angel of Light, Mother Nature, Astrid and… " I paused. Who was the other one?

"So far, so good."

"Oh… " I was stuck. Who in the Hell was the other True Immortal?

"I hear you did the nasty with the Angel of Death."

"I did not do the nasty," I snapped. Was nothing sacred?

"Touché, and you're a terrible liar." He grinned and shrugged. "Your mother is a True Immortal."

"My mother is alive?" My sex life was suddenly forgotten.

"As far as I know, my sweet. I'm sure I would have heard if she bit the big one. Although if you ask me, she may as well be dead considering how she's neglected her duties and the mess she's made."

"Would you like to expound on that?" He was excellent at avoidance, but he was not avoiding this.

"Nope."

I deflated like a flat tire and sagged in my chair. My head fell to my hands and I gave in to the impulse that had been clawing at me for days. I cried. Hard.

"Oh my baby." Grandpa took me into his little arms and rocked me in the same manner most Demons couldn't resist rocking him. He gently wiped my tears, gasped and jerked his hand back.

"What?" I choked out, alarmed by his reaction.

"Your tears." Grandpa looked at his burnt finger with amazement. "They burned me."

"I'm so sorry." I was so confused. I touched the residual tears on my face to see if they burned me.

Nothing.

"Don't be sorry, lovey." He smiled. "It's not your fault. One who has the strength to cry is often the strongest of all. You're more like your mother than I realized."

"About that," I started.

"Don't ask," he cut me off. "Because I can't tell. I can get away with a lot, but not even I can go there."

"What in the Hell is wrong with everybody? What could be so awful? Is she a farm animal or something?" Tired of this didn't even begin to touch on the frustration with the *mom* subject, but I knew a closed door when I saw one. Furthermore, he was laughing too hard at my farm animal or something question to be of much use to me. "Fine," I said, changing the subject, "what are you doing here? I thought all of you were forbidden to communicate with me for a month." If that turned out to be false, Hayden, my own personal Angel of Death's ass was grass.

Grandpa was still enjoying himself at my expense so it took him a moment to gather his cute little self. My jaw clenched and I pressed my hands firmly down on the kitchen table. I had the urge to grab and squeeze him, but I knew I could control it.

"Dixie, Dixie." He sighed the way one does after a good hearty laugh. "Rules don't apply to me."

He giggled and squeezed himself. Holy Hell, he'd better not do that. I wasn't sure I could curb my hugging impulses if he was going to rub my face in it by loving on himself.

"Grandpa." I turned away from him. I was seconds away from smothering him with kisses. "Does Dad know you're here?"

"Not exactly, but Cole and the generals do. Those bastards are everywhere." He got serious. "Your father suspects. He wants me here, but he can't say that since he already laid down the law. Sooo he simply turned his head and pretended he had no idea what my plans were. Furthermore." He grinned evilly. "I don't know if you've noticed, but it's quite difficult to say no to me."

"I've noticed." Amusement colored my voice and I gently touched his face. "Why are you really here?"

"I miss you." It was all I could do not to tackle him and cuddle. "Is that all?"

He tended to save the best for last.

"Um, no." He smiled sheepishly and took another swig of milk. "You have to drink from me again. It takes two times to ensure the Black Magic has taken and I need to implant several random messages into your head."

"Like that wasn't random enough?" I swallowed and attempted to tamp down my gag reflex. Blood after Rice Krispie treats did not sound good to me right now... actually ever.

"I understand how drinking from me doesn't appeal. Hades knows it freaks me out, but you're too important to the world for me not to do this. Not to mention I love you more than all of your sisters put together. You have never broken one bone in my body!"

As immature as it was, I loved knowing I was his favorite. "Grandpa, it's just that blood tastes so... " I shut my mouth. It filled with water and I knew I was close to hurling. I refused to vomit. If I vomited, he'd vomit and I'd still have to drink his blood. Oh, Uncle God, please help me.

"What if I put chocolate syrup in my mouth and then drink your blood? Will that screw anything up?" I asked, praying to Satan that my mouth would stop watering.

He wrung his hands and considered my suggestion. "I don't

see why not. It certainly makes me happier to know that you're happy."

I quickly grabbed the Hershey's Syrup from the fridge while Grandpa slit his throat. I squirted a gob of liquid chocolate into my mouth and latched onto my beloved grandpa's bloody neck.

It really was much better this way. The chocolate-blood mix tasted a bit rank, but it was greatly improved from the first blood suck-a-thon.

A burning heat rushed through my body, but instead of being scared this time I went with it. I held tightly to Grandpa as I started to convulse. I shook violently for about two minutes, then it subsided. The burning and churning was alarming, but doable because I knew it would end. I felt floaty and springy. The magic whooshed through me.

The sound of wind chimes bounced around inside my head and a feeling of absolute power consumed and unnerved me. I pulled back and searched my grandpa's face. He was weaker and I was stronger.

"Am I killing you?" I gasped as I cuddled him carefully.

"No, my love." His smile broadened with love and approval. "You are becoming stronger than me."

"No," I cried out. This was all wrong.

"Yes." His mood was thoughtful. "This is the way it is meant to be. It should have been years from now before we had to do all this, but... " He faded off.

"But what?" I shook him gently. My life and future were spinning out of control.

"But so much is happening, you are the only one to solve it... end it." His smile was sad.

I touched his neck and closed the knife wound. My body automatically knew how to do things that my brain had no idea I could.

"What else do I need to know?"

"Absolute power can corrupt absolutely. People aren't always who you think they are and the old ones have wisdom... most of the time."

"Is that all?"

"For now," he added cryptically.

"Oookay." I shook my head in frustration. "And what am I supposed to do until I understand all your messages and try not to get killed?"

"Oh, you know," he said as he giggled. "Go to community college, make friends, visit your cousin Astrid, practice Black Magic, have fun. The usual."

"Wait. Did you say community college? I've already graduated from a college that rivals most Ivy League institutions."

"You look young and that is where you need to be."

"Holy crap, you're serious?"

"As a heart attack," he replied, tucking my hair behind my ears. "You are so darn pretty, my little one."

Compliments didn't help at the moment. I paced the room and my ire rose to my throat. An utter lack of control consumed me and I turned away from my grandpa's concerned gaze.

Frustration was eating me, and instead of yelling at the little man who had only come to help I slammed my hands down on the table... and it exploded.

"Shit," I screeched. Frantically I ran for the fire extinguisher and in my haste blew up the fridge. "Son of a bitch, help me," I begged before I took down the house.

"Breathe, Dixie," Grandpa demanded in a voice that calmed me. "Control your anger. Don't let it control you."

"I can handle this," I said with more confidence than I felt. Shithellfirebuttholes , I was going with the theory that if I said something aloud enough it would be true. Again, shithellfirebuttholes.

"You can and you will," he replied with an ancient confidence that calmed me some.

"Anger is my trigger?" I asked.

"Somewhat, but the main trigger is imbalance."

"I'm imbalanced?" I snapped. That would have been a lovely thing to have known before I'd left Hell.

"No, no dear." He chuckled. "Your Grandma Gigi is imbalanced, but she has a wonderful bosom. Imbalance in the world is your trigger."

"Could you be more specific?" I asked, ignoring the part about Mother Nature's boobs.

"Lack of balance, injustice, unfairness."

"That seems a bit do-goody for a Demon," I muttered.

"Yes, well, you can blame that on your mother."

"Ahhh, the elusive mother figure that seems to have caused some of the shitstorm up here."

"Correct. Keep your eyes open, child."

"If I didn't adore you so damned much I would incinerate you too," I muttered, hating the rules of being a Demon.

"I love you," he said.

"I love you too." I leaned in to kiss him but paused. "How will I know who the Rogue Demons and Angels are?"

"Trust me, you'll know."

CHAPTER NINETEEN

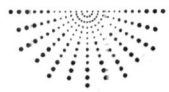

THERE WAS NO WAY SHE COULD BE THAT STUPID. COMMUNITY
college was bad enough without this.

We'd only been going to classes with humans for three days—
how could she do this to me? I ran down the smelly hallway
toward the crowd that had gathered. I was conscious of my speed.
I had to hold back or explain a whole lot of stuff that no one
would believe anyway.

Grandpa had stayed for four days and had left this morning.
He made it abundantly clear to me that I needed to behave like a
human. He told me to dance more. WTH?

Carl was delighted and added ballroom dancing to our fight
training sessions. Myrtle thought we should twerk. Holding back
my speed was literally painful. Not many mortals could run so
fast that they disappeared. There were simply too many things to
remember.

The fluorescent lighting made the paint on the walls appear
puke green. The colorful bulletin boards with lime green sorority
rush notices couldn't hide the fact that the college was over eighty
years old and hadn't been remodeled since the 1970's.

I tried in vain to make my way through a group of the

popular sorority girls sporting Uggs, t-shirts with Greek letters on them and super short minis. They had no intention of letting me by. I could disintegrate them with a single flick of my fingers, but that would be a bad thing and almost impossible to explain to my dad. None of the girls liked me because apparently all the boys did. The college was tiny and all who went here seemed to either be related or buddies since kindergarten. Very *Deliverance*.

I made a huge point of not even looking at the guys once I figured out what was going on. Not only that, but the classes were far too easy for me. I was trying to dumb it down, but it was difficult when I knew I was smarter than my teachers.

The Ugg brigade gave me no choice. I shoved my way through the overly made up mean girls to see what I knew was awaiting me but prayed to Satan was not.

Damn Myrtle, she was that stupid. Of all the dumb things she could have done, she had to do this. Was this payback for the vomit party? I'd apologized for that one repeatedly. It wasn't like she and Janet and Carl weren't trying to kick my ass too. However, it was pointed out to me that getting your ass kicked and being spun till you puked were two different things entirely.

Myrtle was up to no good and was reliving one of the pranks she liked to play in Hell—playing dead. She lay prone on the bluish-greenish-grayish linoleum floor of the hallway between the math and science labs. The horrid lighting pouring out of the science room made her already pale skin even paler . To top it all off she didn't appear to be breathing. Demons could go hours without breathing. I stared at my dear little fake *cousin* on the floor and began to brainstorm the ways I would kill her dead later.

"Oh God, she's dead," one vapid girl shrieked and others followed suit.

Students sobbed and held each other. One had fainted and I was fairly sure one was about to get sick. Myrtle was getting a much better reaction here on Earth than she ever got in Hell. A super-cute guy had begun CPR and I could swear she smirked.

That was about all I could take.

"Excuse me," I said as I pushed my way past the last mean girl.

"Watch it," Blondie hissed. "Can't you see there's a dead girl? Show some respect, for God's sake."

"Like He's ever shown me any," I mumbled.

"What is wrong with you? Are you slow or something?" she asked, completely confused. She was as nasty as some of the ickier Demons in Hell.

"Aren't you a sweetie." I rolled my eyes and confused her even more. Hell's Bells, I wanted to shut Blondie's mouth so badly I felt my fingers tingle. I quickly clapped my hands. "She's my cousin," I informed the bitchy blonde. "And she's not dead."

"Yeah, right." She and her attractive minions looked at me like I had three heads.

Myrtle wasn't the only one I was going to deal with later. Blondie needed to learn some manners. I turned my back on the Meanies and gingerly pulled Cute Guy off of Myrtle. He seemed to be enjoying himself a little too much. I wasn't sure if he was a necrophiliac or if he was simply a good Samaritan.

"She has narcolepsy." They all stared at me blankly. For real? Hades, these mortals were slow. "You know, when you fall asleep without warning," I enlightened the grieving crowd as I yanked the first explanation I could think of out of my ass. I have to say as far as lies went it was pretty good. The group of about thirty gasped and began to cheer. Where were the professors? Hell forbid one had called an ambulance. I was grateful no one with authority was in the vicinity. The students were still crying, but now they were high fiving, hugging and chest bumping as well. These humans were the weirdest and creepiest species ever.

Cute Guy shoved me out of the way and clasped Myrtle to his chest as crocodile tears of joy rolled down his unblemished cheeks.

"Wake up," he yelled. "Wake up, Sleeping Beauty." He shook her and glanced over at me suspiciously. "I think she's dead." He gulped hard and bit back the hysteria that was mighty close to the surface.

The crowd was no longer with me. They were torn between hoping she was alive and hoping she was dead. A death in the math-science hallway would mean no school for at least a week and automatic A's on finals for everyone. Actually, I couldn't blame them. If I were in their shoes I'm not sure which way I'd go. Nevertheless, she wasn't dead and Cute Guy was riding my very last nerve.

My lips thinned in irritation and it was everything I could do to keep my eyes from going red. Myrtle was going to pay. "Give her to me." My stare drilled into Cute Guy and he reluctantly handed her over. She might not be dead now, but she was going to be so dead after I killed her so bad when we got home.

I pressed my lips to her ear. To the crowd of doubting co-eds, it looked as if I was whispering gentle endearments. They were very wrong.

"If you don't open your eyes right now I will kill you myself," I told her with a loving smile on my face for the benefit of our audience. "I will see to it that you end up in the Basement of Hell burning for eternity. I will visit you weekly and pour alcohol all over your open wounds and I will finish that off by dipping you in salt. And if that's not enough, I'll make sure you're placed right next to our skanky hag therapist till the end of time."

That did it.

Myrtle's eyes shot open so fast I dropped her. Actually, I dropped her on purpose. Just for fun.

The crowd went wild and Cute Guy grabbed her and laid a big wet one right on her lips. She squealed, turned bright red, leaned in and gave Cute Guy another smackaroo. The cat calls and whistles came fast and furious. The good will and happiness amongst the jaded and over-it co-eds was contagious. Some of the girls even smiled at me. Maybe I wouldn't kill Myrtle.

As quickly as it started it was over. We all scattered like mice when we heard it. Not the bell to change classes… the ambulance in the distance to retrieve the dead girl.

CHAPTER TWENTY

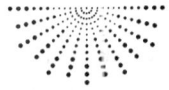

"I'M A FREAKIN' COLLEGE GRADUATE. THIS IS RIDICULOUS," I muttered.

"I like college. You just need to try harder."

"If Grandpa hadn't insisted I be there I'd be cutting classes like my dad wanted me to in Hell."

"Such a good little Demon," Myrtle said as she ransacked my closet for clothes.

"None of that will fit you," I snapped as she hugged my favorite t-shirt to her chest.

"Sure it will. My boobs are bigger." She swiped my shirt and raced from my room.

Her boobs were not bigger and a week and a half of community college on Earth had worn me out. Playing dumb, trying to move slowly and making sure my eyes didn't turn red was hard--plus nobody liked me. Myrtle, an outcast in Hell, had joined a sorority and had a boyfriend. Cute Guy, aka Timmy Smith the necrophiliac, was her man.

I was not asked to join a sorority and I was not popular. I was more of a smart nerd, but even the nerds seemed wary of me. I was grudgingly tolerated by the mean girls because I was Myrtle's *cousin.* They still thought I was after their gross human boyfriends. As if. I had a boyfriend… a soul mate. At least I thought I did. I was counting the minutes until I was allowed communication with Hell.

Even though Myrtle seemed quite happy being popular, a Demon was still a Demon. Besides playing dead in public places, she was also practicing her other bizarre hobby on Earth— shaving and dyeing people's pets in the dead of night to look like wild animals. I had spotted a number of dogs and cats in town resembling lions and tigers and skunks. The townfolk of Eden were stymied. She also joyfully appeared to be pitting the popular mean girls against each other. I couldn't say I minded that one.

As I wandered to my closet I hid my favorite t-shirts. "No way she's swiping these," I muttered to no one, since being alone seemed to be my new MO.

I missed home so much it physically hurt. Thoughts of Hayden made me feel short of breath. He was in my every waking thought. And my dad. Oh, my dad. Thinking of him made my heart ache. I knew he hadn't abandoned me, but the irrational side of me was still hurt and angry. I was sure he was visiting me in my dreams, but in the morning when I woke everything was too hazy to remember.

So here I was, in a place I had no desire to be, with no friends and nothing to do but go to *community college*, come home to get my ass kicked by Carl during fight training and wait for the Balance of Chaos, Angels or the evil Rogue Demons I was supposed to kill. Good times, good times. I used to drive a Porsche, have gobs of friends, family and invitations to everything. This sucked.

I missed my Porsche, but dad had set me up with a cool little Mustang convertible. Driving around Eden had become my new hobby. I had to keep moving or I'd find myself a portal to Hell and go home to be with Hayden. I knew that was the worst thing I could possibly do. My dad would be furious. I owed it to him, myself and Hayden to be brave and do whatever the Hell I was supposed to do.

Again to say Eden, Kentucky was beautiful was an understatement of epic proportions. It was loaded with gardens. Exquisite flower gardens. Every residence, business, school and park boasted landscaping that left you breathless. I wondered if they tested potential residents for green thumbs. Blanche loved the gardens.

Speaking of Blanche, Grandpa hadn't been surprised in the least that the book with the heartbeat turned out to be my invisible best friend. He thought that it was a lot more convenient to have someone tell me the rules instead of having to read them. I explained to him that she hadn't taught me anything and I had no idea where she was and he laughed. Laughed. I almost punched him in his cute little head. However, he did show me how to cloak myself in invisibility and how to transport without a portal. Janet thought it was hilarious that I kept ending up in the bathroom no matter where I tried to transport. She thought possibly my magic system might be clogged. I turned her skin lime green for two hours for that lovely pun. If I was any kind of decent Demon I would have left her green for a week.

I might be a wussy Demon occasionally, but I certainly wasn't a wussy driver. Ever. I topped out at ninety-eight as I made my way down the long country road into town. I needed to kill a couple of hours before I got my ass handed to me by Carl, so I decided to go shopping.

THE CANDLE SHOP WAS CUTE. THE WHOLE FREAKIN' DOWNTOWN area was cute. "Light My Fire", *I'm not kidding,* the uber kitschy candle store was empty. So much for a bustling economy in Eden, Kentucky. It did smell lovely inside. I moved immediately to the grapefruit, lemony-smelling candles and started sniffing. I could spend hours in a candle shop sniffing every candle in the entire store. The good, the bad, and the ugly. I loved them all. Of course I'd leave with a raging headache and reeking of cinnamon and vanilla, but I couldn't seem to stop myself. Stella and I used to do it at least every other week. Hades, I missed Stella.

"Can I help you?'

Crap, I knew that bitchy voice. That voice liked me about as much as I liked it. Damn it, now I wasn't going to be able to sniff my way into a migraine. She was such a buzzkill. I willed my eyes to stay gold as I turned to find Blondie, aka Lucy Adams, glaring at me. Hands on her popular hips and peaches and cream complexion all flustered. All American golden girl and a big fat hairy bitch all rolled into one.

"I don't know, can you?" I narrowed my eyes and considered teaching her a lesson. I had never done anything to her and she was as mean as a snake. Maybe I would give her a gnarly case of acne or perhaps relieve her of her blonde flowing locks. She was so nasty at school I was itching to do something ugly.

"What do you want, Dixie?" she sneered. "This is my dad's store, among others, so of course I can help you. Do I want to help you? No. Do I have to? Yes."

"What in the Hell did I do to you to make you act like such a gaping hole?"

She stopped dead in her tracks and looked confused for a moment. "I don't know." She shrugged to hide her confusion. "I just hate you."

"Well, that's lovely," I retorted with cold sarcasm. "At least I have a reason to hate you."

"Why?"

Was she serious?

"Because." I smiled and flicked her golden locks. "You're a bitch."

She opened her mouth to impart some kind of sage wisdom but got cut short.

"Lucy Adams," a male voice roared from the back storeroom. It sent a chill up my spine and I was from Hell.

"You should leave," she hissed as she frantically pushed me toward the door.

"Can I do anything?" I whispered. I was desperate to get her out of this place, not to mention myself. My fingers tingled. I could feel my power increasing, feeding off the anger, fear and imbalance in the shop.

"Get out," she ground out through clenched teeth. "My father is not your problem."

"But," I started.

"Out." She colored fiercely. "You'll make it worse."

She was about to cry and I was completely undone. My fists clenched at my sides and the tingling in my fingers increased. Why was there such a sense of evil in this place, and why hadn't I noticed it when I walked in? My heart pounded furiously in my chest as I turned to leave.

When she was satisfied I was going, she turned and ran into the back room. I plastered myself against the wall by the entrance and waited. What was I going to do? I had no idea, but I knew I couldn't just leave.

The first thud and gasp made my stomach roil. The second punch and the crying and moaning made my heat rush through my body with a violent jolt. The third made me go numb. Fathers didn't do this to their daughters. Rage flew through my body and burned for release. I knew I could stop this Hell on Earth. I cloaked myself with invisibility and carefully made my way to the back room.

The sounds were bad, but the visual was far worse.

Lucy Adams lay in the corner of the storeroom curled into a ball. Her lip was bloody and her eye was swollen shut. She clutched her stomach and moaned quietly. Her eyes were glassy and she stared into nothingness. She looked like a beautiful broken doll.

"When I call you," her father shouted as he gritted his teeth in fury, "you will come." He stood about six feet tall and was a big burly man. He'd probably been handsome in his youth, but the years and anger had ravaged his looks.

"We had a customer, Dad," Lucy whispered faintly.

"I don't give a goddamn," he said harshly and laughed. He reared his foot back and slammed it into her stomach. He seemed sickly comfortable with the move.

Her eyes rolled back into her head. She bit down on her lower lip, drawing blood, but refusing to scream.

He glared at her. "You're as useless as your mother was."

Her lower bloody lip trembled as she returned his glare. "She's lucky she's dead."

"Well," he growled, "we can certainly remedy that." He went to kick her again with his steel-toed boot.

My power had reached such a frenzy from all the evil and hatred and fear, it was use it or lose it.

Still under the cloak of invisibility, I pointed to his stomach and shot a massive dose of acid-like energy there. He screamed in shock and doubled over, slamming his head on the table as he went down. That was an unintentional bonus. Blood gushed from his hairline. I knew the excruciating stomach pain would last about four hours. How did I know that? No clue... I just did. Four hours of Hellish pain wasn't enough for a bastard like him, but it would have to do for now. I couldn't give myself away, but I wasn't quite through yet. I pinched my fingers together like little chompers. I repeated the motion, gaining speed and grinned delightedly as he started to slap at his body while still writhing around the floor in agony.

The feeling of slimy pinching bugs would stay with him for about twenty-four hours. I was tempted to go farther, but the utter shock on Lucy Adams' face made me stop.

She stood slowly, a bloody bruised mess, and cautiously made her way out of the storeroom, never taking her eyes from the revolting man she called her father. The minute she hit the shop she ran and she didn't look back.

I stared in disgust at the human pig on the floor and I knew why Lucy Adams was so mean. How could she not be, if she lived with this on a daily basis? People thought Hell was bad? It was nothing compared to what I'd seen on Earth.

I gave a last fleeting glance to the pile of shit on the floor, turned and left.

CHAPTER TWENTY-ONE

I REALLY WANTED TO GO HOME. AT LEAST EVIL WAS DEFINED IN Hell. Bad was bad and good was good. The lines didn't cross like they did on Earth and you didn't get away with it in Hell. True evil was punished. On Earth? From what I'd seen, not so much. Lucy Adam's dad just beat her and would probably get away with it. It did not seem like an isolated incident. I didn't like her, but I needed to find Lucy. She needed a hospital. I ran out of the shop and tripped over a big pile of fur.

A dog lay bloody and whimpering in front of the candle shop. What in the Hell was wrong with this town? Fathers beat their daughters and people hit dogs with their cars and drove away? His battered body lay half on the bricked sidewalk and half in the street. I quickly shed my invisibility and knelt down next to the poor creature. His breathing was labored. Looking up and down Main Street for an owner, a person or a car proved futile. The town was deserted. How was it that nobody was out and about at four in the afternoon?

I ran my hands through the fur that wasn't bloody. The animal's body was tense. It didn't trust me. "Dear Satan, what are you?" I couldn't tell if it was a dog or a wolf. It kind of looked like both. Even through the blood I could tell the animal had a beautiful golden coat. It had to be a dog.

The dog-wolf thing wagged its long tail and gasped from the effort. His body was still coiled tight, but he seemed to understand I wanted to help. Although there was no collar he didn't look mangy or flea bitten.

"Okay, big doggie or wolfie, I need to find you a vet. My powers are getting better, but I don't think I can fix this. Plus, I just used a buttload of magic to put a daughter-beating asshole into agony." He looked pathetic lying bloody and mangled on the ground. "You sure picked a Hell of a place to live," I told him. "Full of child abusers and animal killers."

The dog-wolf stared into my eyes for an unusually long moment and then relaxed his body. A spurt of delight shot through me at his acceptance. I wasn't sure what I said or what tone of voice made him happy, but I didn't care. So many people on Earth didn't like me—I wasn't sure if I could take animals not liking me either.

I tried to examine his wounds to figure out the extent of his injuries, but there was too much blood and one of his eyes was swollen shut. Even if I did know how to fix him, I really had temporarily depleted my magic on Lucy Adam's abomination of a father. And I didn't think this animal had the time for me to go find some evil or angry people to refuel.

"Okay buddy, I'm going to pick you up and find a vet."

He sighed and closed his one good eye. I wasn't quite sure how to interpret that but it worried me. Was he close to death? I moved in closer. Most people wouldn't go near a bloody injured dog-wolf, but most people weren't immortal Demons. Short of the thing taking my entire head off, a few bites and scratches might sting but they wouldn't kill me.

As I bent to pick him up my body locked and I was paralyzed with a vision. Oh shit no, please tell me Black Magic didn't include visions. Sloth's life was a living Hell with her visions... Knowing fighting was futile, I closed my eyes and went with it.

In a hazy stream of light Hayden appeared. My breath caught in my throat and I reached out to touch his beautiful face, but my hand went right through him.

He wore all black and his face was sad.

"Hayden? Are you here or have I truly lost it?"

"I'm here, Dixie."

"Why?" I asked. "I thought everyone was forbidden."

"It's not a social call."

I shook my head in confusion.

"The wolf, Dixie. I'm here to take the wolf."

"No," I said, realizing he was acting as the Angel of Death. "No, absolutely not. You can't seriously tell me you take animals to wherever animals go when they die."

"That's correct. I don't."

"Then leave," I yelled. "This is my wolf. He's an animal and I'm keeping him." Why was he being such an asshole? If this was his way of getting around my father's rules to see me it was stupid.

"This one is my gift to you," he said. "Because I love you I will not take the wolf."

"Good," I snapped. He began to fade away and I wanted to scream. "Will you come back? As just Hayden?" I pleaded as he faded farther and farther away.

"I will come to you soon," he promised. "My life is empty without you in it."

"Mine is too," I replied to air since he was gone. This was quickly going down as one of the suckiest days ever. I half expected a gaggle of Angels to pop up out of nowhere and try to off my ass.

The wolf wimpered.

"All right," I told him as I scanned the area for danger. "I'm going to pick you up. I'll try not to hurt you, but you look like you're hurting bad anyway." Damn if that wolf didn't look as if he knew what I was saying. Why did Hayden come for a wolf? One more piece of the puzzle I would figure out... and I would. Soon.

I thought about putting the bleeding animal in my car, but I figured carrying him would be easier on his body. Besides, Main Street wasn't that long—the vet had to be close. I pushed Hayden from my mind and focused on the wolf-dog.

"I'm going to call you Steve," I told him. "I've always wanted to name an animal Steve. It's just wrong in such a good way. You know?"

The dog moaned, either from pain or the fact I was naming him Steve.

"Oh please," I cooed, gently stroking his snout, "it could be worse. I could have said Skippy or Bubba."

I gingerly wedged my arms beneath him and tried to avoid any open wounds. Damn it if this wasn't going to ruin my favorite Sock Monkey t-shirt. I was glad the street was deserted—I would have a hard time explaining how I was able to carry a hundred pound bloody dog-wolf with ease.

I'd find a vet and get him fixed up and I'd keep him. Yep, I'd keep him. The thought made me giddy. I didn't think Carl, Janet or Myrtle would mind. If they did, screw 'em. I was keeping the dog-wolf. Steve needed me. Clearly he was a special dog-wolf if my own Angel of Death had come to get him. Forget Hayden. Save the dog.

Sweet Baby Satan, I hadn't felt so happy in a while. I looked down at my new dog-wolf and I smiled. Bloody mess or not, he was mine. I just needed him to live.

"Do you know which way the vet is?" I asked my wonderful new pet named Steve.

Steve leaned his head to the left. I froze. "Did you just point to the left?" Was I losing it from loneliness and giving an animal human traits, or was my dog simply brilliant? I searched his pain-glazed eyes as he blankly stared back. A bizarre sense of sadness enveloped me. He didn't understand me, but he'd definitely seen some bad things in his short life. I suppose I'd have to label myself lonely and losing it. Nonetheless, I was going to the left.

I wanted to move at Demon speed, but knowing it might freak out Steve I walked. Off we went, moving at a dreadfully slow human pace, looking left and right for an animal hospital.

Holding back on my instinct for speed was making me sweat, or maybe it was the hundred pound bleeding mound of fur I was carrying. Whatever—I didn't like it. You didn't sweat in Hell. Well not unless you were frying in the basement—or having sex. Damn it, forget Hayden. Save the dying dog.

Did this town even have a vet? Steve was so quiet in my arms I was beginning to panic. "Are you okay, sweetie?" I muttered, burying my chin in his fur.

He grunted softly, sighed and laid his big head on my shoulder. I wasn't sure if it was his drool or his blood running down my back. Neither boded well. I needed help. Fast.

The sun bounced off something shiny about two blocks down. The glare was blinding. I took it as an omen and moved toward it. Picking up my pace a little bit, I moved as quickly as I thought was safe for my dog.

It wasn't something shiny—it was someone shiny. It was Blanche. She had some explaining to do.

She was perched on a wooden bench of the lovely if not slightly over-manicured front lawn of Happy Hacienda Senior Citizens Home. She was deep in conversation with an old woman who was either dead or sound asleep. The old woman was slim and had obviously been a beauty in her youth. She was ethereal. Her eyes were closed and her lashes were so long they brushed her cheeks, her long tapered fingers were clasped at her chest and her feet were crossed at the ankle. The topper was they were encased in red sequined Uggs. This little old lady was rockin' some style. However, the turquoise blue housecoat knocked her down a few notches. She had a serene look on her strangely unlined face. She must have some scary good genes. I doubted she'd look so relaxed if she knew a silver-skinned, blue-eyed Demon was spilling her life story right next to her. My dear invisible friend was talking a mile a minute. Clearly she was as lonely as I was.

"Blanche," I called, catching her off guard. "What in the Hell are you doing? And where have you been? You can't keep disappearing when I need you."

"Dixie," she hissed, flinging her arms out in alarm and narrowly missing the old woman's head. "You can't just sneak up on me like that!"

"How is walking up to you in broad daylight carrying a hundred pound bleeding dog sneaking up on you?" I shot back.

"That's a dog?" She got up to examine Steve.

"Of course it's a dog. Well, I think it's a dog," I offered lamely. "Where have you been?"

"I have stuff I have to do," she snapped. She almost beat my grandpa for the top prize in avoidance of questions. She peered at the furry mess in my arms, successfully distracting me from my interrogation. "What happened to it?"

"I don't know, but I love him and I'm keeping him and his name is Steve."

"That's an awesome name."

"I know," I grinned. "Isn't it?"

"Steve looks kind of dead." Blanche circled me, checking Steve from all angles.

"He's not dead," I insisted. "Your friend on the bench looks more dead than Steve."

We both stared at the old woman on the bench for a moment. "She's too pink to be dead. Besides, if you look really close her chest is moving," Blanche whispered, checking the old lady out.

"Fine." I nodded. "She's not dead and neither is Steve. He's hurt. Can you fix him?"

"I don't know," she began.

"What do you mean you don't know?" I narrowed my eyes at

her as I gently laid my dog on the ground at my feet. "You can turn into a book and a tornado. You can disappear and reappear whenever you feel like it. Why in the Hell can't you fix my dog?"

"I don't have healing magic," she retorted angrily.

"What does that even mean? How can there be a difference in mag…"

"But you do," she cut me off.

"I do what?" Lucifer, she was exasperating. Steve was beginning to cough up blood and my heart constricted in my throat.

"You have healing magic from your mother," Blanche informed me.

"Holy Hell," I shouted. Fear for Steve and anger at Blanche was knotting me up inside. "Do you know who my mother is too?"

"No, I don't know who she is for Satan's sake, and if I did I would tell you." She glared at me. "I don't know how I know but I'm sure you can heal things."

"How do I do it?"

She paused for too long. "I have no idea," she mumbled.

"You're joking." I held my raw emotion in check. Surely I misunderstood her. She was supposed to teach me how to use my power.

Her icy blue eyes clouded over with tears. "I'm not joking."

I swallowed the firestorm of swear words I wanted to hurl at her. I knelt down on the ground by Steve and tried to heal him. I closed my eyes, hoping desperately that my healing magic would come to me. I felt no tingle, no spark. Damn it. I tried visualizing my dog whole and healthy… Nothing.

"It's not working, Blanche." I attempted to hide the feeling of dread inside but I couldn't. Why was this dog's future affecting me so much? Was he more than a dog?

"Because you need something to love you," Blanche replied to my thought.

I didn't have the energy to tell her to get out of my head. I wasn't sure if that was even a possibility.

"I'm so sorry, Steve." I gulped hard and tried to hold back my tears. No such luck. Grandpa said tears were strength and I decided to believe him. Steve was dying and despite all my hoo-doo voo-doo gifts, I was useless. I leaned over him and stroked his big head, my tears falling unchecked all over him. I rocked back and forth. The pain I felt was intense. I was still unsure why his death was hurting me like this. I'd known him for less than an hour. Maybe Blanche was right. I did need something to love me.

"No way," Blanche gasped. "How can it be so simple? Heal with pain," she muttered. "Your pain heals."

What in the Hell was she talking about? My dog was dying and she was babbling nonsense. I turned to look at her.

"No," she barked. "Keep your eyes over Steve and cry." She was fascinated. "Your tears are healing him. It's your tears, Dixie. Your tears have magic. Look."

She was right. My tears that had burned my grandpa were healing my dog. His ridiculous cryptic clues were beginning to make sense. Everywhere my tears landed on Steve, his wounds knitted themselves shut. I cautiously began to massage my teardrops all over his broken body—every open wound, bruise and cut. Adrenaline shot through me and sparks began to appear at my fingertips. I quickly clapped my hands as I didn't want to set Steve on fire. My tears had changed to ones of joy, but that didn't matter. The healing properties seemed the same. I had done it. I saved my dog. He looked up at me with gratitude and something else in his eyes. A noise and the scent of gardenias knocked me back from my magic high.

"Oh thank heavens, you found my wolf," the old woman cried joyfully. Her voice was melodic and bizarrely familiar to me. She smelled lightly of gardenias. Was she a retired old Hollywood actress I'd seen in the movies? She was certainly pretty enough. Her long lashes framed the most beautiful violet eyes I'd ever seen. Back in her day she must have been a knockout. As lovely as she was, she was sorely mistaken. Steve was not a wolf—he was a dog and he was mine. Of course Steve picked that very moment to look up at the old woman and wag his tail happily.

"Steve is yours?" I asked quietly, my heart breaking just a little bit.

Blanche stepped in to defend me, like that was going to do any good. She was invisible. "He's not a wolf, he's a dog and Dixie saved his life so he's hers," she insisted, moving to stand between the old woman and my Steve.

"Oh sweetie," the old woman gently touched Blanche's cheek. "It's a wolf and it's not a he. It's a she." She walked around Blanche and squatted next to me. "Thank you, my beautiful child for saving Lucky. My wolf means the world to me." Her violet eyes searched my face. I felt caught. I couldn't look away.

Her voice... what was it about her voice? Steve, aka Lucky, *how I missed that he was a girl I'd never know,* leaned into the old woman and lovingly licked her. She was so happy and I was so sad. It was like a bad dream. Blanche stood there in a stupor.

"You can see me?" she whispered.

"It would be pretty hard to miss you with that silver skin and those gorgeous blue eyes." The old woman laughed.

Blanche was shocked to silence. A first in my experience, but I was speechless too. She should not be able to see Blanche, and if she could see her, she should be alarmed at the very least... terrified at the most. I was quite sure this was no ordinary old lady. She had a wolf for a pet and she could see my imaginary friend. She wasn't a Demon—I could sense a Demon. She hadn't tried to kill me, so I surmised she wasn't an Angel. Plus Angels didn't age. She was something else. I just had no idea what.

"Cat got your tongue, little girl?" The old woman smiled and winked at Blanche. "Lord knows it's been working fine for the last two hours." She chuckled. "You have an extraordinary imagination."

I laughed, partially from shock and partially because of the look on Blanche's face. "What are you?" I asked, wondering if she had any clue what we were.

"Just a crazy old lady with a wolf for a pet." She smiled. My breath caught in my throat and I fought back the urge to reach out and touch her. It was similar to the feeling I got around my grandpa. I could tell Blanche had the same impulse.

The smell of cookies made me look up and I spotted a round, cheery nurse walking toward us. Grinning from ear to ear she moved closer and walked right through Blanche. Holy Hades, I'd never seen that before, but then again Blanche usually showed up when I was alone. I glanced quickly at the old woman to see if she noticed, but she seemed blissfully unaware that a four hundred pound perky gal in a nurse uniform just walked through the silver girl.

"Howdy Miss Evelyn, I see your dog came home." She smiled and shook her head.

"It's a wolf," the old woman named Evelyn patiently corrected her.

"Wolf, smulf, you need to get a collar on that damn dog. It runs off more than it's here." She put out her big beefy hand and tenderly helped Miss Evelyn to her feet. "Who's your little friend here?" she asked as she smoothed Miss Evelyn's housecoat.

"This is Dixie." Miss Evelyn smiled at me. "Dixie, this is Rhonda."

"Nice to meetcha." Rhonda extended her hand and I shook it. She was warm and soft and smelled like vanilla and sugar.

"Nice to meet you too," I replied, watching Lucky get to her feet and press her body to Miss Evelyn. "Well, I'd better go," I said, halfway hoping Miss Evelyn would ask me to stay. I went to shake her hand, but she pulled me into an embrace and hugged me hard. I stiffened. I wasn't used to affection from women. My sisters all loved me, but no woman ever held me. I felt dizzy and a little lightheaded.

Tentatively I wrapped my arms around her and let my head lay on her shoulder. It felt so right. I didn't want to let go.

"Come back and see me sometime, Dixie," she whispered. "And bring Blanche."

She disengaged herself, took Rhonda's big hand in her slender one and walked back into the senior home. Lucky followed close on her heels. The sense of loss I felt was acute. What in the Hell just happened here? I shook my head and ran my hand through my hair. This was going to go down as the weirdest day ever.

"Do you think she's psychic?" I asked Blanche.

"Possibly, or maybe she's just crazy. Really nice, but crazy," she replied. We stood in silence and mulled the options.

"Should we tell anybody about her?" I wondered aloud.

Blanche thought for a moment. "No, I don't think that's a good idea."

"Why?"

Blanche worried her bottom lip with her teeth. "I have no clue, it's just a feeling." She paused and then took my hand. "Dixie, I'm sorry I haven't been around."

I leaned in and kissed her cheek. I could never stay mad at her. "Come on," I said wearily. "It's time to go home and get my ass kicked."

"Haven't you had it kicked enough today?" she asked.

"Metaphorically? Yes. Literally? No." I grinned and squeezed her hand as I guided us toward my car.

"Why don't you just transport us?" she asked.

"One, because my car is parked down the street and two, because we'll end up in a bathroom somewhere."

Blanche giggled and I rolled my eyes.

Life on Earth kind of sucked. I still had over two weeks before I could communicate with anyone from Hell and I wasn't sure I could make it. I wondered if Hayden would have to wait the two weeks to come to me. The thought was depressing and I pushed it to the back of my mind. I would deal with it, but then again it didn't look like I had much of a choice.

CHAPTER TWENTY-TWO

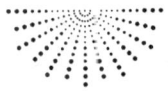

WHEN WE GOT HOME FROM THE STRANGEST AFTERNOON EVER, Blanche nearly laughed herself silly watching Carl hand me my butt during fight practice. I wanted to slap her, but I was too busy defending myself from a two hundred and fifty pound hairy man in gauchos and a rainbow tie-dyed muscle shirt. Carl's fashion choices were appalling yet riveting.

Anyway, I knew I was improving. Hand to hand combat wasn't my strong point, but Carl was determined to change that. Even though it hurt like Hell I loved him for pushing me. Carl was unaware of our invisible audience, so my giggling at the insults Blanche was hurling mystified him. I suppose he thought I'd either lost my mind or I was starting to enjoy the pain.

Blanche stayed with me through the night. We slept like two little babies curled into balls together. I felt safe, happy and warm. I was so grateful she had shared my experience with Steve and Miss Evelyn. I needed someone to verify I wasn't insane. I realized I hadn't told her about Hayden, but when I woke she was gone. Sadly I expected that and idly wondered when I'd see her again.

I yanked on my favorite jeans, a comfy old sweatshirt that said *Hell's Not For Pussies*, some purple Uggs and made my way downstairs for breakfast. I was hoping Janet would make pancakes—she was a killer cook. I paused mid-stair. Something was off... There was a powerful Demonic presence in the house. I was unsure if it was evil or civil. I cloaked myself in invisibility, took a deep breath and continued to the kitchen.

Carl, Janet and Myrtle were prostrate on the floor, foreheads touching the ground and hands placed facedown next to their heads. Janet was trembling, Carl's body was so tense I could see the veins bulging in his neck and Myrtle looked like a coil about to spring. WTF?

The Demon's back was to me. He wore a long black cloak with a hood, total bad B movie get-up. The scene was bizarre and somewhat ominous, but his scent was familiar. I floated around him to see who was making my little family bow to him in servitude. As far as I knew my dad was the only one to receive that honor.

All my fear evaporated and a shriek of happiness escaped me as I shed my invisibility and scared the Hell out of Cole. My father's second in command had come to see me. He shouted a curse and fell backwards into the kitchen table.

"Oh, I am so sorry," I gasped and immediately tried to help him to his feet.

He pushed my hand away and quickly stood in an attempt to maintain his dignity and authority.

"Your Highness." He gave a curt bow and pretended he hadn't just been sprawled on his ass in my kitchen. I bit back my giggles and curtsied.

"Cole," I mumbled, biting hard on the inside of my cheek as his wipeout replayed in my head.

I moved in with Demon speed to hug him and turn him away from the trio on the floor. Their bodies were trembling. Not from fear... from laughter. I was a Demon Princess, daughter of Satan. There was nothing he could do to me, but my little family?... I wasn't so sure. Demons with power could be dangerous and testy. Cole, my father's right hand man, had a lot of power.

He seemed taken aback at my show of affection and carefully disengaged himself. I suppose it was a bit out of character for me to hug him. I'd never done anything of the sort before, but it was the first diversionary tactic that came to mind.

"So I see you have learned to cloak yourself in invisibility." He nodded, stating the obvious. "What other powers have emerged?"

"Well, I can transport, but no matter where I'm trying to go I always end up in the bathroom." I grinned. He didn't. "What are you doing here?"

He adjusted his cloak and looked disdainfully at the Demons on the floor before him. "I was making rounds on Earth and came by to check on your wellbeing, Your Highness." He spoke with rigid formality.

"Cole, it's me, Dixie. What's with all the Your Highness stuff?"

"Of course." He smiled. "Dixie. How are you?"

"Okay, I guess." I paused and looked down at my hands. "Are there any messages for me?"

"No, I'm sorry. None." His tone was gentle. I wondered if my dad had decreed no messages. Satan was such a wad. Cole continued, "I want you to know there are many on this plane that would wish you ill."

"I already got that message loud and clear." I sighed, feeling lonelier than ever.

Cole became alarmed, his voice clipped. "Has anything unusual happened?"

"Um... no." His manner made me uncomfortable. Did he know something I should know? "Well... "

"Yes?" He waited.

I mulled over what I was going to say in my head for a moment. What in the Hell wasn't unusual about my life right now? I was about to tell him about Miss Evelyn, but then I'd have to explain Blanche and her silver skin, the book, the tornado, my black magic, drinking blood from Grandpa and how my tears healed a wolf that I thought was going to be my new dog named Steve. Although what really made my mouth stay shut is that I knew anything I said would get back to my dad. I was pissed at my dad. If he wouldn't let me have access to my old life, he couldn't have access to my new life.

"The girls at college don't like me." I figured I had to say something. Vapid and clueless felt right, so I went with it.

"Oh," he laughed, clearly relieved not to have to deal with anything serious. I could tell he also thought I was a spoiled rotten brat. I'd never noticed his attitude in Hell, but I was never around him very much. "You're a beautiful woman. I'm sure they're jealous."

There was an awkward pause. He stared at the ceiling while I stared at him. He was a very handsome Demon, but he paled in comparison to my father. Then again, who didn't?

"How's my dad?" I asked quietly.

"Very well," he replied. "Does this house have a security system? Is it warded with magic?" he inquired.

"Yeth, my Lord," Carl muttered from his floor-licking position.

"Good," Cole said, barely acknowledging Carl.

"Is Dad still dating Sandra?" I was desperate for any gossip from Hell. I remembered Cole keeping an eye on her as she tried to claim her territory at the Dark Palace. I was hoping to have a laugh about the silicone piece of trash that my father was involved with. Cole wasn't a real talkative Demon but I was hoping for something.

"Amanda—her name is Amanda," he corrected me. "And yes, he is. We are very fortunate that Lucifer has chosen a consort as accomplished and as powerful as Amanda. It is a miracle that she carries his son. You should treat her and speak of her with the respect she is due."

That was the longest group of words I'd ever heard Cole string together in my entire life. You'd think he had the hots for

Amanda. Hell, he probably did. Demons were like that. Whatever my dad had everyone else wanted. Each time my father ended an affair the line of potential suitors for Satan's ex-gal-pal was miles long. Literally.

"Um... sure," I shrugged. I didn't like her and I never would, but being polite probably wouldn't kill me. I didn't believe she would have a boy. If she did, I'd like to see some DNA test results.

"I must take my leave now." His tone was clipped and formal again. Was it because I made fun of the surgically enhanced consort? I knew Cole took his job seriously, but come on. "Remember, there are many who want you dead. Stay alert."

"For what, exactly?" Could anyone from Hell be specific or was I just going to keep getting these generalized death threats?

"You'll know when you see it." He wrapped his flowing black cloak tightly around his body. I wondered if Dad had any idea how cheesy his minions were looking in their bad *Demon attire*. He began to turn to mist.

"Wait," I yelled.

He paused, half of his body had already disappeared into a mist, but the top half was still corporeal. Damn, he was a powerful Demon.

"Will you tell my dad I love him?" I felt dumb sending a message through Mr. Life of the Party, but my need was great.

"Of course, Your Highness." He smiled and disappeared.

The silence in my kitchen was long.

"Ith he gone?" Carl whispered.

"Yep," I helped them up. "Why were you guys on the floor?"

"Becauth heth an athhole," Carl muttered as he brushed the dust from the floor off of Janet's dress.

"He forced us," Myrtle said through clenched teeth. She pulled out a frying pan and slammed it down on the stove. Oh shit, was she going to cook? Last time she cooked the smoke alarm went off, the indoor sprinkler system came on and the Eden Volunteer Fire Department showed up.

Janet's head was bowed and she was staring at the floor.

"Janet, are you okay?" I asked, trying unsuccessfully to take the frying pan from Myrtle.

"No, she's not." Myrtle's pretty features hardened in anger. "Look at her."

I approached Janet and gently lifted her chin. Her eye was swelling shut and there was a deep ugly laceration on her cheekbone. My stomach clenched and Janet refused to meet my eyes.

"What happened to you?" I had a difficult time reining in the fury that was about to set my fingertips on fire. My hair began to float around my head.

"Nothing," she whispered and turned her head away from me.

"What happened to her?" I turned on Carl and Myrtle. It was a huge effort to hang onto my fragile control.

"He slapped her," Myrtle hissed. "With a Hell Fire ring on his hand." She began to crack eggs into the pan a mile a minute. I winced at all the shells she was adding to her egg concoction, then refocused on Janet.

"Why did he hit you?" I squatted down so we were face to face. Her eye looked hideous. I knew it would heal, but it must hurt tremendously. The ring Cole wore carried poison inside it. While it couldn't kill a Demon it was said to be excruciatingly painful. It was fatal if used on a mortal. Worse than the pain was the humiliation of being struck. A Hell Fire ring was a large piece of powerful jewelry, only worn by a few. I hadn't realized Cole had earned one. Janet shuddered and big tears rolled down her delicate cheeks.

I contemplated trying to heal her with my own tears, but they had burnt Grandpa. I was worried I would burn her. I realized my healing powers might only work on animals or possibly mortals. I didn't want to risk causing Janet any more pain. I knew she would heal on her own even if it would take a while. The poison was evil.

Carl wrapped his arms around Janet and rocked her back and

184

forth. "Janet told him we bow to no one but Thatan," Carl said. He handled his mate with exquisite tenderness, but his voice was laced with hatred.

"But that's true," I said. "Why did he make you bow to him?"

"A few of your Dad's flunkies are like that when Satan's not around to control them," Myrtle spat as she shook a ton of salt, pepper and Tabasco into her eggs and shells. I thought she was a vegetarian.

"This happens often?" My stomach roiled and my fingers began to dance with sparks.

"Yes Dixie, this happens often." Myrtle's voice was flat and lifeless. "We're Demons, it's the nature of the beast. The strong prey on the weak. Period."

"That's bullshit," I shouted. My fingertip fireworks show set the tablecloth on fire. "Damn it." I quickly clapped my hands, grabbed the salt from Myrtle and dumped it all over the flames. I certainly didn't want to be the reason for another fire department visit. That was Myrtle's newest hobby.

I paced the kitchen like a caged animal. How dare he abuse his power like that. It was one thing to punish evil. It was another altogether to beat up on someone weaker.

"I'm finding a portal and going to Hell. I'm going to ask my father to have that son-of-a-bitch destroyed. No one hurts my family," I hissed. That's what they had become, my family—and I loved them.

"NO," Carl roared and stopped me dead in my tracks.

"What do you mean, no?" I challenged, turning my ire on him. The room crackled with tension and aggression.

"You will do no thuch thing," he insisted, not backing down. "You are a Princeth, your life has been theltered. You have no idea what life ith like for uth." He shook his head sadly. "If you go to your father about thith, it will be a death thententh for uth."

"He's right," Janet agreed. "When we are done on Earth and go back to Hell, Cole will kill us."

185

"But I'll have him thrown in the Basement. He attacked my guardians. Royal Guardians. That's a capital offense." I frowned in exasperation. I wasn't getting through to them.

Myrtle's expression was tight with strain. "Dixie, you are twenty-one years old. I am two hundred and three. Janet is three hundred and sixty-one and Carl is one hundred and forty."

"I'm a cougar," Janet piped in as she giggled through her tears. Carl kissed the top of her head and grinned.

Myrtle rolled her eyes and tried to suppress her laugh without success. She regathered herself and continued. "My point is that we've been around for much longer than you have. We know what it takes to survive in Hell. Why do you think Carl and Janet and I gravitate together?" She waited. I was silent. "We protect and care for each other." She lifted her head and her eyes bored into mine. "If you're comfortable condemning us to death, then go. Have at it. Go to Hell and try to impart justice, but someday you'll learn. There is no justice—no balance."

I dropped into a kitchen chair. All the energy drained from my body. I was growing up fast and right now I hated it.

"I'm so sorry," I told them as I stared at the burn marks on the tablecloth. I was too ashamed to look at them.

"You've done nothing wrong Dixie." Janet gently rubbed my back.

"I want you to know that I love all of you." I glanced up at their familiar perfectly imperfect faces. "And I want you to know that if anyone tries to hurt you again, Cole or whomever, I will kill them." I knew for the first time in my life I meant it. They knew too.

Another piece of the puzzle clicked. Cole. Cole had randomly come up in my conversation with Grandpa. Cole was up to no good. Way to go, Gramps. Either I was getting smarter or I'd gone insane. I was leaning toward insane. It would take going nuts at the very least to be able to decipher Grandpa's ramblings. Whatever. I was going with it. I would keep an eye out for Cole.

The silence was loud and long. Janet broke it.

"Thank you, Dixie. You are a good girl." She leaned forward and kissed my cheek.

"Well." Carl found his voice after my violent proclamation. "In that cathe we better get back to training."

"I have to go to class," I said. "I'll meet you after."

"No," Janet said, trying to rescue the egg travesty Myrtle had created. "The community college is closed for three days."

"Why?" I was surprised. Was there some human holiday I didn't know about?

"Apparently," Myrtle crowed as she grinned from ear to ear. "Fifteen hot pink, lime green and neon yellow skunks got locked in the school last night. They have to fumigate."

"And how did that happen?" I asked her, already knowing full well how it happened.

"I have no clue," she answered.

She was so delighted with herself I didn't have the heart to tell her how wrong that was. So I didn't. I laughed. I laughed hard.

CHAPTER TWENTY-THREE

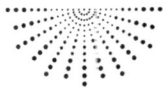

"WHAT THE HELL IS THAT?" MYRTLE ASKED AS WE GAPED AT A HUGE manor exploding with foliage.

"I don't know, but this is the right address," I muttered.

"I think the GPS is smoking crack. No way your cousin lives in that," she continued.

"I have a bad feeling this is exactly where my cousin lives."

Three days off from classes meant I could finally visit my cousin Astrid. Carl, Janet and Myrtle joined me as they'd met her and loved her when she'd visited Hell six months ago. I'd had a horrific dream that Mother Nature met us there. Turns out it wasn't a dream at all...

We cautiously approached and pushed open a huge door covered in ivy and purple parrots.

"I can't find my ass with both hands," Ethan, my cousin's Vampyre mate, bellowed from somewhere deep in the mansion.

"Well, too bad," Astrid screeched. "I haven't seen my hooha in months because my stomach is the enormous house for our four-headed son that is going to live inside me for the next ten years."

"Help me, Jesus," I heard him mutter from somewhere in the jungle that I was sure used to be a gorgeous compound.

"Maybe we should come back another time," Myrtle whispered frantically as she tried to untangle herself from a vine with teeth.

"Who invited your grandmother?" Ethan shouted. "This is a fucking mess."

"I can hear you, Vampyre, and I don't like your tone," Mother Nature's voice boomed so loudly I winced. Maybe we *should* come back later…

"Mother humpin' shithats," my cousin hissed. "I think a flower just grabbed my boob."

I had no clue where we were. The mansion looked like a multi-level jungle complete with monkeys and waterfalls. I could hear Ethan, Astrid and my grandma, but had no real indication as to their whereabouts.

"I really *really* want to leave," Myrtle grumbled as she choked and beheaded the vine that was trying to eat her.

"Me too," Janet whispered.

"Okay. Carl, take the girls to the car. I'm going to find Astrid, say hi and get the Hell out of Dodge." I pushed them toward what used to be the front door.

"Be careful, Dixie," he said as he ushered my little faux family out.

"Will do."

Using my nose I headed toward my cousin, carefully avoiding the quicksand and random bottomless cliffs. Mother Nature had done a doozy on Astrid's abode. I couldn't remember her doing anything this drastic to my dad… ever.

"God damn it," Astrid yelled. "Dixie, do I smell you? Are you here in this leafy shitstorm?"

"Um… yep," I called out. "Not sure how to find you."

"I'll just magic your ass to me. Stay still. It might hurt."

"Awesome," I mumbled as I wrapped my arms around myself and prayed to Satan I wouldn't lose a body part.

"Astrid, don't worry about it," Grandma Gigi shouted. "I have her. We'll come to you."

She did have me and I wasn't sure if it was any safer than having my cousin *magic* me. Violently I was yanked inside a glittery teal tornado funnel and ended up plastered against a cackling insane woman.

"Are we going to die?" I asked my grandma.

"Not today," she screamed over the whistling and shrieking weather pattern we were trapped in.

"Is this your normal mode of travel?"

"Only on Tuesdays," she replied at earsplitting decibels.

"Holy shit, Gigi," Astrid spat as we landed in a clump at her feet. "You'd better have a good explanation for this because I am feeling violent and fat. I don't care how we're related, I'm two seconds away from offing your unstable pole dancing ass."

"I just love how disrespectful you are," Gigi said as she embraced my pregnant cousin in her arms. "It's lovely to be with my two favorite granddaughters."

"Lovely's not the word I'd use at the moment," Astrid griped. I was in shock that she threatened to whack Mother Nature and was still alive. Well, as alive as a dead person could be.

"Excuse me," Ethan ground out through clenched teeth and he uprooted a massive tree to enter the room. He was gorgeous normally, but he was positively breathtaking when furious. "If we're done with the niceties, I'd like you to fix my fucking home and leave."

"Is he always this testy?" Grandma asked.

"Only when monkeys are crawling up his ass," Astrid explained.

"How are we supposed to stay here in this forest?" he demanded.

"Clusterfuck," I muttered.

"What?"

"It's more of a clusterfuck than a forest," I offered.

"I'd call it a clusterfuck of epic proportions, and I am so proud of you, Dixie!" Astrid gave me a thumbs up over her big tummy.

"For what?" I asked.

"For dropping the f-bomb. It agrees with you. Lowers your ridiculously high IQ just a bit and shows the world you're a goddamned Demon."

"Um, thanks. I think."

"You really shouldn't take your uncle's name in vain," Mother Nature tsked.

"And you shouldn't turn my home into a safari adventure," Astrid shot back.

"I didn't mean to," she said as she dropped her head into her delicate hands.

Wait. What? Mother Nature made a mistake? This did not bode well.

"This was an accident?" Ethan roared. "You destroyed my home by accident?"

"Yes," she whispered.

"Fix it," he said in a quiet voice that made the hair on my neck stand up.

"I can try, but the magic in this area is off balance and it's affecting my mojo," she pouted.

"What the Hell are you talking about?" Astrid's eyes narrowed at our grandma as Ethan's ire bounced around the room knocking monkeys from their perches in the flowering trees that protruded from the walls.

"I mean," she whined defensively as she removed a monkey from her head. "That something bad is happening and it put a woowoo wrench in my juju."

"Holy shit," I said and laughed. "That sounds disgusting and painful... and wrong."

"Well, it's about time," Mother Nature crowed.

"I'm sorry. What?"

"It's about time you started growing some balls, young lady. How in the world will you save the day if your testicles haven't dropped yet? Showing disrespect to your elders is a good start.

Ask your cousin," Gigi said.

I truly hoped she was using balls as a metaphor. I discreetly glanced down and sighed in relief. I was sack-less.

"I'm not disrespectful, you crazy old cow," Astrid snapped.

Mother Nature produced a dictionary out of thin air and tossed it to Astrid. "Look it up. You're listed under *Big Balls* and *Vampyre-Demon With a Death Wish.*"

"Nope. I'm listed in the *Guinness Book of World Records* as the only freak in history to have an eight-headed Vampyre-Demon baby after five years of gestation."

Grandma Gigi threw her head back and laughed. The monkeys clapped their hands and danced wildly around her. "Your child will come soon," she said.

"What?" Ethan asked, visibly alarmed. "How soon?"

"Very soon, and I have a lot to tell you people. First of all… "

"No!" an unfamiliar German accented voice bellowed. "You will stop right now unless you want to change the tides of destiny and turn your family to dust. If you persist you will pay," the voice growled ominously.

What the Hell? My fingers tingled and my magic came up fast and violent, making me dizzy. My family was certifiable, but no German douchebag was going to destroy them. They were capable of doing that themselves with no outside help. I turned in the direction of the enemy and let my power rip. A fiery explosion flew from my fingertips and then the screaming started…

"Dixie, no!" Astrid yelled. "It's The Kev and Gemma. Do not under any circumstance kill my friends."

Her friends? Shit. Did I just kill her friends?

"Amazing! This, the cousin of you has the power that is from one with the big balls!" The Kev, who looked alarmingly like Arnold Schwarzenegger, said. "Good aim and the trigger of the finger is impressive."

"Um, not sure I followed that, but are you okay? If I'd known you were Astrid's friends I wouldn't have tried to kill you," I mumbled apologetically. And why was everyone so concerned with my balls? Discreetly I checked again.

"Of course you wouldn't have," a crazily beautiful woman, who I assumed was Gemma, said kindly as she patted out the fire still dancing up her dress. "That was a Hell of a wallop of magic, dude." She grinned at me as she made her way to my cousin. She carried black raspberry chip ice cream along with chips and salsa. Sweet baby Satan… was she unaware that Astrid couldn't eat that?

I was powerful, but my cousin was slightly unhinged at the moment. I glanced frantically around the room and looked for cover. Astrid was nutty under normal circumstances, but flashing food in her face was sure to be ugly. She was pregnant, for Uncle God's sake. As I headed for a clump of bushes, I stopped dead in my tracks. The Kev was wearing a tutu, sparkly tights and a jog bra. Not to mention his scent was a mystery to me. The scent I would figure out, but his outfit… I wasn't so sure. Was he gay? I kind of thought he and Gemma were an item, but who would date a man in a woman's ballet costume?

"And may I ask why you have chosen the Teminator as your cover again?" Mother Nature asked grumpily. "Also, as much as I loathe saying it… thank you."

"You have the welcome from me," he replied to my grandma. He gave me a wink and I couldn't help but giggle.

"What are you?" I asked.

"I'm a Fairy."

"Oh, well that explains a lot," I said and then slapped my hand over my mouth. "I mean, I have no problem with homosexuality—at all. I think everyone's sexual preference is their own business and I'm impressed that you are so comfortable with your um… you know, and your outfit is very sparkly and fun," I stammered and wanted to die. The laughter in the room was mortifying. The Kev laughed the loudest.

"No, no, my little krumecaca. I am a Fairy, as in the magical being. I too have no problem with the homosexuality, but I can assure you that I am not gay."

"Amen to that," Gemma chimed in as she sat next to my cousin and scarfed down the ice cream.

"Sorry about that," I whispered, wondering if I could make a polite exit. I'd already put my foot down my throat. At the rate I was going I didn't want to find out if I could pull it out of my ass.

"She is so young," The Kev said as he took my hand. His touch was gentle, but I sensed he could be very dangerous if he didn't like you.

"I know," Mother Nature snapped. "And if that asswhacking floozy hadn't fallen down on her job… "

"Enough," The Kev ground out. Before my eyes he morphed into a man so beautiful I had to turn away. "How much damage can you do in a day?" he hissed, referring to the jungle.

"I'm leaving," she snapped. "While I enjoy disrespect, there's only so much one can take in a half hour."

In a blinding blast of glitter and sparks, Mother Nature made her exit.

"Son of a bitch." Ethan groaned as he slapped some overzealous monkeys out of the way. "She destroys my home, tells us the baby is coming soon, almost turns us to dust and just leaves?"

"Looks like it," Astrid said as she bit into her friend's wrist. She made little happy slurping sounds as she drank. Hades, my family was screwed up. I was also highly aware that Grandma was referring to my mother. At this point I was fairly sure I wanted nothing to do with my mother. She seemed like more trouble than all my relatives put together. Awesome.

"You have Black Magic," The Kev said as he examined my hands. I tried to glance up, but had to squint due to his redonkulous beauty.

"Turn off the Fairy glamour, babe," Gemma told The Kev. "No one except me can actually look at you and not singe their corneas."

"Whoops." He laughed and morphed back into *Kindergarten Cop*... accent and all.

"Um, does the morph affect your brain?" I asked as I realized I was losing my polite filter in a big way.

"Not at all, my strudel pookie. Why have you to ask the silliness of the question?"

"Because you talk like a dumbass when you're in the Arnold's body," Astrid volunteered as Ethan winced.

"I do that because it makes the fun for me and drives you to the crazy," he told my cousin as he grinned from ear to ear.

"Right now you can do whatever you want. I'm drinking black raspberry chip flavored blood," Astrid announced happily as she went back to Gemma's wrist.

"Wait. What?" Gemma could flavor her blood? I wondered if Grandpa could do that next time I had to suck on his neck.

"Yep." Gemma grinned and held up the pint of ice cream. "Whatever I eat, I apparently taste like. Do not share that info with any Vamps. I only have so much blood to go around."

"Got it," I said. "Do you think that would work with Demons?"

"You want to have the drink of my mate's blood?" The Kev asked, surprised.

"No," I quickly replied. "I, um... " *Shit on a flaming stick.* How did I get out of this one?

"You drank from Grandpa," Astrid said as she watched me closely. "And it tasted like ass to you."

The jig was up and I was actually kind of relieved. I knew Astrid had Black Magic... maybe she could help me with mine. "Well, I wouldn't exactly say ass—more like burnt butt."

"Can you control this magic?" The Kev asked, ignoring the buttocks discussion.

Where the Hell did his accent go?

"Um... "

"Of course she can't. No one in our fucked up family gives

anyone directions, much less a straight answer," Astrid snapped. "I'll help her."

"No, you won't," Ethan said. "We're leaving, which is what I think your whackjob of a grandmother intended when she destroyed our home."

"He's right," Gemma agreed. "The magic in the area is screwed with a capital S and you're about to blow a seven-headed baby out of your hooha. You have to leave for a while."

"I'm not going anywhere," Astrid informed the room as Ethan banged his head against a tree. "And my baby will only have five heads. My cousin is in trouble, and quite honestly left to her own devices she could blow up the continental United States. I'm staying."

"Ethan is correct, my leibchen. You will be leaving. I will be staying and training Dixie. Her magic cannot hurt Gemma or myself," The Kev said.

"Are you a True Immortal?" I asked. Was Grandpa wrong about who my magic affected?

"No, but trust me on this. The ways of the Fairy are a mystery to most other races. I will teach you."

"I call bullshit," Astrid snapped. "Not that you're not a Hell of a teacher with a fist like a Mack truck, but Dixie is mine. I will take care of her."

"No, Astrid," I said, surprising myself and the rest of the room —mostly my cousin. "You're leaving. I belong to no one but me and I would never forgive myself if something happened to you or the baby. I have something to do here. Something I have to do myself and I swear on Hades I will do my best not to blow up the United States, but just in case I think you should go to Europe. The Kev, I accept your offer. I have three Demons with me—Carl, Janet and Myrtle,—and they have been training me."

"Sweet baby Jesus in a thong," Astrid shouted. "Carl, Janet and Myrtle? We're all gonna die."

"Nope, not today," The Kev said. "I know of Carl, Janet and

Myrtle… they are far more than they seem. And I admire Carl's dress sense."

Of course he did.

Several other very attractive Vampyres quietly made their way into the room and bowed to Ethan. Astrid, clearly unused to not getting her way, stomped around the room and tried to find something to break.

"My Liege," a gorgeous dark haired Vampyre said. "We are armed, ready to go."

"We'll be with you momentarily, Heathcliff," Ethan replied.

"Fine," Astrid said wearily. "Dixie, you will call me if you need me. Gigi said the twelve-headed baby boy will be here soon and I have decided to believe her even though she's an unstable, foul-mouthed fucking walking disaster area." Astrid punctuated her description with a resounding crash as she blew out all the windows in the room with a flick of her fingers.

"Pot. Kettle. Black, dude," Gemma said as Astrid giggled and Ethan banged his head on a tree again.

"Now," Ethan growled.

"I'm coming," Astrid said as she took me into a tight hug. "You will be careful and kill anything that looks at you sideways. Do you understand me?"

"Yep."

"You'll kill it? Not just maim it or hurt it a little?"

"I will kill it," I said firmly.

She narrowed her eyes and gave me one last hug before Ethan attempted to pull her from the room. I idly stroked a monkey that had wrapped itself around my waist and gave my cousin a little shove.

"Go. I promise if I need anything I will call."

"Okay, but you will be taking the babies." She reached into her pocket. "Here."

In her palm Beyonce, Abe, Rachel and Ross danced around and

beat the tar out of each other. She was offering me her tiny yet very destructive baby Demons.

"Are you sure?" I asked as I tried not to bounce with excitement. I loved the baby Demons. They were a little difficult to control, but they were as protective as the Hell Hounds.

"I'm sure. Just don't let them go to strip clubs and keep them away from really evil Demons unless you want them to eat them. If that happens, don't watch. Trust me on that. Oh, and I heard you did the nasty with the Angel of Death."

"What the Hell?" I shouted. How did everyone know all the details of my sex life?

"Just use condoms when you nail him or you too could have a ten-headed baby," she warned with a shit-eating grin on her face.

"Dixie and the Angel of Death cannot reproduce unless they bond," The Kev informed the room. It seemed he only used his accent when he felt like it.

"You sure about that?" Astrid asked. "I mean, no one in their right fucking mind would have called my pregnancy."

"Quite sure." The Kev nodded with certainty. "That's the way it goes with two Tru... "

He stopped abruptly and blanched.

"Did you almost just reduce us all to dust?" Gemma shouted. Her skin began to glow and sharp talons burst from her fingertips.

The Kev stood silently and nodded. What the Hell did Gemma turn into? From her claws alone it looked frightening.

"Does anyone know if this turning to dust shit is actually true?" Astrid demanded.

"No," The Kev admitted. "But I refuse to test the theory."

The Kev had almost dropped a huge piece of the puzzle in my lap. I was grateful he hadn't let the entire sentence slip. Turning to dust wasn't on my agenda today. However, I was pretty sure I knew exactly what the rest of his sentence was and I didn't know if that made me happy or freaked out.

"Astrid, are you done?" Ethan asked through clenched teeth.

"Will you have mercy sex with the miserable pregnant lady when we get to wherever we're going?"

"Yes. Yes, I will."

"Then I'm done."

They left.

"All right, my little snickerdoodle. Gemma and I are going to scout to see if we can find anything out about the magical imbalance. You will take the tiny ones and go to Carl, Myrtle and Janet. We will see you in a couple of days."

Gemma *not so discreetly* shoved a box of condoms into my hand and winked. "Better safe than sorry." She giggled and they disappeared.

I stared at the little Demons in my hands.

"If Mommy say no bad booby titty woowoo bars, will you take us to car dealership?" Abe asked sweetly.

"Are you going to eat the car salesmen?"

"Of course we eat the sellers of cars. They tasty," Beyonce yelled.

"Then um, no. However I have a bad feeling you are going to find a lot to eat in the very near future." I knew evil was coming quickly and soon.

"Yayayayayayayay!" Ross and Rachel squealed. "You so fun, Dixie."

"Thank you. I think. You guys ready to go?"

"We be borned ready," Abe informed me.

"That's what scares me," I mumbled as they laughed like little hyenas. I hoped to Hades it wasn't a mistake to take them, but what was done was done.

CHAPTER TWENTY-FOUR

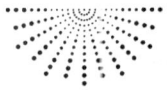

Why did it surprise me that the commissary lunches on Earth were more heinous than the commissary lunches in Hell? While I could occasionally identify the lumps on my plate in Hell, I had no idea what graced my tray today.

Thankfully despite the crowd in the student center I found an empty table. I knew if I sat there it would stay empty. How in the Hell did I become such a pariah? I was starting to get a complex.

Everyone was buzzing about Skunkgate. The aroma of skunk still lingered. Mixed with the culinary delights served by the lunch ladies it was positively nauseating. Watching Myrtle feign outrage at the Skunkgate perpetrators during World Religions made my boring day more tolerable. I glanced down at the mystery meat on my tray and my gag reflex kicked in. Tomorrow I was skipping lunch.

The Ugg brigade stood at the head of the cafeteria holding court and scoping for a table. Lucy Adams, clearly the leader, was barking orders and deciding futures. I glanced up as they made their way across the room. Crap, it looked like they were headed for my table. That was impossible. They had made it abundantly clear I wasn't on their radar which was fine with me.

Wait. She looked the same as she always did. How in the Hell did she look normal after getting beaten four days ago? From where I sat she looked flawless. Surely makeup couldn't cover a beating like that.

I put my head down and waited for them to pass. I was afraid if Lucy said one snarky thing to me I'd zap her bald. She rubbed me wrong and her minions were brainless. I didn't know how Myrtle hung out with them.

I was positive they passed by… they didn't.

"Hello Dixie," Lucy said as she sat down across from me. Her four clones hovered behind her and waited for a command. Where was Myrtle?

"What do you want?" I eyed her warily. I didn't have the time or the energy for her right now.

She nodded to the others and they sat down, two on either side of her and two on either side of me. They had effectively boxed me in. Great.

"I think we may have misjudged you, Dixie," she informed me haughtily.

"Really?" I laughed, pissing her off. Her lips pursed in irritation and she crossed her arms over her chest. What in the Hell did she think my reaction would be? Did she assume I'd bow down and kiss her ass? She was gravely mistaken. "I'm fairly sure I didn't misjudge you, Lucy."

There was a flash of anger, then fear and insecurity in her eyes. She quickly covered it, but it was there. It jerked me right back to the storeroom and the vision of her broken body on the floor while her father beat her. I still didn't understand how she healed so quickly, but my anger began to melt. Shit, why couldn't I be a bitchy unforgiving Demon like my sisters?

I watched her carefully while she considered her next move. Her posse sat silently, unable to function without permission.

"I'm sorry for being a bitch to you," she said quietly. Her minions gasped.

I wasn't sure I believed her, but this was certainly making my day more interesting. I said nothing. I simply stared.

Lucy began to fidget and tried to hold my gaze, but I was Satan's daughter and staring people down came quite naturally. She caved and averted her eyes. Her gal pals watched in fascination. They'd clearly never seen their idol at a loss for words.

In her discomfort, she took a bite from her tray. Her minions squealed in disgust. The look on Lucy's face was awesome—sheer terror and disgust. She gagged and searched desperately for a napkin. Her butt-kiss brigade had no clue what to do. Two of them started crying and one started dry heaving, threatening the table with something far worse than lunch. I rolled my eyes at their ineptness and handed her my napkin. I wouldn't wish that dog chow-looking pile on my worst enemy. She quickly spit and then downed an entire bottle of water.

"You okay?" I grinned.

"No." The beginnings of a smile pulled at the corners of her mouth. "Thanks for the napkin." She eyed her worthless buddies with disdain. "I could have died," she hissed.

I bit down on my lip hard and tried not to laugh. I failed.

"You think it's funny?" she demanded as she smiled at me.

"Yes I do," I said as I tried to figure her out.

"Well," she paused for dramatic effect, tossing her blonde locks over her shoulder. "I do too, and I'm pretty sure that stuff is Alpo."

"I was thinking gravy covered dry cat food."

"No," Lucy said definitively. "It was Alpo and you saved my life."

"I'd hardly call handing you a napkin saving your life."

"You saved my life," she stated firmly, her blue eyes glued to mine.

"Oookay." Why did it sound like she was talking about something else? I was getting paranoid. She couldn't know anything. "You're welcome." I gave her a tight smile. What was her game and why was I playing it? Bizarrely enough, she fascinated me. Anyone who could get beaten nearly to death on Monday and be back at school looking amazing and sporting an attitude on Friday had to have something worthwhile going on. Or maybe I was just a sucker for the underdog.

"You like to save things, don't you?" Lucy said as she watched me closely for a reaction.

I put on my poker face and freaked out inside. Why in the Hell did she say that? There was no way she knew anything about my part in defending her. She had no way of knowing I was in the storeroom with her. Even if she thought I was there, she wouldn't be able to comprehend what I did to her father. She was human, I could smell it. Humans didn't know about Demons and magic. How had the tables turned? Now I was uneasy so I stayed quiet.

There was a large, long, uncomfortable pause.

"Look Dixie," she said, thankfully leaving her former line of questioning alone. "I was mean and uh… you didn't deserve it. No one has given you a chance here, so… I, I mean we," she said as she referred to the idiots who were nodding like bobbleheads. "We would like to start over."

Confusion and wariness warred within me as I searched their expressions for an ulterior motive. I wished one of my gifts was mindreading. What was the old saying? Keep your friends close, but your enemies closer?

"I suppose," I said, knowing I would probably regret it. "We could try."

Did I really need friends so badly that I was willing to give it a go with vapid, overly made up mean girls? Yep, I did. Anyway, if they screwed with me I could easily make them wake up in the morning with twenty-five extra pounds hanging off their trim little bods.

The minions started to babble excitedly and I decided immediately I would not learn their names. Henceforth they would be Thing One, Thing Two, Thing Three and Thing Four.

Now that a truce had been born, I wasn't sure what to do. I pushed my Alpo around with my fork and tried to make sense of the Things' conversation. Two words stopped me cold.

"Angels and Demons," Thing One gushed to all the other Things.

"I'm sorry," I interrupted. "What did you say?"

"Angels and Demons." Thing One's eyes lit up like a Christmas tree—*not that I'd ever had one*. "The theme of the Fall dance, silly!" she giggled.

"We're the dance committee." Thing Two grabbed my hand and squeezed it as if we were best buds. "And now you are too!"

Her excitement was like a rash. What had I been thinking? It was better when they hated me. I extracted my hand and put it in my lap. However, this could be fascinating and until I had to go kill a bunch of evil immortal asswipes this might be a good diversion. I'd have great stories for Stella when I was allowed to see her again.

Shit. Another piece of the puzzle clicked. Grandpa said I needed to dance. Did the Angel Demon dance fulfill that part of my destiny? Considering the fact it would be filled with innocent humans, I prayed to my father and uncle that this was not the case. I briefly closed my eyes and decided that I was definitely going to be part of the dance committee. If anything was to go down at the dance, at least I would have been in the planning stages and would know the lay of the land... or the gymnasium. Also, I promised myself that I would do everything in my power not to turn the Things into mutes. Hard, but doable.

"What kind of Angels and Demons?" I asked.

"Are there more than one kind?" Thing Three was alarmed and confused.

"I don't know," I quickly said. "I was just wondering how this all works."

"Ohhhh," Thing Four squealed. "It's beyond awesome. Half of the gym will be Heaven and half will be Hell." She whispered the word Hell like it was a swear word. I almost slapped her. "Everyone will dress like a Demon or an Angel. I'm going as a Demon," she announced proudly. The other Things gave her a round of applause. Were they for real?

"What are you wearing?" I was starting to enjoy myself immensely, although I felt Lucy's stare. I glanced over and she looked away. My paranoia was getting ridiculous.

Thing Four, oblivious to anyone but herself, went on. "I have a red dress. I'm pairing it with horns and fangs and blood dripping all over me," she explained. "My dress is hot, it shows a ton of cleavage. Then I'm going to decapitate a couple old dolls, cover them in blood and tie them to my legs. You know, so they drag on the floor."

I was beyond speechless. I wanted to laugh, but a bigger part of me wanted to magic up some huge cold sores all over her mouth.

"Don't you think," Lucy chimed in dryly. "That it might be difficult to dance with dead babies attached to your feet?"

"Oooo." Thing Four puzzled it out, completely missing the irony in her leader's snarky tone. "You're right. I'll tie them to my arms."

Lucy rolled her eyes and then turned them on me. "What do you think a Demon looks like, Dixie?"

"I wouldn't know," I told her, wondering what evil I'd committed to deserve this group's friendship.

"I'm going as an Angel," Thing One volunteered. "I'm wearing a white bustier, hot pants and boots with ripped black fishnets."

"Very Miley Cyrus," Thing Three observed. "What about a halo and wings?" Thing Three, the dry heaver, asked while applying way too much lip gloss.

"Totally," Thing One gasped, "I would never forget those. I want my wings to look like Dixie's necklace."

All eyes shot to my neck. Instinctively I covered my beautiful golden feather. These idiots didn't deserve to look at it.

"God," Thing Three said enviously through gobs of lip gloss. "Where did someone like you get something like that?"

"Walmart," Myrtle said from behind me as she drew the attention to herself and away from my neck. "Are you going to ask her if it's real and how much it cost next?" she snapped.

"Um, no, sorry," Thing Three said, duly chastised by my skunk pranking fake cousin.

"Where have you been?" Lucy asked Myrtle as she wedged her little Demon body between me and a Thing.

"Having sex in the science lab closet with Timmy," she said. She gingerly pushed my tray of animal chow away from her line of vision.

"TMI, Myrtle. TMI." Lucy laughed and shook her head.

Myrtle shrugged and grinned. "Whatever. It was awesome. You should all try it sometime."

The Things nodded in unison, hanging on her every word.

"I have to agree with Lucy on this one," I groaned. "Definitely too much information."

"You're just jealous." She shoved me. I shoved her back.

"Girls, girls," Lucy spoke in an excited whisper. "Ten o'clock. Total hottie checking out our table."

"Oh my God," one of the Things said. They were becoming interchangeable. "Who is he?"

"He's new," Lucy whispered loudly.

I didn't look. I'd have to turn completely around and that would be obnoxious.

"He's not scoping our table," Thing Three hissed. "He's scoping Dixie."

"Like every other guy at school," Thing Two added under her breath.

"Shhh." Lucy readjusted herself to get a better view. "She's right." She waggled her eyebrows at me. "Mr. Sex-on-a-Stick is burning holes in your back."

"Whatever," Myrtle said. "Dixie's got a boyfriend and he's

hotter than sin." She nudged me to make sure I got the Hell reference. Hades, she was an idiot.

"If he's hotter than this guy," Lucy challenged, "I'll eat an entire vat of the Alpo they serve here." Her eyes sparkled with mischief. I was kind of starting to like her.

"He's walking this way," Thing Three screeched, frantically smearing on more lip gloss.

"Oh my God." Thing Two was near tears. "He is." She began fluffing her hair.

What in the Hell was I doing? These girls were freaks. Lucy seemed okay, even interesting, but why was she hanging out with these imbeciles?

The feeling of spiders skittering down my spine halted my inner diatribe on stupid girls. Something was very wrong. I glanced at Myrtle to see if she noticed. She seemed tense. I needed to turn and scan the lunchroom. My stomach clenched and serious unease rippled through me. Were Rogue Demons in my college cafeteria? The Things were busy primping, unaware of impending danger, but Lucy's eyes were on me.

"You okay?" she asked, concerned.

"Yep." I smiled, which I was sure came out like a pained grimace. I slowly turned around to see what was freaking me out.

There he was. All six foot something of him. Eyes like midnight and hair as dark as mine, with beauty that made my heart skip. A warning voice whispered in my head and fear knotted up inside me. From across the cafeteria his eyes locked on mine and the world stopped for a moment. My breath left my lungs and an icy chill crawled through my veins. I was shaking. He was coming for me.

His scent was not human and it was definitely not Demon, which could only mean one thing.

I grabbed Myrtle's arm in a grip that would have crushed a mortal.

"We have to go." I hissed. I was panicked.

"What?" Lucy sensed my unease.

"Myrtle has… an orthodontist appointment. Now." I was dizzy. Surely he wouldn't try to kill me in a room full of mortals. I had to get the Hell out before innocent people started dying.

I dragged Myrtle behind me and moved as fast as I could away from him. I spotted an emergency exit in the far left corner. My fingers started to spark and it took supreme effort not to run with Demon speed. Without seeing him, I felt him pick up his pace. I was so not ready to die today.

"What's happening?" Myrtle gasped as I yanked her along.

"An Angel," I muttered through clenched teeth as I tried to avoid knocking all my classmates to the floor in my haste to escape. "An Angel is coming after me and I have to draw him away from here so the humans don't die."

"But… "

"No buts," I replied sharply. "Be quiet and get ready to run." I knew she wanted to say something else but I gave her no chance.

I pushed through the exit and the alarm went off. I laughed at the irony. The blast of fresh air in my face made me hopeful. I just needed to get him as far from the student center as I could. If we got a good head start, maybe we could outrun him. Maybe.

I let go of Myrtle, shut the exit door and bent the lock. That wouldn't stop him, but it might buy us a few minutes… or seconds. "We have to run," I told her.

"What about your car?" She pointed to the parking lot.

"Screw the car," I said tersely. "Stay behind me so my tail wind will pull you along faster."

She nodded.

He was getting closer. The insane part of me wanted to stay and confront him, but thankfully my instincts were better than that. Confronting him on campus could be deadly for a lot of innocent people. The air around me grew warmer and the breeze smelled of sunshine and cinnamon. Who knew impending death would smell so good.

I frantically shoved Myrtle behind me. "Run," I shouted.

We did.

We flew through the fields surrounding the campus at speeds of about two hundred miles an hour. We were headed for our house. I needed weapons or the baby Demons if I was going to have a chance with the Angel. My magic was strong, but I didn't trust it enough to protect both myself and Myrtle. This was the last day I would travel without the baby Demons or a sword in my backpack. Ever.

For a brief moment I debated if I was wrong to have left the school. Would the students have been safer if I stayed? Neither Angels nor Demons were supposed to harm mortals. I said a quick prayer to Satan that in my haste to escape I hadn't mistakenly set up innocents for death. Of course if I didn't haul some major ass Myrtle and I would be facing a permanent death.

I briefly glanced back to check on Myrtle and my world exploded. I ran head first into a granite mountain. The impact of our bodies in motion at over two hundred miles an hour meeting an immovable object was devastating. We went flying, tumbling and rolling over each other and landed in a tangled bloody mess on the ground.

"Damn it to Hell," I moaned as I held my head. Fireworks detonated inside my brain. With much effort, I pried my body off of Myrtle's. She looked bad but she was breathing. Her head was still attached so she wasn't dead, but she was out cold and her shoulder was grotesquely dislocated.

I sucked in a sharp breath, ignored my own pain, and moved closer to my little friend. If I could pop her shoulder back in while she was unconscious I'd save her a world of pain later. Her pale skin was almost white and all I wanted to do was sit back and cry. I smoothed her bloody hair back from her face and kissed her forehead.

"You'll be okay, baby," I promised her. She looked so fragile and small. "I'll take care of you." I was going to kill that fucking

Angel when I saw him again. I smile-grimaced when I realized how delighted Hayden would be with my emerging foul mouth.

The sound was so gross when I popped her shoulder back I almost hurled. Thank Lucifer she was passed out. Now I just needed to pick her up and run. I had no idea where the Angel was, but I knew time was not on my side. Where in the Hell did a granite mountain come from? There were no mountains in Eden, Kentucky. Not to mention, in all my twenty-one years, I'd never crashed into anything.

Something wet and slobbery licked my neck.

"Steve? What are you doing out here?" I whispered. My voice hurt and getting air in my lungs was a challenge.

Steve walked around me and pushed her cool wet nose into my face. She looked down at Myrtle and whimpered.

"It's okay," I tried to comfort her. "She'll be fine. We're Demons, we heal." I knew she didn't understand a word, but she seemed happy with my explanation and gave me another big sloppy wet one. "Steve, you have to go. Somebody is after me. I'll just die if you get hurt again. Go," I shouted the best I could. I tried to do a mean voice and give her the evil eye. "Go, you bad dog-wolf. Go away!" She stood there like an idiot and wagged her big tail.

"Shit," I muttered. Now I was responsible for Steve too.

My neck ached and my body burned, but when life was at stake, those tended to be minor problems. I gingerly turned my head to swear at the mountain that took me out… but my litany of expletives got caught in my throat. At that exact moment I went into shock. I knew this for a fact—because I started to laugh. Uncontrollably.

There was a mountain but it wasn't granite. It was flesh and blood, looked like a male supermodel and wanted to kill me.

CHAPTER TWENTY-FIVE

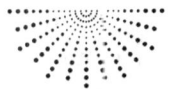

"HELLO DIXIE." HIS VOICE WAS SMOOTH AND SILKY. HYPNOTIC. THE term "voice of an Angel" now made sense.

I refused to speak. I stared warily and moved my injured body so I blocked him from Myrtle and Steve.

"Your friend will be fine," he said. His stance was neutral, legs slightly spread and arms at his sides. He carried no weapon, but that meant nothing. He could have all sorts of things hidden in his clothes.

"Yeah," I snapped. "Until you kill us."

He laughed. Not chuckled... laughed. Hard. What kind of psycho asshole was he? And why did he have to be so pretty? It was distracting.

"What is wrong with you?" My anger eclipsed my fear. I was in no shape to take on the Angel, but my mouth clearly didn't get the memo.

I needed to freeze him, but my body was so damaged from the impact of the crash all my magic was focused on healing myself. Maybe if I could keep his gorgeous murdering ass talking I could heal enough to render him helpless. It wasn't great, but it was the best I could do in a bad situation.

"You're even more beautiful than described," the Angel commented.

"By who?"

"Some people." He smiled seductively. My pulse raced and I looked away.

What in the Hell was wrong with me? Had I lost my freakin' mind? My impulse was to flirt with the Angel who was here to destroy me. Not to mention I already had a soul mate who was equally as beautiful as the Angel standing before me and didn't want to kill me. Talking... I had to keep him talking.

"Do you have a name?" I inquired coldly.

"I do." He grinned and stepped closer to me. Steve growled.

"Since I'll be dead and unable to rat you out, you may as well tell me." I tried to scoot back to counter his advance, but my body wasn't working yet.

He tilted his head, reminding me alarmingly of Hayden. "My name is Elijah. What else would you like to know, Dixie?"

My stupid name sounded like a caress on his lips and his lips were... lips. They were nothing but lips.

"I don't want to know anything about you," I informed him rudely. I tried to stare him down, but the stunning midnight blue of his eyes sucked me in and made my heart flutter. My reaction to him brought an unwelcome blush to my cheeks and my body felt hot.

"But I want you to know about me." My enemy gave me an irresistible grin. I had to fight a major battle of personal restraint to keep from grinning back. Steve growled again and jerked me back to reality.

"Are you psychotic? You want to be friends before you kill me?" I pressed my lips together in anger and self-preservation. I wanted to call him every bad word I knew, but thankfully I remembered I was trying to buy time. My main goal was to protect Myrtle and Steve.

"Oh Dixie, there are many things I'd like to do to you and with you... killing is definitely not one of them." His mouth curved into a smile as his gaze raked over me. "You have nothing to fear from me."

"Only myself," I muttered. Elijah let out a bark of joyous laughter at my comment he wasn't supposed to hear. I should have known Angels could hear as well as Demons. My voice turned to ice. I wanted to slap the smile off of his face. "If you're not here to kill me, then why are you here, Angel boy?"

"To see you, Dixie, and I prefer Elijah." He stooped down in front of me. His nearness made me dizzy. I wanted to blame the wooziness on the massive concussion I'd just received, but that would be a lie. "I've waited a very long time to make your acquaintance," he said softly.

My breathing was uneven and it wasn't from my injuries. There was something about this Angel, an enemy of my race, that was mesmerizing. His gaze dropped to my lips and his hand gently cupped my battered face.

"Will you let me heal you and your friend?" His eyes searched mine. He was so close my brain shorted out. Little bits of silver mixed with the dark blue of his eyes. It looked like flecks of diamonds in a deep blue night. "Your accident was my fault and I want to make it right."

"Okay." Much to my chagrin, I was sure I would have said okay to any question he asked. My lack of morals and self-control appalled me. I tried to look away, but he gently held my face still.

Very slowly, with his eyes locked on mine he leaned forward. Warning bells went off in my head. "No. Stop. I can't."

"This is the way it has to be, Dixie." His voice flowed over me like honey. "I'm an Angel. I will heal you with love."

He didn't wait for my reply. There was a tenderness and longing in his gaze that made my heart flutter wildly in my chest. He closed the space between us and pressed his lips to mine. His kiss was slow and drugging.

Against my will, and to my disgust, I found myself responding.

He moaned into my mouth and my pulse skyrocketed. He broke the kiss and planted small kisses along my jawline and neck. I refused to put my arms around him, but my traitorous body leaned into his.

A shot of warm soothing heat coursed through my body and my injuries slowly disappeared.

"Are you going to kiss Myrtle now?" I asked as I stood and put some distance between us.

"Nope." He smirked and pointed a finger at my little friend. A fine golden mist engulfed her body and her bruises, cuts and lacerations disappeared. She slowly began to come to.

"Wait a minute," I sputtered as I stood and tried to shove the big liar. "You didn't need to kiss me, did you?"

"Nope." He smiled as he backed away from my ire.

"You tricked me," I yelled, forgetting about the differences in our race, height and weight. I was going to kill him.

"I'd do it again in a heartbeat." Elijah was so serious it halted my pursuit of destroying him.

"I have a soul mate," I told him.

He approached and fingered my beautiful necklace with interest. He leaned down and whispered in my ear, sending shivers all through me. "Tell him he has competition. Until you're bonded, you're a free agent."

He stepped back and with a panty melting smile he disappeared in a glittering burst of gold. I was healed, confused and off balance.

"What in the Hell happened?" Myrtle, finally awake, asked groggily.

"I have no idea," I told her truthfully. "I really have no idea."

We walked the rest of the way home with Steve at our heels.

"Where'd you find the wolf?" Myrtle asked as she examined her bloody clothes.

"She's not mine. She belongs to an old lady in town. Her name is Lucky, but I call her Steve."

"Oh."

"Is that all you have to say?" I snapped. I knew I was taking my anger at myself out on her, but I couldn't help it.

"No, but you made it clear you didn't want to hear what I had to say back in the commissary."

"When has that ever stopped you?" I came to a halt and yanked her around to face me.

"Okay, fine." She laughed at my tough girl stance and winced. "Why does my shoulder hurt and how did we get all bloody and gross?"

"I crashed into the Angel when we were running. It was like hitting a concrete wall. You got knocked out and your shoulder got dislocated. I popped it back in and the Angel healed us."

"Thanks," she said as she rotated her arm.

"Aren't you shocked he didn't kill us?" How was she so nonchalant about our brush with death? Maybe the impact rattled her brain.

"No."

"No?" I laughed. She was definitely concussed.

"Dixie," Myrtle explained as if I were five. "Eden, Kentucky is neutral territory. He can't kill us here."

I gave her a brutal stare. "You people suck. Is anybody going to keep me up to speed on the rules here?" I yelled.

"Do you really think Lucifer would have sent you into a war zone before you were ready?" she asked as she tried to bite back her laugh at my tantrum. She failed.

That stopped me and made me miss my father terribly. "No, he wouldn't."

"Dixie," Myrtle said gently as she took my hands in hers. "You were justified in doing what you did. The world is a bad place right now and the rules can't be trusted."

Steve wedged herself into me and whimpered. I sat down on the ground and stroked her soft fur.

"I need to know everything from you that won't turn us to dust. Can you do that for me?" I asked, idly making circles in Steve's coat.

"I can."

"Thanks."

"We're looking for Rogue Demons, but the Angels are not our friends either," Myrtle reminded me.

"I don't think he would have hurt me," I murmured as I laid my head on Steve.

"Not here he wouldn't." Myrtle joined in on the Steve love-fest.

"No," I said softly. "I'm quite sure he would never hurt me anywhere. Neutral or not."

"You're crazy," Myrtle huffed and petted Steve.

"Possibly." I smiled at her. Guilt about Hayden tugged at my heart as I remembered the kiss from Elijah. "But I really don't think he would."

CHAPTER TWENTY-SIX

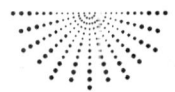

BLANCHE WAS WAITING ON THE FRONT PORCH STEPS WHEN WE GOT home. Steve ran over to her, wagging her big tail.

"Why are you here?" I smiled tiredly, happy to see her even though my question sounded snarky.

"Nice to see you too." She grinned as she scratched Steve. "What in the Hell happened to you guys?"

"Are you talking to your invisible friend?" Myrtle asked as she watched Steve's fur be manipulated by what appeared to be nothing.

"Yep," I said as I plopped my exhausted body down next to Blanche.

"Well, tell her I said hi." Myrtle made her way to the front door. "I can't stand myself." She groaned and attempted to rub the dried blood off her arms. "I need a shower."

She went inside. Blanche and I sat quietly petting Steve.

"I like Myrtle," she said, absently massaging a very happy Steve.

"Me too. Did you know Eden was neutral territory?" I asked as I found a tickle spot on Steve's belly. Her leg started dancing and I scratched faster.

"I assumed it was," she replied. "Your dad's not an idiot. Why do you ask?"

"I had a run-in with an Angel." I sighed and wrapped my arms around myself. "I thought he was going to kill me."

"Did he try?"

"No, he… " I didn't have the energy to rehash every sordid detail. "Can't you just get inside my head and see everything?"

"Only with an invite." She smiled evilly.

"What are you talking about?" I laughed. "You get into my head all the time."

"True," she agreed. "When I'm with you it's easy. I'm allowed to be privy to the here and now, but the past is a different story."

"It wasn't even an hour ago," I said, trying to get it straight.

"Doesn't matter if it was five minutes ago," she explained. "If it's in the past you have to invite me in."

"Fine, I invite you."

It was weird. For the first time I could feel her inside my head. Definitely an odd sensation—like a breeze floating in my mind. My head felt full and my body tightened in resistance.

"You have to relax, Dixie, or it won't work."

"Okay." I took a deep breath. "I'll try."

On its own my body went limp. I slumped forward onto Steve's soft furry body and I heard a click in my head. It was working. Unfortunately for me, the entire scene played back in full color with surround sound. I had to relive every moment as Blanche watched.

My head clicked again when she pulled out. I thought I was tired before…

"Great Balls of Hell." Blanche shook her head. "That's screwed up."

"Tell me about it. And by the way." I pinched the bridge of my nose trying to ward off the headache that was blooming rapidly. "We are never doing that again. It hurt."

"What are you going to do about him?" she asked.

"Do? Nothing. It was a physical attraction, not a soul deep one," I said truthfully. "I have Hayden."

"Good luck with that," she drawled as her mouth quirked with amusement. "It doesn't look like he plans to give you much choice in the matter. Damn, you go from never having a date to having the two hottest and most powerful Angels in the universe after you."

Warning bells clanked in my already throbbing brain. "What do you mean?"

"I mean." Blanche grinned. "They are H-O-T hot."

"I got that part," I interrupted in frustration. "What do you mean the most powerful?"

"Well," Blanche lowered her voice being purposefully mysterious and incredibly annoying. "Hayden is the Angel of Death and Elijah is the Angel of Light."

"Is that a big deal?"

Blanche looked at me like I sprouted horns. Big ones. "Dixie," she gasped. "They are True Immortals... two of the True Immortals."

I knew Hayden was—that was why my dad couldn't kill him. Everything was starting to make sense and I wasn't sure I was happy about that. Knowledge might be power, but sometimes the less you knew the better off you were. Hayden and Elijah both had to be thousands of years old. That was a little freaky to wrap my mind around. What in the Hell did they want with a twenty-one year old girl? Unless The Kev had been right about me... My headache was two minutes from being full blown.

"That's not even the best part." Blanche rocked back and forth in excitement.

"What else could there possibly be to tell?" I thought seriously about putting my hand over her mouth so I could find some duct tape to keep her from talking until my aching head could take it, but that could be a very long time. She was going to announce something whether I wanted to know or not. I definitely did not want to know.

"They're brothers!" she blurted. She grabbed me as I tumbled backward in shock.

I didn't know why that information made me feel so raw, but it did. I knew Hayden had a brother. He told me he did. He said they didn't get along...

"Do you think Elijah knows my boyfriend is Hayden?" I asked Blanche as she settled me back on the steps after my near pass out. Damn, it sounded ridiculous to use the term boyfriend about someone who'd been around before mortals roamed the Earth. And he wasn't just my boyfriend. He was my soul mate.

"Absolutely." She nodded. "Do you remember him touching and looking at your necklace?"

I did. I remembered it clearly. "So is this just a competition between brothers?" The thought of that hurt and pissed me off royally. I was nobody's contest prize.

"If I hadn't seen the whole thing I would have said yes, but he meant business and his feelings rang true. As true as Hayden's. You can't fake that," she added, making me feel sick to my stomach on top of my headache. "So," she took on a very matter of fact tone, "two of the most powerful beings in the universe are head over heels in love with you... what are you going to do?"

"I'm going to Disney World," I snapped sarcastically. "Wait," I gasped as I doubled over. "Grandpa said God begat two True Immortal Angels." My body trembled as I put two and two together. "God is their father, which means they're my cousins." I stood up on shaky legs and began to pace the front yard, stepping all over flowers and plants. "Holy Hell, I'm in love with one of my cousins and just kissed the other one!"

And I thought I was nauseous before.

"Hold on," Blanche yelled, stopping me in the middle of a bed of petunias. "Technically you're right, but you're actually wrong."

"Have you been hanging out with Grandpa?" I shouted. "You're making no sense." I continued to destroy the beautiful garden with clumsy feet and a broken heart. Did Hayden lie to me?

"Sit!" Blanche demanded as she put a temporary kibosh on my hysteria. I sat in the bluebells and narrowed my eyes at her. "You are not related by blood to Hayden or Elijah."

"How in the Hell do you know that?" I shrieked.

"I have no idea." She was bewildered, "I didn't know it an hour ago, but I know it as true now."

"That's completely screwed." I was quieter now. However, for no good reason I knew she spoke the truth. "Go on."

"In the beginning, when True Immortals first came to be, they weren't born of a woman and a man like you were. They were created."

"But my father has parents and so does God." This made no sense. "My father and God share the same mother."

"Mother Nature didn't give birth the traditional way. She used power from your grandpa and God's father to create Satan and God."

"Not to be rude, but that sounds like a pile of shit." I rolled my eyes.

"It does," Blanche agreed. "But it's not. So while God and Satan were raised as brothers, they are not blood related."

I was so confused. "Which means everybody is adopted?"

"Simplistic, but yes. Think of everyone as found and lumped together with caretakers."

"So freakin' typical for my family… Spell it out one more time —in English."

"It means you are not related to the ridiculously hot Angels who are after your ass."

This was too much to take in. What had started as a bad day just kept getting worse. First, Lucy and the Things wanted my friendship, then I almost died, then to top it all off my not-by-blood-related kinda cousin, The Angel of Light, hit on me instead of killing me. Could it get any stranger? Nope.

"So, my dad and his brother were hatched from pods without the benefit of sperm or eggs from their True Immortal parents… just some power and some magic hoodoo. Which by the way is really stinkin' hard to buy," I huffed in disbelief and continued. "Then God and Satan had children the traditional way, the way we learned about in science class. They had sex. Hayden and Elijah are brothers born of my Uncle God, who I suppose isn't really my uncle if we get technical. I am born of his non-blood related brother Satan, even though they have the same mother who didn't physically give birth to them. Therefore all of this bullshit boils down to the fact that I am not related to my boyfriend, who is apparently older than dirt, or his brother who I just swapped spit with an hour ago. Who, by the way, is also older than dirt." I took a huge cleansing breath. "Is that about right?"

"Pretty much," Blanche said. A grin replaced the open mouthed reaction to the Cliffs Notes version of my family history. "The pod part is kind of off, but whatever." She pulled me up and away from the decimated bluebells and wrapped her silver arms around me. "Are you going to be okay?" She held me tight.

"I don't really have a choice, do I?"

"No," she agreed. "You really don't."

"Do you know what the most screwed up part of all of this is?" I pulled out of her embrace and ran my hands through my hair. "The fun hasn't even begun yet. I'm supposed to find a freakin' sword and kill a buttload of Rogue Demons and restore or find the Balance of Chaos." I started to laugh.

"When you put it like that, dating your cousin doesn't sound that bad, you know?"

"I know. I really do know. I need to shower and change." I sighed as I looked down at my torn and bloody clothes. "And then we'll drive Steve back to Miss Evelyn. Keep an eye on Steve while I change. I wouldn't be surprised if Myrtle starts feeling the need to take scissors and dye to her."

~

I'D BE HARD PRESSED TO IMAGINE THE REST OF THE UNITED STATES was as beautiful as Eden, Kentucky. It had a magic that made me feel calm--lush fields, wildly colorful gardens, thoroughbred horse farms and old Southern mansions. Perfect. I really wanted to see other parts of the country, especially New York, the Grand Canyon and Disney World, but that would have to wait until I kicked ass and took no prisoners here.

Blanche tried to con me into letting her drive, but allowing your invisible friend to drive your car could cause all sorts of unwanted attention in town. She begged and pleaded. In the end I compromised, mostly so she would shut up. I let her drive the country roads till we were about a mile out of town. She was a horrible driver—even Steve whimpered in terror.

A party was in full swing when we pulled up in front of the Happy Hacienda Senior Citizens Home. Around twenty really old people wearing brightly colored leis and hula skirts over their housecoats and slippers mingled on the front lawn. Some were eating from the trays of food piled high on a buffet table decorated with tiki statues, twinkle lights and fake palm trees. Hawaiian music blasted from a speaker. Several gals were doing a geriatric hula, and two of the women were dancing in their wheelchairs.

I watched from the car in rapt fascination. I'd never seen so many old people in my life. I'd never seen old people at all till I came to Earth. Demons stopped aging anywhere between twenty and thirty. It had never seemed unusual that my father could pass for my brother, or that his own father looked like his brother. That was my normal. This was not. These people were bizarrely happy to be so close to death.

The concept of dying was foreign to me. Of course I'd considered it more often lately because running from Elijah earlier had scared a healthy dose of *desire to live* into me. My own mortality hadn't occurred to me in Hell and I wondered as I watched the aged bodies of these smiling people how often they thought about dying.

Steve nuzzled my neck with her big wet nose. "Okay girl." I scratched between her ears and wondered if I was confusing her by calling her Steve. "Let's go find Miss Evelyn."

As we walked through the throngs of eighty year old hula dancers, a cute little old lady in a pale peach robe and matching slippers grabbed my arm. Her skin felt papery and fragile but her grip was strong.

"Hey darlin', let's dance." Her laugh was infectious and she swung her terry cloth covered hips in a circular motion, reminiscent of a really bad stripper.

I giggled at her dancing but was drawn to the lines around her eyes. They crinkled when she smiled, yet her watery blue eyes sparkled. I froze and realized those were laugh lines. I'd never seen them before. I wanted to touch them, but I knew that would be rude. She wore her lifetime of joy and sorrow proudly on her face. She was beautiful. Every line etched in her skin was a story.

"Come on, sweetie pie," she urged, doing moves that would make Carl proud. "Dance with me."

"Okay," I muttered, rocking back and forth feeling like an ass. Blanche stood beside me and laughed. Nobody was going to make her dance. Nobody could see her.

"I like chicken," my little dance partner yelled above the music. "Do you like chicken?"

"Um... yes." Was she senile?

"I'm gonna sit down, sugar puss. Would you get me some chicken?" She took my hand and we wound our way over to a bench. "I'm not as young as I look." She grinned and eased herself down with a grunt.

"I'd be happy to get you some chicken," I told her.

There were three kinds of chicken on the buffet table, so I piled a plate high with all of them. I glanced around for Miss

Evelyn but couldn't find her. I very carefully made my way back to my new friend. I held the plate high... walking through a group of hulaing seniors could be dangerous.

"Thank you, sugar buns." She took the plate gratefully. I was curious how many nicknames she had stored up in her brain. "Would you like some chicken, sweet cheeks?" She offered her plate to me.

"No thanks."

"Well, sit your pretty fanny down and talk to me for a minute. Not many younguns come around here much."

I watched her eat her chicken with gusto. She made happy little noises with each bite, reminding me of Astrid as she slurped on Gemma. I had no idea what to talk about, so I sat quietly and let her enjoy her chicken.

"I like cheese too," she informed me between bites.

"Would you like me to get you some cheese?" I smiled, starting to understand her game.

"Nope." She grinned. "Maybe later. What's your name, sweet potato? Mine's Miss Sally." She extended a chicken grease covered hand.

I gingerly took it. "I'm Dixie." I retrieved my hand and wiped it discreetly on my jeans.

"Oooo, what a pretty name for a pretty girl. I used to know a sweet little thing named Dixie a long time ago."

"I suppose in the South Dixie's a common name," I said as I took her now empty plate and tossed it in a nearby trashcan. Miss Sally could put back some food for being such a little thing. That plate had been full.

"No," she mused. "Not really. She was a darling little girl, like sunshine."

"Can I get you something else to eat? Some cheese?" I asked as I searched the crowd for Miss Evelyn. Steve sat curled at my feet.

"No, thank you." A tired look of sadness passed over her features. "She was such a happy little girl. I loved her."

"Who?" I asked, distracted by my search.

"Little Dixie," she replied, lost in thought. "She was a precious thing."

I gave her my full attention. She was lonely. The least I could do was listen to her. It was odd to hear about another Dixie. I'd never come across anyone with my name before. "Do you still see her?"

"Oh heavens no," she said. "She died. Saddest funeral I've ever been to." She shook her head, her voice lost all of its spark. "Never found her little body. I don't think her momma was ever the same after that."

"I'm sorry." I didn't know what to say. Clearly little Dixie's death still affected Miss Sally to this day.

"I like cake more than I like chicken," she said slowly as a mischievous smile lit her eyes.

I was grateful for the change of subject, but her abrupt emotional turnaround made me curious again about her mental state. "Would you like me to get you some cake?" I used her napkin to wipe some chicken grease from her chin.

"You got me all figured out, sugar dumplin'." She giggled. "But no, if I'm gonna have cake, I need to get my fanny up and get it myself. Give an old lady a hand."

She reached out and I gently pulled her to her feet. She took my face in her hands and kissed my nose.

"Miss Sally?" I asked as she began her trek to the dessert table. "Do you know where I could find Miss Evelyn?"

"The new gal?"

"New?" I was surprised. For some reason I'd been under the impression Miss Evelyn was from here. It wasn't anything she said… it was just what I'd assumed.

"Oh yes, sugar pie, she moved here about two weeks ago with her nurse, Rhonda." Miss Sally shook her head and chuckled. "That Rhonda can play some poker. She won nine dollars off me the other night and I cheat!" She chuckled with delight and slapped her thighs. "If they're not out here they'll be out back. Miss Evelyn kinda keeps to herself. Come back and see me, pretty little Dixie."

As she beelined to her cake, I thought about Grandpa's cryptic advice. The old ones have wisdom. Learn to dance... was it the dance at the college? Was the dance with Miss Sally important? I looked around and scanned the area for Angels or Demons and sensed nothing. I'd be hard pressed to find any wisdom in Miss Sally's diatribe about chicken and cheese and long lost little girls who shared my name, but I sure did like her.

CHAPTER TWENTY-SEVEN

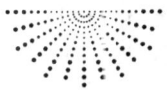

MISS EVELYN STOOD VERY STILL ON THE STEPS OF THE WRAPAROUND porch of the senior center and watched our approach. A happy smile played on her lips and her violet eyes danced. For a brief moment I could swear she was a young woman—a blindingly beautiful young woman. I blinked my eyes and she was old again. It must have been the angle of the sun or my recently acquired concussion. Blanche grabbed my hand.

"She's so pretty it's weird," she muttered.

"I know."

She was tall and regal. Her long grey hair hung loose and blew gently in the breeze. She looked like a Grecian goddess even in her lavender housedress and slippers.

"Hello girls." She smiled warmly. "I'm so glad you came back."

"We found Steve, I mean Lucky," I stammered.

"You know," she mused. "I think Steve is a very fitting name for my wolf. From now on she shall be known as Steve."

Steve woofed in dismay. My eyes shot to Miss Evelyn's in wonder. "Did she understand you?"

"Animals are much smarter than you think. Oftentimes far superior to their human counterparts." Steve's tail wagged in approval. "Would you young ladies like to come to my home for some tea?"

"Yes," Blanche and I replied in unison.

"Very good." Miss Evelyn laughed. "Follow me."

Rhonda appeared out of nowhere and put out her big beefy arm to steady Miss Evelyn as she walked. Steve followed at Rhonda's heels and Blanche and I brought up the rear. We were an odd little group. My heart pounded rapidly in anticipation of spending time with Miss Evelyn. What was with that?

"Do you like tea?" Blanche whispered.

"Hate it," I muttered. "And where in the Hell did Rhonda come from?"

"No clue, it's like she poofed out of thin air," Blanche marveled. "Is that possible?"

"They're too old to be immortals, so no," she replied.

"About the tea," I said as I grabbed Blanche so we separated ourselves from them by a few paces. "Just drink it and be polite."

"Fine, but if I hurl it's your fault."

MISS EVELYN'S HOME WAS A BUNGALOW IN BACK OF THE SENIOR center. There were about fifteen charming little places all in a circle facing an elaborate flower garden with a large fountain in the middle. Her home smelled of gardenias, just like she did. Although it didn't look like my bungalow in Hell, it had the same rose, chocolate and cream color palette. I was immediately comfortable.

"How do you take your tea?" Miss Evelyn asked.

"Mostly milk, about eight sugars and a minuscule splash of tea," Blanche replied with utmost sincerity.

I groaned and gave her the evil eye as Miss Evelyn turned away to hide her grin. Blanche shrugged her shoulders helplessly.

"Whatever's easiest for you would be fine," I said politely, hoping to counterbalance Blanche's gross request.

Miss Evelyn pressed her lips together in amusement. "How about lemonade instead?"

"Yes!" Blanche shouted in relief.

"That would be lovely," I cut in before Blanche went into a dissertation on our hatred of tea. We were never going to be asked back at this rate.

"Four lemonades coming right up," Rhonda said.

"Wait. Four?" Blanche gasped. "You can see me?"

"Only from the front," she informed my dumbstruck friend, her eyes twinkling. "Oh my stars, sorry for walking through you the other day. Your back was to me." She winked and left the room, going to what I assumed was the kitchen.

"I'll help you with that, dear," Miss Evelyn told her as she followed Rhonda out of the room.

"How in the Hell are they human?" Blanche quietly hissed at me.

"I don't know, but they are. I think," I said, bewildered and unnerved. "I can sense a Demon and now that I've been around Elijah, I can sense an Angel. They're neither."

"What else could they be?" Blanche sounded freaked out, which did nothing for my state of mind.

"You're supposed to know this stuff." My eyes narrowed in disgust. "You're the direction book, for Satan's sake."

"I'm your fate, dumbass. I do not have all the answers," she huffed. She crossed her arms over her chest and pouted. "Do you think we're in danger?"

"No, we're safe here. Eden is neutral and even if it wasn't, Miss Evelyn would never harm us."

"You're sure?"

"Very sure." I knew I was right. I could feel it in my gut. I knew it the same way I knew Elijah would never hurt me.

"Something is burning." Blanche sniffed the air and pointed toward the kitchen.

"It smells like it," I agreed. "But it smells good."

The scent reminded me of a bonfire of sugar or a mountain of slightly burnt cookies. It was definitely coming from the kitchen.

"They're going to come back in here, grind us up and turn us into baked goods," Blanche informed me solemnly.

"You so did not just use the term baked goods," I groaned.

"I did." She smirked. "And I'm serious."

"Sweet Baby Satan, you've been reading too many fairytales."

"Possibly, but this place is weird."

"Yep." I nodded. "But I like it."

Miss Evelyn and Rhonda came back carrying a tray of lemonade and cookies. Blanche eyed the *baked goods* and raised her eyebrows as high as they would go. It was all I could do not to laugh. Rhonda put the tray down and I swear there was a tendril of lavender smoke floating out of her nose. I blinked and it was gone. Now I was seeing things—first, Miss Evelyn as a young woman and now Rhonda as a smoke snorting cookie dealer. Great. I needed a good night's sleep. Today had simply been too much.

"So, what have you ladies been up to?" Miss Evelyn asked as she served the lemonade.

"Nothing," I muttered as I took a huge gulp of my drink and hoped she couldn't tell I was lying. How on Earth could I possibly explain being chased by what I thought was a killer Angel and healing from wounds that would kill a mortal ten times over?

"Same 'ole, same 'ole," Blanche added, quickly shoving two cookies into her mouth.

Miss Evelyn sat back on her loveseat and watched us, clearly amused by our pathetic attempts at deflection. "Hmm, sounds kind of boring."

"It is," Blanche agreed as she tried to swallow and talk at the same time. "Totally boring. Nice bracelet," she added, steering the conversation toward the delicate piece of jewelry on Miss Evelyn's arm.

It wasn't just a nice bracelet. It was a beautiful bracelet. There were three burnished gold strips woven together like a braid and set in breathtaking pink diamonds. An intricate scroll covered the bands that I assumed was decorative, but on closer inspection I realized they were words. Words of a language I didn't know... how odd. Miss Evelyn was one big mystery after another.

I leaned forward pretending to examine the bracelet, but really trying to cover up the pieces of chewed cookie that had flown out of Blanche's face when she spoke with her mouth full.

There were definitely words on the jewelry, and I definitely didn't understand them. I glanced up and caught Miss Evelyn's eye. She winked and put her hand back in her lap, effectively hiding the unfamiliar language from me.

"So," Miss Evelyn turned the tables back on us while graciously ignoring Blanche's cookie crumb explosion. "Tell me about yourselves, girls."

Damn, I was a bad liar, but Blanche was worse. I decided to take the reins.

"Well, we just moved here a couple of weeks ago," I said as I tried to figure out how to bypass the particulars.

"From a tropical area," Blanche volunteered.

"Yes... um, very tropical," I cut her off before she announced we were from Hell and Miss Evelyn asked us to leave. Rhonda sat quietly and watched. I kept stealing glimpses at her to see if any more smoke floated out of her nose. Nothing. I was losing it for sure.

"What do your parents do?" Miss Evelyn inquired as she kindly reloaded Blanche's baked goods plate.

I almost choked.

"Well, you know... um, my dad runs kind of... well, I guess you could say, um... a corporation of sorts. And my mom—I don't know my mom," I mumbled, wondering why in the Hell I told her that.

"Oh, I'm sorry." She took my hand and gave it a squeeze. "I'm sure she would be quite proud of you if she knew you."

"Well, maybe." I shrugged my shoulders. "She didn't want me."

"Did your father tell you that?" Miss Evelyn asked sharply. Rhonda huffed and rearranged all the cookies on the tray. It was getting a little bizarre here.

"No," I quickly replied. I'd clearly hit a sore spot with the ladies. Maybe they'd been abandoned too. And my dad never said she didn't want me. He just never said anything. Period. "No," I repeated. "He never talked about her."

She shook her head sadly. "That's too bad."

"Did you get dumped by your mom too?" Blanche asked as she pocketed a few cookies and fed several others to Steve. Where in the Hell did she learn her manners? In a barn?

"No!" Miss Evelyn was taken aback. "Why do you ask?"

"You just seem a little wonky about the whole no mom thing."

"Oh." She shook her head and laughed. Her laughter sent happy shivers of delight through me. "I simply find it unfortunate that families these days can't find ways to stay together."

"Do you have a family?" I asked. A zing of jealousy shot through me as I imagined Miss Evelyn with a bunch of beautiful, well-adjusted children and a handsome husband.

"I do." She sighed happily and clasped her hands to her chest. "I have two lovely daughters."

Envy set fire to my insides and I exerted great effort for my eyes to remain gold. I needed sleep badly. This was ridiculous. I felt like crying about not being included in a family of people I didn't even know.

"Do you see your daughters much?" Blanche asked as she held out her glass to Rhonda for more lemonade. I idly wondered when she'd last eaten. Hell, I didn't even know she could eat.

"Occasionally," Miss Evelyn answered. "It's some of the most precious time I spend. It brings me true joy."

That was all I could take. The walls closed in around me and I needed to breathe fresh air. "We have to go." I stood abruptly and gave Blanche a look.

"We do?" She was surprised and clearly not ready to leave.

"Yep, we do," I insisted tightly, letting her know I meant business. "Thank you for your hospitality, Miss Evelyn and Rhonda," I blurted. "But I have homework and stuff."

"Can't you stay a bit longer?" Miss Evelyn asked.

"No," I bit my lip so I wouldn't cry. Steve whimpered in the corner and Blanche stood up uncertainly.

"Dixie," she pouted while pocketing a few more cookies. I wanted to deck her for her hideous etiquette. "I want to stay."

"Well, you can't," I snapped. *What was wrong with me?* I knew I was being rude, but my need to leave was overwhelming.

"It's okay, Blanche," Miss Evelyn said gently. "You can visit again soon."

"With all due respect, Miss Evelyn," I stated firmly even though my insides quaked. "I'm quite sure we won't be back."

"Dixie," Blanche gasped. "What is wrong with you?"

That was an outstanding question. My behavior was appalling. I only knew being around Miss Evelyn and Rhonda made me want things I could never have. Things I'd longed for my whole life… things I would continue to long for. Always. I couldn't be distracted by this. It was consuming me and making me weak.

I was a Demon Princess. Daughter of Satan and I was here for a reason. I was here to find The Balance of Chaos, The Sword of Death and to kill Rogue Demons. Processing that thought made my stomach roil.

I was not here to turn an old woman into a mother figure, flirt with Angels who have agendas or make friends with mean mortals. I was a Demon. I thrive on chaos, anger, hatred and pain. Acceptance of my nature would only make me stronger.

237

The regret I felt about ending a relationship with Miss Evelyn was physical, but I wasn't here to be happy.

"It's all right, Dixie." Miss Evelyn's voice was soft and soothing. My body involuntarily leaned toward her warmth and light. "I will be here if you'd like to visit again. You are always welcome."

She gently took my face in her hands and pressed her lips to my forehead. I stiffened and backed away. I didn't think witches existed, but the spell she had cast on me felt unmistakably real.

Blanche tentatively stepped to her. "Will you hug me goodbye?"

"Of course." Miss Evelyn smiled. Her eyes lit up and she took my friend into her arms.

"I need to touch your face," Blanche told her.

Miss Evelyn hesitated and put an arm's length between herself and Blanche. It was a bizarre standoff and I was lost. Rhonda moved to Miss Evelyn's side with a grunt.

"No, Rhonda, it's necessary. I invite you in," she told Blanche.

What in the Hell was going on? My feet were rooted to the floor as I watched a surreal episode of *The Twilight Zone* unfold. Something bad was about to go down, but I couldn't for the life of me figure out what. The danger was real. I was unsure if it was life threatening or life changing, but I'd already had a shitty day and one more bit of crazy was not going to work for me.

Rhonda and Miss Evelyn definitely had some magic hoodoo going on. It wasn't Demonic or Angelic, but I was now positive it wasn't mortal either. The simple fact that they could see Blanche was a dead giveaway.

Why didn't I listen to Blanche? These crazy old women were probably going to grind us up and turn us into brownies. My gut screamed to tell Blanche not to touch her, but my mouth stayed silent.

Rhonda took my friend's hand and placed it on Miss Evelyn's cheek. Blanche's skin began to glow and a silver mist swirled around her. Her sharp intake of breath, followed by violent shaking ended my silence.

"No," I shouted as I tried to pull her away.

Rhonda blocked my path as Blanche continued to convulse.

"Stop it," I screamed and clawed at Rhonda. "You're hurting her."

Miss Evelyn stood serenely with her eyes closed while she killed my friend. Rhonda's grip on me was insane. She was a Mack truck. My fury spiked and I fought Rhonda like a rabid animal. Sparks of red and lavender flew from my fingertips mixing with Blanche's silver mist, creating an alarming light show of magic that should have scared the old women to death. They ignored it.

I wanted to kill them. However, somewhere in my subconscious I knew that was wrong.

Blanche collapsed at Miss Evelyn's feet. Her body still convulsed. A fury like I'd never felt consumed me and a chant in a language I didn't know flowed seamlessly from my lips. Hot flashes of rage burned in my gut and the chant turned vicious. Much to my shock and delight all several hundred pounds of Rhonda went flying across the room. She slammed against the wall with a sickening thud and I threw my body over Blanche's.

"Don't any of you touch her," I ground out through clenched teeth. "She's done nothing to hurt you. If you touch her again I'll…"

"Dixie." Blanche was shaken and her voice was weak. "Stop. They're not hurting me."

She began to fade away.

"No, no, no." I shook my head as tears threatened. "Don't you dare disappear on me now."

"It's okay," she whispered. "Miss Evelyn is good. Weird, but good." A small laugh escaped her lips. "We're not going to end up as baked goods."

"Blanche." I pressed her transparent body to my own. All

thoughts of anyone else in the room ceased to exist. "You can't leave me. I need you."

"Dixie, I'm your fate. I take you where you need to be. Trust me, you're supposed to be here. You are so much stronger than you think. Believe me."

"If I'm supposed to be here, you have to stay with me," I insisted desperately. The tightening in my chest made it hard to breathe.

"I will be back very soon." Her voice faltered and she shook her head sadly. "These women are important. And guess what?" She grinned. "We were right—they're not quite mortal."

"What are they?" I looked up and locked eyes with Miss Evelyn.

"Everything will reveal itself when it's supposed to. Don't even say it," she cut me off before I could explode. "There are too many rules in this damn game." She giggled faintly as she began to fade away. "Stay true."

She was gone.

I sat motionless on the floor and stared at the spot where Blanche had been, willing her to come back. She knew who or what Miss Evelyn and Rhonda were and she couldn't tell me. And I'd bet my eternally damned soul these ladies weren't going to talk.

"I don't know what Blanche meant," I said cautiously as I ran my fingers through the glittering silver dust on the floor. "But if she trusts you… I will give you the benefit of the doubt."

I raised my eyes to Miss Evelyn's and a sense of peace washed through me. Rhonda helped me to my feet.

"Are you okay?" I asked Rhonda, worried that I may have broken some of her bones or cracked her skull. "I thought you guys were, you know… killing her."

Rhonda gave me a big toothy smile. "I'm fine, child. That was one heck of a body slam though," she grunted and rubbed her neck.

How she wasn't dead was beyond me, but Blanche said they were not mortal. What in the Hell were they? They were old, so they couldn't be immortal. Clearly there was another species I didn't know about. That would explain the language on Miss Evelyn's bracelet.

"I'm really sorry, Rhonda," I told her. "I'll try not to throw you across the room anymore," I added lamely.

She belly laughed. "Aww sweetie, I gotta say I enjoyed it. Not many people can give me a run for my money. It makes me real proud of you."

"Okay… well, thanks." A compliment was a compliment, no matter how bizarre.

I glanced around Miss Evelyn's trashed home and winced. I was as bad as my therapy group in their heyday. I wished Stella was here to restore the house… wait a minute. I could do it!

"Miss Evelyn, would you like me to clean up the mess I made?" I asked, halfway hoping she'd decline my offer.

"That would be lovely, dear."

Craptastic… Here goes nothing. I took a huge breath and closed my eyes. I'd never done this before, but how hard could it be? For Satan's sake, I could freeze people, throw Mack trucks around and blow up tables and refrigerators. Certainly I could use a little magic to clean a room.

I began to chant the same one I'd used earlier. I wasn't sure what I was saying but it felt good and right. It was interesting to know that I could create magic without anger. As the chant grew the energy of the room whirled and crackled around me. My hair blew wildly around my head tickling my nose. Steve barked as her wagging tail beat against my leg. An intense excitement coursed through my body and I heard Miss Evelyn and Rhonda giggle with delight. I felt happy and light. Behind my closed lids, fireworks burst in a rainbow of sparkling colors. As my chant continued, I idly wondered what the Hell language I was speaking, but it felt so good I didn't care.

I was done.

I opened my eyes and gasped in dismay. The glitter was gone and the hole in the wall from Rhonda's crash was repaired, but all was not well. I had cleaned the room, but I also completely rearranged it. The chairs were on the coffee table, the pillows sat atop the television, the couch cushions were backwards and oh so much more…

"Holy Hell," I moaned. "I am so sorry."

"Oh my." Miss Evelyn laughed joyously. "That was wonderful."

Was she on crack? Rhonda was laughing so hard she snorted. It wasn't cute. I ran around the room and tried to right all my wrongs. I was so embarrassed I wanted to die.

"Dixie, Dixie." Miss Evelyn grabbed me around my waist and turned me to face her. "It's the little things. Enjoy the little things." She smiled and gave me a quick peck on the cheek.

I stood still and my mortification slowly melted away. She was right. I looked around the room and I saw the humor of it. It was funny. I took a deep breath and smiled. As my smile grew broader and I owned the ridiculousness of the room I'd created… I giggled.

"Just take life a moment at a time," she whispered in my ear.

"Yes." I moved into her embrace. "A moment at a time."

CHAPTER TWENTY-EIGHT

I GOT HOME AND SLEPT FOR FOURTEEN HOURS. WHEN I AWOKE AT ten the next morning Myrtle was curled up next to me. Janet was sound asleep in the chair next to the bed and Carl snored lightly in a makeshift sleeping bag on the floor. So much for going to class today.

I carefully sat up and looked at my little family who had come to Earth willing to die for me. My breath hitched and my eyes welled up with tears. As out of control as my life was spinning, I knew I was lucky. Starting today all of the pity parties were over. I would be ready to protect my little tribe and make my father proud.

Blanche's absence made my heart hurt, but I was beginning to understand the pattern. She was my guide, leading me where she knew it was necessary. I was unclear how the old women figured in, but I didn't doubt that they would.

The world and the people around me were somehow instrumental in why I was here. I was positive that Eden, Kentucky had not been a random choice by my father. With no direction book and only my twenty-one year old wits to guide me, I had a feeling that my path was being dictated by those around me… or at the very least they were providing clues. It frustrated the Hell out of me that everything and everyone was so damn cryptic, but that was the way of the immortal world. I could learn or burn. I decided to learn.

The pieces were clicking quickly and I knew the darkness loomed close. Instead of scaring me, I felt invigorated and excited.

I was having a difficult time wrapping my brain around how Thing One, Thing Two, Thing Three and Thing Four could be anything but annoying, but I wasn't going to question anymore. They had to be connected to the dance. The dance from Heaven and Hell… how hideously appropriate.

I also realized why my dad had forbade any contact with Hell. There was no way I would have come this far on my own if I'd had a major support system. Hayden, Stella and Sloth would have caught me every time I fell. I would be no stronger or wiser with that kind of help. I was still angry with Satan but I understood.

Myrtle's small hand clasped mine. "Are you feeling better?" she asked in a sleepy voice.

"I'm not sure." I wrinkled my brow in confusion. "I don't remember crawling into bed last night."

"You didn't." Myrtle rolled over and stretched. "You walked in the front door and collapsed. Carl carried you up."

Well, that explained why I was still dressed in the clothes I'd worn yesterday. Janet opened her eyes and smiled while Carl snored and snuggled deeper into his thrown together bed.

I patted the space beside me. Janet bounced over and hopped in next to me. I hugged her tight and dragged Myrtle over with my other hand.

"What the… " Myrtle groaned as I pressed her close to my side.

Carl's bald head popped up at the end of the bed, a big grin splitting his sweet face. "Can I join the love fetht?" Damn, his dimples were cute.

"Yes, you can." I grinned, then moaned in agony as I realized he was shirtless. "Oh, Sweet Underworld Carl, please tell me you're wearing pants."

He chuckled and raised a hot pink terry cloth covered leg. I rolled my eyes and made room for my dear, hairy, style-impaired friend.

"I'm starting to figure the clusterfuck out," I told them.

"Lucifer's Bouncing Balls." Janet laughed. "You already knew what you needed to know."

I reached down and checked myself for balls. Thankfully there were none to be found.

"The'th right," Carl added, giving me a noogie like a third grade boy. "And The Kev and Gemma will be coming today." He continued his noogie fest.

"Quit it, Carl." I smacked his hand away and tried to noogie him back. "The Fairies are coming?"

"Yep."

He laughed and dodged me, cracking his bald noggin on the headboard and knocking Myrtle to the floor. Janet shrieked with joy and began jumping on the bed.

"Damn it to Hell," Myrtle yelled. "You people need to act your age."

She crawled back up on the bed, knocked Janet's feet out from under her, effectively ending her trampoline time while simultaneously popping Carl in the back of the head. She was good.

"Janet's correct." Myrtle's voice was calm with certainty. "You already have everything you need. Put it together." She smoothed out the comforter and shoved Carl off the bed. "You're shedding," she informed him.

Ewww. I threw myself back onto the mountain of pillows. My mind registered the significance of her words. I knew it was time. "Are you sure?"

"Yes, I am sure that Carl is getting chest hair all over your sheets," she replied matter of factly.

"No," I snapped. "Are you sure I already have everything I need?"

My mind reeled and my stomach clenched with excitement. Who cared if I couldn't restore Miss Evelyn's room correctly? Did it really matter that I blew up tables and fridges? No, it didn't. I did protect Lucy from her awful father and I healed Steve with my tears. I kept waiting in vain for everything to come together... to feel powerful and knowledgeable and to understand what in the Hell was expected of me.

Waiting was for weenies. There was no more time to wait.

"Dixthie," Carl said as he tried to help Myrtle remove his chest fur from my bed. "You have to trutht yourthelf. Find your balanth." The chest hair was going nowhere fast. "You have the thkillth we taught you, you chant in a language we've never heard and you potheth Black Magic."

"You know I have Black Magic?" My eyes narrowed dangerously. No one was supposed to know. Carl blanched and backed away.

"Oh sweetie." Janet giggled. "You can freeze Demons, and your strength in a matter of a couple of weeks has quadrupled." She tucked my hair behind my ears and placed her soft little hands on my hot cheeks. "Regular Demons can't do that—only the strongest Demons with Black Magic are capable of such power so quickly."

I sucked in a huge breath and blew it out slowly. "I'm a True Immortal," I said. My heart pounded in my ears. It was the first time I'd said the words aloud.

"It's about time," Myrtle shouted.

"Why is it so important I figure it out for myself?" I asked as I rolled my eyes. "Will we really turn to dust if the story gets told before its time?"

Myrtle sat back and clasped her small hands in her lap. "Honestly, we really don't know about the dust thing, but it would suck ass if it was true. The real reason has to do with destiny as opposed to pre-destiny."

"Explain."

"If you knew you were a True Immortal because we told you, you would have done things in a different order and screwed up destiny's timeline. You are the master of your destiny and you have to determine how it plays out."

"Do you already know what's coming or what will happen?" I asked, feeling stronger and more powerful with each passing second.

"No, but it's coming soon," she said and the other two nodded.

"I come from here," I said. "This is where I was born. It's why it feels familiar and it's why my father sent me back here."

"I think you're right," Janet said.

"There was an old lady who told me a story about a little girl named Dixie who died. That was me." I stood and paced. Was that little old lady my mother? She certainly didn't seem like someone my father would have mated with, but what the Hell did I know? It felt wrong, but I was going back there to find out. "Shit, as I figure it out, the ball starts rolling faster," I muttered. "Will this mean all the Angels and Demons will descend and wreak havoc?" Shitdamndamnballs. Again, I checked for balls...

"Relax your crack," Myrtle rolled her eyes and scooted over next to me. "Very few immortals, Demonic or Angelic, can destroy you... but you, on the other hand, can do a buttload of damage to them."

"It really would have been fucking awesome to have known this a little earlier." I shook my head in disgust.

Myrtle shrugged and grinned. I wanted to slap her. "Why do you think your father sent us with you?"

"So you could drive me insane?"

"Nooo," Janet clapped her hands together in glee. Her cackle bounced around the room. I bit my lip to hide my smile. "Our gifts are different from other Demons," she continued. "It's why we were shunned in Hell."

"We are caretakerth." Carl climbed back on the bed, gauging

my mood with caution. "Ath you can imagine, thath not a great quality for a Demon."

I nodded and waited.

"We can read the intentions and powers of others," Janet's voice changed. For the first time I was aware of her true age. "That's a dangerous power to have." All of her mirth disappeared. "Most of our kind have been destroyed."

"We behaved like circus show freaks in Hell," Myrtle explained. "We were dismissed as weak, stupid and inconsequential. It was our cover."

Wait," I interrupted as I tried to piece their story together. "Why were you in therapy with me? Was that a set up?" I gasped. My head swirled with doubt and distrust.

"No!" Carl bellowed. "No thet up." He rubbed his bald head, a sure sign of distress. "Dixthie, we have been athigned to you from birth. We were created hundredth of yearth ago for you."

"We never knew our purpose until you were brought to Hell." Janet grasped my arm, determined to make me understand. "When I saw you as a beautiful little toddler, it was the greatest day of my life."

"We've stayed hidden most of our lives," Myrtle said quietly. "To be recognized by our Lord and King as protectors to his most beloved child is an honor beyond anything we could have hoped or imagined for ourselves."

"We love you, Dixthie," Carl added shyly. "We will protect you and die for you."

"So the volunteering in Hell to come with me to Earth?"

"Was just for show, in case any traitors were in the midst," Janet said.

"Therapy?" I asked.

"So you could know us better," Myrtle said.

I was speechless. As the pieces of my life puzzle clicked together I wanted to laugh. I stared at the three Demons waiting patiently on the bed for my reaction. My brain was racing with whys, hows, what ifs and WTFs. I took a deep breath and in a moment of both perfect calm and utter insanity... I decided to just go with it. One moment at a time.

"I love you guys too," I told them.

"Thank Satan!" Janet giggled, expelling the breath she'd been holding. "Now that we have all that sorted out, there's something odd I've noticed in Eden, Kentucky. The mortals here are not what they seem."

"What do you mean?" I asked, hoping she could shed some light on Miss Evelyn and Rhonda.

"I haven't been able to put my finger on it." She sighed unhappily.

"Is there a species on Earth that I don't know about?" I turned to Myrtle, the Keeper of Secrets. If anyone knew, she did.

"Shifters," she said and my brain clicked so hard it hurt. "Mortals are mortals, but I do believe some of them possess significant magic."

"Demonic or Angelic?" I asked.

"Neither," she replied as she shrugged her shoulders.

I ran my hands through my tangled hair and realized I had a few very important visits to make today.

"So," I said, examining the remarkable amount of chest hair on my comforter, "I have several people I need to surprise today. Is there anything else we should be doing?"

"We keep doing what we've been doing... going to school, fight training, planning the dance, having sex in the science closet with Timmy." She smirked, but then on a dime turned deadly serious. "I believe the trouble will come to us. We don't need to look for it."

"Eden is neutral territory," I reminded her as I wondered if I was going to have to throw my bedding away. I suppose I could take it outside and beat it before I washed it.

"Neutral won't mean anything to pure evil. They will come," Carl said, getting off my bed and putting on a t-shirt. Why in

Satan's name couldn't he have covered the hair rug on his chest before he shed all over my bed?

"He's right," Janet added disgustedly. "True evil plays by no rules."

"Everybody off the bed," I instructed. "I don't want to set any of you on fire."

"What in the Hell are you going to do?" Myrtle asked, wasting no time removing herself from my bed.

"I'm going to use Black Magic to get rid of the massive gift from Carl that's covering my sheets and making me want to hurl." I eyeballed Carl who sheepishly grinned. "If I'm gonna save the world, I'd better be able to clean a comforter."

"Holy Baby Beelzebub." Janet was in a panic. "Be careful and don't blow up the house."

She plastered herself against the wall and began inching her way towards the door.

"Janet, if you try to leave this room I will freeze you and zap you bald," I calmly informed her.

She stopped and gave me a guilty smile. "Sorry," she whispered contritely.

"No prob."

I closed my eyes and began to chant, but this time it was different. I narrowed all the thoughts in my mind to encompass exactly what I wanted to happen. I let myself completely relax... I trusted myself.

I continued to chant and tried something else new. I opened my eyes. Maybe if I watched what I was doing, it might go a little better.

A glittering black mist mixed with lavender and gold engulfed my bed. It smelled of citrus and wind. It tickled and I scrunched my nose to stifle the sneeze that was threatening to escape. Myrtle, Janet and Carl's eyes were wide with anticipation and a healthy dose of fear. I laughed with delight and reached out to run my hands through the mist. It was warm and silky.

I felt right and strong and joyous. I closed my eyes, raised my arms and stopped chanting. As good as I felt, I hesitated to open my eyes.

"Is it gone?" At the very least, I knew I hadn't blown up the house. I would have heard that.

"Yeth!" Carl shouted, tackling and tickling me.

I opened my eyes and screamed, trying to swat Carl away. Janet ran across the room and started bouncing on my clean hairless bed. It was utter chaos and I loved it.

"I'm so proud of you," Janet trilled, jumping so high she touched the ceiling with each bounce.

I glanced over at Myrtle. She stood quietly against the wall, arms crossed with a wide, open smile on her pretty face. "You done good, my friend."

Satisfaction and pride burst through me. I was happier than I'd been since coming to Earth.

"Myrtle, are shifters immortal?"

"Not sure. Why?"

"I was just curious."

"We can teach you many things." Myrtle approached the jump-fest on my bed. "But the trust part is all you. This may seem small," she said as she referred to the hairless bedding. "However it's really quite monumental. You can do what needs to be done as long as you trust yourself and believe."

The room quieted and my friends curled up with me. A cool calm floated through my mind and for the first time I knew I could do it. Do what? I still had no real clue, but it was coming and I would be waiting. And I would win. Maybe Dad had picked the right Demon...

Eventually the Rogue Demons would arrive and wreak havoc. They wanted to kill God and Satan. They were currently in possession of the Sword of Death. That was going to change.

The Balance of Chaos was still a mystery to me. Was it a thing or a person or a state of mind? Maybe killing the Rogue Demons would restore the balance between good and evil. Could it be that simple? Not that killing Rogue Demons would be easy... And Cole? He was a sneaky fucker and I was sure he wasn't clean. Elijah? Another problem along with Miss Evelyn and Rhonda. They were part of the puzzle. But first things first.

"I have to go see a girl about a dog," I said as I eased off the bed and headed for the shower.

"Are we supposed to understand that?" Janet asked.

"Nope." I grinned. "It's my turn to be cryptic."

CHAPTER TWENTY-NINE

SHE WAS EASY TO FIND AS SHE FLITTED FROM THE ENGLISH BUILDING to the science labs. I wondered where her minions were, but it was far better to catch her alone. She adjusted a huge banner advertising the upcoming dance. *"Get your boogie on at the Heaven vs Hell on Earth Dance"* was block printed in black and red. I rolled my eyes at the utter unorginality, but what did I expect?

Most of the students had cleared the area and gone to class. Instinctually I scanned the grounds for danger. I was expecting a visit from Elijah soon. There was no way he wasn't going to show himself again. The campus was calm and I quietly approached Lucy from behind.

"Hey Steve," I said. "How you doing?"

Lucy froze.

"I was wondering if you had a moment, *Steve.*"

She turned and grinned. "Took you long enough," she said as she looped her arm through mine and led us away from campus to a clump of trees.

I shook my head and removed her hand. "Were you going to tell me?"

"I was a little afraid because of the turning to dust rumor," she said as she plopped down on the ground at the base of a tree.

"That one's a bitch," I agreed. "Where are the Things?"

"Things?"

"Your fan club."

"Oh my God." She burst out laughing. "You named them the Things?"

"Yes. I did. It was far too complicated to remember their actual names. Where are they?"

"Well," she said, still laughing. "They found some tiny people and went car shopping."

My stomach descended to my toes. I dropped down to the ground next to Lucy and grabbed her by the shoulders. "What did the tiny people look like?" I demanded.

"Um… they were very cute in a hideous way. I'd have to say they looked like some of the characters from that show *Friends*. The other two looked like Abe Lincoln and Beyonce."

"Shit," I yelled. "Text the Things and tell them under no circumstances can they go to a car dealership or a strip club."

"Why?"

"They're baby Demons and they like to eat car salesmen," I snapped. I'd forgotten about my cousin's little friends. This was bad. Lucy quickly and frantically texted the girls to explain.

"Done. It's fine." She heaved a huge sigh of relief. "And just so you know there are no strip clubs in Eden."

"How is it fine? How in the Hell will humans understand salesmen-eating baby Demons from Hell?" I stood and paced a tight circle around the tree. Astrid was going to have my butt. However it was good news to know I didn't have to worry about strip clubs.

"They're not mortal. Most of us in Eden are not human."

That stopped me.

"You're all shifters?"

"Yep. And you're a Demon."

"Can you tell by scent?" I asked her.

"No. It was when you saved my life."

"You knew I was in the room with you and your dad?" What kind of *sight* did these shifters have?

"No. No, I didn't know you were there. It was outside the shop when I had shifted to my wolf."

Hades, so much was making sense now—her healing and my feelings of paranoia about her knowledge.

"Dixie, you did save me."

"I just screwed with your father," I muttered. "He's a real asshole, by the way."

"True, but that's not what I meant," she said quietly.

The click was fast and it was painful. Hayden hadn't come for a wolf at all. He'd come for Lucy and he let me have her. Why did he let me keep her if it was her time to go?

"Lucy, if Hayden—I mean the Angel of Death, let you stay it means I need you."

"I figured—that's why I've kept following you. What's happening?" she asked as she paled a little. "That hot dude you crashed into the other day was an Angel, wasn't he?"

"Yep. And the dude who let you stay was an Angel."

"And your boyfriend?" she asked with raised brows and a smirk.

"Something like that," I admitted.

"Angels are hot. I would so date an Angel."

"Beware of what you wish for," I told her. "Can I ask you something else?"

"Sure."

"Why did you hate me so much in the beginning?"

"I was jealous... not of how pretty you are or anything so superficial. I'm not even sure I can find the words to explain. It was deep and it hurt. I still don't understand it."

I watched her inner struggle and I believed her. We were connected and I was going to find out how.

255

"Have you ever fought a Demon?" I asked. What good would she be to me if I got her killed?

"I'm not just a pretty face," she snapped and tossed her blonde hair. "I've never had the opportunity to fight a Demon, but I'm deadly around Rogue shifters."

"Are there Rogues in every freakin' species?"

Of course there were. That was how balance was met. The problems cropped up when evil or good outweighed each other. My guess was that evil was winning at the moment... but why?

"Looks that way," she said as she stood and shifted back and forth on her feet. "What's next?"

"Do the Things know about me?"

"No. For some reason I told no one about you."

"Good," I said as I grabbed her arm and led her to my car. "Let's pay a visit to your owner."

She blanched and violently pulled her arm from my grasp. Damn she was strong. "I won't go to my father. Never again."

"I wasn't talking about your father, I was talking about Miss Evelyn and Rhonda."

She paused and tilted her head to the side. "I only met the old ladies two weeks ago when they showed up. They don't own me."

WTH? Just when things start adding up they begin to fall apart. Shit. "But I assumed... "

"Don't assume—makes an ass out of you and me." She giggled and punched me in the arm.

"Oh my Hell." I groaned and punched her back. "You're a dork. Why did you go to them then? I wanted to keep you."

"I can leave them and shift back to my human version. I wouldn't have been able to do that as easily with you. You seemed kind of needy." She grinned and shrugged. I wanted to deck her, but she was correct. "Plus, there's something about them that I'm wildly attracted to. Especially Miss Evelyn."

I was wildly attracted too.

"She has two daughters," I mumbled and then grabbed my head as the headache blossomed quickly.

"Are you okay?" She gasped as I dropped to my knees.

"Been better," I shot back sarcastically as the pain in my head slowly receded.

"How do you know she has two daughters?"

"She told me."

"And you think we... "

"Yes, I think," I hissed. "And if there was any doubt the explosion in my cranium has put it to rest."

"Oh my God. You're my *sister*? Who's your dad?"

"Satan."

She paled considerably and I laughed. "According to most he's really hot and he's not as evil as reported. Oh, and while we're dissecting family trees... my other sisters are the Seven Deadly Sins."

"Fuck to the no," she choked out. "I'm related to the Seven Deadly Sins?"

"Technically no, but you can certainly have them if you want them. They're a pain in my ass."

"This is a lot to take in," she whispered.

"Yep." I grinned. "And that's only the beginning."

CHAPTER THIRTY

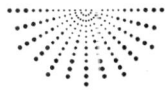

"She left? That's impossible," I told the little chicken-eating senior citizen, Miss Sally. "She didn't say goodbye."

"Oh sweetienumnum, I'm so sorry. Was she your grandma?" she asked kindly.

"No. She was just someone I think I used to know."

What did I do now? Lucy stood trembling beside me. *Was she going to cry?*

"Did Miss Evelyn or Rhonda leave a forwarding address?" she inquired icily. She wasn't going to cry. She was furious.

"Um no, little one. I'm afraid she didn't," Miss Sally said, either ignoring Lucy's ire or not noticing it. "I have to go to pottery class. Would you pretty gals like to join me?"

"No, but thanks. We have to go."

"Well, come back and see me, Dixie." She sighed and shook her head. "Such a tragedy. That little girl died too young."

"She's nuts," Lucy hissed in my ear.

"Isn't everyone?" I shot back. As Miss Sally wandered away, I called out to her. "How did little Dixie die?"

"She was taken by Angels—two of them. I saw it. They fought with each other like the Devil himself. The golden winged one beat the black winged one. The golden Angel won and he flew away with her. No one believes me, but I saw it."

"What the fuck?" Lucy mumbled and I elbowed her.

"Was the child scared?" I asked.

Miss Sally considered me for a moment to decide if I was making fun of her. She shook her head in confusion. "No. She wrapped her little arms around his neck, kissed his cheek and laid her head on his chest. Her poor mother saw the whole thing. She stood there paralyzed and cried. Eve was a good woman. She just broke after the Angels took her baby."

Miss Sally gave us a wave and walked away. My heart constricted and black spots danced in front of my eyes. I'd bet my Immortal life that Elijah had black wings and that Hayden was the Angel who took me to Hell. And my mother was Eve. Eve was one of the True Immortals. Was she *that* Eve?

"Your last name?" I asked Lucy.

"Adams," she said slowly.

"Coincidence?"

"I don't think so," she ground out as her body continued to shake. "Why would she leave me with that monster? Screw her. She left me and let some psycho Angels steal you. Fuck her." Her tears flowed freely and I realized I was missing a piece of Lucy's puzzle. I wasn't ready to deal with the abstract of our mother's abandonment of us, so I'd stick to fact finding.

"How old are you?"

She looked at me like I was nuts. "In the upper thousands somewhere. I lost track hundreds of years ago."

It was hard to throw me, but she did. "You've lived in Eden for thousands of years?"

"I told you, we're shifters. Immortal shifters. This is where you live if you're a freak like me," she snapped. "Mortals rarely come here, and if they do they don't stay. We don't have to explain ourselves."

"Community college?"

"We get bored. We have to do something. I sold real estate for a while and I tried to be an actress in Hollywood back in the thirties, but when people noticed I didn't age I had to come back here." She sighed and chewed on her lips. "How old are you?"

"Twenty-one."

"You're shitting me." Her eyes grew wide and she threw her hands up. "For real?"

"Yep."

"And you're gonna save the world?"

"Yep."

She paused for at least a minute, shrugged her shoulders and then smirked. "Well, all right then. Let's go."

I began to walk to my car with Lucy, *my sister*, close on my heels.

"Where are we going now?" she asked.

"To hang with some Fairies."

"Fairies are real?" she asked doubtfully.

"As real as shifters, Demons and Vampyres."

"Vampyres are real too?" She came to an abrupt halt and smacked herself in the forehead. Her blonde hair flew around her head like a halo.

"Dude." I grinned. "For being older than dirt, you sure don't know very much."

She nodded her head in agreement. "I gotta get out more," she muttered and pushed me toward the car. "Do Fairies bite?"

"No, not that I know of, but I hear they punch like a freight train."

"Cool."

I shook my head and laughed. Weird was weird, but my life was turning insane.

CARL AND THE KEV TANGOED ACROSS THE BACK YARD DRESSED IN brightly colored sequined dresses while Gemma painted Janet and Myrtle's fingernails. The baby Demons were thankfully back and they jumped around the fray, pummeling each other happily as they grunted out a bizarre rhythm for the tango. Just another normal day at my house.

"Which ones are the Fairies?" Lucy asked as she tried to take it all in.

"The one who looks like the Terminator in a gown and the gorgeous one doing the manicures. The rest are Demons, but you already knew about Myrtle."

"Is she really your cousin?"

"Nope, but I love her like family and I'll kill anyone who screws with her," I told Lucy as I pulled her into the circus.

"Krumecaca," The Kev yelled with delight as he dipped Carl. Carl squealed as he righted himself and slid slowly into the splits. "And look! You brought your sister!"

Everyone shrieked, froze and frantically examined their bodies.

"It's okay, guys," I reassured them. "I already knew. No one is turning to dust... yet." I eyed The Kev distrustfully. "You sure are a deadly fountain of info."

His grin was contagious and I looked down to hide my smile. Fairies were something else altogether.

"Can I tell you a little secret?" he asked.

"Will I live through it, big guy?" I shot back.

He threw back his head and laughed heartily. "If you added a few curses I would have mistaken you for Astrid."

"Astrid?" Lucy asked.

"My foul mouthed, kickass, take no prisoners, pregnant Vampyre cousin," I explained as I preened under The Kev's compliment.

"What's the secret?" I asked.

He pulled me to the far corner of the massive yard and

narrowed his eyes. He made me uncomfortable, but I knew he was a premeditated man. He wasn't about to tell me something I didn't need to know.

"The turning to dust thing. It's bullshit."

"What?" I shouted as the crowd in the distance winced. "You have got to be fucking kidding me. Why in the Hell... ?"

"Shhhh." The Kev put his finger to his lips and winked. "If there was no need for the story it would not exist—would it?"

"Why are you telling me?" I snapped. My life would have been a whole Hell of a lot easier if everyone, good and bad, had been able to clue me in.

"How can we balance anything if there are no repercussions? Why should it be necessary to hold the future and destiny sacred? Why, little True Immortal? Why would that be important?"

I was still stuck on the fact that the dust story was false and that everyone believed it. Who even started it? The Fairies? The Kev stood quietly and waited for my answer. I knew it was a test —a huge one. However I also knew I would pass.

"Because I create my own destiny. Any one of us, no matter how powerful, could be controlled by someone or something else unless we let destiny play out in its own time. But how do you know I won't screw with people—change destiny now that I know the secret?"

The Kev squatted down until we were nose to nose. "Because you are Balance, Dixie. That is your job. All True Immortals have one: God is Good, Satan is Evil, Mother Nature is Emotion, your Grandfather is Wisdom, The Angel of Light is Life, The Angel of Death is Death, Astrid is Compassion and you are Balance."

"Holy Hell, The Kev, that was one overload of info, but you forgot someone. What is my mother?"

"What do you think your mother is?" he asked as he pulled me farther away and led me to a stone bench in a grove of flowering trees.

"A nightmare? A craptastic parent? How am I supposed to

know what the Hell her job is? All I've ever heard is that she hasn't been doing it well."

"Sometimes people become incapable of what they are asked to do. What do you think of her?" he asked.

"Are you everywhere?" I asked. "How do you know I know who she is?"

He expelled a sigh. "My life is nothing like yours or any other Immortal you know," he said wearily. "Secrets cannot be hidden from me—dreams, wishes, desires. This is not a bonus. It is a burden. Until I found Gemma, my life was one of vast painful emptiness and very soon I will have to fight for her very existence."

"How is that fair?" I demanded. I barely knew the crazy man sitting in front of me, but he touched me deeply and I knew he was good.

"Be careful, child," he advised. "I am not all good nor am I all evil. I am a person who gets done what needs to be done. Do not elevate me or anyone to more than what they are."

I considered his words and I understood, but it still made me sad. "When the time comes to fight for her, I will be there if you need me."

He was taken aback by my words and pulled me into an embrace I never wanted to leave. He was beautiful, kind and fair. I knew for certain there was no such thing as good or evil in its purest sense, and the desire to attain it was impossible and wrong.

"I will remember your words, Balance. Your time draws near and the stakes are high. Your success will depend on looking at all sides with clear eyes."

"Um, since we both know the dust thingie isn't true... you wanna let loose with a little more?" I asked as innocently as I could without giggling.

"The dust *thingie* was created for a reason, little one. Just because you know we'll live through it, do you really want to know my version of the future when you still have the ability to change it—make it yours?"

Damn, I was so tempted I itched, but he was right.

"Is there anything else you can tell me without fucking with the future?"

"Astrid will be so proud of your mouth," he said as he contemplated my request. "The Balance of Chaos is not an abstract notion. It breathes and is temptation personified."

"Hmmm. A little vague, but more than I knew a few seconds ago, Fairy Man." I leaned in and kissed his cheek. "Are you gonna punch me like you punched Astrid?"

"Heavens no! I trained Carl over seventy-five years ago. His instruction is outstanding!"

"You trained Carl?" I was flabbergasted.

"I have trained many. Have a chat with your father or uncle sometime," he said as he grabbed my hand and pulled me back into my yard of warped reality. I shook my head in disbelief. Fairies were nuts and I liked them. A lot.

"You okay?" Myrtle asked as she offered snacks to our guests. I hoped like Hell she hadn't prepared them. She was a disaster in the kitchen.

"I'm good."

"Lucy's your sister?"

"Looking that way." I grinned and shrugged. "And Timmy your boyfriend is a wolf shifter?"

"Oh no," she whispered. "He's a bear shifter, and I can't even begin to tell you the things a bear can do with its tongue."

"Please don't," I begged as I made a quick escape. I'd thought all shifters were wolves. Don't *assume*. I found Lucy off on the side of the yard by herself.

"Do you want me to stay here?" Lucy asked, not making eye contact.

"Where have you been sleeping?" I asked, knowing she wasn't going home to her father anymore.

"My car," she answered.

"Then yes. You now live here. Period," I stated as a look of relief washed over her features. "Why didn't you stay with a Thing?"

"They're vultures."

"Yeah. And?"

"No, I mean they're seriously vultures. They shift to vultures, and when they're not at school they usually take their bird form and sleep in caves." She wrinkled her nose in disgust.

"I can see how that wouldn't appeal," I muttered. "Why are you friends with vultures?"

"I got bored with the wolves and bears and lions. The vultures showed up about a year ago and they make good little followers." She laughed.

"You like having followers?"

"Breaks up the monotony," she said.

"I suppose. Do you remember the little girl named Dixie?" I asked.

"Kind of. I was climbing Mt. Everest for a couple of years back then."

"Years?"

"Yeah." She chuckled. "I could do it in a day, so I had to figure out ways not to freak all the mortal climbers out. It was a blast. I almost got hitched to a sherpa, but it would suck to outlive someone and there are just too many questions when they get older and you don't. It was colder than a witch's tit, but beautiful. Oh my God, do witches exist? Wait, what the Hell did you ask me? I forgot."

"Do you remember little Dixie? And I have no clue if witches exist."

"They do and they're mean as snakes," The Kev yelled from across the yard as he examined the snack Myrtle had insisted he eat.

"Thanks," I yelled back.

"Damn, his hearing is good," Lucy said appreciatively.

"My question?" I reminded her.

"Right. I remember a little girl died and there was no body. I had no clue you were a Demon. I thought you were a shifter. I vaguely recall a ceremony and a marker placed in the cemetery."

"Eden has a cemetery?" I asked with an excitement that made me tingle.

She looked at me strangely and then her eyes lit up. "It's not in Eden proper, it's outside. Immortals don't often have much use for cemeteries."

"It's outside of neutral territory?" This could be risky.

"Yeah." She nodded as she pondered the pros and cons of us visiting territory without safeguards. She closed her eyes and inhaled deeply. "You wanna go?"

"I believe we might find what we're searching for if we do."

"I think you might be right."

"I'm going to transport us," I told her. "It will be faster."

"Is that safe?" she asked as she chewed her lips in distress. "I do recall hearing when I was shifted that you tend to end up places you didn't mean to."

"Yep, I do. You with me?" I grinned and held out my hand—to my sister.

Her own smile matched my grin and she put her hand in mine. "You're crazy, but I'm crazier. Let's go."

CHAPTER THIRTY-ONE

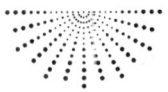

"Is this the right place?" I whispered as I glanced around at the decrepit headstones and overgrown weeds. Early twilight in a graveyard was freaky—even for a Demon.

"This is it. I told you Immortals don't have much use for cemeteries."

"Are there mortals buried here?' I asked as I stepped over the decapitated stone head of an Angel statue.

"No clue. Doesn't smell mortal, but I haven't sniffed a lot of dead ones. Do you think she's here?"

I closed my eyes and quietly chanted. I let my magic fly away from me a bit as I searched for my mother.

"What are you chanting?" Lucy asked as she involuntarily shivered.

"Some dead language," I muttered.

"Do you even know what the Hell you're saying?" she asked, aghast.

"Do you want me to lie?"

She put her head in her hands and tried not to laugh. "Yes."

"Oookay, then I know exactly what I'm saying and exactly

what I'm doing and little monkeys are going to fly out of your ass in twelve seconds."

"You suck," she moaned and checked her backside for primates.

"You looked." I laughed and then froze. "She's here."

Carefully and silently we made our way across the graveyard. The last of the setting sun cast an eerie orange and red glow on the crumbling stone tombs. Our mother sat on a bench next to a large headstone labeled *Dixie* and wept. Rhonda stood beside her. Tendrils of colorful smoke wafted from Rhonda's nose and her eyes glowed purple.

"What in the Hell is Rhonda?"

"If I had to guess I'd say dragon shifter," Lucy whispered unhappily. "I've never seen one before. Most shifters don't believe they exist. They're supposed to be seriously deadly."

"Awesome. Hi Mom," I yelled across the cement jungle. "You forgot to say bye. Again."

"Let her be," Rhonda growled. "She is in pain."

"Like I've been in pain, stuck with my bastard father for thousands of years?" Lucy spat.

"You don't understand," Rhonda insisted and put loving arms around Eve. "I told you to leave. I don't want to have to make you do it," she threatened.

"You can't," I said.

"Do you want to try me?" she asked ominously.

"Do you want to *try* me is the question you should consider," I countered. A very brief flicker of fear shot across Rhonda's face, but I saw it and I smiled. "We aren't here for a bogus family reunion. You already had that with us over the last few weeks. We're here for answers, Mom."

"It's all right, Rhonda. I owe them as much."

Lucy growled and I put my hand on her arm. As much as I hated the woman on the bench, my impulse was to go and comfort her. Was I so desperate for her love and acceptance that I'd become pathetic?

"Who are you?" I demanded.

"I'm Eve, the Balance of Chaos."

My knees buckled and I grabbed onto my sister for purchase. I'd been looking for my mother all along? What kind of sick joke was this? She was the Balance of Chaos and I was Balance? How did that make sense? I glanced around warily. I'd found Chaos. Did that mean the Sword of Death-wielding Rogue Demons weren't far behind? Shit, why didn't I bring the baby Demons? I wanted to do damage, but the feel of my sister's skin beneath my fingertips helped me hold on to the thin shreds of sanity I still possessed.

I closed my eyes and thought and it slowly became more clear. They all knew she wouldn't be able to resist finding me if I came to Earth. My father, grandfather, Mother Nature, the rest of the True Immortals... but who else? How could her presence kill my father and God?

"Balance of Chaos can't be your job. It doesn't work. What's your job?"

"You don't have to tell her anything," Rhonda hissed.

"Are you fucking kidding me?" Lucy yelled. "Shut your Dragon cakehole or I'll shut it for you—with my foot."

If the situation wasn't so wrong I would have laughed at the expression on Rhonda's face. As hard as I tried, I couldn't hold back a snort—neither could Lucy. Much to my amazement and wonder, Rhonda and Eve began to giggle.

"Well, they're certainly your daughters," Rhonda muttered and sat down next to the now grinning Eve. "Go ahead. Show yourself."

Eve began to glow in a vivid haze of pink and gold as she transformed before our eyes into the exquisite woman I'd seen on the porch of the old folks home.

"Blanche and I weren't seeing things," I gasped.

"Who in the Hell is Blanche?" Lucy asked, looking around in alarm.

"She's gone as you knew her," Eve said quietly. "You don't need her anymore."

"You did kill her," I said.

"No. She was here to serve a purpose. You created her and you let her go when you were ready," Eve said.

"I didn't let her go. You turned her to dust," I accused.

"Dixie, she's you. She just won't manifest outside of you anymore because you were ready to take her in and own her. You are now the true master of your destiny and fate."

It made sense, but it made me angry. I created her to replace a lot of the things Eve should have done for me as a mother, but didn't because she wasn't there. However I was grown now and I had a choice… wallow in the past or try to understand the woman who went away.

"Your job?" I asked.

Eve hesitated and wrung her slender fingers. "I control temptation. I am temptation. I feel it and I cause it… thus creating chaos."

"Well, that must suck," Lucy blurted out.

"Why in the Hell would a True Immortal's job be Temptation?" I asked as I approached her. "Why?"

"It keeps good and evil in check. It keeps the thirst alive for wisdom and the need for emotion honest." She bowed her head in shame. "And I have let them all down. I can't do it anymore."

My draw to her made more sense. Everything that should have repulsed me about her was appealing. "Was my father this drawn to you?"

"Yes, and so was his brother." Hmm, that was interesting.

"Were you what caused the rift?"

"I was part of it. There were many more issues than desire for me," she explained.

"And my father?" Lucy demanded.

"I'm sorry." Eve looked away as tears rolled down her lovely cheeks. "I'm so sorry, Lucy."

"Sorry doesn't really cut it, Eve," Lucy said acidly. "However, I'd like to thank you for finally revealing yourself. I will no longer glorify you in my dreams."

Eve was silent, and as harsh as Lucy's statement was I agreed. My mother was weak. Maybe more in Lucy's case than mine, but she was weak. Her Dragon protector now made sense.

"Everyone is looking for you," I told her. "You have fallen down on the job and now some big clusterfuck is looming and I have to fix it."

Her eyes went wide and she gasped. "What?"

"You heard me, Mom. Why have you not done your duty?"

"It hurts," she whispered.

"Tough titty." Lucy shook her head with disgust. "Pain sucks and then you go eat dinner. I've been doing it for thousands of years, Mommy. I don't buy this poor me crap. You're selfish and playing some kind of game, but if my sister... *who I just freakin' found* dies because you're too narcissistic to do your damn job, then I'll kill you."

"We're True Immortals," I whispered to Lucy.

"You can't die?" she asked, relieved.

"Not really, but neither can she."

"Whatever," Lucy snapped. "I'll just fuck her up real good then."

I realized in that moment how bad my sister's existence had been. I'd been without a mother for twenty-one years, but I had a father and sisters and grandparents who loved me in their own warped way. Lucy had none of that. She had nothing, yet she was still here. She still laughed and felt compassion, love and anger. She climbed Mt. Everest and sold real estate... She was amazing and would never be alone again as long as I was around.

"That'll work," I told her and hugged her to me hard.

"One more question, Mommy," Lucy said emotionlessly. "Why did you abandon us?"

Eve shook her head and sighed. "I couldn't take care of you."

"Couldn't or wouldn't?" she snapped.

"I..." Eve was cut off by a violent explosion.

"Motherhumpinshithatscocksuckercrap," a welcome and familiar voice shrieked as the owner fell from the sky in a massive cloud of glitter and sparks. "I am missing *Downton Abbey* for this shit and I'm not happy," Mother Nature shouted as she righted herself. "Hi Dixie." She giggled and waved.

"Hi, Grandma Gigi." I waved back and blew her a kiss.

"That's your grandma?" Lucy whispered in a strangled voice.

"I prefer Gigi, but you can also call me Mother Nature, sweet child," she said as she bestowed a wet kiss on Lucy's cheek. "I've been watching you and I think you would make a fabu pole dancer. I officially invite you to Nirvana. You are tough as nails and I do believe you could help me knock Dixie's sisters Lust, Wrath and Greed into line. What do you think?"

Lucy was speechless, but she nodded her head vigorously. I grinned as I thought about Lucy handing it to the nastiest of the Seven Deadly Sins.

"Good. That's settled," Mother Nature said as she adjusted the neckline of her gown that was showing an obscene amount of cleavage. "Now about you," she hissed as she turned to my mother.

"Don't," Rhonda warned shakily.

"Don't what?" Mother Nature asked pleasantly. "Don't turn your Dragon ass into a handbag and matching pumps? Or how about a skintight bustier and booty shorts for my upcoming pole humping competition?"

"Pole dancing," I corrected her.

"That's what I said."

Lucy giggled and I gave her a quick elbow.

"Gaia," Eve said, using Mother Nature's given name. "She is just protecting me."

"From what? Yourself?" Gigi sneered. "You have played with my boys and my granddaughter. That gives me gas, but now you're playing with destiny. I won't even begin to tell you what malady that causes my lower regions."

"Thank Hades," I mumbled and Lucy choked.

"I have done what I needed to do to survive." Eve stood and faced my grandma. "I have done nothing wrong."

"No, my dearest temptress... you have simply done nothing at all. There's a big difference. While you've wallowed in your perceived pain, those that wish to destroy balance have been quite busy. Your lack of balls has put your daughter, my sons and the mortal world as we know it in peril. Plus," she hissed, "I'm missing my program. If I miss *Long Island Medium*, there's no telling what will happen to Asia."

My family's obsession with balls made me involuntarily check to make sure I hadn't physically grown any.

"What are you doing?" Lucy asked as I discreetly grabbed my crotch.

"I'll tell you later," I whispered, relieved that I was still nutsack free.

"What do you expect of me?" my mother cried. Her distress was real, but it didn't move me. Rhonda went to her and held her gently.

"I expect you to do what you were created for," Mother Nature said in a voice that was chilling. "I expect you to dump your baggage and step up. Now," she roared as the tombstone bearing my name crumbled to the ground. "Your daughter is not dead. She will not die, but you, my little temptress, are walking very close to the edge."

"We will not listen to this," Rhonda said angrily. "Eve does not deserve this. We will take our leave."

The Dragon threw her huge arms in the air and my mother and her protector vanished.

"Well, that was stupid and shortsighted," Mother Nature quipped and giggled.

"What are you talking about?" I asked as Lucy's mouth gaped open.

"It's not wise to fuck with Mother Nature," Gigi said.

"I thought it was fool," Lucy whispered.

"It is," Mother Nature agreed. "But fuck is simply more fun to say. Don't you think?"

"Yes," Lucy acknowledged. "It is."

"My kind of girl," Gigi said as she patted a happy Lucy on the head lovingly. "Well, my job here is done." She lifted her arms and prepared to blast off to somewhere.

"Wait," I yelled. "Do you have anything else to tell me?"

"Absolutely not," she sniffed incredulously. "I have no intention of turning us all to dust. I won the last fifteen pole dancing marathons. I'm on a roll. Not gonna screw with those odds."

"But… " I stopped myself and swallowed back the words that had almost left my lips. The Kev was right. I was in charge of my own destiny. I would discover the rest of the journey. Alone. "I love you," I told her instead.

"And I you," she cooed. "And you too, Lucy. I take you on as a step-Gigi. Can you cook?" she inquired.

"Kind of," Lucy answered.

"Good enough," Gigi shouted as a funnel of turquoise glitter engulfed her. "I'll expect you next month. You'll teach me to cook and I'll teach you to hump a pole like a stripper. Dixie, you come too and bring your man. He has a wonderful ass and I'd enjoy grabbing it."

On those alarming parting words she disappeared.

"Holy shit," Lucy uttered.

"Yep. That about covers it."

CHAPTER THIRTY-TWO

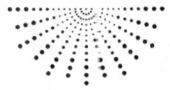

Lucy slept soundly in her new room after Janet fussed over her for an hour. Myrtle was on a date with Timmy the Bear shifter doing Satan knew what, Carl was sewing sequins on matching tutus for himself and The Kev and the baby Demons were watching a monster truck marathon and beating the Hell out of each other. All was right with my world at the moment. I was exhausted. All I wanted was my bed and my dreams about Hayden. The thought of Gigi grabbing the Angel of Death's ass brought a smile to my lips. I wouldn't mind grabbing his ass either. Another week till I could see him. I couldn't wait.

Pulling on some clean panties after a quick shower was about all I could muster up the energy to do. I fell to my bed, yanked the comforter over my head and sighed with pleasure.

"Hello Dixie."

WTH? How could a bad day get worse? Let me see... the Angel of Light could show up in my bedroom when I was wearing nothing but panties.

"Leave," I snapped as I secured the comforter around me.

"Now that's just rude," he replied.

"No. It's rude to show up uninvited when I've had a shitty day."

"I didn't think I'd get an invite," he said sulkily.

"You were correct, Angel boy."

"So I invited myself."

"Look, Elijah. Hayden is my soul mate. You're hot and all, but I'm good with the man I love," I told him.

"You kissed me," he informed me triumphantly.

"No, actually you kissed me," I shot back.

"Semantics," he said dismissively.

"Elijah, I love Hayden."

His eyes flashed and he advanced on the bed. "You think the Angel of Death is capable of love?"

"Yes, I do."

"You never had a chance," he said sadly. "You have so much good in you from your mother, but it's been tainted by your evil side."

I could certainly tell him a few things about my mother's goodness, but I was too pissed off about the rest of what he'd said.

"You think you're not evil?" I raised an eyebrow and waited.

"I'm the Angel of Light. I am goodness and love," he insisted.

"Blah, blah, blah. It seems a little evil to me to hit on your brother's soul mate."

He was taken aback at either my snarkiness or my accuracy.

"I never had a chance with you," he pouted. "You could have been perfect and good."

"Give me a break." I rolled my eyes and groaned. "There is no such thing as pure good or pure evil."

"Of course there is," he huffed indignantly. "I'm pure goodness."

"Nope."

"I am."

"Nope."

"Yes. I. Am," he roared and knocked all the pictures from my bedroom walls.

"That wasn't very good," I muttered and grinned.

"All right. Fine. I'm just pissed that I never had a chance." He crossed to the other side of the room and dropped into a beanbag chair.

The simple fact that the Angel of Light was sitting in a rose-colored beanbag chair was enough to keep me giggling for a while.

"What?" he demanded.

"Nothing. Is it because I'm a True Immortal?" I asked. "Is that why you want me?"

"No. Yes. I don't know," he admitted. "You're beautiful and you're Balance. I was hoping to tip the scales."

"And that's good?"

"No," he said sheepishly. "I suppose not."

An alarmingly depressing thought crossed my brain. Did Hayden want me for the same reason?

"No, he doesn't," Elijah ground out morosely.

"Did I say that out loud?" I gasped.

"No. I can read minds, especially when they yell as loud as yours does. As much as I loathe to admit it, my bastard brother loves you. The evil part and the good part."

"Was that so hard?" I asked, smiling. A huge weight lifted from my heart and if I wasn't mostly naked I would have hugged the Angel in my room. As annoying as he was, I did kind of like him.

"Actually it was. However, he will be pissed." Elijah grinned evilly.

"Why?"

"He'll be able to scent that I was here."

"Now that *is* evil," I informed him and wondered how angry Hayden would be.

"It is, isn't it? That was fun." He threw his head back and laughed. He really was beautiful, but he wasn't for me. "Dixie, I may not win your hand, but I will do my duty to help you keep balance. If you ever need me, just think of our kiss."

"Are you for real?"

"No, but it is fun being a *little* bad." He grinned like a naughty child. "You simply have to call my name and I will always come."

"Thank you. Elijah, are your wings black?"

"You're most welcome and, irony of all ironies, they are. It figures that the Angel of Death would get the golden wings. I have to go. I do believe evil is on his way."

He stood and vanished in a shower of golden mist.

I sighed as I realized that it was very true that he and Hayden had been the ones who had fought over me as a child. I pulled my covers tightly around me and wished the other part of his statement had been true, but there was still a week before Hayden was permitted to see me.

"Where is he?" a furious voice demanded.

"Oh my Hell," I shouted as I jumped up and banged my head on the lamp next to my bed. "What are you doing here?"

"Is he under the bed?" Hayden demanded, his eyes narrowing.

"Are you being a dick?"

"Did you just call me a dick?"

"No, I asked you if you were being one," I replied. I wanted to jump him so badly it hurt, but he was going to have to lose the 'tude.

"You are practically naked and I can smell the bastard's scent. I am going to kill him and then I will spank you," he snapped as he looked under the bed.

"Will you make love to me after my spanking?" I asked as I watched him tear up my room.

"Yes, of course."

He froze and then slowly glanced up.

"Would you like to talk before you completely destroy my bedroom?" I inquired politely.

His chest heaved and he barely held onto his control. Bad boys were freakin' hot. I smiled and waited.

"You're different," he said as he slowly made his way toward my bed.

"I had no choice. I grew up."

His eyes flashed red and his movement ceased. His desire was extremely evident, but he held back.

"Did anything happen between you and my brother?"

"What do you mean by that?"

"Hell Dixie, I'm hanging on by a thread here. You've got to help me out." His breathing was labored and the muscles were taut in his neck.

"Are you sorry for being a dick?"

He ran his hands through his hair and sighed dramatically. "Yes, I'm sorry for being a dick."

"Nothing happened with your brother. I'm in love with you."

His grin set my panties on fire, but I backed away. "You cannot storm in here and accuse me of cheating ever again. There will be times work will keep us apart and you will lose panty privileges if you behave like a Neanderthal. We clear on that, buddy?"

"First you call me a dick and then you call me buddy. Do you think that's wise?" His expression was feral and I was losing my inner battle with making him wait.

"Will it get me a spanking?" I asked sweetly.

Yes," he said in a gruff voice. "It will."

"Then I suppose it was very wise then."

The sexual tension in the room was almost suffocating and I was happily drowning in it. Hayden unhurriedly pulled his shirt over his head and tossed it on the floor. He kicked out of his shoes and went for his jeans. His broad chest and six-pack abs were gorgeous and made me shiver all over. Need coursed through me, but I wanted the rules to change.

"Freeze," I said as he glanced up at me in confusion. "I want to undress you."

His smile was sinful and he dropped his hands to his sides. "Be my guest."

I crawled off the bed and approached. As I ran my hands lightly over his torso, my fingers tingled and my stomach clenched with desire. I pressed my naked aching breasts to his chest and rubbed my body on his, eliciting the exact response I wanted. However the plans I had for him would fly out the window if I didn't pull back. Regaining what little composure I had left, I unbuttoned his jeans and slid them and his boxer briefs down his long muscular legs. The blond hair teased my fingertips as I massaged his thighs.

On my knees, I came face to face with something huge and beautiful. I squeezed my legs together tightly in anticipation what was to come. I'd dreamt of Hayden taking me over and over and I planned to live that fantasy tonight.

Learning the ropes by the seat of my pants had become my normal and I decided to keep going with that method. I took his erection in my hand and licked it softly. He tasted like the best kind of sin and the drop of liquid on the head was salty and delicious. His sharp intake of breath and muttered curses made me bolder.

I wrapped my lips around the head of his cock and sucked gently. My cheeks hollowed and I swirled my tongue around the tip.

"I won't break," he ground out through his teeth as he threaded his hands in my hair. "Suck me harder."

I did.

And he went wild.

The sheer potency of having a being so powerful at my mercy was heady, but loving the person I was giving pleasure was far more staggering on levels I could have never imagined. The sounds coming from deep within his chest sent white-hot sparks of heat through my body and I increased my speed.

"Dixie, stop," he demanded as he pulled himself from my mouth with a pop. "I want to come inside you." Dropping to his knees in front of me and pressing his forehead to mine, he held my head immobile as he brushed sweet kisses on my lips.

"I am a jealous man," he hissed as he took my aching nipples between his fingers and applied pressure I could feel between my legs. "You're mine."

"That's okay." I moaned as I bit down on his neck and sucked. "I accidently blow up kitchen appliances and I like expensive shoes."

"I can live with that," he growled as he picked me up and threw me on the bed. "I rarely use the clothes hamper and I suck at leaving the toilet seat down."

"That's not gonna work," I said as I took his throbbing erection in my hand and stroked it.

"I'll try and do better with that one," he grunted as he took my distended nipple into his mouth and sucked hard.

"I don't really cook." I moaned and ran my nails lightly over his testicles.

"I like Chinese takeout," he muttered as he slid down my body and did sinful things between my legs.

"I like Indian, but we can compromise," I squealed as his teeth and tongue sent me into a violent orgasm.

"I need to fuck you." His eyes were wild and his hands were everywhere.

"I wanna be on top."

"No need for a compromise there." He grinned and rolled to his back. All six foot six of my beautiful lover was laid out before me and I trembled with need. His eyes blazed red as I slowly and deliberately straddled him. Taking him in my hand, I put him right where I wanted him and slid him inside me. The stretch and slight burn was like coming home and my head dropped back to my shoulders as I sheathed him completely.

"I love you, Dixie," he promised as my body rocked on his. "I will love you to the end of time."

Tears welled in my eyes as the magnitude of what I felt for this beautiful complicated man overwhelmed me. "I love you too," I whispered as my desire escalated and the time for slow and easy ended. His grip on my hips as his body merged with mine would leave marks, but no less than the ones I left on his chest with my nails as I screamed through the mother of all orgasms.

My body clenched around his as ripple after ripple of heat tore through my abdomen and Hayden growled as he came. Collapsing on top of him, I felt him grow rigid again inside me.

"I don't think I can," I gasped as he rolled me to my back.

"Trust me." He grinned as he rotated his hips making my brain short out. "I know you can."

He was right.

I could. And I did.

Four more times.

CHAPTER THIRTY-THREE

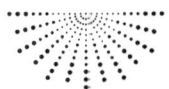

"I HAVE TO GO," HAYDEN MURMURED AS HIS FINGERTIPS RAN LAZY circles over my sore and very satisfied body. "Your father will want my ass on a platter for breaking the rules."

"He's not the only crazy Immortal who wants your ass." I giggled as I traced his full lips with my finger.

"You?"

"Of course me," I said as I rolled my eyes. "But there is another."

"Care to explain?"

"My grandma likes your ass and told me she wouldn't mind grabbing it."

Hayden closed his eyes and pinched the bridge of his nose. "I have no words. None."

"It is a little disconcerting," I agreed as I tried to roll off the bed.

"Wait," he said. He grabbed me by the waist and hauled me on top of him. "We forgot something."

"I'm pretty sure we covered a lot of territory last night." I pressed my lips to his. He ran his large hands down my back and rested them on my ass.

"This is one of my favorite parts," he murmured as he squeezed my booty and then slapped it.

"Ow!" I laughed and tried to escape.

"I promised a spanking and a spanking you shall have," he purred as he lightly smacked my ass again. I ground my hips into his and his eyes went from green to red in a hot second. "You like that?" he asked as he smoothed his hands over my bottom in preparation for another little spank.

"I actually do." I bit on his bottom lip and writhed on his naked body. "Do it again."

"My pleasure... ah, Dixie?"

"Yes?" I asked as I moved down his body and flicked my tongue over his nipple.

"There are four tiny smiling Demons with a large dagger staring at us. You know them?" he asked in a bemused tone.

"Dixie get the spank spank on the bumbum!" Abe yelled joyously as he hopped on the bed and cuddled close. "Can me spank the bumbum too?"

"Nope, that's my bumbum," Hayden told him. He gingerly removed Abe from my left butt cheek.

"Awwwwwwww, that no be nice! " Abe grunted and the rest of the motley crew jumped onto the bed.

"Um guys, this is kind of bad timing," I told them while I yanked a sheet over Hayden and myself. "And is there any particular reason you're wielding a knife?"

"I think we no tell you unless we get to smacky on the bumbum," Ross pouted.

"How about you smacky each other on the bumbum after you explain why you're holding a gnarly looking weapon?" I suggested nicely.

They conferred quite violently and loudly while Hayden and I watched.

"Me say ooooookaaaay!" Beyonce screamed.

"You takey big knife." Rachel instructed. "Put pointy part on hand and make hole! Okiee dokeee?"

"Why should we do that?" Hayden asked the little monsters as he again removed Abe from the vicinity of my rear end.

"To make the bond of the lovers of the bumbum spanky," Abe said logically.

"You want us to bond?" I asked. My eyes shot to Hayden's.

"Yayayayayayayayayayay," Rachel sang as she tossed the dagger in the air.

Hayden grabbed the knife mid-air before it dropped and decapitated one of my cousin's babies. That would have sucked.

"You makey bond and we watch and then you do the naked jiggy," Abe informed us.

"And we watch," Ross added solemnly.

"And help," Rachel chimed in.

"And video for YouTube," Beyonce explained as if that would seal the deal.

"Um, no. That doesn't sound like a plan," I said as I picked up the little Demons and walked to my door. "You guys go play and we'll let you know how it turns out."

"Can me touch you bumbum?" Abe asked sweetly.

I glanced over at Hayden who closed his eyes and shrugged. "For one second," I told him. "And then you little dudes have to go bother Myrtle. Okay? She would love for you guys to touch her bumbum."

"Yesssssssssssssss!" They hollered and all took turns quickly touching my bumbum with their tiny little hands.

"Enough," Hayden demanded as he shooed them out the door. "You're done with Dixie's bumbum. You will never touch her bumbum again. Understand?"

"You big silly Angel sex man," Beyonce screeched. "Me touch you bumbum now!" She dove and smacked Hayden's ass with glee. The look on his face was priceless and he chased the little devils from the room while trying not to laugh.

"Are you keeping them?" he asked as he pressed the heel of his hand to his forehead and squeezed his eyes shut.

"No, I am not. They belong to my cousin Astrid and I will give them back when I see her again."

Blowing out a rather large sigh of relief, Hayden carefully examined the knife the baby Demons had gifted us. What the Hell —why did it look so familiar? The handle was encrusted with diamonds. It twinkled and winked at me. My mouth filled with water and my stomach cramped—Grandpa.

"Hayden, I can't bond with that knife," I said, quickly slapping my hand over my mouth just in case I hurled in memory of drinking my grandpa's blood.

"It's ancient. I've never seen anything like it," he said and then noticed my pallor change. "You okay?"

"No, not really. Suffice it to say that dagger brings some icky gastrointestinal memories."

"You want to expound on that?"

"Not right now," I gagged out.

"Got it," he said as he put the knife aside and took me in his arms. "I don't want to be interrupted by ass-grabbing tiny Demons anyway."

Something clicked and I inhaled deeply through the pain. I disengaged myself from Hayden's embrace and walked over to the dagger. Astrid gave me the baby Demons. The baby Demons gave me my grandfather's dagger. Mistakes in life were rare. There was no more time to put life on hold. I held my breath for a brief moment and made my decision. "I love you, Hayden. Bond with me. Now."

I placed the blade of the dagger on my left palm and sliced. Hayden quietly took the jeweled handle from me and cut an identical incision in his own left hand.

"I love you, Dixie and I will honor our bond until we cease to exist and beyond." He took my hand in his and our blood mixed. Sparks flew from both our bodies and we held each other as we collapsed to the floor. Our combined magic swirled around us and the room blazed with a rainbow of blinding light.

"Stay with me," Hayden insisted urgently. "Look into my eyes."

I did.

And in his eyes I saw his pain and joy. I saw horrors and beauty—desires and dreams. So much of his life passed before my eyes it hurt—it was brutal. The man I loved had a duty that was filled with pain and death. I was his light and he was my dark—my perfectly imperfect darkness. He would help me find the Balance. Even with my Demon heritage, I leaned toward the light. Purity of good and evil was a myth… both existed in every living being. My job was to know it, own it and keep it that way.

The magic receded and we both caught our breath. "Is that all?" I whispered hoarsely as I tried to stop trembling.

"Hell, I hope so," he said. He held me firmly to his chest. "I'm so sorry."

"Why?"

"Because of what you had to see," he whispered sadly.

"I'm not. I saw you. I love you. Nothing can change that."

"I do not deserve someone like you," he said quietly and gripped me tighter.

"And I don't deserve someone as wonderful as you, but we were lucky enough to find each other, and according to the blood brother act we just pulled, we get to keep each other."

His laughter lightened my heart and I knew we'd done the right thing at the right time. "Do you think there will be any aftershocks?" I asked.

He was silent for a moment as he considered. "It feels like that was the worst of it."

"You need to go," I told him. "I no longer fear my father's wrath, but I think there was a reason he set the boundaries." I paused and shook my head in confusion. "Is it weird that I feel normal after what we just did?"

"I was thinking the same." He grinned and shrugged. "I'll come back on Friday."

"Oh my Hell, do you wanna be my date at the Angels and Demons dance on Friday?"

"Are you serious?" He chuckled as he slowly pulled on his clothes. "We just tilted the axis of Heaven and Hell with our bonding and you're asking me to a dance?"

"Yep." I grinned and grabbed my own.

"I've never been to a dance before. I accept. What does one wear to an Angel and Demon dance?"

"Jeans," I said as I ran my finger along the jewel encrusted handle of the dagger that had just rocked my world. "I do suspect some will be sporting wings, bustiers, fake blood and dead babies tied to their feet."

"Lovely." Hayden winced and shook his head. "Can I feel you up during a slow dance?"

"Only if you spank my bumbum first," I teased.

His bark of laughter sent shivers of delight through me. "I'm leaving. If I don't, I will spank your bumbum and we won't leave this room until next Friday. This would of course piss off Satan, which I normally enjoy… however he is your father."

"He is," I agreed and laid a big smackeroo on my soul mate's lips. "I love you, my Angel of Death."

"And I you, Balance. I have a present for you," he said as he conjured a book out of the air.

"What's that?"

"The original copy of *The Beginning of Time*." He grinned at my squeal of joy and placed it in my hands. "It's in a dead language, but it's still strangely beautiful."

I flipped gently through the ancient pages and a feeling of wonder and excitement consumed me. "Can you read it?" I asked.

"No, but it comforts me."

I nodded in understanding and placed it gently next to the dagger. "I'll miss you."

"Come here, beautiful girl."

His kiss held promise, love and our future. I clung to him and breathed him in. After a light tap on the bumbum and a crooked smile that melted my panties, he disappeared in a beautiful swirling mist of black glitter. A little piece of my heart left with him.

CHAPTER THIRTY-FOUR

THE THINGS HAD BEEN BUSY...

"This looks fucking stupid," Myrtle huffed indignantly as we stood in Hell.

"Yep," I agreed as I laughed at the seven foot Satan that the Things had created from papier-mâché, red sequins and black feathers. My father would have a shit fit if he saw it.

"Heaven's no better," Lucy sniffed as she crossed to the other side of the gymnasium and kicked a huge puffy cloud made of toilet paper and cotton balls. Silver and white streamers floated down from the ceiling in Heaven and red and black from Hell. The walls of the *Underworld* half of the gym had been smeared with fake blood and a sound track of screaming and wailing played ominously in the background. Of course Heaven had an absurd amount of wind chimes hanging from large plastic wings and an industrial fan to make sure they never stopped tinkling.

Lucy was right. Heaven was heinous, but Hell was just as bad. I idly wondered what Hayden would think and giggled. The gash on my hand from our bonding had healed but I still felt the sting keenly. Thankfully the week had flown by. I was on high alert for Rogue Demons and evil in general, but nothing happened. Eve hadn't shown back up, but I didn't really expect her to. Carl and I continued to train and Lucy joined us. Her magic was fierce and her strength was astounding. Carl was besotted after she knocked him out cold for the sixth time. He and Janet were secretly hatching plans to adopt her and take her back to Hell.

"We need Stella," I muttered as I almost tripped over an ugly little red doll with enormous plastic fangs.

"Is that supposed to be a Demon?" Myrtle yelled as she picked up the abomination by an eye tooth. "I have never been so insulted in my life." She dropped the doll and crunched it under her boot.

"Who's Stella?" Lucy asked as she tossed Myrtle another Demon doll.

"My BFF. You'll love her. She creates lightning storms and can change decor in no time flat."

"Is she coming to the dance?" Myrtle asked as she decapitated several offending dolls with the flick of her pinky finger.

"Yep."

"Good, this is a clusterfuck waiting to happen," she muttered disgustedly as she stomped out of the gym, but not before she zapped several more Demons and a few Heavenly chimes.

"Dixie, come here," Lucy said. Her tone was off and her body was stiff. She stared at the floor and her normally rosy complexion had gone pale.

"What?"

"Look," she whispered.

On the wooden floor of the gym, partially obscured by a ridiculous fluffy cloud was a bracelet. A lovely delicate bracelet. Eve's bracelet—the one with the language I couldn't read engraved into the woven bands. A ray of sun shining through the skylight caught it and it glistened.

"That's not a mistake," Lucy said as she squatted down and examined it. "It's her bracelet. She was here."

"Or someone took the bracelet and put it here," I said as I

picked it up and held it. The magic that flowed from it was strong and it carried my mother's signature clearly. "Do you feel that?"

"I do." Lucy nodded and ran her fingers over it. "She put it here. I only can scent her. No one else has touched it. Do you think she's dead?"

"No. She'd have to have the Sword of Death, but... " Holy Hell, did Eve steal the Sword of Death? Was she going to kill herself? No. She was too selfish to kill herself. She might be *tempted*, but it would all be for show.

"But what?"

"She's not dead. We would know. She may win the Asstastic Mother of the Millennium Award, but she's still our blood and we would feel her death."

"You sure about that?" Lucy asked doubtfully.

"Yep. It's a story my father told me as a child—we know when our blood dies. We will feel it. All these years I've lived with the pathetic hope that I would meet her because I never felt her death."

"That certainly turned out to be a disappointment," Lucy snapped.

I turned the bracelet over in my palm and realized the script was the same as the text in *The Beginning of Time*. This was no mistake, but was it a trap? Was Eve part of my purpose or was she the harbinger of my downfall? I was Balance, but she was the Balance of Chaos. Were we natural enemies? I carefully slipped the bracelet on my arm and a searing shot of pain sliced through my head. I dropped to the floor and curled to a ball. Damn her. Damn her to Hell.

"Oh my God," Lucy screamed. "I don't care if she's a fucking True Immortal. She is so dead. Dixie, don't die. Let me take that thing off of you."

My sister tried in vain to remove the bracelet. The moment I put it on, it became a part of me and it was going nowhere fast.

"I'm okay," I mumbled as I got to my knees and looked at my arm. "What the Hell was that?"

"Oh my God," Thing One screeched from the far side of Heaven. "Do you love it or what?" She barreled into the gym followed by the other chattering Things.

Lucy pulled me to my feet and stood slightly in front of me, effectively covering my throbbing red arm. "I wouldn't say *love*," Lucy quipped.

"Thank you!" Thing Three gushed, completely missing Lucy's sarcasm. "We worked for a whole hour on the Devil."

"I'm sure he would appreciate that," I muttered.

"You are so funny, Dixie," Thing Two sang as she turned circles in Heaven and giggled up a storm. How Lucy spent any time with these girls was still a mystery to me. From the look on her face it was a mystery to her too.

"Oooookay," Thing One said as she straightened out some tangled wind chimes. "The dance committee has to be here early tomorrow. Six o'clock sharp. We get to help the band set up and they are hotter than sin!" she screamed at decibels meant to attract strays.

Thing Three whipped out her lip gloss and applied it as she doled out the rest of the instructions. "Now you two can't be late. Come in the side door because the front will be locked until eight. Bring your costume so you don't mess it up. I'll bring hairspray and extra faux blood in case anyone needs it."

"I'm bringing vodka and Percocet," Thing Four volunteered. "Is anyone bringing Oreos?"

"I will," Thing Two said. "Ewww, what happened to the Demons?"

They stared in horror at the decapitated and crushed dolls.

"Um… Myrtle didn't feel they look quite right, so she fixed them," I said sincerely.

"I think it's perfect," Lucy said and nudged me.

They paused in confusion for a minute and then began to hop around like bunnies. "Me too," they shrieked in unison.

Help me Satan, they were almost too stupid to live.

"We're skipping class tomorrow to get our hair dyed green," Thing One explained. "So we'll see you two at six!"

"Toodles," they yelled as they exited the gym en masse.

"Green?" I asked.

"Green," Lucy answered.

"Gonna be fun."

Lucy grinned and shrugged. "It won't be boring."

CHAPTER THIRTY-FIVE

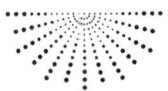

THE BRACELET ENABLED ME TO READ *THE BEGINNING OF TIME*. I'D
spent a good part of the evening before and the entire afternoon
trying to piece together the stories. I no longer thought Eve had
sabotaged me. I believed in her own pathetic way she was trying
to help. Lucy didn't buy it and had tried for hours to remove the
bangle from my arm. The book made me feel itchy and antsy.

"Leave it be, Lucy," Janet said. She ruffled Lucy's hair and
looked over my shoulder at the book. "What does it say?"

"Even though I can read it, I can't make sense of all the words,"
I admitted. "But I'm pretty sure there are more True Immortals
than the ones we know about. There's a bizarre passage about a
child that will encompass all the Immortal traits."

"Are there more True Immortal traits than the ones we already
know?" Myrtle asked.

"What in the Hell are True Immortal traits?" Lucy asked as she
eyed my bracelet distrustfully.

"God is Good, Satan is Evil, Dixie's grandpa is Wisdom,
Mother Nature is Emotion, Angel of Death is Death, Angel of
Light is Life, Eve is Temptation, Astrid is Compassion and Dixie is
Balance," Myrtle rattled off the list by rote.

"So there are more?" Janet mused.

"I'm not sure. It doesn't say here, or it's just tied up in the language I don't understand."

"Maybe the other True Immortals running around are spare heirs," Lucy said.

"That's freakin' genius!" Myrtle slapped Lucy on the back and she went flying across the room. "Whoops. Sorry."

"You are one strong little skinny girl," Lucy grumbled as she got up.

"I said sorry." Myrtle grinned and flexed her little arms.

Myrtle was such a little shit. I grinned and rolled my eyes.

"I agree," Lucy said.

"With what?"

"That Myrtle's a shit," she replied.

"I didn't say that out loud," I stammered.

"Yes, you did," Lucy insisted.

"No, she didn't. I would have kicked her Demon princess ass if she did," Myrtle informed us. "But now that the cat is out of the bag, I'll kick your ass after the dance. I'd do it now, but I got a manicure and I don't want to mess it up. Plus she still deserves a beating for sending the baby Demons to spank my bumbum." With that she flipped us off and left the room.

"You really heard me?" I asked Lucy.

"I really did."

Was she like Elijah? Was I yelling in my head? Why didn't anyone else hear me? Damn, I was really going to have to watch my thoughts…

"It's five-thirty, you gals need to get a move on," Janet said and handed me my purse.

"I'll see you at eight. I refuse to be around the Things without killing them. For real killing them," Myrtle yelled from down the hall.

"Alrighty then, we'll see you at eight."

"I CAN'T WAIT TO SEE HAYDEN AND YOU'LL MEET STELLA TONIGHT. Who knows? My dad might even show up. Shit, he'll blow an aneurysm when he sees his red sequined likeness," I babbled to Lucy. "Did you bring a costume? Did you know Myrtle is coming dressed as a bear and..." WTF?

We both froze as we entered the gym. We entered cautiously and the heavy door slammed shut behind us. Heaven was still heinous and Hell was still an abomination, but something was wrong—very wrong. The air was thick with malevolent magic and an icy wind whipped through the cavernous room. Shitshitshitshitshit.

"What are the Things' names?" I asked Lucy frantically.

"Veronica, Velda, Vivian and Varsha."

"Are you fucking serious?"

"They're vultures. What did you expect?"

"Not that," I hissed. "Veronica? Are you guys here?" I called out.

Nothing.

Not good.

No one answered and my body tightened. The need to crawl out of my skin was intense and little sparks lit the tips of my fingers. The spot on my palm that I had sliced with the dagger tingled and burned.

"What's going on?" Lucy whispered.

"I'm not sure, but this isn't your fight. I want you to go." I pushed her toward the door, but she pushed right back.

"Nope. Not going anywhere."

"Lucy, leave," I ground out through clenched teeth.

"Dixie, no," she shot back. Her eyes glowed a brilliant green and a gauzy film of magic like I'd never seen glowed around her.

"Is Steve the only form you shift to?" I asked as I took in the power of the magic she was throwing off.

"Not even close." She snorted and rolled her neck on her shoulders.

"What else do you shift to?" I demanded. Could she hold her own in whatever clusterfuck was about to happen?

"Do you have nightmares?" she asked.

"Yes."

"Think of the most horrific nightmare you've ever had. I'm ten times worse."

"For real?" My grin split my face and I wanted to hug her and smack her.

"For very real." Her grin matched mine and I gave up on making her leave. I knew she wouldn't go anyway.

"Hello Dixie, I see you brought your dog," Cole's voice boomed and bounced off the walls. His eyes were slightly wild and he was armed to the teeth. He wore a long cheesy black cape, black pants and a red ruffled shirt. "So nice of you to come to my party."

What the Hell was Cole doing here and why was he dressed like a Demon from a bad B movie? He muttered and laughed and he walked quickly in circles so his cape flowed behind him. This was bad, but I knew I could take him. He was stupid and arrogant. I was a True Immortal. He could do me damage, but he couldn't kill me. Lucy was another story.

"Didn't realize it was yours," I greeted him politely. "I would have torn up the invite and spit on it if I'd known. I'm guessing this is a family affair—you will let Lucy leave."

"But she's your sister," he sneered. "Family is family, no matter what the breed."

"I already told you, I'm not leaving," Lucy hissed under her breath.

"See?" He laughed. "Your dog likes to heel."

"Shut up, asshole," I snapped.

"I've always said you were a spoiled rotten brat and I can see things haven't changed."

I was right about Cole being a shitbag, but I still didn't

understand the game. Lucy stood quietly beside me, but her body was as tense as a coil about to spring.

"Everyone should be arriving soon, so make yourselves comfortable."

"We'll do that," I said nastily.

The door we'd entered through flew open and Demons of the sort I'd never seen entered and spaced themselves around the gym. There had to be at least two hundred. The odds were looking slightly craptastic. Even though the Things were vapid and worthless, I hoped like Hell they would sense the danger in the gym and stay away. There was still two hours before innocent people would arrive. Pus and blood oozed from open sores on the faces and necks of the all male Demon army. Their breathing came out in short bursts and their black teeth protruded over bulbous lips. Rogue Demons were butt-ass ugly—and they looked hungry. Awesome.

I pulled Lucy away from the perimeter and into a clump of trees made out of coat racks and tissue paper. I said a quick prayer to my father that what happened earlier wasn't a fluke...

"*Lucy, can you hear me?*" Her eyes shot to mine and I closed my eyes for a brief moment in relief. "*Cole is my father's second in command. Or he was... He's a powerful Demon and he clearly has delusions of grandeur or a massive death wish. I'm unsure what's going down, but all the stinky asshole wallflowers are Rogue Demons.*"

Lucy gave me a quick wink.

"*You don't want to go at Cole under any circumstances. I'm pretty sure he has some Black Magic and he wears a Hell Fire ring. It could kill you, and if you die today I will hunt your ghost ass down and kill you again. Do you understand me?*"

She gave me another wink and a smirk.

I discreetly reached into my purse and smiled. I had told them they couldn't come, but I was delighted they blatantly disobeyed me. I pulled my baby Demon saliva covered hand from my bag and patted it gently. I had no clue if they could eat two hundred

Rogue Demons, but the less I had to destroy would leave me more time to deal with Cole.

"So killing me gets you what?" I asked as Cole paced Heaven with an authority and stature that belied his true status.

"Kill you?" He laughed and gave me a condescending glare. "I can't kill you. She would be upset if I did that. You've been granted a reprieve." Thank Hades he thought I was killable. He was unaware of my True Immortal standing.

None of this was adding up. Where was the Sword of Death and was I just supposed to annihilate the room of bad guys? How would that balance anything? The Kev told me to see things clearly and make a balanced decision. All I saw were badly dressed smelly evil dudes. Did they tip the balance?

The waiting was worse than anything I'd ever experienced.

And then it happened.

All at once.

The vultures came crashing through the skylights and landed at Cole's feet. He cooed to them and pet their hairless heads.

"Motherfucker," Lucy muttered. "The Things are bad guys?"

"Looking that way," I replied as I brushed shards of glass from the skylight off of my sister and pulled us farther back to the relative safety of the seven-foot papier-mâché Satan.

The Demons surrounding us wailed and moaned. They rocked back and forth—their teeth clicked and snapped ominously. The sounds and smells made my stomach roil.

"Such good little vultures," Cole purred to the Things. "You brought your daddy the evil ones right on time."

"They're related?" Lucy was flabbergasted.

"Cole's their dad?" I was shocked.

"My children are hungry," Cole bellowed. "Who will make the ultimate sacrifice for me?"

The Demons began to fight each other. Their long claws stabbed through open wounds and the screams were horrific. I felt their shrieks all the way to my toes. They pushed each other forward and fought to go back to the wall. Clearly no one wanted to be dinner.

"You," Cole cried out to a smaller Demon who had landed in a heap on the floor. "You will serve me. Disrobe."

The hideous Demon disrobed reluctantly and his comrades against the walls hissed and laughed maniacally. His muscular body was covered in open wounds and dried flakey blood. My gag reflex rose quickly.

"Oh fuck no," Lucy grunted and turned her head as the Demon laid himself at the clawed feet of the Things.

The sounds were Hellish and the screams from the peanut gallery made the entire show more macabre. The vultures viciously tore into the live body of the Demon as he screamed in agony. Cole clapped his hands with delight and the Vultures ate hungrily. If this was the warmup act the evening was going to be very bad indeed.

The magic in the air of the gym thickened and Cole's eyes widened in excitement. His pacing became erratic and his cape blew around him making him look like he was ready for takeoff. "She's here," he announced loudly over the roar of the Demons and the shrill keening of the vultures.

The crash through the ceiling and the explosion of glass, wood and metal made me hope for a short moment that Mother Nature was making a violent entrance, but that would have been too easy. I didn't need my grandma. I didn't need to be saved—I simply needed to figure out what the Hell was going on. A Dragon the size of an SUV barreled down from the sky holding a beaten, bloody and barely breathing Eve in her sharp talons. She wasn't dead. It would take far more than a beating to kill Temptation. The Demons danced wildly and the vultures in their ecstasy coughed up chunks of bloody Demon. The bile rose in my throat and I realized that half the battle would be to keep from vomiting.

"You're late," Cole shouted as he ran to my mother's crumpled body and pulled her from Rhonda's claws. He ran his hands possessively over her in such a sexual way I had to turn my head. Could no one deny temptation?

"Silence," Rhonda the Dragon roared so loudly I winced in pain. I yanked Lucy behind a cardboard boulder and watched the disaster unfold. Before I could act I needed to be sure. More plaster and metal fell from the ceiling, impaling and beheading several Demons. "I said silence," she screeched. The walls trembled and the floor shook, but she accomplished her goal. The room went quiet.

"You hurt her," Cole accused as he ran his open mouth down my mother's neck.

"I'll hurt you if you don't shut up. Where are they?" she demanded. She stomped around Heaven and crushed two Things to death beneath her massive feet. Cole barely noticed his feathered children had died as he was too engrossed with my mother.

"Soon. Amanda is luring him. Where is the Sword?"

Amanda, my father's consort, was luring who? Was she luring my father here? Were they planning on killing my father in front of me?

"She has the Sword," Rhonda snapped. My mother did have the Sword. It was strapped to her back. Had Mr. Rogers caved to temptation too? "Where's God?" Rhonda's beady eyes swept the room.-

"Won't be coming," Cole said as he backed away from the furious fire-breathing Dragon.

"Can you not get anything right?" she hissed as an explosion of flames burst from her nose and destroyed a clump of Demons cowering in the corner. "I have spent a year weakening and brainwashing the bitch to make her steal the Sword and neglect her job and you can't do the simple things I asked?"

"We don't need him. We'll have Satan. When he sees Eve he will break. He has loved her for millions of years. He lives for the day she will come to him and stay," he rasped as he cupped my mother's breast in his hand. "We all do... She will do as told or we will kill her daughters in front of her."

Well now I knew why we were here. Lucy gripped my arm and growled.

"You think that will work?" Rhonda asked so quietly my hair stood on end. "We needed them to fight over her to destroy each other. We need a heart to break so the Sword of Death will work. This is a folly you've created." She stomped her foot and took out the other two Things.

"It will work," he said as he gazed at my mother with such longing I felt ill. Was she such a temptation to all that she could end the world? Did balance mean the end of my mother?

"Her denial of him will break him?" she demanded as she advanced on Cole.

"Yes, and the lives of her spawn will guarantee her compliance. All we need is a mere second of heartbreak and the Sword of Death and Satan's life is vanquished. Forever."

They were correct. It was so simple and so very wrong. If Eve was sprung on my father and her denial of him hurt badly enough —even for a moment, it could be over. His momentary wish for death and a broken heart would be all the opening they would need.

"Are we just gonna hide behind a rock or are we gonna kick some ass?" Lucy asked with disgust.

"Just needed a minute to figure out who had to bite it," I snapped.

"Who did you decide on?"

"Pretty much all of them."

Lucy's grin was evil and I bit back the most inappropriate laugh that had almost ever left my body. I bit down hard and a thin stream of blood dribbled down my lip.

"Lick my chin," I told Lucy. "Now."

"What the... is that some kind of Demon lesbian thingie? I like guys," she stammered.

"My blood," I hissed. "Take some of my blood. It will make you stronger. Just do it." I yanked her mouth to mine and she licked the blood from my lips and chin. "You might have a quick seizure, but go with it."

She nodded and gulped. "Go kill those bastards," she choked out as her body convulsed.

No such thing as pure good and pure evil. I was both and I would own it. My power rose rapidly and with a great deal of pain. Sparks flew from my fingers and Lucy rolled away. The roar in my ears was like an ocean during a hurricane and I vaguely heard Rhonda ask about my and Lucy's whereabouts. My skin grew hot and my palm burned. I would spare my mother, but the rest had to go.

"I'm here," I said as I walked forward toward the abomination that wanted to rule the world. Cole was simply a minion—a weak worthless piece of shit that had helped to tip the scales. His obsession with my mother had been used wisely. Rhonda was the brains. Rhonda had to go.

My feet barely touched the floor as I advanced and the bracelet on my arm heated just as the scar on my palm added to the pain ricocheting through me. Instead of debilitating me, I let the pain empower me. The good inside me warred with the evil, but I controlled it. Neither would ever control me.

"Why, what have we here? A little baby Immortal with some mommy issues?" She bared her long sharp teeth and spit a stream of fire at me.

Lifting my left hand, I caught the fire and threw it back at her. The look of horror on her face was gorgeous as her own fire singed off a good portion of her shoulder.

"No," she screamed as she doubled forward and grasped her arm. As quickly as the shoulder disappeared, it grew back and her fury increased tenfold. "Get her and the other one," she bellowed so loudly several girders fell from above.

My mother's shout of agony rang in my ears, but her need and

weakness would not tempt me ever again. I focused on my prey
and all Hell broke loose.

It felt like slow motion. The Demons sprang from the walls
and the Dragon increased in size. I heard the delighted squeals of
the baby Demons as they went to work on the meal of the
century. The groaning and cursing mixed with the wet sounds of
bodies being torn apart didn't even bother me. The Dragon's
claws were sharp as they tore into my skin, but the sense of calm
inside me enabled me to take each blow as I dealt my own.

My hair whipped wildly around my head. I flicked my fingers
and a vicious wind blew up. I laughed as Demons flew through
the air into a pile for the babies. The fear in the Dragon made her
fight erratically. I stilled my body and let her think for a brief
second she could win. Arrogance created carelessness and I was
not arrogant.

"No one shall defeat me." She came at me with hatred and
desperation. I shifted slightly and her body weight took her
forward into a wall. The sound of a Dragon taking down steel
beams with her head was delightful, but I wasn't done.

"I'm not no one," I roared and let my body relax. "I am Balance."

From the core of my being I pulled up a magic so strong I felt
sick. I raised my hands above my head and I chanted. Never
before had I understood what I was saying, but now I did. My
mother had left her bracelet for me on purpose. No matter how
she had fucked up, she clearly felt remorse. She could not take
back what she had done, but she could give me the tools to put an
end to it.

My voice was strong and the storm in the room kicked up to
tornado level. The wind on my skin was cleansing and healing. I
smiled at the chaos around me and I spoke with my eyes and heart
wide open.

"Without balance there is no peace.
Without peace there is no reason.
Without reason there is no purpose.

Good and evil shall exist, but never in its purest form.

There are no true absolutes.

Absolutes must be abolished.

And I shall, for I am Balance."

The explosions that flew from my fingertips were targeted and deadly. The Demons burst into flames and fell to dust on the ground, but the Dragon... the Dragon's demise was something much more fitting.

Her screams of madness were the things of which nightmares are made, but I felt no mercy—no regret. Rhonda detonated and fireworks erupted from every orifice. Her body shattered into millions of shiny fragments and embedded themselves in the walls of both Heaven and Hell. I had blown her to Kingdom Come and she was never coming back.

CHAPTER THIRTY-SIX

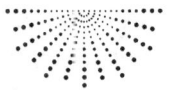

"Impressive," Cole snarled.

I had dropped to the ground in exhaustion. How in the Hell had I missed Cole? The sound of his voice was an unwelcome intrusion. I glanced up and froze. He had Lucy in a chokehold. Her face was bleeding and I recognized the mark. He had ripped her cheek open with his Hell Fire ring. How was she still alive? Were shifters immune to Demon magic?

Her face was bad but the Sword of Death pointed at her heart was far worse—a simple prick of the Sword was all it would take to kill a regular Immortal. Our mother lay in a clump at Cole's feet and wept. For herself? For Lucy? For me? Who knew...

"You are a surprise," Cole purred. "Didn't see that one coming, but no matter. My plan will still work."

"Let her go. Take me."

His laugh grated on my ears and I ground my teeth together to keep from saying something that could hasten my sister's death. "Do you think I'm stupid?" he barked and it took all I had not to answer. "You're unkillable. The mutt is not. I need insurance that your beautiful mommy will do as she has been told. I'm actually glad you killed the Dragon—now Amanda and I will rule Hell ourselves."

"Even if you destroy my father there are quite a few people in line for the throne, Cole."

"Yes, but none of them carry the son of Satan," he informed me haughtily.

"You think that child is his?"

"I know the child is *not* his, but once he's gone there will be no way to prove it. He has told all in Hell that Amanda carries his son. His son is the rightful heir and his son shall rule with me at his side."

He wasn't as stupid as I thought, but Lucy was.

The Black Magic that I'd given her had made her bold and I cried out as she made her move. Before my eyes a horror worse than anything I could have imagined unfolded. It happened so quickly I was helpless. She twisted out of Cole's deadly embrace and shifted into a monster so large and frightening she made the Hell Hounds look cute. She went for his head, but Cole was too fast. He plunged the Sword of Death through her neck and she collapsed next to our mother at his feet as blood spurted profusely from her neck. He had killed my sister.

The red of her blood mixed with the hatred in my soul and came out in a scream that ripped my throat raw. My palm burned and my head felt like it would fall from my body. A searing shot of pain flared up through my back and my skin separated. The agony was intense and I shot forward to the ground. The only thing that kept me conscious were the gasps and muttered curses from the Demon who'd taken the life of my sister.

Glancing up I saw the terror in his eyes as he backed away and stumbled over Lucy's dead body. Had my father shown up? Why was he so terrified? I struggled to my feet. My body felt much heavier than it had a moment ago. With a quick look back to see what had made Cole feel the need to run, I gasped.

No one had arrived, but something had. I had another gift. A beautiful new savage gift. Wings had erupted from my back. My left wing was golden and shot red fire and my right wing was black. Gold and silver flames blazed from the black wing. I laughed. I was good and evil. I was life and death. I was Balance. I bore the mark of Angels and my dream of flight was no longer a dream—it was real. And it was Cole's turn to die.

I whooshed up into the air and flew at him like a bullet from Hell. His shrieks and cries would never bring my sister back, but he would not rule Hell and he would never lay a finger on my mother or father again.

He writhed and howled in pain as the fire from both of my wings sent wave after wave of acid poison into his traitorous body. I watched his bones pop and his skin tear from his body dispassionately. The pain he felt as his life force left him matched the pain in my heart of seeing him kill my sister.

It was over too fast. But it was done. He was broken and burned, but still identifiable. I wondered how long it would take him to turn to dust.

"Dixie." My mother sounded small and pathetic. I wasn't even tempted.

"Don't speak to me right now. I can't listen to your voice."

Her whimper didn't move me. Nothing could move me right now. I sat next to Lucy as her body shifted back to human and I gently closed her beautiful eyelids over her unseeing eyes. And then I cried.

CHAPTER THIRTY-SEVEN

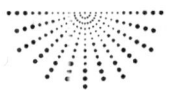

"WHAT IN THE NAME OF MY HOMELAND AM I LOOKING AT? AND where in the Hell am I?" my father bellowed as he examined the seven foot sequined and feathered statue of himself. "If this is supposed to be me, there will be some asses frying in the Basement tonight."

Through my tears I saw my father and Amanda. The next to arrive was Hayden, followed by Stella, then Elijah. Myrtle, Carl and Janet appeared in a puff of glitter and everyone looked terribly confused.

"What the fuck?" Myrtle gasped and took in the carnage.

"This is certainly one Hell of a decorating job," Stella muttered as she kicked a pile of dust that used to be a Demon.

"Dad," I whispered. My voice was still raw from screaming, but he heard me and so did Hayden.

"Dixie." Hayden ran for me and stopped short when he really saw me. "You have wings," he whispered reverently and knelt down to take me in his arms. I wrapped my arms around him and let my tears fall freely.

"I see your power finally came in," my father said sardonically as he gently ran his hands through my wings. "You seem to have had some fu…" His speech halted when his eyes found Eve. He stood mesmerized and then slowly approached her. "You. Why are you here?" He struggled with the words and I knew without a doubt that Cole had been correct. Satan loved Eve. I had never seen my father at a loss for anything—until now.

"I have failed, Lucifer. Don't look at me," she sobbed and curled into a ball on the hard floor.

"What have you done?" he asked in an awestruck voice I'd never heard.

"Who is she?" Amanda demanded as she sidled up to my father and grasped his arm in possession. Her eyes shot around the room as she tried to ascertain what had happened. Her quick shocked intake of breath was not lost on me as she spotted Cole's dead carcass. Her brain clearly worked fast and she developed another plan.

"I am nothing," Eve choked out. "Nothing."

"That's right—you're nothing," Amanda hissed. "I carry the son of Satan in my body. I will be his queen."

"About that," Satan said silkily as he removed Amanda's claws from his arm. "You'll be nothing of the sort. You'll be lucky if you live through the night."

"What do you mean?" Her voice was shrill and her eyes blinked rapidly. "I carry your child."

"You carry *a* child. Not *my* child. Do you take me for a fool?" Satan bellowed and more of the ceiling caved in.

"Look at me." She whimpered and clutched her stomach. "I am round with our baby boy."

My Father stood as still as a statue. His words were clipped and shards of ice dripped from each syllable. "I have lived for millions of years and I have eight children. Only eight children. I am very aware when I impregnate someone and I did not put my seed in you."

"But I don't understand," she blubbered as she dropped to her knees before my Father.

"Oh, but I think you do. I keep my friends close, but my enemies far closer… *Amanda*."

He raised his hands above Amanda. I knew what he was going to do, but it was wrong.

"Stop," I said harshly. "You will not destroy her."

The shock on my father's face would have been comical if the situation wasn't so dire. "What did you say?"

"I said do not kill her."

"You think she is innocent?" he hissed.

"No, I don't." I got to my feet and stood toe to toe with Satan. "She is guilty, but the child is not. Give her reprieve until the baby is born and then do with her what you will… or give her to me and I will destroy her, but not while she carries an innocent life."

My father stared at me with surprise and wonder. He lifted my chin and kissed my forehead. "As you wish, Balance. As you wish."

Amanda began to crawl from the room, but Elijah froze her with a flick of his hand. Satan gave him a brief nod of approval and let his gaze wander back to the woman that had been the downfall of so many.

"Motherhumpinshitballsonfire," Mother Nature shrieked as she fell from the sky with my grandpa on her back. "Can't I ever get a fucking break? Bill and I were testing out my new spinning sex swing and I catch wind that the Apocalypse is looming." They landed with a thud and Grandpa rolled across the room.

"Dixie has it covered," Satan said with pride as he righted his father and hugged his mother.

"Well, of course she does," Gigi snapped. "She's smarter than the lot of us."

Hayden stepped close and I leaned into his warm comfort. Right now I didn't care if I was smarter than anyone. I just wanted a bath—and to take my sister's body to a safe place.

"It was Cole and a horrid Dragon named Rhonda. They planned to use your love for Eve against you and take your life."

My father was silent, but my grandmother was not. "Where is

that worthless assbag?" she demanded. "I have had it up to my ears with this bullshit nonsense."

"Mother," Satan warned.

"Enough," she spat. "Enough of you." She slowly turned and faced my mother. "What do you have to say for yourself, Eve?"

"I don't know," Eve replied.

"That's what I thought." Gigi shook her head in disgust. "You are done. Your duties have been revoked. You are weak and selfish and you have been since you bit the damned apple."

"But the balance," I said as I took my grandma's hand in mine. "Temptation is part of what balances us."

"Who said I was eliminating balance? I'm simply taking it away from Eve."

"And what True Immortal will you put in her place?" Elijah demanded, speaking up for the first time. He kept a healthy distance from Hayden, but his question was pertinent.

"Why, her daughter, of course," Mother Nature replied as if we were all idiots.

"Her daughter is Balance," my father said angrily. "You shall not condemn Dixie to holding more than one trait."

Hayden stiffened beside me. He liked the idea no more than my father. Quite honestly I didn't like it either.

"Not Dixie, you assknuckle. Lucy. Lucy is Eve's daughter too. She is the logical and only choice."

"She's dead," I said. "Cole killed her. I saw it. He used the Sword of Death." My knees buckled and Hayden caught me before I fell.

"For God's sake! Sorry, son," she shouted to the Heavens. "Lucy's not dead. And where the Hell is God? Is he too good for every family meeting?" she yelled as she stomped over to Lucy's lifeless body. "Wake up, child," she said lovingly. "It's time to get up."

Suddenly the realization that I hadn't felt Lucy's death left me breathless. Lucy hadn't died. I would have known. *The Beginning of Time* was correct. There were True Immortals floating in our midst and Lucy was going to become the product of her own genius—she was the spare heir. She would become Temptation.

"She was stabbed with the Sword of Death," Elijah said loudly. "The Sword of Death kills True Immortals."

"For the love of my big bosom, it has to be a three part finale," Mother Nature shrieked and stamped her foot. Vines and trees erupted out of the cement and brightly colored parrots flew through the fractured ceiling. Gigi was getting pissed. "Lucy did not have a broken heart, she did not want to die and she was stabbed in the neck from the looks of it. Not the heart."

"Sorry—my mistake," Elijah muttered and jumped out of the way of a massive tree that exploded through the ground where he was standing.

"At least this one isn't weak," Gigi said as Lucy slowly came to. "She won't cave to anyone and she will do her duty as it should have been done in the first place. The reason Eve failed is that she took the easy way out and only dealt with the sexual side of temptation. Temptation in its truest sense embodies much more than sex." She aimed her derisive words straight at Eve.

"Give me the Sword of Death," my mother cried. "I will end myself so all of you can have your happily ever after."

"Oh no, dearie. That would be far too light of a punishment for you. You shall not forfeit your life. You will live for eternity to make amends for your transgressions."

My mother slumped forward, dropped her head to her hands and silently wept. There was good in her, but it had been eclipsed or her will had been bent by evil. She wasn't fit to lead, but Gigi was right not to let her die. A large part of me wanted her to get well and become who she had been a long time ago. I wanted to know the woman who rocked back and forth on the floor. I wanted to earn her real love and I wanted her to earn mine.

"I'll take her to Hell," my father said.

"No, you won't," Grandpa informed him. "She is your weakness. She will go with Mother Nature. Someday she might go free, but until then she will be dealt with by one who is not tempted by her."

"Why are all you people staring at me?" Lucy demanded as she stood shakily and took in all the unfamiliar faces. "Who in the Hell are all you people?"

"That's no way to talk to your step-Gigi," Mother Nature admonished a shocked Lucy. "Your mother has fallen down on the job, so you get to be Temptation."

"But…" Lucy stammered.

"Don't thank me now. The job's a bitch, but you can handle it. Just remember that sex is fun, but temptation has many faces."

"But…" Lucy choked out.

"I know. I know. You'd rather be emotion or death or something more stable, but you get what you get and you like it. You are a True Immortal, Lucy. I've known for ages, but until you are called to serve you cannot be privy to the gift. The expense account is divine and the family dinners would be wonderful if all the bastards would show up." She cast an evil eye to my father who ran his hands through his hair and looked at the sky. "So darling, what do you say?"

"Do I have a choice in the matter?" Lucy asked, still dazed by the motherload of info that she'd just been presented with.

"No, you don't. In the same way I have no choice about being beautiful," she said.

"And insane," Satan muttered.

"I heard that, you little shit," she snapped at my father and then turned her attention back to Lucy. "We all have a choice, child. You are Temptation whether you want to be or not. The choice is if you will step up to the plate and do the job. Sink or swim, baby."

"I'll swim. I always swim," she replied.

"Good! I'm outta here," Gigi said. "Bill, are you with me?"

"Always, my love. I'm always with you," Grandpa said as he gave me a quick kiss and hug.

Mother Nature grabbed Eve with one hand and Grandpa with

the other. "Later," she shouted as they disappeared in a blast of iridescent glitter.

"Um, I think people are arriving for the dance," Stella said as my classmates slowly wandered into the gym.

"Oh my God," a girl dressed in a white tube top, mini, thigh high boot and wings squealed. "The decorations rock!"

My father magically disposed of Cole's body and sent Amanda to some padded cell in Hell before they were noticed. He took me in his arms and held me tight. "You might want to retract those wings," he told me. "They're kind of conspicuous."

I quickly pulled them toward me and they disappeared into my back. "Thanks, Dad."

"No problem. Will you come back to Hell?" he asked.

I glanced over at Hayden and I grinned. "Yes, we will be coming back to Hell very soon."

"He's part of the package now?" Satan asked as he gave my Angel of Death the evil eye.

"Yep. He's definitely part of the package."

My father sighed dramatically. "Fine. I suppose it could have been worse."

He disappeared in a cloud of black glitter and the crowd of co-eds clapped wildly. They thought he was a magician... if they only knew.

Elijah walked right up to Lucy and stared. "Would you like to dance?"

"My eyes are up here, douchebag," she said as he tore his gaze from her chest.

"Sorry," he muttered.

"You'd better be. I'll dance with you, but if you try any funny business I will knee your balls into your mouth."

"Duly noted." He grinned as he held his hand out to her.

"There's a match made in Heaven," Hayden said dryly as he pulled me onto the dance floor that had recently been a bloody scene of destruction.

I glanced around the room and smiled. Carl was waltzing with Janet. Myrtle was making out with Timmy by the broom closet. The baby Demons were at the snack table beating the Hell out of each other, much to the dismay of several faculty members who were at the dance. Stella had about ten young men vying for her attention and Lucy warily danced with Elijah. I laid my head on Hayden's chest and sighed.

"Can I feel you up?" Hayden asked with a glint in his eye. "It's a slow song."

"You have to spank my bumbum first." I giggled and snuggled closer.

"That could be arranged," his whispered in my ear as he lightly tapped my butt followed by a semi discreet body massage that should have taken place in private.

"I love you, my Angel," I told him.

"I love you too. Are you having fun?" he asked as he kissed me.

"Yep, but I want to go."

"Home?"

"Eventually, but I want to do something first."

"Can I guess?" he asked as he led me to the exit.

"Go ahead," I challenged.

"You want to fly."

I grinned and nodded. He led me out into the crisp cool evening and with a running start we launched ourselves into the night.

It was magical.

It was perfect.

And it was just the beginning.

EPILOGUE

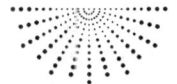

THREE WEEKS LATER...

"LET ME TELL YOU SOMETHING, VAMPYRE," ASTRID HISSED BETWEEN her screams of labor. "If you ever pull out your penis again in this lifetime I will remove it with a dull butter knife."

"That will be fine," Ethan muttered. "Now breathe through the pain."

"Come over here," she grunted. "I'll show you how to breathe through my fist."

All the men in the sitting area outside of Astrid and Ethan's suite winced in solidarity. The Vampyre compound had been restored by Mother Nature as a gift for the arrival of the baby. Plus Ethan had threatened her with baby visitation rights. Now that the danger had passed, everyone had come home.

The ornate sitting room was filled with those who loved Astrid and Ethan. The Kev and Gemma sat close to each other and held hands. Pam, Astrid's strikingly beautiful and foul-mouthed Guardian Angel, and her mate, Ethan's father, paced the room with excitement. Satan and Sloth sat in a corner and quietly played cards. Astrid's cousins, Heathcliff and Cathy, along with their father smiled at everyone as they passed around refreshments. Mother Nature held court with the baby Demons as Grandpa looked on approvingly. Janet and Myrtle were folding a pile of onesies they had brought and Carl was bejeweling a tiny baseball cap. I sat on Hayden's lap as he traced little circles on my back and we waited.

And waited.

And waited.

"This baby is not coming out," Astrid ground out. "I will be pregnant for a thousand years." Her breath came out in spurts and she cried out when it became too much.

"Oh my God," Gemma said. "Does it always hurt like that?" Her face was ashen and she clung tightly to The Kev.

"I just squatted in a field and they fell out," Pam informed the room.

Her announcement was greeted with appalled silence.

"Everybody in here. NOW," Astrid demanded. "If I have to go through this, you do too."

The men held back, but the women rushed forward.

"Guys, come up here by my head," she instructed as she stiffened and groaned. "I have no problem with nudity, but I'm fairly sure Ethan will lose it if everyone gets a peek at my hooha. Ladies, I don't care where you stand, but watch out. If he ever comes out, he's liable to eat all of us."

"Get your shit together, asshead," Pam said as she lovingly pushed Astrid's hair from her face. "You ain't the only woman in the world to blow out a baby."

"Yeah? How many women do you know that blow out eight-headed babies?" she grunted and tried to punch Pam in the nose.

"I thought it was six heads," Mother Nature added unhelpfully.

"It's twelve," Gemma chimed in, and then ducked as a vase of roses came flying at her.

"It's ten heads," Astrid snapped, and then screeched in agony.

"Darling niece," Satan said calmly as he approached the bed. "You can take down armies. I don't really see the problem here."

All the women in the room gasped and went for cover.

"He does have a point," Grandpa backed up his son. "Pam said she squatted in a field and dropped it right out."

"Should we take her outside to a field?" Ethan's father inquired politely. "Maybe if she stood up and jogged around a bit it would fall out."

"Outstanding point," The Kev agreed.

"Get out." Astrid's voice was murderous. "If you don't leave right now I will magic a fifteen-headed baby into the stomachs of all the penis-owning bastards in this room."

I'd never seen men move so quickly in my life.

"Not you, Ethan," she hissed at her mate as he tried to make his escape on the tail end of the exodus. "You will experience every joyous moment with me."

"Of course," he mumbled as he slunk back in the room.

"He's coming," she wailed as her grip on the bedpost snapped it in half.

We gathered around my cousin as she pushed with all her might.

And he came.

"Sweet baby Moses in a mesh tracksuit," Pam squealed as she took the baby and cleaned him. Ethan cut the cord and Pam placed the screaming child in his hands. His look of astonishment and joy brought tears to my eyes.

"What?" Astrid asked. "What's wrong with him?"

"Nothing," I said as I gazed at the small perfect bundle in his father's trembling arms.

"How many heads?" she demanded.

"One head, my love. One beautiful head," Ethan whispered reverently as he gave the little baby boy to her.

Astrid was silent for once as she gazed at her child. Her lips quivered and her magic swirled through the room. "He's ours?" She spoke in a voice so soft I barely heard her.

"He's ours," Ethan replied as he sat on the bed next to his mate and child.

"He has one head," she murmured as she traced the tiny lips, toes and fingers of her child.

"That doesn't mean he won't sprout a few more in the next couple of days." Pam snorted as she kissed Astrid and then the baby. "Put that little son of a bitch on your boob. He's gonna be hungry," she instructed.

"Vampyre-Demons can nurse?" Astrid asked, surprised.

"No clue, dumbass. Try it and see," Pam said.

Vampyre-Demons could nurse. The baby suckled with delight from his mother and Ethan watched rapt with a dreamy expression on his handsome face. He stroked the back of his child's head as the boy drank from his mother.

"What shall we call him?" he asked.

Astrid looked down at the baby and sighed happily. "Samuel. We will call him Samuel."

Samuel stopped drinking for a brief moment at the sound of his name, looked up and smiled a gummy baby smile.

"Did that just happen?" Myrtle asked, shocked.

"Yes, it did," Mother Nature said knowingly. "This is no normal child. Samuel will… "

"Stop," Astrid cut her off. "I don't want to know. Right now I have a perfect one-headed baby boy and I love him more than I thought possible. I can feel he is special and different, but I just want to hold him and be with him. I don't want to know his future… yet."

"Come on, let's leave them alone," Gemma said as she ushered us out.

The last thing I saw as I left the room was the passionate and loving kiss Ethan gave Astrid and two tiny little hands resting on the chins of his parents.

Hayden's arms were open and I ran into them. "Is that something you would like to do?" he asked as he pressed his lips to my hair.

I paused and considered. "Yes, but not yet."

"Should we go practice until we're ready?" His smirk made me tingle.

I giggled and took his precious face between my hands, then whispered in his ear. "I think that is a very good idea… a very good idea indeed."

THE END (for now)
Go HERE to grab the next book in the series!

EXCERPT: FASHIONABLY DEAD IN DIAPERS

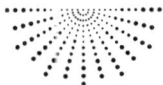

THE HOT DAMNED SERIES, BOOK 4

CHAPTER ONE

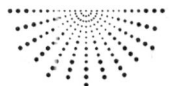

ONCE UPON A TIME THERE WAS A LITTLE BOY. HE WAS LIKE NO OTHER. His power knew no bounds and he was destined for greatness. However, he had to get through teething and diapers first.

"ETHAN, COME HERE. HE LOOKS WASTED."

I sighed with joy as I caressed the beautiful baby at my breast. He looked up at me with lazy eyes and a milk-drunk grin. My heart clenched. His little fangs peeked through his full pink lips and I was relieved he knew better than to chomp down on my boob—those fangs were sharp little suckers. My baby was freakin' brilliant and he was mine. I pinched myself constantly to make sure this was all real.

"I love you so much it hurts," I whispered as I buried my face in the wisps of curly blond hair on his head. Samuel had grown much faster than a regular child. It was as alarming as it was fascinating. At the rate he was going, he'd be a toddler in a month.

Our bedroom suite at the Cressida House had been turned into a massive nursery—complete with a crib, mobiles, playpens and more stuffed animals than I knew existed. There was also a large pile of nylon dog bones. It was the only thing that he could chew and not destroy in thirty-three seconds—it took him at least a half hour. I felt a little unsettled about giving my child canine toys, but I figured whatever worked was okay. It was better than him chewing on the furniture. The loss of two couches and a seven hundred year old priceless coffee table made me search out an alternative method for him to relieve the pain of teething— hence the truckload of dog bones. However, whenever someone inquired about the neon green and purple toys, I lied and told them we'd gotten a pet Hell Hound for Samuel.

"He's a smart boy," Ethan said quietly as he took in the scene. "I'd stay at that breast for eternity if I could."

"You're a pig." I grinned with delight at my mate as my insides tingled at the thought of him near my breast or any of my private parts. Having Sammy had put a bit of a crimp in our over-active sex life and I was ready for that to be rectified.

"Actually, I'm a Master Vampyre and a Prince, but pig will do for the moment." He winked, which made me want to jump him, but the precious child in my arms put a stop to that.

I mumbled grumpily as I watched him walk away.

"*Silly, silly—pretty lady, I hate fucking naps. Asswaffle, shit-monster, Jesus in booty shorts. Boobies, boobies, boobies.*"

"What did you just say?" I hissed at Ethan. My eyes narrowed and I put Samuel down on the bed.

"I'm fairly sure I just gave you permission to call me a pig. A rare first for me," Ethan said as he sauntered back in and tried to cop a feel.

Not happening.

"That is not what you said." I crossed my arms over my naked chest and gave him the stink eye. My temper had been short lately, most likely due to not getting laid…but calling me names was not working for me. "You called me an asswaffle shit-monster!" I snapped.

"I beg your pardon," Ethan said as he bit down on his lip to stifle his grin. "I most certainly did not."

"You most certainly did," I shot back as I yanked a tank top over my head. "Along with saying my Cousin Jesus wears booty shorts and then calling my knockers boobies—three times."

"Interesting," he commented as he plopped down on the bed and wrapped Samuel in his strong embrace. The baby cuddled up to his father and cooed as he grabbed a fistful of Ethan's hair and shoved a chubby thumb into his mouth.

If I wasn't so pissed I would have joined the two men I loved more than anything in the world, but I wasn't done yet.

"Did I say anything else?" he inquired casually.

"As if you didn't know." I rolled my eyes and got up in his perfectly gorgeous face. "You said you hate fucking naps...Oh shitballs," I shrieked and slapped my hands over my mouth. "Impossible. No fucking way."

We both stared at Samuel. Ethan was thoroughly amused and I was horrified. My perfect little three month old son glanced up and winked. If I could have hurled I would have. However, Vampyres can't puke.

"Ohmygodohmygodohmygod, I am an unfit mother," I shouted as I paced the room frantically. "I give my son dog bones and he already curses like a fucking sailor. Vampyre- Demon social services will take him away. We have to get out of town and you have to watch your language around him. Do we have duct tape?" I demanded.

"I'm sure we can find some," Ethan said as he watched me race around the room like a lunatic.

"That's good. I need to strap my mouth shut for about a year and then everything will work out fine. Samuel," I said sternly. "You just said some really shitty words. We do not fucking speak like that in this house. Do you understand Mommy?"

Samuel giggled hysterically and flipped me off.

"Sweet Baby Jesus in a thong," I screeched. "Where did he learn that?"

"*Gamma Gigi,*" a sweet voice bounced through my head. Ethan sat up with a look of utter shock on his face.

"Did you hear that?" I demanded as he stared at his son.

"I did," he said reverently. "Amazing."

"It's not amazing. It's bad. Very bad. He's three months old. He's the size of a nine month old according to those dumb-ass human baby books and he can flip the bird. What is amazing about that?"

Sparks began to fly from my fingertips and my hair began to float around my head. This was so not happening.

"This is a fine excuse to forbid your grandmother from coming to visit him anymore," Ethan volunteered logically.

That gave me pause. Maybe this wasn't *all* my fault. My crazy ass family had been around constantly. Uncle Satan. Pam aka my guardian angel. Mother Nature aka Grandma Gigi. My cousins, the Seven Deadly Sins. Son of a bitch—I was an unfit mother. No child should hang out with Satan on a daily basis. I mean he was fun and all, but he was still the Devil.

"We're having a meeting," I said as I shoved all the dog bones under the bed. "Every last one of them is going to sit here and listen to the new fucking rules. No more swearing or bird flipping." I froze. "Do you think the Baby Demons took him to a strip club?"

My stomach dropped to my toes. I didn't deserve this child. We were the most dysfunctional lot imaginable. He would be better off with normal parents who didn't swear, fly and destroy cities with the flick of a finger.

"I'm going to lay down the law and if anyone disagrees, I'll tear their head off or at the very least maim them thoroughly."

"You're not serious," Ethan said. A look of horror marred his ridiculously handsome features. "That will be a clusterfuck of epic proportions."

"*Clusterfuckclusterfuckclusterfuck,*" Samuel gleefully bellowed in our heads.

My eyes narrowed dangerously at my mate and my son.

"Fine." Ethan sighed dramatically. "But get ready for life to be over as we know it."

"First of all, we're already dead, so that part of the argument doesn't work, Little Mister Master Vampyre. And if we keep going at the rate we're traveling, we'll have a depraved convict with absolutely no morals on our hands."

Samuel pulled his wet thumb from his mouth with a pop and grinned. "Bite me, assjacket!" he yelled at his father in an adorable voice that was no longer confined to our heads. It was loud and clear and I had to bite down on my cheek to keep from laughing. Of course the laughter died a violent death in my throat as my perfect son wiggled his chunky fingers and set the curtains on fire.

"Call everyone. Now," Ethan ground out as he gently laid the fire starter on the bed and doused the flames with magic. "We have a bit of a problem on our hands."

— Visit The Web Page For More Info —

ROBYN'S BOOK LIST

(IN CORRECT READING ORDER)

HOT DAMNED SERIES
Fashionably Dead
Fashionably Dead Down Under
Hell on Heels
Fashionably Dead in Diapers
A Fashionably Dead Christmas
Fashionably Hotter Than Hell
Fashionably Dead and Wed
Fashionably Fanged
Fashionably Flawed
A Fashionably Dead Diary
Fashionably Forever After
Fashionably Fabulous
A Fashionable Fiasco
Fashionably Fooled
Fashionably Dead and Loving It
Fashionably Dead and Demonic
The Oh My Gawd Couple
A Fashionable Disaster

GOOD TO THE LAST DEMON SERIES
As the Underworld Turns
The Edge of Evil
The Bold and the Banished
Guiding Blight

GOOD TO THE LAST DEATH SERIES
It's a Wonderful Midlife Crisis
Whose Midlife Crisis Is It Anyway?
A Most Excellent Midlife Crisis
My Midlife Crisis, My Rules
You Light Up My Midlife Crisis
It's A Matter of Midlife and Death
The Facts Of Midlife
It's A Hard Knock Midlife
Run for Your Midlife
It's A Hell of A Midlife

MY SO-CALLED MYSTICAL MIDLIFE SERIES
The Write Hook
You May Be Write
All The Write Moves
My Big Fat Hairy Wedding

SHIFT HAPPENS SERIES
Ready to Were
Some Were in Time
No Were To Run
Were Me Out
Were We Belong

MAGIC AND MAYHEM SERIES
Switching Hour
Witch Glitch

A Witch in Time
Magically Delicious
A Tale of Two Witches
Three's A Charm
Switching Witches
You're Broom or Mine?
The Bad Boys of Assjacket
The Newly Witch Game
Witches In Stitches

SEA SHENANIGANS SERIES
Tallulah's Temptation
Ariel's Antics
Misty's Mayhem
Petunia's Pandemonium
Jingle Me Balls

A WYLDE PARANORMAL SERIES
Beauty Loves the Beast

HANDCUFFS AND HAPPILY EVER AFTERS SERIES
How Hard Can it Be?
Size Matters
Cop a Feel

If after reading all the above you are still wanting more adventure and zany fun, read *Pirate Dave and His Randy Adventures*, the romance novel budding novelist Rena helped wicked Evangeline write in *How Hard Can It Be?*

Warning: Pirate Dave Contains Romance Satire, Spoofing, and Pirates with Two Pork Swords.

NOTE FROM THE AUTHOR

If you enjoyed this ebook, please consider leaving a positive review or rating on the site where you purchased it. Reader reviews help my books continue to be valued by resellers and help new readers make decisions about reading them.

You are the reason I write these stories and I sincerely appreciate each of you!

Many thanks for your support,
~ Robyn Peterman

ABOUT THE AUTHOR

Robyn Peterman writes because the people inside her head won't leave her alone until she gives them life on paper.

Her addictions include laughing really hard with friends, shoes (the expensive kind), Target, iced coffee with a squirt of chocolate syrup in a Yeti cup, bejeweled reading glasses, her kids, her super hot hubby and collecting stray animals.

A former professional actress with Broadway, film and TV credits, she now lives in the South with her family and too many animals to count.

Writing gives her peace and makes her whole, plus having a job where she can work in her sweatpants works really well for her.

Want More Info About Robyn? You can find her here...
www.robynpeterman.com